P9-DFK-051

ALSO BY CATHY HOLTON

The Secret Lives of the Kudzu Debutantes

Revenge
of the
Kudzu
Debutantes

Revenge

of the

Kudzu
Debutantes

—— A NOVEL

Cathy Holton

BALLANTINE BOOKS
NEW YORK

Revenge of the Kudzu Debutantes is a work of fiction. Names, characters, places, and incidents are the products of the author's imagination or are used fictitiously. Any resemblance to actual events, locales, or persons, living or dead, is entirely coincidental.

2007 Ballantine Books Trade Paperback Edition

Copyright © 2006 by Cathy Holton
Excerpt from *The Secret Lives of the Kudzu Debutantes* by Cathy Holton
copyright © 2007 by Cathy Holton

All rights reserved.

Published in the United States by Ballantine, an imprint of The Random House Publishing Group, a division of Random House, Inc., New York.

BALLANTINE and colophon are registered trademarks of Random House, Inc.

Originally published in hardcover in the United States by Ballantine Books, an imprint of The Random House Publishing Group, a division of Random House, Inc., in 2006.

This book contains an excerpt from the forthcoming book *The Secret Lives of the Kudzu Debutantes* by Cathy Holton. This excerpt has been set for this edition only and may not reflect the final content of the forthcoming book.

ISBN 978-0-345-47928-0

Library of Congress Cataloging-in-Publication Data

Holton, Cathy.
Revenge of the kudzu debutantes : a novel / Cathy Holton.
p.   cm.
ISBN 978-0-345-47928-0 (pbk.)
1. Women—Southern States—Fiction.   2. Man-woman relationship—Fiction.
3. Southern States—Fiction.   4. Revenge—Fiction.   I. Title
PS3608.O494434R488 2006
813'.6—dc22
2005048275

Printed in the United States of America

www.ballantinebooks.com

4 6 8 9 7 5 3

Book design by Susan Turner

For Mark

Revenge
of the
Kudzu
Debutantes

CHAPTER

ONE

*O*NE WEEK BEFORE THE DINNER PARTY WHERE SHE FOUND out the truth about her cheating husband, Eadie Boone sat in her car outside the offices of Boone & Broadwell waiting for Trevor and his new girlfriend to appear. She was parked in a no-parking zone across the street from the old columned mansion that housed her husband's law firm. It was five o'clock in the afternoon and Ithaca's thin stream of rush-hour traffic moved sluggishly along the street.

Sunlight fell from a wide blue Georgia sky and slanted through the arching branches of the live oaks. The air was cool and sweet with the scent of wet grass. Fall was Eadie's favorite time of year. It reminded her of football games, and new school bags, and the hope and promise of good things to come. Other people think of spring as the season of renewal, but there was something about autumn's dark wet corruption that appealed to Eadie's nature. In the damp sunshine of an autumn afternoon Eadie felt there was nothing she could not do. Even become one of the greatest artists of the twenty-first century. Even make her husband love her again.

Not that Trevor had ever stopped loving her. Eadie knew, deeply and intuitively, that he had not. Eadie believed a good marriage was a fight to the death, a long slow clamp on the jugular by two equally determined adversaries, and given this definition, she and Trevor had one of the best marriages around. Trevor liked a good fight as much as she did. But somewhere along the way, he had forgotten all this. Waiting in her car, protruding like a jetty into the slow-moving stream of rush-hour traffic, Eadie felt it was her duty to remind him.

Still, the sight of the girl with her husband stunned her. They appeared minutes later, walking arm in arm, heads close while they shared some secret moment. Looking at the two of them, Eadie realized how much reminding Trevor needed. The girl could not be a day over twenty-two. She had the pliant, eager look of someone with low self-esteem. Eadie bet she didn't even argue with Trevor. She probably listened intently and did as she was told and wasn't even selfish in bed. Poor Trevor must be bored senseless.

She watched them disappear around the back of the building, and a few minutes later Trevor's old Mercedes rattled past, shooting out a plume of dark smoke that disappeared lazily among the arching branches of the trees. Eadie started her car and followed them. Five minutes later Trevor parked in front of the Pink House Restaurant, and Eadie pulled to the side of the street and watched them cross between traffic, holding hands and laughing like a couple of teenagers. A woman with less self-confidence than Eadie Boone would have been crushed, seeing how much they seemed to enjoy each other's company. But Eadie was feeling nothing more than a growing sense of impatience with Trevor's stubborn stupidity.

She waited for thirty minutes, until she was sure they were seated and beginning to enjoy their meal, and then she picked up her cell phone and called the Pink House and asked to have Eadie Boone paged. It was one of her favorite tricks. She'd follow Trevor and then have herself paged, knowing he would spend the rest of the evening looking over his shoulder to see if she was there. She also liked to call his apartment when she imagined him in the middle of sex, and leave loud messages on his machine—*Bad news, Trevor. The sheriff called. That client who vowed to kill you has jumped bail,* or *The lab called with the results of the herpes test. You might want to call me.*

Her phone beeped. Eadie checked the caller ID but stayed on the line with the Pink House hostess. The call was from Lavonne Zibolsky, who was ringing, no doubt, to beg Eadie to help her plan the Boone & Broadwell party that had been dumped on Lavonne just a week before.

The annual dinner party that was only a week away, and that Eadie wasn't even invited to, now that Trevor had left her for his secretary. She could hear the hostess's footsteps and a minute later her tired voice. "Sorry, there's no Eadie Boone here."

"Thanks," Eadie said and hung up. She had her work cut out for her, but she wasn't discouraged. She hadn't dragged herself up out of a life of poverty and adverse destiny by thinking like a defeatist. She hadn't overcome a tragic childhood and become an artist by thinking it couldn't be done. To admit she might have made a mistake about Trevor Boone would have been like admitting the whole code by which she had lived her life up to now was wrong, and this was something Eadie Boone just wasn't willing to do.

She waited ten minutes and then called the restaurant again. She imagined the two of them crouched guiltily over their entrées, afraid to look around. *Not laughing now,* she thought, closing up her phone. She considered going inside and causing a scene, but decided against it. She was tired. She decided to go home and take a hot bath instead.

Following a wayward husband was hard work. Trying to convince that same husband that what he needed was not a change of wives but a change of careers was even more exhausting. Trevor would never be happy until he quit practicing law and moved home to write the Great American Novel he had always promised himself he would write.

Eadie knew this even if Trevor didn't.

NITA BROADWELL SAT IN THE CAR-POOL LINE READING *CAPTIVE Bride of the Choctaw.* The love scenes were graphic, and made her feel restless and slightly queasy. She had started out reading Harlequin Romances but had quickly progressed to the harder stuff, and now she read about masters and slave girls, Indian braves and captive white women. No matter how hard she tried, she just couldn't stop. She had seen women like herself on afternoon talk shows, sad women who were addicted to alcohol, or food, or the Home Shopping Network. She wasn't sure what a woman addicted to soft porn romance novels would be called, but she was pretty sure there was a name for it. She was pretty sure Oprah or Dr. Phil would know what it was called.

Nita slid the novel down behind her steering wheel so Susan Deakins couldn't look in her rearview mirror and see what she was reading. Nita was certain there must be other women in town hopped up on soft-porn romance novels; she just didn't know who they were. Being addicted to soft-porn romance novels in Ithaca, Georgia, was like filling a prescription for head lice or genital herpes. It just wasn't the kind of thing you went around bragging about, not if you were a good Southern girl, anyway, from a good Southern family.

Nita read for a while and then closed her eyes and leaned back against the headrest of her seat. Her heart pounded like a piston. There was a sound in her ears like water running in a sink. Lone Wolf, a full-blooded Choctaw Indian chief, had his captive white slave, a red-haired beauty named Lydia, staked out in the middle of his teepee. Nita imagined herself as Lydia. She imagined Lone Wolf's hard, muscled chest. He reminded her of Jimmy Lee Motes, the twenty-six-year-old carpenter she had hired to fix her pool house. Jimmy Lee had dark hair and dark eyes. He looked like he could be part Choctaw.

Behind her a horn honked and Nita opened her eyes and sat up suddenly and slid the novel into her purse. She put the car into drive and followed the slow-moving traffic as it inched toward the school portico, trying to clear the gyrating images of Lone Wolf and Lydia that drifted through her mind like an X-rated hologram.

She had started reading soft-porn romance novels with the idea of trying to put the zip back into her sixteen-year marriage to Charles Broadwell, but so far the only person Nita had been able to fantasize about was Jimmy Lee Motes.

Sunlight glinted off the Gothic towers and red-bricked façade of the tall buildings circling the courtyard. A throng of bored children stood around the school fountain, an exact replica of the Little Mermaid of Copenhagen, lethargically tossing quarters into the foaming water and waiting for their mothers to come. Nita searched the crowd anxiously for her children but could not see them. Far off in the distance, past the polo field and the lacrosse practice field, the sharp-edged shape of a scull glided on the river, oars moving rhythmically.

Nita's children, Logan and Whitney, attended Barron Hall, the old and prestigious prep school for which Ithaca was famous and which Nita's husband and his father before him had attended. Nita, born

Juanita Sue James, had grown up in Ithaca, too, but she had attended public school. Charles Broadwell was four years older than she, and she'd known who he was, of course, but he had existed in a world so alien to her own that she'd never paid much attention to him. The Broadwells lived in a big columned house out by the river that Judge Broadwell had built and filled with the mounted heads of numerous murdered animals. They belonged to a small select group who lived in big houses, sent their children to Barron Hall and weekend dances at the country club, then off to small liberal arts colleges in Atlanta and Richmond and Birmingham. If growing up with money and attending one of the finest prep schools in the Southeast had been enough to guarantee happiness and emotional stability, then Nita's husband and children should have been happy and well-adjusted people. Unfortunately, life was not that simple.

She could see her children waiting beneath the school portico. Logan stood with his jacket slung over one shoulder, his fourteen-year-old face fixed in its usual expression of disappointment and adolescent rage. Whitney stood with Miss Carlton, the car-pool monitor, idly plucking at the torn hem of her uniform skirt that hung down around her plump legs like a flag at half-mast. She saw her mother and launched herself off the sidewalk, stumbling toward the car with an odd rolling gait, laboring beneath her overfilled backpack and holding her arms out stiffly in front of her as a counterweight. Logan saw Nita, and scowling, slouched toward the car. Watching her children drag themselves toward her, Nita smiled and gave a hopeful little wave. As a child, she'd dreamed of a happy family, the way some girls dream of wedding days and Miss America crowns and award-winning performances on the silver screen.

"Shotgun," Whitney shouted breathlessly, reaching the car.

"Get in, retard," Logan said to his little sister.

They followed a long line of expensive imported cars and SUVs through the expansive school grounds to the highway. Nita glanced at Whitney and adjusted the rearview mirror so she could see Logan. Still smiling, she said tentatively, "Did you have a good day?" Other than trying to put the zip back into her marriage, the one thing Nita wished she could do above all else was to make her children happy.

Logan slumped against the door and stared bleakly at his reflection in the window glass. A pimple had risen in the thick brush of his left eyebrow, he had not made the cut for the fencing team, and he was too cynical to believe that life would ever get any better than this. His mother's false enthusiasm brought out the worst in him. "I flunked my algebra test," he said despondently. "And Mr. Johnson gave a pop quiz in history and I probably flunked that, too."

Whitney, at eleven, was only slightly more encouraging. "Madison DeVane's having a slumber party," she said, "and I'm not invited."

They drove for a while in silence. Nita was pretty sure that whatever was wrong with her children had something to do with her. In between her soft-porn romance novels she had read numerous books on childrearing written by psychologists and psychiatrists and counselors and experts who didn't even have children but who had managed to pick up a lot of information by studying them in labs. Nita must have read over fifty books on how to raise happy, well-adjusted children, and so far the only thing she'd managed to learn from these books was that she had done everything wrong.

Someone had asked her once if she was raised Catholic, and she'd gotten kind of confused and flustered and said, "No, Baptist," and the woman said, "Because you wear your guilt like a hair shirt." Nita didn't know what in the world she was talking about. She didn't even know what a hair shirt was. All she knew was that when her children felt sad or lonely or got left out of slumber parties, she felt bad.

"How about some ice cream?" she said brightly. "We can stop for ice cream if you like."

"Can I go to a different school?" Logan said. "I hate this place."

"Rocky road, bubble gum, mint chocolate chip—it's my treat," Nita said, holding tightly to the steering wheel.

"I'd give anything to go to a public school," Logan said.

"Butter pecan, almond delight, blue moon . . ." Nita felt like a drowning woman clinging to debris in the middle of a stormy sea. "How about you, honey?" she said, looking desperately at Whitney. "Would you like some ice cream?"

Whitney played with the edge of her skirt and thought about it. "Charlie Mosby had a fit in Latin class," she said finally, "and they had to stick a ruler in his mouth to keep him from swallowing his tongue."

Nita slumped against the steering wheel of the big car, exhausted. She hadn't done a thing all day, but being with her children always made her tired. She remembered she had to call Lavonne Zibolsky to discuss details for the firm's party next weekend. Charles had been very specific about this. She made a mental note to remember to pick up Charles's shirts at the dry cleaner. She had forgotten yesterday and he had been sullen and rude, standing in the doorway this morning in his undershirt and bare feet while she made breakfast for the children.

"Is it too much to ask?" he asked politely from the doorway while the children cowered behind their cereal boxes. "Could you possibly find time in your busy day of shopping, bridge, and tennis to stop by the dry cleaner and pick up my shirts?" Charles prided himself on his skillful use of sarcasm, but today he could see it was having little effect on Nita. She continued to stir the eggs, her eyes fixed dreamily on the skillet, a slight smile on her lips. She was imagining herself hunched over an open fire, while in the teepee behind her Lone Wolf slumbered peacefully. She could see his smooth chest rising and falling with each breath. His black hair spread out on the animal skins beneath his head like wings. He looked peaceful and content. *That's what Jimmy Lee Motes looks like when he sleeps,* she thought.

"Nita," Charles said sharply.

She jumped. The wooden spoon in her hand clattered to the floor. "I'll pick up the shirts," she promised her husband. "I won't forget."

Nita turned the Mercedes left on Main Street and headed toward the newer section of town where the Broadwells lived in a massive new house of indiscriminate architecture, surrounded by other massive new houses of indiscriminate architecture. The area was called River Oaks and it was popular among the young upper middle class and corporate transferees who came in through DuPont. As she drove, Nita was remembering the way Jimmy Lee Motes looked this morning when she left him standing out by her pool, his tool belt slung low on his hips and a kind of rumpled, sleepy-boy look about him. He had smiled drowsily when she came out to ask if he wanted a cup of coffee.

"No thanks," he said. "I don't drink coffee." His hair was brown and glossy and he kept it tucked behind his ears. Watching him smile, something tugged deep in her belly.

"I have to run some errands," Nita said, trying to sound casual. "Will you still be here when I get back?"

He smiled again. His eyes were dark and opaque as a mirror. "I'll be here until four," he said.

Remembering, Nita clamped her foot down heavily on the accelerator. If she hurried, he might still be there. The big Mercedes glided over the bricked streets, past restaurants, shops, and antique stores, past the small upscale laundry where her husband's shirts hung, neglected and forlorn as orphaned children, behind the big plate-glass window.

LAVONNE ZIBOLSKY HAD DREAMT AGAIN OF HER DEAD MOTHER, and she spent the following day struggling with the feelings of foreboding and remorse that these dreams always brought. At forty-six, Lavonne considered herself too old for psychotherapy, but there were times in between her eating binges when she realized that the increasing frequency of her dreams might foreshadow something life-altering. There were moments when she wondered if the dreams and the startling memories they evoked might be universal, times when she questioned whether middle age might be nothing more than long-submerged guilt and regret rising to the surface of the mind like corpses in a rain-soaked field. There were other times when she wondered if maybe she didn't have a hormonal imbalance brought on by menopause or food allergies or blood sugar fluctuations.

The afternoon after the latest dream, Lavonne stood in her sunroom eating Rocky Road ice cream out of the carton and watching her neighbor, Myra Redmon, plant azaleas. Lavonne was supposed to be planning her husband's firm's dinner party, but after a morning spent making futile phone calls, she had pretty much given up. The party was less than a week away and she had yet to find a caterer. She had called everyone she knew between here and Atlanta, and no one could do it on such short notice. The party, an annual affair put on for the firm's clients and office staff, was a very big deal to Leonard and his law partners, Charles Broadwell and Trevor Boone. Lavonne knew if she didn't find a caterer and the party was a disaster, the blame would fall squarely on her shoulders. Never mind that Charles's mother, Virginia, who had handled the party for the last fifteen years, had decided at the last minute to dump it on the wives. Never mind that Nita Broadwell, who went around these days in her own dreamy little world, and Eadie Boone, whose marriage to Trevor appeared to be finally crumbling to dust, had been no help whatsoever. None of that would matter if the party turned out to be a disaster. The blame would rest solely on Lavonne's big round shoulders. Hence the Rocky Road ice cream.

Lavonne finished off the ice cream and took the empty carton into the kitchen and tossed it into the trash. She stood at the refrigerator with the door open and tried not to think about the party. After awhile she decided on a bagel. A bagel might be just the thing to fill the creeping emptiness that threatened, at times, to overwhelm her. She took the cream cheese out of the refrigerator and shoved a bagel into the toaster. When it had crisped, she smeared it with cheese, put it on a plate, and went back to the sunroom.

Gray clouds scuttled across the blue sky. Sunlight fell sporadically through the long windows. Lavonne finished the bagel and licked the cream cheese off her sticky fingers, feeling the usual sense of regret and longing she felt after returning from Shapiro's Bakery. She hadn't had a decent bagel since she left Cleveland. *Shalom Ya'll* the sign in Shapiro's window read, but in nearly eighteen years of patronage Lavonne had yet to purchase a bagel that even remotely tasted like the ones she had grown up eating at Finkelstein's down on Third Street.

Lavonne ran her finger along the edge of her plate and sat despondently at the window watching Myra Redmon work. Myra had bleached blonde hair and a misshapen upper lip, the result of a bad collagen job that she tried to disguise with an elaborately drawn line of lipstick. Myra and Nita Broadwell's snobbish mother-in-law, Virginia, had grown up together and were tight as Siamese twins. They had married well and spent their earlier years climbing Ithaca's wobbly social ladder, and once at the top, banded together to exclude the daughters of people they considered unworthy for membership in the Ithaca Cotillion and the Junior League. Myra's father had truck farmed and Virginia's had worked for the railroad, but Myra's great-great-grandfather had built a sprawling plantation long before the Civil War and Virginia's had once owned two dozen raggedy slaves. In the South, it didn't matter what your father did or whether you grew up with money. All that mattered was the kind of people you came from, and if you went back far enough, Myra and Virginia had come from gentry, and everyone in Ithaca knew it. Myra was sixty-three years old and had a heart as rusty and sharp as barbed wire, but she played tennis four times a week and had legs like a college freshman.

Lavonne went into the kitchen, put the plate in the dishwasher, and opened her Daytimer to the list of things she must accomplish today. Across the top of the page she had written *Find caterer or leave town.* Beneath that she had written, *Find caterer or have nervous break-down.* Underneath that she had written, *Call Eadie and Nita and beg them to help me find caterer.* She called Eadie and left a message on her cell phone. She glanced through her kitchen bay window to the Broad-well's big house next door, but Nita's Mercedes was not in the drive. She would call her later. But if she called her later she might acciden-tally get Charles Broadwell on the phone. This was a chance Lavonne wasn't willing to take. She went to the phone, called Nita, and left a message on her machine.

Lavonne supposed it was not unusual for a woman to hate her hus-band's law partner. She would have preferred to tell Charles Broadwell to go fuck himself years ago, but, as Leonard was constantly reminding her, *We live in the South now and you can't go around saying things like that, Lavonne. My God, you'll ruin me if you don't learn to keep your mouth shut.*

The move south had not been her idea. Leonard had inherited enough money when his father died to go looking for a needy partner-ship, but he had done so without consulting her. She had been too busy running her own accounting practice to worry about what her husband was doing. It was tax season and he had left her enshrined in her office happily going over her clients' receipts and payroll records. Too fo-cused on her business to keep up with anything else, she had thought he was going south for a vacation. He returned several weeks later, tanned and happy, and announced they were moving to Ithaca, Geor-gia. He had found the perfect firm.

Boone & Broadwell. The firm was old and prestigious, the founders' sons respectable but cash-poor; it seemed a match made in heaven. Leonard Zibolsky dreamed of moonlight and magnolias, soft subservient Southern girls, and the white columns of Tara. Lavonne sold her accounting business, packed up her books and remaining office goods, and went into mourning. Eight months later they were living in a big expensive house in a small south Georgia town where everyone had known everyone else's secrets for generations. Life moved placidly, heat shimmered over the lush green landscape, and Cleveland, Ohio, seemed as far away as the gray cratered surface of the moon.

It was hard to believe she had been here eighteen years. Eighteen years in the Banana Republic, and what did she have to show for it? A husband who was rarely home, two daughters who were nearly grown and didn't seem to need her anymore, and a life that felt increasingly like somewhere she didn't belong.

Through the bay window she could see the good-looking carpenter Nita had hired to fix her pool house loading his tools into the back of his truck. He had long black hair and wide shoulders. From this distance, he looked a little like Johnny Depp. Lavonne wondered if there was anything she could find for him to do around her house.

The phone rang and she went to check the caller ID. It was Leonard. She let it ring. The last person in the world she wanted to talk to was her husband. She and Leonard could go days without having a conversation, but in the week since Virginia Broadwell dumped the firm's party in Lavonne's lap he'd been calling her relentlessly to see if she had found a caterer for the party. Every night when he returned home from work it was the first thing he asked her. It was bad enough she had to attend the damn party, bad enough she had to squeeze into a new dress and stand around making small talk with people she saw only once a year. But now she also had to be responsible for making sure the wretched dinner was a success and be hounded by her husband in the process.

The feeling of grief she had carried with her since awakening from the dream about her mother lengthened and grew into a kind of emptiness she could not fill no matter how hard she tried. She was not hungry, but she needed to eat. Lavonne closed up her Daytimer. Louise was picking Ashley up at cheerleading practice and they were having dinner at the mall. She glanced at the clock and thought about making a run to Burger King. A Whopper might be just the thing to settle her queasy stomach. A cheeseburger might be just the thing to take her mind off the party, the idea of which hovered at the edge of her consciousness like a bad dream, a promise of impending disaster, gunfire on a darkened street, a hint of smoke on the Hindenburg.

As soon as this party's over I'll go on a diet, she thought, leaning to take her car keys out of her purse. *As soon as this party's over I'll go on a diet and lose sixty pounds and figure out what I need to do to make me happy again.*

She went out through the garage door, waving once at Nita's good-looking carpenter, who smiled and waved back.

IMMY LEE MOTES WAS STILL THERE WHEN NITA ARRIVED home, loading his tools into a small blue pickup truck with a bumper sticker that read *American by Birth, Southern by the Grace of God.* Nita liked that. It made her feel warm and slightly patriotic. She parked beside him in the driveway and the children climbed out and Whitney said, "Hey" and gave him a little wave.

"Hey," Jimmy Lee said.

Logan put his head down and slouched into the house, ignoring Jimmy Lee.

Nita slid out of the car. Jimmy Lee closed the lid on his tool chest, clamping down the combination lock. His arms were thick and hard as strands of coiled wire. He was singing softly to himself, *And I want to lay with you in the desert tonight with a million stars in the sky. . . .*

"How'd it go today?" Nita said, half-recognizing the song. It sounded like something the Eagles would sing. The Eagles were one of her favorite bands. She liked the way he could sing like that, right out in the open without being self-conscious or shy about it at all. He sang as good as he looked.

"Okay, I guess. I should be able to finish up and get out of your hair maybe as soon as tomorrow."

"Oh you aren't in my hair," Nita said quickly. She blushed crimson and wondered why, when she was around him, her mouth seemed to work like it was disconnected from her brain. He had been working at her house for nearly three weeks now.

He grinned and said, "I wish everyone I worked for was as nice as you."

She could stand here talking to him all day but she realized he was probably in a hurry to get home. He wore no wedding ring but she imagined he had at least one girlfriend. A man who looked like him probably had at least a dozen girlfriends. She swung her purse strap up on her shoulder, but as she did the soft-porn romance novel slid out and landed with a loud *smack* on the driveway between them.

Jimmy Lee leaned over and picked up the novel and handed it to her, glancing at the title. He grinned, a long slow grin that made her feel like something heavy rested on her chest. A furniture truck rumbled down the street. Great flat-bottomed clouds hung from a blue sky. Nita's face glowed like a space heater. She stuck the book in her purse and pretended to look for her keys.

"Good reading?" he said.

"It's for a friend," she said.

His teeth were white and straight. "Well, I'll see you in the morning then."

She smiled and looked at his chin. "Okay," she said.

NITA FED THE CHILDREN EARLY, HELPED WHITNEY WITH HER homework, and then went upstairs, still thinking about Jimmy Lee's grin and the way it made her feel, hollow-stomached and light-headed, the way you feel when you climb to the top of a swaying ladder or stand too close to the edge of a tall building. She opened her closet and rummaged around until she found a black see-through camisole she had bought weeks ago at the Victoria's Secret at the mall. Nita had never been one to wear sexy underwear, but under the influence of her porno romance novels and Jimmy Lee Motes's intoxicating presence, she was beginning to loosen up a bit. She was beginning to feel like there were whole parts of herself coming to light, parts she only suspected before but had never clearly appreciated—a certain luminous quality to the skin of her wrist, the velvety feel of her earlobe, the way her breasts felt nestled beneath a silk nightgown.

She ran herself a hot bath, lit a few candles, sprinkled the water liberally with lavender oil, and then climbed in to wait for her husband to come home.

NITA DIDN'T EVEN KNOW SHE WAS SEXUALLY REPRESSED UNTIL she went to Lee Anne Bales's Passion Party. It was one of those parties where instead of Tupperware the hostess sells flavored skin lotions and edible panties and a variety of innovative sex toys. Only Lee Anne didn't call them sex toys, she called them Passion Playthings. Lee Ann served light hor d'oeuvres and mimosas and after awhile she dimmed the lights and pulled the drapes and gave a little talk about how these parties weren't for single women or sex perverts, but were for "Christian married ladies who wanted to put a little good clean fun into their sex lives within the bounds of holy matrimony, of course."

Helen Haynes said "Whoeee!" and knocked her mimosa over, and they all had a good laugh about that, and then Lee Anne passed around a silver tray covered in these little silver bells. Lee Anne called them her Jeza-bells. The idea was that Lee Anne would read from a script provided by the Passion Party people, and anytime she hit on a subject where one of her guests had firsthand knowledge, some kind of spicy sexual escapade she might have participated in with her husband, the guest would ring her little bell. Nita was thirty-eight at the time, the same age as Lee Anne, but most of the other women at the party were younger, in their late twenties and early thirties, and it occurred to Nita, listening to all those little silver bells going off as the party wore on, that sometime between her generation and theirs, a lot of sexual liberation had been going on. Nita had found herself wishing that Lavonne Zibolsky was here. Lavonne was seven years older than Nita and she was from up North, where people kept to themselves and women didn't seem to feel a need to attend Passion Parties. Nita guessed that Lavonne and Leonard Zibolsky's sex life was probably even more uninspired than her and Charles's, which wasn't something that made Nita particularly happy; it just would have been nice to have a little support. She wished her best friend, Eadie Boone, had been invited but Lee Anne hadn't asked Eadie, naturally, because no one wanted to listen to Eadie's bell ringing continuously, no one wanted to put up with that kind of pressure.

Lee Anne passed around another pitcher of mimosas and after awhile the bell ringing got louder and more sustained and the women quit putting their hands over their mouths when they rang, and some of the bolder ones even launched into personal stories that no one really wanted to hear. Nita sat quietly on the sofa, listening, while humiliation rolled over her like a cloud of insecticide. That whole evening she rang her little bell only twice.

The Passion Party had been a year ago, when Nita was still reading her Harlequin Romances, and immediately afterward she graduated to the hard-core heaving-bosom novels she was addicted to now. She told herself she read these to come up with ideas she and Charles could use at home, but so far she hadn't worked up the courage to suggest anything.

Still, Nita was determined to sexually liberate herself no matter what it took. She was pretty sure there was nothing sadder than a thirty-nine-year-old woman who had never had an orgasm. She watched endless television talk shows that dealt with sexual intimacy, and late one night she happened across a show for twenty-somethings run by two good-looking young men, one of them a doctor and the other a tough-talking New Yorker who looked and sounded like a Mafia hit man. The studio audience would stand up and ask about things that made Nita squirm and cover her mouth in embarrassment. The sex therapists answered the questions calmly, as if they were telling someone how to break down a carburetor or fix a horse race at Pimlico. Nita pulled the covers up to hide her face while beside her in the darkened room Charles clicked and snored and hummed like an old generator.

The more talk shows Nita watched, the more she realized she had a lot of studying to do if she was ever going to catch up with the rest of the sexual revolution. There were times she thought it just might not be possible. There were moments she felt like a ten-year-old trying to cram for a college physics exam. After awhile she decided it might be best if she quit watching the talk shows and maybe found a sex therapist who was a little closer to her own hang-ups and insecurities. The last thing Nita wanted was a sex therapist who talked openly about sex, so after a few weeks of furtively poking through the shelves of local bookstores she worked up the courage to get on the Internet and order a book written by Dr. Simon Ledbetter. Dr. Ledbetter billed himself as a Christian sex therapist and his books were explicit but based on biblical scripture, which somehow made it more acceptable to Nita. Oral sex, for example, was okay based on Dr. Ledbetter's reading of several obscure passages from Joshua, and variations in position were allowable according to his interpretation of Proverbs.

Nita studied Dr. Ledbetter's books diligently, highlighting passages she thought pertinent with a yellow marker, and in addition to the numerous variations in sexual position and multiple orgasms and assorted fetishes, she managed to learn quite a bit about the Bible, too.

NITA FELL ASLEEP IN THE TUB AND AWOKE WHEN THE BOOK SHE had been reading sank with a heavy thumping sound into the water. The book was *The Joy of Married Christian Sex*, and she had fallen asleep during the chapter on bondage. She quickly retrieved the book and tried to dry the pages with a towel. From the back cover Dr. Ledbetter, a balding, middle-aged man wearing Coke-bottle glasses and a tweed jacket, watched her sadly.

She put the book on the floor register to dry, slipped on her bathrobe, and went downstairs to check on the children. They were playing video games in front of the big-screen TV.

"Did you two finish your homework?" Nita asked.

"Why are you wearing your pajamas?" Whitney said, clutching her controller to her chest. "It's not bedtime."

Nita went to the bar and poured herself a glass of wine. She figured she had a two-hour window of opportunity to seduce her husband, between the time the children finished their homework and immersed themselves in video games and the time they went to bed, and if Charles didn't hurry, the window would be closed. It was six-thirty and he should be home by now. Sometimes he had dinner at the club. If he played golf with a big client he might have stayed to buy the client dinner. She checked the answering machine, but the only message was from Lavonne Zibolsky, reminding her about the lunch meeting tomorrow to discuss the firm's dinner party. Lavonne's voice sounded hard and nasal. Even after so many years in the South, Lavonne still clung stubbornly to her Yankee accent.

Nita loved Lavonne in spite of the odd clipped way in which she spoke and the strange phrases she persisted in using, like calling a Coca-cola a "pop" and saying "you guys" instead of "ya'll." Nita loved her in spite of the way Lavonne used four-letter words with shocking regularity and said whatever she thought no matter who she offended. It was her Yankee ways that kept most of the people they socialized with at arm's length, just like it was Eadie Boone's flaunting of social conventions that kept her on the outlaw fringe of Barron Hall society. "I've asked Eadie to come, too, but I won't blame her if she doesn't, given her current situation with Trevor and all," Lavonne said and hung up.

Nita couldn't imagine Eadie coming to the lunch meeting either. Eadie had never been very good about helping with firm functions, even when she and Trevor were happily married, and Nita couldn't imagine she'd bother to show up and help plan one she wasn't even invited to. Nita and Eadie had graduated from public high school in the same class but they'd never really been friends until after Eadie had married Trevor Boone and moved back to Ithaca from Athens. In high school, Nita had always been afraid of Eadie Wilkens. She ran with a rough group of kids who wore heavy eye makeup and nose rings and were always in trouble for things like painting the school mascot black and setting fire to the home ec room.

Nita had been a good girl all her life, an honor roll student and student council representative who sang in the church choir; a girl like Eadie Wilkens was a mystery to her. It wasn't until Nita's senior year of high school, when she was being crowned Homecoming Queen and Eadie stole the show by standing on her head in the bleachers (she wasn't wearing any underwear), that Nita had a sudden epiphany and realized for the first time why Eadie Wilkens was the way she was. Anyone else would have hated Eadie for stealing the show the way she did, but Nita understood with a sudden flash of insight that everything Eadie did was just her way of protecting herself. Eadie had grown up without a daddy or brothers or male cousins to look after her, and a rebellious reputation was the best chance she had of putting up a force field. Standing on the fifty-yard line with the overhead lights shimmering through her crown like a halo, Nita realized if she'd been raised the way Eadie'd been raised, without a good home and a good family and a decent place to live, she might've turned out the same sad way. For the first time in her life, she felt sorry for Eadie Wilkens. Years later, after Eadie had married Trevor Boone and returned to Ithaca, she'd walked into Boone & Broadwell where Nita was working as a secretary and, taking one look at Nita, grinned and said, "Hey, I remember you. You were the only girl who was ever nice to me in high school." Eighteen years later she and Nita were still friends.

Nita climbed the stairs with her glass of wine. Dr. Ledbetter was where she had left him, lying facedown on the floor. She picked him up and put him on the bed and then went around the room dimming the lamps and lighting a few candles, which she placed on the tables closest to the bed.

After awhile she climbed into bed and lay staring at the ceiling and trying to imagine her husband coming through the door. She rehearsed several seduction scenes in her mind. Dr. Ledbetter was a big believer in using fantasy to put the zip back into a stagnant marriage, and he had set up several scenarios, including dialogue, to use during foreplay. The only one she could even remotely imagine Charles agreeing to was the Lion Tamer and the Naughty Trapeze Girl. For some reason she could imagine Charles wearing boots and carrying a whip. But this fantasy required installation of some ceiling hardware that Nita would never be able to explain to the children.

She read the other scripts, finding that the dialogue pretty much followed the same format. After awhile Nita realized that she had been reading the same monotonous dialogue in numerous soft-porn romance novels. She had always assumed that porno romance novelists must have incredibly varied and innovative sex lives, but now she had a sudden image of a middle-aged librarian locked in a small room poring over sex manuals and entering the dialogue, verbatim, into an endless stream of repetitive novels. It was shocking. It made her wonder if she had wasted a year of her life immersed in a world of false sex and romance. Nita let the book drop. She crossed her hands on her chest and stared at the ceiling. She wondered how hard it would be to install a trapeze. She wondered which way the ceiling joists ran.

She wondered what Jimmy Lee Motes would say if she asked him to hang a trapeze from her bedroom ceiling.

* * *

"NITA, WHAT IN THE HELL ARE YOU DOING?"

She awoke with a start. Charles was standing in the doorway, illuminated by the light falling from the hallway and the stairwell behind him.

"It's nine-thirty and the kids are still playing video games," he said. "They're completely unsupervised."

"Sorry," she said, sitting up on one elbow. Drool had collected at the corner of her mouth and run down along her chin and the front of her black silk camisole. She wiped her face with the back of one hand.

"Do you have the flu?" he asked suspiciously. He stood in the doorway, a dark and slightly menacing figure.

"No," she said. "I don't think so."

"I told the kids to go to bed," he said, coming into the room. "I didn't know what else to do."

"Okay." She pulled her hair away from her mouth, trying to make herself wake up, trying to remember why she was lying in bed wearing sexy lingerie.

"Why is it so dark in here?" he said, hitting the switch to the wall sconces. Light flooded the room and Nita shielded her eyes with her hand, swaying on one elbow, her hair wild around her face, lipstick smeared in a red arc around her mouth, mascara oozing beneath her eyes and down one cheek.

Charles stared blankly at his wife, who resembled a deranged circus clown. The sexual aspect of her lying in bed didn't occur to him. He hadn't thought of her that way in years, not since the birth of the children. He had a stack of pornographic magazines in a box in the back of his closet that he masturbated to, but he wouldn't have thought of doing to his wife what men in the magazines did to those women. Sex with his wife was a sacred trust; a covenant based on two thousand years of faith and history. After a minute, he turned and went into the bathroom.

She could hear him running water in the sink. She had been dreaming she was locked in a decrepit old house and the sewer had backed up and was steadily filling the house with green stinking water and a kind of brown sludge. She kept running up the stairs and hollering for everyone to get out, and the sewage kept following her up one flight after another, filling floor after floor of the sinking house.

"Nita, what did I tell you about the toothpaste?" Charles said, leaning around the bathroom door and holding the tube out in front of him like a relay runner holds a baton. Charles was very particular about his toothpaste. There was a right way to squeeze it and a wrong way. The right way was to start at the bottom and roll it. The wrong way was to grab the middle of a full tube and squeeze. He had taught her this years ago, but somehow, during the past few weeks she had spent trying to figure out how to put the zip back into her marriage, Nita had managed to forget.

"Sorry," she said.

He went back into the bathroom and a minute later she heard him humming to himself as he brushed his teeth.

Nita caught a glimpse of herself in the dresser mirror. She wet her fingers and tried to remove the mascara smudges beneath her eyes. She rubbed her mouth on a Kleenex. Dr. Ledbetter was lying there, faceup on the bed, and she quickly slid him into her nightstand drawer.

"I saw Leonard at the office today," Charles said, coming out of the bathroom and wiping his hands on a towel. "He says you and Lavonne have a lunch meeting tomorrow to talk about the firm party. He seemed to think Lavonne was getting pretty close to finding a caterer." Nita pulled the sheet to her chin. She didn't know what to say to this. She wasn't very good at lying. She nodded her head slightly.

"Good," he said. "Is it one of my mother's caterers?"

Nita nodded again. She tried to imagine her husband as a lion tamer or a pirate. She tried to imagine him with long hair and an eye patch and a curving cutlass strapped to his waist.

"Why are you squinting like that?" Charles said, frowning. "Is there something wrong with your eyes?"

Nita opened her mouth to explain about Dr. Ledbetter's Christian lovemaking, but then thought better of it. Charles stared at her suspiciously. In the hallway behind him, Logan's door closed softly. "You might want to make an appointment to get your eyes checked," he said. "You're getting to that age when people start needing to wear reading glasses." He stepped out of his slacks and folded them neatly over a chair. "I'm going to jump in the shower," he said. "I had dinner at the club so don't bother to make me anything."

She waited until she heard the water running and then she went into her closet and took off the black camisole and put on her favorite flannel nightgown and her slippers with the pig faces the children had given her last Christmas. She stuffed the camisole in the back of a drawer where she would never find it again. She was thirty-nine years old. Her eyes would be going soon. Her breasts would sag. Her thighs would dimple. All that time she had spent reading soft-porn romance novels and going to Passion Parties and reading about how to explore her sexuality, she should have been developing a hobby. Something safe and matronly like collecting spoons. Or scrapbooking.

From inside her closet, Nita heard him climbing out of the shower. She wrapped herself in her bathrobe and noticed Charles had hung his Orvis hunting jacket in her closet, near the front where she would be sure to see it. He was scheduled to leave four weeks from now for his annual hunting trip, and Nita supposed he had hung the jacket there to remind her to take it to the dry cleaners. She reached to move it, and as she lifted the hanger, a long slim package of condoms fell out of the pocket.

"Nita!" he called from the bathroom. "Make sure my mother's at that lunch meeting tomorrow. She may be able to help you with some of the details for the party."

Nita stood there looking at the condoms and feeling like someone had kicked her in the stomach. They were in a blue cellophane wrapper with the picture of a rhino on the front. *Ribbed for her Pleasure!* it read across the front. She'd had her tubes tied eleven years ago and this thought clanged through her head, insistent as an alarm bell. She looked down at the little blue package in her hand. The voice in her head said, *What does this mean?* But she knew what it meant. She closed her fingers tightly over the condoms and stood, clenching both fists. Something monstrous rolled beneath her breast like a heavy wheel, like a stone rolled across the mouth of a cave. All her life she'd been a good girl. All her life she'd done what was expected of her. It was too late to change now. She opened her hands and looked blankly at the palms, at the fresh crescent nail marks. Already the heaviness in her chest was receding, leaving in its place a creeping numbness. She slipped the condoms back inside her husband's jacket.

"I hope you remembered to pick up my shirts at the cleaners," Charles shouted, wrapping a towel around his waist. "I have to be in court in the morning and I need my lucky blue shirt."

Nita had read once that denial was unhealthy, but so far she had found it to be both practical and safe.

Charles quickly combed his hair and checked his teeth in the mirror. "Honey?" he said, stepping out into the bedroom, but Nita was gone.

RETURNING HOME FROM HER STAKEOUT OF TREVOR AND HIS NEW girlfriend at the Pink House Restaurant, Eadie Boone poured herself a tumbler of scotch and took a hot bath. She was sitting up in bed drinking a second glass of scotch and contemplating a midnight call to Denton Swafford, her personal trainer, when the phone rang.

"Eadie."

"Yes?" She recognized Trevor's voice. She smiled and snuggled down in the covers, resting her drink on her stomach.

"Stop following me and Tonya."

"My God, is that her name?" Eadie wondered if the girl was with him. He sounded nervous.

"You know there are laws out there protecting people from stalkers."

"You flatter yourself," Eadie said. She didn't like to think about the girl lying in bed with her husband. All in all, Eadie had been pretty patient about the whole situation, but her patience was beginning to wear a little thin.

"And stop calling wherever I am and having yourself paged. After awhile it loses its effectiveness."

"I guess I'll just have to start showing up in person."

Tonya had climbed on top of Trevor and was doing things that, given the fact he was talking on the phone with his wife, made him very uncomfortable. "What is it you want, Eadie?" Trevor made a movement with his hand for Tonya to stop but she ignored him.

"I want you to come home."

"That's impossible," he said.

"You know she can't make you happy. She can't give you what you need to make yourself happy." Eadie wondered if Trevor was getting any writing done with Tonya around. When they were first married and lived in the basement of the house in Athens, they used to spend whole weekends shut up in the bedroom. He always kept a stack of books on the bedside table, and after they made love, he would open a book the way some men would light a cigarette. He would read for a while, and Eadie would sit on the edge of the bed making charcoal sketches of him reading, Vivaldi playing softly in the background. After awhile he would put the book down, and reach for her.

"I want you to get on with your life." Trevor put his hand on Tonya's shoulder and shook his head. The girl sat back on her heels, frowning. "I want you to get on with your life and stop following me around."

"Come home, Trevor. It's too hard to fight when we're not living under the same roof."

"You're crazy," he said.

"That's why you love me."

"My mother was right."

"Your mother was crazy, too. That's why you fell in love with me. Boys always marry girls like their mothers."

He laughed. Eadie could always make him laugh. Tonya rolled off him and stalked off, her high-heeled slippers clicking loudly against the hardwood floor. She slammed the bedroom door as she went out.

"What was that?" Eadie said.

"Nothing." He knew Tonya wouldn't leave. She never left, no matter how angry he made her.

Eadie said, "I've got to go." She put her fingers over the receiver and said loudly, "Stop it, Denton."

"What was that?" Trevor said.

"Nothing."

"Is that goddamn personal trainer there now?"

"Of course not."

"You tell him I said to get the hell out of my house," Trevor shouted. "You tell him I said—"

"Come home and tell him yourself," Eadie said, and hung up.

❀   ❀   ❀

AT A TIME WHEN MANY WOMEN SHE KNEW WERE STRIKING OFF ON
their own, leaving the scattered wreckage of twenty-year marriages behind them, Eadie Boone struggled daily with the undeniable certainty
that she was still in love with her own damn husband. It took courage
to admit this, and a steady belief in the infallibility of her own judgment, especially in light of the fact Trevor had left her for another
woman.

He had left her but he had never stopped loving her. Eadie knew
this. He had convinced himself that it was over between them, but
deep down inside he was still as hooked as he had been that day she
rode by on the Georgia Homecoming float, desirable and aloof. In
those days, she was an art major attending the University of Georgia on
a scholarship. Trevor, a second-year law student, had looked up at her
as she passed above the crowd and gallantly announced to his drunken
fraternity brothers, "Boys, there goes the girl I will marry." She had
thought him somewhat mild at first, and incapable of sustained combat,
and it was not until their first argument in the dining room of the Chi
Phi house, when she had thrown a dessert plate at him, and he ran his
finger through the sticky mess on his face, licked it, and calmly announced, "Blackberry, my favorite," that she knew she would marry
him.

She was eighteen and he was twenty-four. They were from the
same small town, but had grown up without conscious knowledge of
the other. She had grown up in a single-wide trailer on the wrong side
of town and no one had expected much of Eadie Sue Wilkens except
early motherhood and disgrace. Trevor was descended from landowners
and pine barren speculators and had been raised by his widowed
mother in a huge old mansion on Lee Street. They married that same
year, against the wishes of his mother, who could not forgive Eadie for
being a trailer trash girl and, even worse, an artist. Eadie sculpted
women out of clay, headless things with huge breasts and private parts.
Eadie's sculptures started out small, during the first few years after she
married Trevor and came to live in his mama's big house, but over the
years they got bigger and bigger until Eadie had to start selling off
the furniture to make room for them. Mrs. Boone had died, from
shame some said, soon after watching Trevor slip an heirloom platinum

diamond wedding ring on Eadie Wilkens's finger, and after graduating from law school Trevor had returned to Ithaca to his mother's big house and his grandfather's law firm. Even in those early years, there was something about Eadie's dedication to her art that drove Trevor crazy. Every time he came home to find another big-breasted woman in his house, he'd get mad as hell and shout at Eadie and she'd shout back and then, next day, she'd start on a bigger one. After awhile Eadie and her big women chased Trevor out of the house and he got himself a girlfriend, a cocktail waitress out at Bad Bob's saloon, and an apartment over on the other side of town. But even with Trevor gone, Eadie found ways to make trouble. She started sleeping with a bouncer out at Bad Bob's and eventually fell in with a bunch of artistic types from Atlanta who would come down on weekends and sleep in Trevor's big house and drink his whiskey and talk about Kafka until four o'clock in the morning. After that, she used a big chunk of his money to open up a house on Fourth Street for women and their kids who needed a place to hide out from their bad husbands. After awhile, Trevor got tired of trying to live without his wife, and he moved back home to Eadie and her big women.

And now here he was, years later, caught up in the throes of some embarrassing midlife passion, and here Eadie was again, trying to save him from himself. She would not give up on him. At least not yet, although she could look down the road and see an end to her patience. Eadie was an optimist, but there were limits to what even she was willing to take.

THE MORNING AFTER TREVOR'S PHONE CALL, EADIE AWOKE TO find herself in bed with her personal trainer. She didn't usually let Denton stay the night, and when she awoke, she lay very still, trying to accustom herself to the unfamiliar sensation of waking up next to someone, trying to figure out how she had managed to get herself into this predicament. She was pretty sure it had something to do with the amount of scotch she had consumed the night before. She was pretty sure it had something to do with the fact that her husband was sleeping with his goddamned legal secretary. Letting Denton Swafford stay the

night was not something she had planned on, and was sure to compli-
cate matters. Still, she thought, turning to look at the sleeping Denton,
who lay on his back with one well-muscled arm thrown over his head,
what was done, was done. She might as well make the best of it. She
poked him in the ribs with her finger.

He moved slightly and opened his eyes. He turned his face toward
her and grinned. "Morning," he said, his hair falling boyishly over his
forehead.

Eadie yawned and rolled over on her back. "I'll take mine black,"
she said.

"What?" He raised himself on one elbow. He was adorable, but he
knew it, which kind of killed the whole effect for Eadie.

"My coffee," she said. "I'll take it black."

Denton was her latest attempt to get Trevor's attention and circum-
vent the boredom and inertia that inevitably set in when she wasn't
working. She had heard Lee Anne Bales going on about him after a
doubles match at the club, and she had thought, Why not? Spending
five hundred dollars a month on a personal trainer was just the kind
of thing to send Trevor Boone's blood pressure soaring. Denton had
shown up at her house with his bag of equipment and his charts and his
notebook and she had taken one look at him and immediately decided
on the exercise routine that was best for her. So far he hadn't complained.

Outside in the street a tourist bus chugged by, its exhaust plume
billowing in through the partially opened windows with a smell of
diesel and burnt rubber. Faint music drifted from the traffic stopped at
the light. Eadie lived in the home built by her husband's great-great-
grandfather along a street of equally impressive old antebellum homes.
Southern Accents had done an article on the "Gracious Old Homes of
Ithaca" a few years ago, and now busloads of tourists drove down from
Atlanta to gawk at these fine examples of Southern graciousness. From
time to time Eadie liked to appear scantily dressed on her balcony to
give the tourists something else to gawk at. Standing on the porch of
that fine house with the tourists gazing up at her in admiration and de-
votion, Eadie Wilkens Boone, last of a long line of gypsies and itinerant
house painters, was reminded just how far she had managed to come.

As a young girl, Eadie had never wanted anything except to go to Paris and be a starving artist, but Eadie's mother said no, the Wilkenses had been starving for generations; it was time one of them made something of themselves. Eadie was extraordinarily pretty, even as a child, and her mother had entered her in beauty contest after beauty contest, driving her to Birmingham and Mobile and Atlanta. Because she did not care at all about winning, Eadie won them all. She won because she had an arrogant and careless deportment that made her stand out among all those eager and desperately servile young girls like a serpent in a chicken yard. Her insolence was irresistible.

At fifteen she won the Miss Snellville Beach contest; at sixteen she was named Miss Boll Weevil; and at eighteen she was smart enough to realize her looks were her ticket out of Ithaca and poverty via a pageant scholarship to the University of Georgia. Two years later, she'd returned to Ithaca as Mrs. Trevor Boone.

Now, nineteen years later, the Boone House was hers. Old Mrs. Boone's high-ceilinged rooms, once filled with overstuffed mahogany furniture and oil portraits of dead ancestors, were filled with Eadie's giant fertility goddesses. She liked to look around the house and see them scattered like the monoliths of Easter Island. They made her feel powerful. They reminded her she was a woman who could do anything she set her mind to.

In the street below, the tour bus chugged away with its cargo of enthralled tourists. Eadie lay back on her pillow and yawned and stretched and looked at the clock. Denton took her stretching as an invitation, but she rolled away from him and said, "You need to get going. It's almost nine o'clock." She was supposed to meet Lavonne Zibolsky for lunch to discuss the damn firm party that no one wanted to attend, much less plan. If it weren't for the fact that Lavonne was one of her best friends, Eadie wouldn't have agreed to help. Eadie wasn't even going to the party now that Trevor and his pubescent legal secretary would both be there. Eadie was quiet for a moment, considering this. The clock ticked steadily. A damp breeze heavy with the scent of wood smoke blew through the room. She rolled over and faced Denton again. "What are you doing next Saturday night?" she said.

He reached his hand out to cup her breast but she pushed it away.

"I don't know," he said, grinning. "I'll have to check my appointment book."

She imagined the shocked expressions of the crowd as she entered the party. She imagined the drama of the moment. She imagined Trevor and Tonya, stunned and running for cover. Eadie smiled at this pleasant vision. "You're going to a party," she told Denton, having just decided. "Put it on your calendar or in your book or whatever the hell you have to do. You're going."

Denton put his arm under his head and stared intently at the huge, headless torso that stood in front of the opened window. "Just what exactly is that thing?" he asked, frowning. It was Eadie's newest piece. She was rather proud of it.

"You tell me," she said, looking fondly at the goddess. Having decided to crash her husband's firm's party, Eadie could relax now. She had a plan. She only wondered why she hadn't thought of it before. "What is it?" she said, pinching Denton's thick bicep. Each sculpture was unique and yet each carried the same features; huge pendulous breasts, bulging bellies, headless torsos.

"Well, I'm not sure." Denton's handsome brow wrinkled. He stuck his lower lip out and squinted his eyes slightly. He had the slack, perplexed look of a small boy asked to solve a complex algebraic problem in his head. "I'm not sure but it makes me feel sad."

"Sad?" Eadie frowned and sat up on her elbow. Anyone else lying beside Denton in bed would have thought him adorable, but Eadie felt nothing but a growing sense of irritation with his lack of intelligence and artistic vision. "Why in the world would it make you feel sad?"

"I don't know." He sat up in bed and wrapped his arms around his knees, sucking his lower lip, his eyes narrowly following the curves of the goddess. He chewed his bottom lip. He tilted his head. "It looks kind of like a sad walrus or a seal," he said finally. "Like one of those seals you see in *National Geographic Magazine.* The ones that lie abandoned on the ice waiting for some Eskimo to come and beat them to death with a club."

Eadie stared at his silly handsome face. She felt as if someone had driven an ice pick into her chest. Her breath seeped out of her punctured lungs and collected in her throat like poison gas. She wondered at the possibility of sustaining a lasting relationship with a stupid person. She wondered if Trevor would be able to do it.

"I think it's a seal," Denton repeated, grinning.

"Well, I guess that's why you're not paid to think," Eadie said, and rolling out of bed, she went to get ready for her lunch appointment with Lavonne Zibolsky.

*L*AVONNE'S MEETING WITH NITA WAS SCHEDULED FOR noon, so she arrived at the Pink House Restaurant at eleven forty-five. Lavonne prided herself on her ability to be early for any appointment. It was one of those things she did really well. Now that her daughters were nearly grown and no longer needed her, now that Leonard was well-established in his Big Important Career, the things that Lavonne did really well had been whittled down some, but she clung to them stubbornly. She was punctual. She was precise. She could add columns of numbers in her head. It was a small list, but for the time being, it would have to do.

She had lain awake most of the night worrying about the party. Lavonne didn't like to fail at anything, even something she didn't really want to do, and somewhere between the panic attack that set in when she imagined telling Leonard and Charles Broadwell that she hadn't found a caterer, and the pleasant time she spent imagining herself running away to the beach, she had decided she would no longer worry about the party. She would do the best she could, and if the dinner turned out to be a disaster, well, too bad. If Leonard and Charles wanted to get mad at someone they should get mad at Charles's reptilian mother, Virginia, who had decided at the last minute to bail and dump the party on the wives.

This early morning revelation had been noble and courageous, but the reality, of course, was that in the cold hard light of day, Lavonne was still worried. She hoped that the meeting with Nita would be productive. She hoped that this feeling of heaviness in her chest, this shortness of breath, would go away once she and Nita had had a chance to discuss what they must do. But when she saw Nita pull to the curb outside the restaurant and climb wearily out of her car, Lavonne's hopes plummeted like a spent rocket and she realized Nita would be no help whatsoever. Nita's face, in the bright slash of winter sunlight, was pale and haggard. There were dark circles beneath her eyes.

Anyone who had known the lovely, luminous girl Nita had once been would not have recognized the woman now climbing out of her car. She had been a secretary at Boone & Broadwell when Leonard first joined the firm, and had been secretly dating Charles Broadwell for three years. In those days there had been a radiance about Nita, a good-hearted optimism that affected all who knew her. But sixteen years of marriage to Charles Broadwell had tarnished that brightness. Nita was still an extraordinarily pretty woman, with her slender figure and large gray eyes, but there was a faded quality to her now, like old cloth, as if she might be slowly wearing away.

She came into the restaurant looking forlorn and bent forward at the waist as if she dragged something heavy behind her. Looking at her, Lavonne had a sudden memory of her mother struggling to carry a basket of wet clothes to the clothesline on a wintry day.

"Sorry I'm late," Nita said, sliding into a chair.

"You're never late," Lavonne said. The memory of her mother gradually faded. She raised her hand to get the waiter's attention, and as he began to make his way across the crowded room she leaned forward and said to Nita, "I can see you didn't sleep last night worrying about this damn party. I'm telling you, though, I have it all under control. You don't need to worry about a thing."

Nita smiled but she didn't say anything. It was true that she hadn't slept much last night, but it had nothing to do with the firm party. She had dreamed she was being chased by little blue fish. She'd spent all night swimming in slow motion, trying to escape the shiny blue piranhas before they ate her alive. The dream had left her tired and depressed. "Is Eadie coming?" Nita asked, slipping her purse beneath the table.

"I don't think so." Lavonne lifted her glass and sipped her tea. "It's just you and me."

Nita thought, *Well, not exactly*. She didn't have the courage to tell Lavonne that Charles had insisted she invite her mother-in-law to the meeting. Lavonne would find out soon enough and in the meantime, maybe she'd be able to eat a little something before Virginia arrived.

THEY HAD JUST ORDERED LUNCH WHEN EADIE BOONE SHOWED UP. She swept into the restaurant wearing dark sunglasses and a long white knit dress with high-heeled sandals. Over in the corner a group of tourists quit looking at glossy brochures of Ithaca and looked instead at Eadie. She stood by the hostess desk waiting for everyone to get a good look at her. Eadie was aware that the entire town had been gossiping about her and expecting her to do something desperate after Trevor's latest infidelity. It was hard to be confident when the whole town was against you, but Eadie was used to it by now. She liked a challenge. She had spent her whole life proving that she was up to any obstacle fate could throw in her path. So far she had overcome poverty, a tragic childhood, and loneliness. Handling a wayward husband was nothing compared to all that. She saw Lavonne and Nita and waved.

Lavonne was glad to see her. Eadie looked pretty good considering her husband had left her and her life was rumored to be in ruins. Lavonne had always assumed the Boones would make it, they'd been so crazy about each other, and their marriage, although unconventional, had seemed to work for them.

"I didn't think you'd come," she said to Eadie as she sat down.

"You sounded desperate on the phone," Eadie said, grinning. Now that she had decided to crash the firm's party, she felt helping Lavonne plan the fiasco was the least she could do. Not that she had any intention of telling Lavonne about her party-crashing scheme. Lavonne would just try and talk her out of it, and Eadie was too far along to change her plans now. She knew this party might be the last chance she had of convincing Trevor Boone that he still loved her, before he made the mistake of his life and filed for divorce.

"I guess I am pretty desperate," Lavonne said, thankful that Eadie had shown up. No one knew how to plan a party better than Eadie Boone.

Lavonne had been going to Boone parties for years. The first Boone party she'd attended had been a "get acquainted throw down" the Boones had hosted to welcome the Zibolskys to town. Lavonne had thought Eadie the most beautiful woman she'd ever seen, and the most genuine. She had thought Eadie was wasting her time in Ithaca, Georgia, when she could be out in Hollywood making movies. In those days Eadie and Trevor had a lot of bohemian friends from Athens and they'd come down on the weekends for wild parties that kept the rest of the town scandalized. It was only the fact that Trevor was a Boone, and that still meant something in this town, that kept Eadie and Trevor from becoming social outcasts.

"Hi Nita," Eadie said, settling her purse under the table.

Nita gave her a little smile. She was playing with her fork, tapping it against the table like she was sending a telegraph, some kind of frantic S.O.S.

Eadie leaned forward and peered intently into Nita's face. "Honey, I'm worried about you," she said. "Are you feeling okay?"

Nita stopped telegraphing with her fork. She plucked idly at her hair. She had decided last night that she would stop reading romance novels, and she had awakened this morning to a feeling of hopelessness and pessimism about the future. Where once there had been color, now there was only drab black and white, and without her rousing adventures of love and sex on the high seas, in castles, in teepees, in harem tents, to distract her, Nita was being forced to take a good hard look at her real life. And she didn't much like what she saw. "I'm just tired is all," she said.

"Uh-huh," Eadie said, looking at her suspiciously. She had tried to talk Nita out of marrying Charles Broadwell. "He's a control freak. He's a snob. He'll make you miserable." But by then Nita had already dated him past the time she would have felt comfortable breaking it off. Going together longer than two years implied something deeper than casual dating, or at least it did in Nita's code of behavior, and she had felt bound by social convention and by the fact that he had defied his own mother to become engaged to her. There had been nothing else she could do but marry him.

"Is there anything we can do to help?" Lavonne asked.

"Cut his brake line? Poison his soup? Push him down the stairs?"

Nita flushed and looked at her hands. "Let's talk about something else," she said.

The waiter came to take her order and Eadie said, "I'll have a glass of your house merlot and a chicken salad plate." She leaned forward on her elbows and looked around the table. "Am I the only one drinking?"

"I never drink in the middle of the day," Lavonne said. "I have to keep my wits about me." Her dress strained and creaked like a sail in a gale wind. She wondered how she would be able to eat and breathe at the same time. She wished she hadn't quarreled with Leonard this morning over wearing the dress. She wished Leonard hadn't said something stupid that turned wearing the dress into a big challenge.

Eadie took a piece of paper out of her purse and handed it to Lavonne. "Okay, here's my advice for the party," she said. "I wrote it all down so you can follow along with me," she said, pointing to the neatly numbered items on the page. "I went ahead and called the tent and awning place." The party was held every year in the Broadwells' backyard beneath a huge white tent. The waiter brought her a glass of wine and Eadie smiled at him and went on. "The awning people said there must have been some kind of a mix-up because somebody had called and canceled the tent. I know the manager personally and I talked him into reinstating the order ahead of the Donaldsons' wedding so you don't need to worry about that. You can get the tablecloths and the tables and chairs there, too. Nita, here's the name of the guy who carves the ice sculptures. He's expecting your call. Just call him and tell him to carve whatever shape you want. I always order flowers in bulk from the Plantation Greenery and they'll make up centerpieces for the tables. If you can't find a caterer, call one of the restaurants in town—"

"I already did that," Lavonne said. "No one can do it on such short notice."

"Okay, then call the deli manager at the Piggly Wiggly and order a whole lot of party trays and take them home and put them on your best silver. Then call the Salty Dog and order a frozen margarita machine. Trust me, once the tequila starts flowing, no one will notice or care where the food comes from. And for Christsakes get a disk jockey. Don't hire that goddamn string quartet Virginia hires every year. Nothing kills a good party quicker than classical music."

Lavonne looked at Eadie like she might be a genius. "My God, I hadn't even thought about the tent," she said. "I just assumed Virginia had ordered it." She hadn't thought about the ice sculpture or the flowers either. "I don't know about the margarita machine though," she said to Eadie. "The only one who ever rents a margarita machine is you and look how wild your parties get."

Eadie tapped her fingers against the table to give Lavonne a few minutes to think about it. She smiled sweetly and said, "Do you want your guests standing around critiquing the food or do you want them down on the floor gatoring to 'Gimme a Pig's Foot and a Bottle of Beer'?"

"Point taken," Lavonne said.

Nita played nervously with her silverware. Eadie smiled and closed her purse. She hoped Lavonne would remember later how much help she had been in planning the party and forgive her for the scene she was planning on creating. It was unfortunate that the party-crashing had to take place on Lavonne's watch, but it was unavoidable. Eadie lifted the glass of merlot to her lips, frowned, and then set it down with a sharp clanking sound against the table. "Oh shit, what's she doing here?"

Lavonne swiveled around to see who Eadie was staring at. Nita glanced up, her eyes skittering away from the front door, across the rose-colored walls, and coming to rest finally on the pine-planked floor.

Virginia Broadwell stood at the hostess desk. She saw Nita and began to make her way across the crowded restaurant, a small slim woman with a spine as straight and rigid as rebar. She nodded slightly, regally, to people she knew, ignoring those she didn't.

"Ya'll, I'm so sorry," Nita said, still looking at the floor. "Charles made me ask her."

Virginia reached the table and stood waiting for the waiter to pull out her chair. She smiled pleasantly at Eadie and Lavonne, but it was obvious she didn't mean it. "Hello, Eadie," she said, sliding into her seat.

Eadie picked up her wineglass. She thought, *Hello Satan.* She said, "Hello, Virginia."

Virginia nodded. "Lavonne."

"Virginia." Lavonne had disliked Virginia Broadwell from the moment she first saw her presiding over a meeting of the Ithaca Garden Club, smiling in her false, pleasant manner and politely squashing the suggestions of the new members like the benevolent dictator she was. Virginia was a snob, a fact that made her greatly appreciated in the small, closed social set of Ithaca, Georgia. Her great-great-grandfather's property had been nothing more than an overgrown island in the middle of the Black Warrior River, his slaves no more than a handful of ragged, scrawny men who would hail the passing steamboats for food. Virginia's great-grandfather had lost the island in a card game. Her father had worked for the railroad. The old-moneyed aristocracy of Ithaca laughed at Virginia. They laughed at her snobbish manners, and her big house filled with animal trophies, and her dead husband, the judge, who was himself an upstart, his own grandfather having been nothing more than a tenant farmer.

Virginia was ridiculed by the old aristocracy, but she was revered by the people she detested the most, fellow members of the Ithaca Garden Club and the Junior League, many of whom hailed from places north of the Mason-Dixon but who, once settled in the old mansions lining Lee Street, became even more fiercely loyal to the ideals and prejudices of the Old South than their native-South neighbors. Tacky Yankee Corporate People, Virginia called them. They were the scourge of the new South, Virginia maintained, worse even than the carpet-baggers had been. She had never forgiven DuPont for opening up a plant on the outskirts of town ten years ago and bringing with it prosperity and droves of Tacky Yankee Corporate People who came from nothing yet lived in big houses, drove expensive cars, and sent their children to the best private school in town.

"I hope I haven't kept ya'll waiting," Virginia said, unfolding her napkin on her lap. She was dressed impeccably in an Ann Taylor suit and dark pumps. Her hair was cut in a fashionable bob. "Have you already ordered?" Without waiting for a reply, she waved the menu away and said to the waiter, "I'll have a Caesar salad and a glass of sweet tea."

He looked at Eadie and smiled. "Another merlot?"

"I'm going to need one of those big frozen margaritas," Eadie said, holding up two hands to show him the size. "The bigger, the better."

"You better bring me one, too," Lavonne said, closing up her Day-timer.

Virginia leaned her elbows on the table, laced her well-manicured fingers together and rested her chin there, looking expectantly from one to the other. "So what did I miss?" she asked. She smiled broadly, showing a row of sharp little teeth. When no one answered, she put her hands in her lap and said brightly, "Well, I'm sorry I'm late but I had a meeting at Bitsy Manchester's. She has a new Cambodian yard boy, and honey, her yard is just lovely. Not a weed in sight. Roses everywhere. Dogwood trees that look like they sprang up overnight. You should see about getting yourself one, Nita." She turned to her daughter-in-law, patting her arm the way you'd pat a colicky baby. "You could use some help with your lawn. You could use some help with the weeds and that brown mold you have growing all over you rhododendrons." She stopped patting Nita. Nita slid her hand into her lap. "I wonder where you go to find a Cambodian yard boy?" Virginia mused to no one in particular.

"Gee, I don't know," Lavonne said. "How about Cambodia?"

Virginia pursed her lips and let her eyes rest, briefly, on Lavonne. She leaned over the table and said, lowering her voice confidentially, "So, have you found a caterer yet?" She pretended to be concerned but secretly, of course, she hoped they had not. She had overheard Charles two weeks ago bragging to someone that the firm's party basically ran it-self and she had immediately decided to teach him a lesson. Virginia had handled the details for this party for the last fifteen years, and it had been a monumental and thankless task ripe with the potential for disaster. She could only hope that this year Charles would discover this for himself. Perhaps it would make him more grateful and less boastful. When she heard he had turned the planning over to Nita and Lavonne she had secretly crowed with delight. Everyone knew there were no decent caterers in this town and to hire one from Atlanta required months of advance scheduling. Virginia had promptly fired the Atlanta caterer when she decided to teach Charles a lesson (she had lied to him and said it was the caterer who backed out at the last minute). Now all she had to do to succeed was pretend to be helpful, and sit around and watch Nita and Lavonne turn the party into a disaster.

"We're working on it," Lavonne said.

Virginia sighed. "I'm so sorry I had to withdraw for health reasons and then that idiotic caterer in Atlanta backed out at the last minute. I had *no idea* Charles would expect ya'll to come up with a caterer at the last minute, it really doesn't seem fair at all, and what *good, good* sports ya'll are being about this whole wretched affair."

No one said anything. The waiter brought their drinks. Virginia glanced around the table to get a good look at what everyone was wearing. Virginia was very particular about appearances. She was one of those Southern women who cannot imagine why a woman would let herself go the way Lavonne had let herself go. To give way to obesity suggested deep-seated unhappiness and MoonPie binges. It hinted at poor breeding and a tendency toward white-trashery. Seeing as how Lavonne was a Yankee, Virginia figured she might not know all this. Virginia figured it was her duty to suggest methods for improvement. "You know, Lucy Metcalfe went on that Atkins diet and lost sixty pounds," she said to Nita.

"Lucy Metcalfe went to Atlanta and had her stomach stapled," Eadie said, lifting her big margarita. "Any idiot can do that." She grimaced and sipped her drink. She'd had about all she could take of Virginia Broadwell. Another ten minutes and things were going to get ugly.

Virginia was accustomed to ignoring Eadie Boone. "Lavonne, have you lost weight?" she said, smiling sweetly. "You look like you have."

Unperturbed, Lavonne buttered another roll and took a big bite before answering. In June, she had gone on Weight Watchers and gained ten pounds. Then in August she went on the Palm Beach Diet and gained fifteen more. If she kept dieting at this rate, she would put on forty pounds by Christmas. "No, Virginia," she said finally, still chewing. "I haven't lost weight. Thanks for asking though."

Eadie touched her big margarita glass to the rim of Lavonne's glass. She motioned for the waiter to bring them another round.

It made Nita nervous the way Eadie and Lavonne were draining their big drinks. The last time Eadie and Lavonne drank tequila around Virginia, they'd gone out to her house in the middle of the night, stolen her lawn jockey, and painted him to look like Bozo the Clown, then returned him to his rightful place in the middle of the front flower bed. It had taken Nita a week of steady pleading to talk Charles and Virginia out of hiring a private investigator to find out who defiled the jockey.

"So what's your plan for finding a caterer?" the irrepressible Virginia said, trying to sound like a coconspirator. She rested her sharp little chin on her palm and looked from one to the other.

"My plan is to get the hell out of town," Lavonne said. "My plan is to throw my suitcase into the back of my car and head for the beach."

Eadie thought this was funny. "Now you're talking," she said. "I'll go with you."

"I haven't been to the beach in so long," Nita said wistfully. The last time had been six months ago for their sixteenth wedding anniversary. Remembering, Nita felt a vibration of guilt in the pit of her stomach. Charles had ordered room service and they'd eaten on their balcony overlooking the Atlantic Ocean. *Maybe the condoms weren't even his,* Nita thought suddenly. Maybe he'd found them on the ground and picked them up and put them in his pocket.

Virginia looked at her daughter-in-law as if she were noticing her for the first time. "Nita," she said sharply. "What's wrong with you? You look terrible."

Nita blanched and knocked her water glass over. "Charles hung his hunting jacket in my closet," she blurted out, mopping the water with her napkin, "and I had to move it." She looked around the table. They were all watching her now, Lavonne and Eadie above the rims of their big-as-a-cereal-bowl margarita glasses, and Virginia with a pinched expression on her face, as if she'd just caught a whiff of something unsavory.

"Maybe you should try sleeping pills," Virginia said.

Nita said, "Sleeping pills?"

The frustration of watching this exchange grew inside Lavonne like a tumor. She'd been watching it for years, Virginia, cruel and manipulative, and Nita, soft and yielding as butter. Lavonne felt Nita's life would be better if just once she told her mother-in-law to fuck off. Except for Nita's steadfast refusal to join the Junior League, Lavonne could not think of a single time Nita had openly opposed Virginia. She took everything Virginia had to dish out, and never said a word in her own defense.

"Maybe you should try Prozac."

"Prozac's not the answer for everything, Virginia," Lavonne said.

"It's the answer for most things," Virginia said.

"Well, you should know," Eadie said.

"I don't have to sit here and be criticized by an adulteress," Virginia snapped, feeling her façade of sympathetic good cheer beginning to slide.

"Well, fuck me," Eadie said.

"I think that's her point," Lavonne said, sipping her drink.

Nita had had enough of this bickering. She couldn't handle open conflict. She put her hands on the table, palms down, and leaned forward slightly. "Maybe we should just concentrate on making this the best firm party ever," she said with the forced fervor of a cheerleader.

Lavonne smiled and said, "Hear, hear." Virginia took a deep breath and regained her composure. Eadie sipped her margarita and thought, *Oh, this'll definitely be the best party ever. They'll be talking about this one for years.*

The waiter brought their food and they settled down to eating. While they ate, Virginia droned on about the Ithaca Cotillion Ball she had attended two weeks ago. The Ithaca Cotillion Ball was one of the oldest debutante balls in south Georgia. People from all over rural Georgia sent their daughters to be presented here, people from towns like Moundsville and Sandy Hook and Shubuta. In Eadie and Nita's day, the only way you could be presented was if your grandmother had been presented or you were nominated by some rogue chairwoman who was herself a member of the committee but who didn't follow the traditional rules of decency and good breeding by allowing new girls in. Mothers worked furiously for years to assure their daughters a berth on the coveted list of twenty-five debs. But over the years the prestige of the ball had begun to diminish. Some of the girls whose grandmothers had been debutantes didn't care about such things now. They refused to participate, leaving room for daughters of doctors and lawyers and corporate executives who were swarming into Ithaca like a horde of nouveau riche barbarians. Getting an invitation to attend the ball was almost as hard as getting an invitation to be a debutante. Lavonne had lived in Ithaca eighteen years and had never been invited. Nita and Eadie had only been twice. Lavonne guessed, unless her daughters somehow managed to be asked as debs, she might spend her entire life without ever attending a debutante ball.

"I don't even think we have debutantes in Cleveland," Lavonne said suddenly.

"Probably not," Virginia murmured.

"Or if we do I don't know about it." Even after eighteen years of living in the South, Lavonne was still trying to work out the complexities of the social scene. Southern society could be broken down into two broad groups: those who were debs, and those who weren't; those who went to private school, and those who didn't. When someone down here asked "What school did you go to?" they weren't asking about college.

"The South is a place of tradition and culture," Virginia reminded them, lifting her sharp little chin.

"Tradition and culture," Lavonne said, raising her glass in a toast. Eadie grinned and lifted her glass. Nita put her face in her hands. "I'm reminded of it every time I'm asked to *mash* an elevator button or *carry* someone to the store," Lavonne said. "Every time I'm asked to *chunk* somebody the remote control."

"Or *tote* a watermelon to a picnic," Eadie said. "Or *whomp* somebody up side of the head to get their attention."

Lavonne grinned and tapped her glass against Eadie's. "I'm reminded of the tradition and culture that is the South every time I drive to the Git n' Gallop or the Honk 'n Holler to pick up a quart of milk."

Virginia had had enough of this conversation. Lavonne was obviously intoxicated. Virginia could tell from looking at the woman that she'd been sampling the frozen margaritas a little too freely. Virginia had been raised to avoid open conflict, she had been taught that no matter how deep an antagonism may run, surface civility must be maintained at all costs. Virginia could hug an enemy to her bosom with one hand, and disembowel her with the other. This was obviously not a skill taught up North.

Virginia lifted her chin slightly and turned to her daughter-in-law. "Nita, did your yard man finish the pool house?" She took her napkin out of her lap and placed it on the table. "You know Charles won't like it if there are scraps of lumber everywhere. You know he likes the yard to look nice the week of the party."

"Jimmy Lee finishes up today," Nita said, remembering. He was finishing up even as she sat here. She'd probably never see him again after today. She picked up her spoon and gazed down into her tomato basil soup. She felt light-headed. Her stomach bounced around her rib cage like a hyperactive gymnast. She wondered if her dream of little blue fishes had something to do with the condoms she'd found in her husband's hunting jacket. She wondered if she was coming down with the flu.

"Jimmy Lee?" Virginia said, frowning.

"Jimmy Lee," Lavonne said. "The south Georgia yard boy."

Nita swirled her soup with her spoon. Jimmy Lee should be loading his tools into his truck right now. She stared into her soup like she was staring into a crystal ball. She could see him reflected there, standing with the sun shining on his dark glossy hair. If she hurried maybe she could get home before he left.

Virginia clucked her tongue and looked around the crowded restaurant. She wished now she hadn't overheard Charles and gotten her feelings hurt. For one brief moment she wished she hadn't turned the party over to her daughter-in-law and her drunken friends. It was sure to be a disaster, and then Virginia would have to spend weeks explaining to everyone who'd listen that she hadn't had a thing to do with it. "Look," she said to Lavonne, opening her purse and taking out a business card. "Call this woman. She works out of her home in Valdosta. I haven't used her, of course, but I understand she did the Chasen girl's engagement party when the girl got herself in the family way and her parents didn't have time to plan a decent function."

Lavonne could feel a muscle twitching above her right eye. She felt like someone had tied a plastic bag around her head. She had a sudden vision of her mother lying dead on the frozen ground, a basket of wet clothes strewn around her like the petals of some monstrous flower. "She won't use it," her father had said, when Lavonne asked him why he hadn't hooked up the new dryer she'd brought her mother for Christmas. "Why hook it up when she won't use it."

"Do you want it or not?" Virginia repeated, holding the card out to Lavonne like she was offering entrails to a rabid dog.

Lavonne shook her head. "Keep it," she said. "I'll find my own damn caterer."

*O*N THE WAY HOME FROM THE LUNCH MEETING, LAVONNE DE-cided to stop at Shapiro's Bakery for a cream cheese brownie. She was feeling depressed and anxious and she figured a cream cheese brownie might be just the thing to take her mind off the party. The traffic was light and she found a spot in front of the bakery and parked.

Lavonne hadn't even known there were Jews in the South when she first moved here. She had been amazed to learn that Dixie Jews went by names like Junior and Bubba and prided themselves on being Southerners, first, and Jews, second. The South was like that. It could take in any ethnic group, culture, or religious sect and pretty soon they'd be saying "ya'll" and fixing greens and corn bread for supper. Maybe it was the drinking water filtered out of murky lakes where alligators slept, maybe it was the sultry, siesta-prone climate or the way the jasmine smelled blooming on a moonlit night. Whatever the reason, within a generation of arriving here from Bialystok in 1886, the Shapiros were as Southern as they come.

Lavonne pushed open the door and went in, the little bell above her head tinkling merrily. Mrs. Shapiro came from the back, wiping her hands on a clean white apron. "Oh, hey, Miz Zibolsky," she said. She was a small round woman with red cheeks and wisps of gray hair that escaped from her hairnet and fell in wild profusion around her face. She had a lazy left eye, the result of a childhood accident involving her brother, June Bug Rubin, and a shovel. "You doing all right?" Mrs. Shapiro's bad eye shifted slightly to the left of where Lavonne stood contemplating the glass case of baked goods.

"I'm fixing to get a whole lot better," Lavonne said. She could talk Southern when she wanted to. Everything in the display looked wonderful. The Texas sheet cake looked especially good. "You got any of those cream cheese brownies in the back?"

"I sure don't. If I'd known you were coming in, I'd have made up a batch this morning," Mona Shapiro said, patting her hair. "The Texas sheet cake is real good." She moved the cake closer to the glass front so Lavonne could get a good look at it. She'd been selling baked goods to Lavonne Zibolsky for a long time and she knew what she liked.

While she waited for Lavonne to decide, Mona said, "Did you hear about Velma Boggs?" Her bad eye skittered and careened off the walls like the headlamp of a runaway train. Lavonne hadn't heard, so while she tried to decide between the Texas sheet cake and the kugel, Mona told her all about Velma, how Velma had a swelling in her stomach the size of a Texas grapefruit, how she went up to Emory and they opened her and she had what you call a benign tumor, meaning it won't kill you but it'll suck the nutrients out of you so's you wind up skinny as a bed slat.

Lavonne listened and clucked her tongue in the right places. After eighteen years of patronage she was used to Mona's tales of woe and mayhem. Mona collected bad news the way some women collect spoons. "How's the Peach Paradise?" Lavonne said finally, pointing at the display.

"Oh, honey, it's delicious. Those peaches are frozen fresh from Mr. Skidmore's orchard," Mona said, bending over to move the Peach Paradise a little closer to the glass window.

"Okay," Lavonne said. "Wrap it up."

Mrs. Shapiro went in the back to get a box, then came back out to wrap up the Peach Paradise. Lavonne stared at the dessert and tried to cheer herself up, imagining the anticipation, the excitement, the sweet taste filling her mouth, but no matter how hard she tried, all she could think about was Leonard's face when she told him she would have to use Piggly Wiggly deli trays for the party. She felt sure the unsettling dreams and visions of her mother, the constant sense of impending disaster, were somehow tied to the stress she was feeling trying to handle last-minute details for the party. She tried to remember a time when her life had been about more than worrying whether she could find a caterer, but those days were a distant memory. She wondered if what she was feeling now might stretch back farther than her marriage to Leonard. She wondered if the spreading roots of her discontent might be imbedded somewhere deep in her childhood.

An only child, she had spent her lonely childhood fantasizing about belonging to a family like the ones she saw on TV. Her father, Raymond, was a clerk down at the local hardware store where he had worked since high school. He was a quiet, morose man accustomed to a degree of sameness in his life. He liked the same beer, ate the same food, sat in the same plaid easy chair, and drove the same sad Buick he had driven for twenty years. Lavonne and her mother, Margaret, spent most of their time moving carefully around their own home so as not to disturb Raymond Schwagel's rigid and meticulous routine. Margaret Schwagel worked as a clerk typist at Bieder & Assoc., an accounting firm located only four blocks from the little house on Hennipen Street where the Schwagels lived. Lavonne would go with her mother to the office on the occasional Saturday mornings when she had to work, and noting Mr. Bieder's plush office and the deference her mother showed him, it was here Lavonne first decided she would be an accountant when she grew up.

"Is there anything else I can get you?" Mona Shapiro asked, beginning to tape up the box.

"Not today," Lavonne said, thinking *But probably tomorrow.*

Maybe she wouldn't tell Leonard anything. Maybe she would call Eadie and Nita and go to the beach instead. She imagined the three of them loading their suitcases into the back of her car and turning off their cell phones. She imagined driving three and a half hours with the windows down and Jimmy Buffet singing on the CD player. She imagined them lying on the beach in the bright sunlight drinking margaritas while Trevor, Charles, and Leonard, forced to organize the party themselves, plundered Ithaca like marauding Huns, seizing take-out tubs from Jimmy's Chicken Shack, snatching deli trays from the Piggly Wiggly, and commandeering massive quantities of alcohol from Merv's Shake Rattle & Roll Liquor Store. Actually, Jimmy's Chicken Shack wasn't such a bad idea. Lavonne made a mental note to call them later.

There was a bookkeeping ledger open on the counter, one of those heavy old-fashioned books Lavonne hadn't seen in years. Mona saw her looking at it and she groaned. "I can handle the baking but the ledger book gives me fits. Marvin always kept the books. Since he's been gone things are kind of sliding downhill fast. I never could tolerate numbers. All those long columns staring me in the face night after night. I just can't seem to concentrate. I'm hoping Little Moses can move back and take over that part of the business for me." Little Moses was Mona's only child, a good-looking, clean-cut boy who used to help her in the shop. Lavonne hadn't seen him since he graduated from high school and went out to California to cut a demo tape with his Jewish reggae band, Burning Bush.

Mona put the last piece of tape on the box. "You probably want to keep this in the refrigerator," she said. "That way it'll stay fresh until you have a chance to eat it all."

Lavonne was pretty sure that wouldn't be a problem. The last time she bought a pie from Shapiro's she'd eaten it in one sitting. She shifted her weight from one foot to the other. She thought about Mrs. Shapiro entering long columns in a ledger book. Hadn't she heard of personal computers? Hadn't she heard of accounting software?

Lavonne checked her watch again. Louise had an after-school fencing class. Ashley had cheerleading practice. They would most likely eat dinner at school. Lavonne hoped they would make better food choices than their mother. Like all reformed career women Lavonne took her parenting seriously, volunteering for play groups, turning her kitchen into a craft center, driving her daughters to preschool, and soccer, and horseback riding, and, later, to school, to slumber parties, and to school sporting events. But now the girls were seventeen and sixteen and no longer seemed to need her to drive them around or make dinner for them. Lavonne was left with large blocks of time to sit around eating Peach Paradise and Rocky Road ice cream out of the carton and spy on her neighbors. There were moments in the middle of the afternoon when she thought, *Maybe I should adopt a child.* She thought, *Maybe*

I should join the Peace Corps. Lately, she had begun thinking, *Maybe I should get a job.*

Mona pushed the box toward Lavonne. She sighed and pulled her hairnet into place. A bus rumbled by in the street outside. "If I can't talk Little Moses into helping me with the business, I might as well go on and sell to Mr. Redmon."

"Mr. Redmon?"

"You know Mr. Redmon, don't you?" Mrs. Shapiro said, shaking the flour off her apron and turning to ring up the purchase on the cash register.

"Yes," Lavonne said. "I know him." Redmon was Leonard's biggest client. Around the office he was known as the Strip Mall King. He was single-handedly responsible for buying up family farms along the interstate that ran through Ithaca and turning the pastoral landscape into a garish jungle of fast-food restaurants, truck stops, and strip joints. In the process, he'd made himself fabulously wealthy. Leonard worshipped him. When Redmon said "Jump," Leonard said, "How high, Mr. Redmon, sir."

"He's been after me for years to sell. You know I own this building," Mona said, lifting her hand to indicate the shop around them. "And the building next door, too. Marvin bought them back in sixty-seven, right after his daddy died and left us a little money. Back then it was nothing more than a dusty storefront and I couldn't see the point of buying something downtown—all the businesses seemed to be moving out to the interstate back then. But Marvin's daddy had a dream right before he died. He dreamed they'd find gold buried beneath the streets of downtown Ithaca, and Marvin was a big believer in dreams. The ink wasn't even dry on the probate documents before he plunked down the money to buy this place." She chuckled and shook her head, remembering. She looked fondly around the room. Her bad eye rolled and bounced in its socket like a bobber on a fishing line. "Still, I don't know why Mr. Redmon would want it. I don't know what he would want with a bakery anyway."

Lavonne looked through the plate-glass window at the steady stream of tourists moving along the sidewalks. Across the street a crowd gathered on the porch of the Pink House Restaurant. Five years ago, a big Atlanta developer had discovered the charm of Ithaca's old downtown and had begun a steady renovation. Now, Mrs. Shapiro's crumbling building must be worth at least a half million dollars. Redmon would no doubt buy it and turn it into an upscale restaurant or women's clothing store.

"Mrs. Shapiro, do you have an attorney?" Lavonne took her wallet out of her purse and counted out the bills.

"An attorney?" Mona frowned. Her eye took off like a rocket, flaring off the walls, the ceiling, and coming to rest finally on a spot just to the left of Lavonne. "Well." She shook her head. "Marvin always took care of all that. He used his second cousin, Solomon, over in Valdosta."

"No, I mean an attorney to look over any contract Redmon might want you to sign."

"Actually, Miz Zibolsky, Mr. Redmon said your husband might be able to help me." She closed the old-fashioned cash register with her hip, and counted out Lavonne's change.

Lavonne had a sudden image of Leonard and Redmon bent over a contract in Leonard's office, laughing and rubbing their hands together like villains in a vaudevillian play. The thought that Leonard might make his living by taking advantage of trusting widows, that the big house they lived in, the grand private school her daughters attended, the everyday luxuries she herself enjoyed might be built upon the backs of sweet, gentle women like Mona Shapiro occurred to Lavonne like a blow to the head. Staring into Mona Shapiro's kindly face, Lavonne felt an odd swelling sensation that started low in her abdomen and traveled up through her chest cavity into her throat. Her breathing quickened. She wondered if she might be hyperventilating. The effect was fleeting but alarming. She took a deep breath and put one hand on the counter to steady herself.

Seeing her discomfort, Mona hurried around the corner and put her arm around her. "Sugar, are you all right?" There was something comforting and familiar about the little woman, something motherly. Lavonne wondered why she had not noticed it before. "I'm okay," she said. "Just a little short of breath."

"Do you want to sit down?"

"No, I'm okay." She took another deep breath. There was a sound in her head, loud and insistent as rain drumming on a tin roof. After awhile she said, "Have you ever heard of conflict of interest?"

Mona Shapiro stood looking up into Lavonne's face with her good eye, trying to read her expression, trying to figure out if she was all right. "You sure you don't want to sit down?" she said.

Lavonne took another deep breath. "I'll be okay. But listen, Mrs. Shapiro, don't sign anything with Redmon or my husband before you get your cousin Solomon to look it over."

Mrs. Shapiro let go of her. She seemed puzzled by Lavonne's request, but she nodded her head in agreement. "Okay," she said.

Lavonne was breathing normally now. She picked up the Peach Paradise in her arms, cradling it like she would a baby. A thought occurred to her suddenly, and she shook herself and said, "Mrs. Shapiro, have you ever done any catering?"

Mona went back behind the counter. Her bad eye shot off like a steel ball in a pinball machine, and rolled slowly back to rest on Lavonne. "Well, I do a lot of bar mitzvahs and bat mitzvahs," she said hesitantly.

Lavonne was a little surprised. She hadn't realized there was such a thriving community of Dixie Jews in Ithaca. "I need a caterer for next Saturday."

Mona's face turned pink. She smiled and shook her head. "I've never cooked anything but kosher food for big groups," she said. "I wouldn't know how to cook anything else."

"Cook whatever you like," Lavonne said quickly. She was afraid Mona would refuse and now that she'd stumbled on the idea, she didn't want to give it up. "I'm sure it'll all taste great. I'll make a few things myself, maybe some crab and artichoke dip, cheese straws, things like that. Finger food." Using Mona Shapiro was the perfect solution to the problem of the firm party, and Lavonne wondered why she hadn't thought of it before. Her pulse stopped drumming in her head like the voice of doom. Her stomach settled down. The feeling of anxiety lifted, and for the first time in a long time she began to feel almost optimistic. "Could you do it? We'll probably have about one hundred people."

"Well." Mona thought about it a moment. She seemed to be warming to the idea. "I suppose I could."

"Do you know anyone who could help you serve?"

"Usually I hire some of the girls from the temple to help me out, but Little Moses is coming in tomorrow. I can ask him and some of his friends. His record deal fell through so he and the boys are coming home to work and save some money and maybe move up to Atlanta to get something going. They could probably use the money. And my cousin Mordecai has a tux shop out at the mall. He could probably get the boys some uniforms to wear."

"Great. I can tell you right now my husband's law firm will pay whatever price you decide is fair."

This seemed to make Mrs. Shapiro happy, which in turn made Lavonne happy. The only ones who would not be happy were Charles and Virginia Broadwell and, possibly, Leonard. Virginia had always used the same tired list of caterers every other hostess in Ithaca had used. By using Mona Shapiro, Lavonne was breaking with tradition and reminding Ithaca that she, an outsider, and a Yankee outsider at that, could do things her own way and not be bound by the same narrow-minded constraints that bound them. It wasn't as good as telling Virginia Broadwell to fuck off, but it was close.

"I'll call you tomorrow with the details," Lavonne said, looking down into Mona's sweet, kindly face. Using Mrs. Shapiro was a small blow struck for social freedom, but it was a blow nevertheless. And it was a blow struck for something else, too, although Lavonne could not quite put her finger on what it was exactly. "We can do this, Mona, I know we can."

Mona grinned and tugged at her hairnet. "Well, all right then," she said.

COMING HOME FROM THE SHAPIRO BAKERY, LAVONNE THOUGHT she saw her mother standing in a queue at the bus stop. The experience left her light-headed and short of breath, again, and it was not until she was almost to the stop that she realized the woman, a small, stoop-shouldered black woman wearing a maid's uniform, looked nothing like her mother. Lavonne blinked her eyes, wondering if she might be on the edge of psychosis, and drove on. The feeling of optimism she had carried with her since leaving the bakery began to dissipate and something else took its place, fluttering in her abdomen like a persistent moth. The feeling intensified as she pulled into the driveway and saw her husband's car. She checked her watch and realized it was only two-thirty. She pulled slowly into the garage and turned off the engine, pondering this development. Leonard never came home early from the office. She and the girls were accustomed to eating dinner alone. She and the girls were accustomed to doing everything alone. Leonard was not a big part of their everyday lives and to find his car parked in the garage at two-thirty in the afternoon was troubling. She wondered if there had been a catastrophe at work. She wondered if there had been an emergency involving one of the girls.

Lavonne grabbed the pastry box from the front seat and hurried into the house. She could hear the TV blaring in the family room. Leonard was sitting on the sofa with his hunting trunk opened at his feet, carefully going through his gear.

"Are the girls okay?" Lavonne said breathlessly, standing in the doorway.

"What's for dinner?" Leonard said, without looking up. "I know it's early but I didn't have lunch and I'm starving." He was whistling cheerfully, running his freckled hands over neatly stacked camouflage gear and rain ponchos and boots and wool socks. Every year Charles, Trevor, and Leonard went to Montana to sleep in feather beds, eat gourmet food off good china, and hunt anesthetized wildlife at a game ranch called, incongruously, the Ah! Wilderness Game Ranch. Lavonne could not remember the last time Leonard had gone on vacation with her and the girls, but he never missed the annual hunting trip.

"Are the girls okay?" she repeated loudly.

He put his hands on his knees and swiveled his head around so he could see her clearly. "What do you mean, are the girls okay? I don't know where the girls are. You're supposed to know where the girls are."

"So there's no emergency?" Lavonne came into the room and slid down on the big overstuffed chair facing him. She stretched her legs along the ottoman, her arms collapsed at her sides, letting the Peach Paradise box balance precariously on her stomach. "Jesus, Leonard, you about gave me a heart attack."

"How'd I do that?"

"Coming home early on a Friday afternoon. I figured something was wrong. I figured one of the girls had been hurt or something."

He looked at her for a moment and then turned around and went back to work checking his hunting gear. "My golf game got canceled," he said.

It didn't really bother her that Leonard rarely came home for dinner anymore. Lavonne thought it was probably a good thing he spent so much time away from home. It was probably the only reason their marriage had lasted as long as it had. "Why are you packing for your trip four weeks early?" she said.

"I'm not packing, I'm just checking to see if there's anything I need to buy."

She opened the pastry box. Mrs. Shapiro had thoughtfully included a plastic fork. Lavonne figured that besides her daughters and Eadie and Nita, Mrs. Shapiro probably knew her better than anyone else in town.

"So, what's for dinner?" he repeated.

"I'm having Peach Paradise," Lavonne said. "What are you having?"

He got up and went into the kitchen to make himself a sandwich. She picked up the remote control and began to flip through the channels, chewing mechanically as she watched scenes of mayhem and destruction, TV pitchmen selling juicers and jewelry, co-eds whining about their love life, talk-show guests hurling chairs at each other, and finally, settling on reruns of *Leave It to Beaver.* It had been one of her favorite childhood shows. The bland normalcy of the Cleaver household had filled her with hope and a sense that anything was possible, even a happy childhood. Even a father who didn't raise his voice, or a mother who could clean the oven wearing pearls and a petticoat, and be happy about it.

"Lavonne, do we have any bread?" Leonard shouted from the kitchen.

"Look in the bread box."

"The bread box?"

She chewed the Peach Paradise, trying not to think about her sad mother standing in a queue at the bus stop, trying not to picture Mona

Shapiro's innocent face as she considered selling her building to Redmon and Leonard. Lavonne made a mental note to ask Leonard about this proposed sale after the trauma of the party had faded.

She could hear her husband helplessly slamming cabinet doors. Lavonne felt a slight tremor of conscience over not rising to go into the kitchen to make his dinner. Really, Leonard was not so bad. She reminded herself of this at least three times a day. He didn't bully her like Charles Broadwell bullied Nita. He didn't run around with other women like Trevor Boone. If you took away the fact that he was boring, self-indulgent, and sexually unappealing, Leonard was not such a bad husband.

"Goddamn it, we're out of mustard!" he shouted from the kitchen.

"Look in the pantry!" she shouted back.

She and Leonard had met their senior year of college and had dated long-distance for three years while she finished her master's and he attended law school at the University of Georgia. Lavonne should have known when he returned home to Ohio, tanned and dreamy, wearing knit golf shirts and loafers without socks, that their relationship was changing, growing into something she might not appreciate or accept. Instead, she threw herself into her practice, and when Leonard graduated from law school, they married. Three years later his father died and Leonard accepted a partnership with Boone & Broadwell. They were both twenty-eight. Lavonne sold her fledgling accounting business and they headed south.

Leave It to Beaver had gone to commercial, so Lavonne flipped back through the channels, stopping for a minute on *Oprah*. She had watched yesterday and had been shocked to learn that a young blond guest with long red fingernails was actually a financial adviser, and had been brought on the show to advise women on how to protect themselves from the financial disasters of divorce and the death of a spouse. "Make sure all the bank accounts are in both your names," the girl had said in her wispy little voice. "Make sure all the real estate is in both names." She giggled and wagged her finger at the audience. "Don't leave all the financial decisions to your husband. Don't let him handle all the checkbooks. Knowledge is the best form of protection." It occurred to Lavonne, watching the girl, that in the eighteen years she had spent at home as a wife and mother, the world had changed. While she had been changing diapers and teaching a four-year-old to read, the workforce had become filled with young, attractive, well-educated women.

Leonard came into the room carrying a sandwich and a mound of potato chips on a plate. He set the plate down on the coffee table and settled himself on the sofa, opening a napkin on his lap. "Where's the remote?" he said.

"I'm watching this," Lavonne said, switching back to *Leave It to Beaver* and turning up the volume. June Cleaver was advising Ward how best to deal with the boys, who were selling shoe polish door to door against Ward's advice. Her pearls shone like alabaster. Her starched apron flared modestly around her twenty-two-inch waist. June watched Ward, wide-eyed, her chin dropped submissively. Her face was vacuous but pleasant. June was not a woman of wild emotional swings. Lavonne wondered if June had ever questioned her decision to stay home with Wally and the Beave.

Leonard put his sandwich down and opened the trunk again. A strong but peculiar odor rose from the interior, musty and sharp and faintly sweet. The scent reminded her, curiously, of something else, some distant, just out of reach memory.

"Is this all that's on?" Leonard said, pointing at the TV screen.

"That smells like the stuff they used to use to clean the girls' locker room at school," she said, wrinkling her nose. "Why does your trunk smell like that?"

Leonard's face flushed suddenly. He put his sandwich down and closed the lid of the trunk, carefully fastening the latches. Then he sat back, stretching his arms along the length of the sofa. "Turn it to CNN," he said.

It was not entirely fair to blame Leonard for her decision to give up her career for the children. Staying home with the girls had been something she wanted to do. She had been there for their first steps, their first drooling attempts at language, their first lost baby teeth; what career could be better than that? She had two beautiful, smart, strong-willed daughters and they were who they were because Lavonne had raised them.

"Here, watch what you want to watch," she said, waving the remote at Leonard. Their marriage, if not exciting, was at least predictable. Secure. How many twenty-one-year marriages could you say that about?

Leonard looked at her suspiciously, munching his sandwich.

Lavonne shrugged and laid the controller down on the coffee table. The truth of the matter was, the girls were nearly grown and she still had twenty years to figure out what she wanted to do with the rest of her life. Twenty years was a long time. Twenty years was time enough to lose sixty pounds and find a job and figure out a way to fall in love with her husband again.

Jimmy Lee's truck was still in the driveway when Nita arrived home. She went around through the side gate, letting it bang shut behind her so he'd know she was there. She was too embarrassed to call out his name. She could hear him whistling as she came down the stone path between the rhododendrons and the azaleas. Jimmy Lee was standing by the pool with a couple of two by fours balanced across one shoulder. Shafts of sunlight fell from the wide blue sky and pooled around him like a spotlight. His hair curled damply around his neck. He saw Nita and waved.

"Well, hello there," he said, shifting the weight of the studs. The muscles of his shoulders strained beneath his Rodney Foster T-shirt.

"Hi," Nita said.

"I wasn't sure you'd get home before I finished." He looked like he had just crawled out of bed. He had that rumpled, sleepy-boy look that made her legs feel like she was standing on wet sand.

"Would you like something cold to drink?"

"What've you got?" He swung the lumber down off his shoulder and set it on a pile at his feet. A small gold earring dangled from his right ear. With his dark hair, tanned skin, and dangling earring, it wasn't too hard to imagine him as a pirate. It wasn't too hard to imagine him in any of the fantasy scenarios set up by Dr. Ledbetter.

"I've got sweet tea," she said. "Juice. Coca-cola."

"Sweet tea would be fine."

She climbed the steps to the deck and went into the kitchen

through the screened porch. She was humming to herself, thinking how smooth his skin was, like baby skin, really, tanned to a light brown except for his chin and lower cheeks, which were stubbled with dark beard. Five o'clock shadow, they called it. She wondered how it would feel against her skin. She imagined him rubbing his face across the places where Lone Wolf had kissed his captive bride, and her stomach spasmed and her heart ricocheted through her rib cage like an emergency flare. A strange sensation of heat rose into her head. She breathed with difficulty and her skin felt hot to the touch.

She went to the refrigerator and filled the glass with ice and poured him some sweet tea from a pitcher. She crossed the room and stood at the French door that led out onto the porch, watching him drag his materials into a neat pile. From time to time he would stop and push his hair behind his ears and stand with his hands on his hips looking at the pool house. His jeans were bleached by the sun and torn below his left knee. She imagined him standing in the middle of her yard wearing nothing but a loincloth. She imagined the sculptured contours of his chest and belly. Her hand shook so badly the cubes rattled against the glass, and she raised it and touched it to her burning face, but it gave her no relief. She set the glass down on the counter.

She was worse than those lecherous old men who sit outside the Jim Dandy Barber Shop ogling the high school girls who pass by. She was beginning to feel like a stranger to herself. She wondered if she was on the edge of a nervous breakdown. All her life she had fought against the urges of the flesh, she had bound up that part of herself with ropes and chains of iron link and buried it deep, and now here she was reading dirty novels and daydreaming about acts of sexual perversion with a boy who wasn't even her husband.

She thought, *What's wrong with me?* She thought, *Where will this end?* She pushed her forehead against the cool window glass and stretched her arms out and placed her feverish palms against the glass, too. She reminded herself that she had given up porno romance novels forever. She remembered she had sung in the church choir and been a Crusader for Christ. She recalled she was a wife and mother.

She told herself that he would leave her house today and she would return, gradually, to her old life, to the way she had been before, heavy and slumbering. Jimmy Lee glanced up at the house and saw her watching him from the door.

He smiled and waved.

Nita peeled her forehead off the glass. She dropped her arms at her sides. Like a sleepwalker, she lifted her hand, and waved back.

The children were going home with Virginia after school and Charles would not be home until six o'clock, so Nita sat out in a lounge chair beside the pool all afternoon drinking sweet tea and watching Jimmy Lee work.

She liked the way he handled his tools, the way he measured carefully so all his cuts were clean and precise. He was a craftsman, and she could see he took a certain careful pride in his work. Accustomed to the rantings of her husband when he was involved in a particular case, she found Jimmy Lee's quiet perfectionism comforting. He reminded her of her daddy, Eustis James, a stonemason who built walls and foundations so well-crafted and sturdy they looked like they'd been there since the beginning of time. "A man has to be able to stand back and take pride in what he has built," he had explained to her once. "Otherwise his life won't mean a thing, and he'll know that in his heart, and it'll eat away at him until nothing is left but bitterness and regret."

Nita sometimes wondered if this was not Charles's problem. She wondered if his frustration and growing bitterness were not caused by the fact that he could never stand back and see what he had built, as if he, too, had realized the practice of law was nothing more than a shifting morass of boredom, incomprehensible language, and resentful clients. Nita sometimes thought Charles would be a much happier man if only he knew how to swing a hammer.

"So, what do you think of your Taj Mahal?" Jimmy Lee asked, looking up at the pool house. He had taken a break and was squatting in the shade of the live oak with his forearms resting on his knees.

"Taj Mahal?" she said.

He grinned and lifted his drink. "I'm just kidding," he said. His back was smooth and sleek. He had the shoulders of a movie idol. Nita couldn't remember boys having bodies like that when she was young. It must be something they were eating these days, some superior genetic trait coming through, sure and certain proof of the beauty of evolution.

"I think it's beautiful," she said from her lounger. "It's just what I wanted."

"Thanks." His eyes moved critically over his work. He chewed an ice cube and thought about ways he could have made it better. "I think we should trim out the eaves," he said, pointing to the roof of the pool house. "We should trim it with some kind of cornice work. Something to dress it up a bit."

"Okay," she said. It looked perfect to her but if it would keep him around a few days longer, she'd agree to anything.

He shook his head and set his glass down on the ground at his feet, grinning at her over his shoulder. "You're just about the nicest person I've ever worked for," he said. "I wish all my customers were like you."

She didn't know what to say to this so she just stretched her legs out along the lounger and looked at her toes. She was wearing a short skirt and a cashmere sweater. She reddened, thinking that a thirty-nine-year-old woman probably shouldn't wear a short skirt. Only thirty-nine-year-old women who looked like Eadie Boone could get away with short skirts. She wished she had Eadie's long legs.

Jimmy Lee looked at her legs like he thought they were just fine. "Hey, aren't you Eustis James's daughter? Billy's sister?" He put the glass to his mouth and tipped his head back, looking at her over the rim.

"Yes. How did you know that?"

"I worked with Eustis and Billy on that new Piggly Wiggly out on Black Warrior Road a couple of years back. I was working on a framing crew at the time and they were doing all the stonework. Is Billy still working with your dad?"

"Yes." Billy was Nita's youngest brother. He was twenty-six and Eustis James had done well enough in business to bring him in as a partner six years ago. Nita had grown up in a little ranch house close to the public high school. They had not been wealthy, but Nita and her brothers, Billy and Lyman, had never wanted for anything. By the time she graduated from high school, Eustis's business had done well enough that he could afford to buy her a brand-new Volkswagen and send her to two years of community college, and by the time Lyman graduated four years later, he'd been able to afford to send him off to Emory University in Atlanta. By the time Billy graduated from high school, Eustis and Loretta James had built a new home on a private lake out from town. The house was not big by River Oaks standards, but it was nice and spacious and Nita liked to take the children out there to spend the night and fish when Charles was out of town and wasn't there to protest.

"But how'd you know I was Eustis's daughter? Billy's sister?"

Jimmy Lee dangled his glass of tea between his knees. "You probably don't remember this, but I went to school with Billy," he said, looking up at her again. "We graduated in the same class and I was there the night of the game with Tyner, the night they were crowning you Homecoming Queen."

Nita had a sudden memory of five-year-old Billy bouncing around the bleachers with a group of round-cheeked boys in baseball caps while he waited for his big sister to accept her crown.

Jimmy Lee took another ice cube in his mouth. He sucked it awhile and when it was small, he went on. "I was just a young punk then, but I thought you were just about the prettiest thing I'd ever seen. A fairy princess." He stood up and stretched, grinning at her. "I told my mama I was going to marry you when I grew up and she used to tease me for years after that."

A chilly breeze blew from the east. Nita looked at her toes and thought *I probably used to babysit him.* The depression that had troubled her since last night, and all through her lunch with Eadie and Lavonne and Virginia, returned. Something heavy swung from her collarbone, swaying over the pit of her stomach like a pendulum.

He finished his drink. He grinned and put the glass down on the patio table. "It just about killed me when you got married," he said.

He was making fun of her now, she was sure of it. Teasing her the way a little boy teases a babysitter. When she was twenty, the year she finished a two-year secretarial program at the community college and accepted a job at Boone & Broadwell, he was still playing Little League Baseball. He was still riding a bike and fishing in the creek when she went to work for old Judge Broadwell and first met Charles, home for the summer and clerking at his father's firm. When she married Charles at twenty-three, two years after Judge Broadwell died, Jimmy

Lee had been a carefree ten-year-old, most likely a Boy Scout or newspaper delivery boy.

He looked at her and frowned. "Did I say something wrong?"

"No." She put her glass down on the patio and swung her legs around to plant her feet. She sat there for a few minutes looking down at her Tahitian Pink toes. "I probably should get dinner started," she said, too embarrassed and self-conscious to rise. The Zibolskys' cat, Pumpkin, crouched on the top of the tall fence, watching them curiously. "I'm thinking of starting a hobby," she said, thinking *Why did I say that?* "Maybe scrapbooking, maybe conversational French. I don't know—maybe piano lessons."

"How about woodworking?"

"Woodworking?" She was embarrassed by her sudden outburst about the hobby. Her mouth seemed to be working without any guidance from her brain. "Where would I learn to do that?"

"I could teach you. I've got a shop at my house." She glanced at him to see if he was kidding. He watched her steadily. Great billowy clouds sailed across the blue sky like an armada. Pumpkin twitched his tail lazily against the fence. "Just think about it," he said, finally. He put his hands on his hips and leaned back, stretching. Bright slabs of sunlight fell across his face and chest. There was a small scar beneath his lower lip, intricate as a coiled thread. "I best get going so you can get supper started for your family. Ask your husband about that trim on the eaves," he said, all business again. "If he wants me to do it I can come back next week."

He began to load his tools into his toolbox, picking up scraps of lumber and dropping them into the burn barrel. Nita sat there, trying not to feel self-conscious while she watched him clean up, not sure if she should go into the house or offer to help, not knowing if he was serious about the woodworking or just making pleasant conversation with a lonely housewife, something he probably did at least once a week.

He closed the lid on his toolbox. "Okay," he said. He picked up his toolbox, but just stood there looking at the pool house.

She tested her weight, leaning first on one foot and then the other, but not rising. "Okay," she said.

Without a word he reached his hand out and took her arm to help her rise. The electricity of that touch traveled up her arm like a lightning strike, blasting all other thought from her mind, and in the moment of clear-headed emptiness that followed, Nita felt herself weightless, freed from the burden of gravity and duty, and she was suddenly floating up over the patio and the pool house and the arching branches of the trees toward the deep blue sky. She was definitely having an out-of-body experience. She had seen episodes of *Unsolved Mysteries* that talked about out-of-body experiences and she was definitely having one now. She looked down on the top of her head and Jimmy Lee's head. She saw the sparkling water of the pool and the steep-pitched pool house and the green grass of her yard and the Zibolskys' yard spread out below her like she was looking through the lens of a telescope. *Bump, bump, bump* went her head against the moss-draped branches of the live oak where a curious woodpecker watched her ascent. *Thump, thump, thump,* went her heart.

He let go of her arm. There was a whirring sound in her ears and Nita felt herself being sucked down from the blue sky and the arching branches of the live oak and back down to earth. It happened in the blink of an eye. One minute she was up bouncing in the top of the live oak and the next she was standing on the patio beside Jimmy Lee.

"I meant what I said about the woodworking. You have my number. Call me." He grinned and walked away, whistling, the gate banging shut behind him, leaving her to stare in astonishment at the glittering water of the pool, and the azalea bushes, and the woodpecker perched and shining like a jewel in the top of the tall tree.

CHAPTER

FIVE

*T*HE DAY OF THE PARTY DAWNED UNSEASONABLY HOT AND muggy for early October. Sunlight fell oppressively over brown lawns like a bad omen. Flies as big as fruit bats darted in the bright, still air. Lavonne, who had not slept the night before, sat despondently at her kitchen table sipping a cup of lukewarm coffee and watching for the arrival of the Shapiro van with a feeling of dread that coalesced and spread through her abdomen like an oil spill. Above, she could hear Leonard's footsteps as he crossed from the bathroom to the bedroom. She could feel each footstep deep in her belly, low and rhythmic like the clacking of railroad cars, like the ticking of a time bomb.

What had she been thinking? She asked herself this as she sipped her coffee, her bleary eyes fixed on the street where, at any minute, the old blue Shapiro van would come careening around the corner. After that lunch meeting with Virginia Broadwell she had convinced herself that Mona Shapiro would be the perfect choice to cater. She had assured herself that given the fact she couldn't find anyone else at this late date, she had no choice but to hire her. But now, a week later, with the reality of her decision weighing heavily on her conscience, Lavonne realized there had been a deeper, more profound motive to hiring Mrs. Shapiro. Her plan had seemed so perfect, her revenge so noble, a blow struck for her mother and Nita, and Mrs. Shapiro, and all the other sweet, docile women she had known in her life who seemed incapable of fighting back. It had seemed so courageous that day and now it all seemed foolish and immature and extremely disloyal to Leonard. What exactly did she have to complain about? She asked herself this again, trying to pinpoint the exact cause of her unhappiness. She lived in an expensive house, her daughters attended an expensive private school, her husband saw to it that they lacked nothing in the way of material comforts and still she was unhappy. Her problems, which had seemed that day so burdensome, seemed to her now, observed in the bright, clear light of her husband's coming embarrassment, insignificant and petty.

She was not a champion of downtrodden women. She was a bored housewife with nothing better to do than plan petty revenges on a husband who did not deserve them.

NITA ROSE FROM BED WITH A DULL HEADACHE. HER EYES FELT swollen. Her skull felt like it had been stuffed with cotton. Images seemed hazy, sounds seemed muffled. Below her in the kitchen she could hear Charles shouting at the children. This was a big day for him and he was as nervous as a crippled bridegroom. *Poor Charles,* she thought dejectedly. *Poor, poor Charles.*

"Goddamn it, boy, get that mess cleaned up! There's a party here today! You don't have the sense God gave a grasshopper!" Nita listened to him shouting at their son in much the same way she imagined Charles's father had shouted at him.

Everybody in town knew stories of the old judge, how he'd been born the grandson of a tenant farmer, the son of a hardware clerk; how the boy had bettered himself through a scholarship to the Barron Hall School and later the University of Georgia, and later still, the University of Georgia law school. Everybody knew how he'd built that big old house out on the river and filled it with the carcasses of animals he'd killed in far-off exotic places like Zimbabwe and Montana; how in thirty-five years of marriage the judge and Mrs. Broadwell had managed to produce only one child, Charles, who cried when he lost at sports and never bagged anything bigger than a goat. When the judge died, Charles locked himself in his bedroom and wept for two days. He had refused to eat and refused to sleep. Virginia had gone away shaking her head as if she had no idea what troubled him, but Nita had known. His daddy had died before Charles could prove himself a man. Now, eighteen years later, he was still trying to prove himself, surrounded by his daddy's old friends and clients, trying to prove to the people of Ithaca he was every bit the man the old judge had been.

"Go to your room, boy!" Charles shouted from the kitchen. "Go to your room and don't come out until I tell you to."

The feeling of weightlessness that had occurred that day in the garden with Jimmy Lee was gone. In the week since she saw him last, she had awakened every morning to a feeling of heaviness and melancholy. He had told her to call him but Nita knew she wouldn't. She couldn't.

All she wanted was a good marriage. All she wanted was a marriage like the one her mama and daddy had shared in the little house she grew up in, with its atmosphere of quiet and unrepentant love. Her father still called her mother "baby." He still held her arm when they crossed a street. Nita had watched her parents love each other all her life. Love and happiness and a simple life. That's all she ever wanted.

"Goddamn it, boy, are you stupid? I said move it," Charles roared.

Nita listened to Charles fulfilling his family legacy. Her head hurt. Her heart felt like a wasteland. Nothing would ever grow or flower there again. The best she could hope for was a quiet life. The best she could hope for was a husband who tolerated her, and children who grew to adulthood without hating her too much.

EADIE AWOKE EARLY AND MADE ONE LAST CALL TO DENTON TO GO over the plan for tonight's party. She had rehearsed him twice now because she was afraid he would forget his lines.

"Yeah, yeah, I know what to do," he said, sounding sullen and sleepy. "Make your husband crazy with jealousy. I get the picture."

"I'm counting on you," Eadie said. "Don't fuck this up." She hung up. Eadie had spent a week planning tonight's little fiasco, but for some reason she couldn't get excited about it. She was tired of Denton, tired of living in this big house all alone, tired of not being able to work. She wanted her husband home in her bed. In their bed.

She lay on her back and watched the sun climb across the ceiling. After awhile she rose and went to stand next to her goddess, looping one arm around the torso's shoulders and staring wearily at the slow-moving tourists passing on the sidewalks with their guidebooks and their blank upturned faces. The windows were open and a balmy breeze blew through the room. In the street below a little girl saw her and waved. Eadie raised her hand and waved back. Against her hip, the goddess swayed slightly.

She had not worked in months, not since Trevor left. A kind of lethargy had overtaken her, an anxious feeling that left her tired and listless. It occurred to Eadie that the only times in her adult life that she hadn't been able to work were after Trevor left her for another woman. Both times she had been seized with aimlessness and inertia. He was the only man she had ever met who she thought strong enough to survive loving her, and yet here he was again making her miserable and desperate and killing her creative spirit in the process. Making her unable to work for long periods of time. Making her doubt herself. She wondered if he was aware of the effect his cheating had on her art.

A thin ragged dog slunk down the street poking his nose under the public trash cans. "Don't touch him," the mother said to the child.

"Here doggie, doggie," the child said.

If Trevor didn't come home, would she ever work again? What was it Denton had called her goddess—a sad abandoned seal lying on the ice waiting to be beaten? Eadie pushed her hair out of her eyes and scratched dejectedly at her hip. After awhile she shook herself and stood up straight. No, she wouldn't think like a defeatist. She hadn't won the Miss Snellville Beach contest by thinking like this. She hadn't dragged herself up out of a life of poverty and adverse destiny by thinking it couldn't be done. She hadn't made Trevor Boone fall in love with her by pretending it couldn't happen.

And he did love her. Goddamn it, he did love her. Eadie knew this even if Trevor didn't. Even if he had somehow managed to forget. She wrapped her robe tightly around her waist and gave the goddess a hard slap on her contoured rump. Her natural self-confidence and optimism was returning. Trevor would come home where he belonged and she would work again. Eadie was sure of it. She smiled, thinking of her plans for the party.

Trevor had managed to convince himself he didn't love her anymore, but tonight she would remind him just how much he still did.

BY TEN O'CLOCK, UNABLE TO BEAR THE SUSPENSE OF WAITING FOR the arrival of the Shapiros, Lavonne suggested Leonard and Charles go out to the club for a round of golf. She watched them walk to the car, Leonard swinging his golf bag over his shoulder and whistling like a chubby choirboy, and Charles dragging his bag behind him like a crucifix.

Fifteen minutes later the Shapiros arrived and Lavonne went next door to greet them. Mona Shapiro climbed out of the van wearing a faded cotton housedress and tennis shoes. "We got the good clothes in the back," she explained, pointing toward the van with her thumb. Lavonne stared at the driver, who had climbed out and was sauntering up the driveway in front of a ragged group of boys wearing baggy shorts and flip-flops.

"Let me introduce you to the Burning Bush boys," Mrs. Shapiro said proudly to Lavonne. There was Little Moses Shapiro, no longer clean-cut but sporting a goatee and a Bob Marley T-shirt. There was the Finklestein boy, whose real name was Isaac but everyone called him Johnny. There was the Goldfarb boy, who went by the name of Weasel, and there was Goodman Singer, who wore a bandanna and a long gold earring shaped like the Star of David in his left ear. They all wore their hair in dreadlocks.

Stunned and speechless, Lavonne stood looking at them. "So what exactly is Jewish Reggae?" she asked finally, wondering what in the hell she was going to do.

"It's kind of a blues and reggae mix based on the words of the Torah," Little Moses said.

"Do you want to hear some?" Weasel said. "I've got my guitar in the van."

"Maybe later," Lavonne said, struggling against a rising sense of desperation. She wondered if she could talk Ashley and Louise into serving. She wondered if she could pay them and some of their friends to work the party. She could feel a strange humming vibration behind her right eye. She reminded herself she needed to have her blood pressure checked, but decided it was probably high right now given the fact that the firm party was fixing to turn into a disaster and she was in charge of it and all.

Little Moses whistled, looking up at the Broadwell's big house. "Damn, Miz Zibolsky, is your old man a doctor or something?"

"A lawyer. And I live next door."

"No shit," Johnny said. "I may need me a lawyer."

"Okay boys, let's discuss our pending court cases later," Lavonne said, turning around quickly before she had a chance to change her mind. "Follow me and I'll show you where to get set up."

The truth of the matter was she only had eight hours until the party started. It was too late to find other servers. *I didn't have any choice, Leonard. No one will remember who catered the party. Let's take a trip somewhere and forget this ever happened. From now on I'll be a good wife, I promise.* She rehearsed her excuses, running them together until they whined through her head like a chain saw.

TEN MINUTES BEFORE THE GUESTS WERE SCHEDULED TO ARRIVE, Charles saw Mrs. Shapiro and the Burning Bush boys standing out by his pool, and he said, "Who in the hell is that?" The boys had changed into their good clothes, which Lavonne now saw had been a mistake. Cousin Mordecai had sent over what he considered perfect catering attire; four powder blue tuxes with wide lapels trimmed in black velvet. Looking at them, Lavonne thought, *All they need are platform shoes and pimp hats.*

"They're the caterers," Nita said.

"You're not funny," Charles said. "Who in the hell are they?"

Nita looked at Lavonne. They were standing on the Broadwells' screened porch, overlooking the pool and the patio that had been set with long tables of flowers and silver serving dishes and bowls of exotic-looking fruits. The ice statue, a three-foot replica of Tara replete with garlands of ivy and Star of Bethlehem lilies and even a small carved figure of Scarlett O'Hara standing on the steps in a hoopskirt and wide hat, had arrived and the boys were busy trying to hoist it into place in the center of the main table. *Gone with the Wind* was Nita's favorite movie. When the ice artist asked her what she wanted the sculpture to look like, she hadn't even hesitated. Nita had spent her whole life wanting to be exactly like Scarlett and knowing she never would be.

"They're all we could get, Charles," Lavonne said, waving her hand vaguely at the Burning Bush boys. "On such short notice and all."

"Those are not the caterers from Atlanta." Charles ignored Lavonne and spoke directly to his wife. There was something wrong with one of his eyes. It stuttered and blinked while the other one stayed stationary, focused hard on the Burning Bush boys.

"They're the only caterers we could find, Charles," Nita explained in a small voice.

Lavonne hoped Leonard would take it better than Charles was taking it. "Calm down, it's not the end of the world," she said to Charles. "If you act like nothing's wrong, your guests will follow suit."

His look of disbelief was childlike and almost touching. "Those can't be the caterers," he said.

Lavonne grimaced and sucked her lower lip. Nita looked at her feet. The setting sun hung over the yard like a bare bulb suspended from a cord.

"But they don't even look like caterers." Charles shook his head stubbornly. He was beginning to catch on, but slowly. "What are they wearing on their heads? Oh my God, is that their *hair*?"

"It's not as bad as it looks," Lavonne said.

"Oh my God, I'm ruined." His nostrils flared. A vein pulsed in his temple like an emergency flasher.

Lavonne said, "It'll be over before you know it. My advice to you is to just sit back and relax and let it happen." At least Leonard had a slight sense of humor. Balding and fat, he was used to being laughed at, whereas Charles Broadwell, the golden boy, obviously was not.

"They'll think I was too cheap to hire decent caterers!" he shouted at Lavonne. He stopped and took a deep breath. Moisture clung to his upper lip. "All I asked was that you handle one simple little party," he said, lifting his arm to wipe his face. "This isn't brain surgery, it's a party. When my mother said—"

"Yes, let's talk about your mother," Lavonne said.

"You leave my mother out of this! My mother loves me! My mother wouldn't sabotage this party when she knows how much it means to me! My mother . . ."

The doorbell rang and Nita jumped and dropped a glass on the floor. A terrible revelation came gradually over Charles. His nose quivered. One eye drooped at the corner.

Lavonne said, "Once the margaritas start flowing no one's going to notice who we got to cater."

Nita swung around and went to answer the door. Crows settled like vultures on the ridge of the Zibolskys' garage.

Charles said, "Margaritas?"

FORTY-FIVE MINUTES LATER, VIRGINIA BROADWELL ARRIVED TO find the party in full swing. Loud music blared from the patio speakers, some kind of grating monotonous music that Virginia didn't recognize, although some of the guests seemed to know it well. A small group clustered around the pool throwing their hands in the air and moving their hips in a shocking manner. In the yard, Mavis Creal, the firm's bookkeeper, danced the macarena. Standing on the porch and looking down at the vulgar chaos below her, a slight smile of satisfaction appeared on Virginia's face.

Charles stood on the deck clutching the railing and looking morosely down at his guests who seemed to be multiplying like rabbits. A pale harvest moon rose slowly over the trees. "Love Shack" blared from the speakers. His mother never served anything other than wine and cocktails and the event always ended promptly at nine. But it was already seven-thirty and this party showed no sign of winding down anytime soon. The classical music Virginia provided encouraged the guests to be sedate and moderate in their drinking. The B-52's did not have the same effect. At the edge of the lawn, two of the girls from word processing stood on chairs and danced like go-go dancers in a wire cage. Dillon Foster took his shirt off and swung it around his head like a man swatting bees. Under the influence of the music and the little silver machine that cranked out its endless stream of lime green poison, things were getting quickly out of hand. *Lord let it rain,* Charles prayed. *And if you can't let it rain, then at least let the margarita machine break down.*

Virginia moved up beside her son at the railing, sipping her wine, and thinking how sweet revenge could be, how it gave shape and meaning to a life that might be otherwise drab and uneventful. Charles had made his bed, so to speak, and now he must wallow in it. She prayed he was conscious of his wallowing. She hoped, by now, he had realized that the firm party did not run itself, that it was a meticulously orchestrated event that must be carefully planned or run the risk of deteriorating into the train wreck they saw going on around them now. Virginia sipped her wine and tried not to gloat openly.

Looking down at a group of associates and their wives who sat at one of the tables whooping and hollering like cheerleaders at a pep rally, it occurred to Charles that perhaps they would drink past the point of remembering, perhaps they would fall victim to some sort of mass amnesia, perhaps there would be earthquakes, pestilence, flood, nuclear annihilation. Anything was possible. Hope, a rare and fragile thing, flared in his breast for the first time that evening.

Below them on the lawn Little Moses passed carrying a tray of blintzes over his head.

"Oh my," Virginia said, her little hand fluttering against her chest like a deformed bird. "Are those the *caterers*?"

Hope flickered, and died. Doug Clark and the Hot Nuts opened up with "Baby Let Me Bang Your Box" and a crowd of younger guests whistled and stamped their feet and began to shag around the pool, followed soon enough by the older set who wanted to get in on the fun. On the far side of the pool, Grey Spradlin picked up his wife, threw out his back, and went down like a rhino felled by a tranquilizer dart. Mavis Creal bumped and ground her way across the yard like an overweight stripper. Charles sighed and pushed himself off the railing. He knew he'd have to stop them or they'd be gatoring before the evening was over, flopping around on their backs like morons until one of them got hurt, and then he'd be facing a lawsuit in addition to public humiliation.

"Excuse me, mother, I have to put a stop to this," he said, lifting his hands, and it wasn't clear whether he meant the dancing or the party itself. It occurred to him as he pushed his way through the crowd toward the stairs that maybe the Zibolsky woman was right, maybe his guests would take their cue from him. If he acted like nothing was wrong, if he acted as if the music, the margarita machine, and the caterers were intentional and not some kind of monstrous mistake, perhaps his guests would follow suit.

His mother's loud voice followed him doggedly across the crowded deck. "Oh dear, hide the silver," she said, watching Weasel slice through the crowd carrying a tray of drinks. "That one looks like a Puerto Rican."

LAVONNE HURRIED TOWARD THE CLUSTER OF DANCERS WHO WERE shagging dangerously close to the edge of the pool. She had heard of parties where someone drowned and the body wasn't discovered until morning, and it occurred to her that this was quickly turning into one of those parties. Looking around her, she had to admit Eadie's idea to use a disk jockey and a frozen margarita machine had been brilliant. This party was definitely changing from a function into a throw-down, and it was too bad Eadie couldn't be here to see it for herself.

Still, from a containment standpoint, the margarita machine might not have been such a good idea. Lavonne hurried toward the shaggers, feeling like a lone fireman trying to put out multiple fires. So far this evening she had talked Braxton McCracken out of riding his electric scooter into the pool, had convinced Mavis Creal to dance the macarena *without* throwing her skirt over her head, and had tactfully tried to convince Leonard's secretary she might want to go easy on the tequila for a while. In the process Lavonne had managed to drink a good number of frozen margaritas herself, trying to shake the feeling of calamity that clung to her like a bad odor, saturating her hair, her clothing, the pores of her skin, all to no avail. An hour into this party, she was still sober and she still had the disturbing feeling that, despite her best efforts, this evening was going to end badly.

It took her about two minutes to realize there was nothing she could do to prevent one of the shaggers from drowning him- or herself if they felt so inclined. She gave up the minute Charles Broadwell showed up, trying in his jovial pompous way to convince everyone to settle down. Just knowing she was on the same side of the fence as that asshole made Lavonne feel like a hypocrite, and she left the pool patio in disgust.

Crossing the yard, she waved at Mona Shapiro who gave her a motherly grin and a thumbs-up sign. Lavonne was glad for Mona's sake that the crowd seemed to be genuinely enjoying the food. The Burning Bush boys kept bringing it out and the guests kept wolfing it down, jostling one another over platters of barbecued beef brisket, roast chicken with matzo farfel dressing, artichokes, and squash fritters. The barbecued beef brisket was especially good. Lavonne had already been back for two helpings. The secret was Grandma Ada's Kosher Barbecue Sauce. Lavonne was pretty sure Mona could bottle the stuff and make a fortune.

She spotted Leonard fluttering among the guests like an obese hummingbird, stopping to clap one on the shoulder, leaning to kiss one on the cheek, his loud voice rising above the hum of the crowd. Mona Shapiro crossed the yard carrying a tray of vegetable latkes. Leonard, seeing her, tried to duck behind a camellia bush, but Mona didn't notice him, and after a moment he slunk from behind the bush and stood watching her disappear into the buffet tent. Leonard acted like a man with something to hide and Lavonne reminded herself to ask him about the Redmon/Shapiro deal later. She reminded herself that there was much she and Leonard needed to discuss, and it wasn't just Mona Shapiro and Leonard's redneck client Redmon.

Leonard had his arm around his secretary and his head bent close, trying to hear her above the noise. Lavonne had not spoken to him since the party began and she wasn't sure how he was handling the Burning Bush boys and the music and the margarita machine, but she was sure he had to be handling it better than Charles Broadwell. She waved at her husband, but he didn't seem to notice her.

She had read somewhere that marriage was a series of stages. If this were so, she and Leonard were entering their Golden Phase, that long, sedate, financially secure period between grown children and death. Maybe they could travel. Maybe they could take up skydiving. Maybe they could sell the big house and move to the south of France.

Moths as big as dragonflies fluttered around the Japanese lanterns, and far off in the distance, old Buddy, the Redmons' sad cocker spaniel, howled mournfully at the moon. Lavonne tried not to see Buddy's sad howling as an omen. She drank her margarita and told herself that in only two more hours, one if she was lucky, it would all be over.

Then she could put this party behind her and move on with the rest of her life as if it had never even happened.

STANDING NEAR A CAMELLIA BUSH, LEONARD IGNORED HIS WIFE AS gracefully as he could given the fact his secretary had just made an extremely improper suggestion in his ear. At least he *thought* it was an improper suggestion. Christy was from Soddy-Daisy, Tennessee, and even after eighteen years in the South, Leonard still had trouble understanding her. *Creesty,* as she called herself, followed the suggestion with a flicker of her tongue in his ear, leaving no doubt as to her intent. The suggestion, not to mention the swelling tightness in his groin, made it extremely difficult for Leonard to respond casually to his wife's wave.

"I'll be right back," Christy said, handing him her drink. "Hold my beer, sweet cheeks."

Leonard couldn't remember the last time a woman had stuck her tongue in his ear. In his whole life no woman had ever called him "sweet cheeks." Across the yard he could see his wife grinning and waving and wearing a dress two sizes too small. No doubt she was congratulating herself on pulling the wool over good old Leonard's eyes. Hiring a Jewish caterer no one had ever heard of and her criminal assistants— he knew a parolee when he saw one, and that boy Johnny had parolee written all over him—making a fool of Leonard in front of his clients and law partners. And worse than that, bringing the Shapiro woman here, where she might see him and spill the beans about him and Redmon and their bid to buy her out. Leonard had to keep all that quiet. No one in town trusted Redmon anymore, so Leonard went in as his front man, lowballed the seller, closed the property, and then turned around and sold it at an agreed-upon profit to Redmon. The arrangement wasn't illegal; it was just unethical. It wasn't something Leonard wanted getting around town. Small Southern towns were hotbeds of gossip and innuendo; even a hint of scandal could ruin a person socially and economically, and Leonard knew this, even if his wife didn't.

Lavonne was the only woman he had ever seriously dated. He'd given her two children, a huge house, and a life of leisure, and all she'd ever given him was ingratitude and resentment. But all that was about to change. Now he had women like Christy sticking their tongues in his ear. He had women who knew how to appreciate the things he could give them, throwing themselves at him. All he had to do was be patient. All he had to do was set up his dominoes and watch them fall. Lavonne was smart about money and she'd know where to look, if he wasn't careful. He'd already met with Dillon Foster, the associate who handled the firm's divorce clients, and they'd come up with a game plan.

"You have to be like a commando behind enemy lines," Dillon said, leaning back in his chair and putting his feet up on the desk. "She can't know a thing is wrong until you serve her with the papers. If she gets wind of what's up, she'll freeze your assets before you have time to move anything. Does she have any idea what you're planning?"

"She doesn't have a clue," Leonard said.

"Good," Dillon said. "Keep it that way."

AROUND EIGHT O'CLOCK, TREVOR BOONE SHOWED UP WEARING blue jeans and a white shirt rolled at the sleeves, looking tanned and fit and happy. Lavonne, who had spent the last five minutes trying to talk King Stanton out of doing a swan dive off the cabana roof into the pool, was disappointed to see that Trevor had brought his secretary with him. She decided to let King kill himself after all and started across the lawn toward Nita, who was sitting alone at a table looking up at the moon. Trevor saw Lavonne and gave her a big charming grin, but Lavonne just nodded and went on. She was glad Eadie wasn't here. It was one thing to hear about your husband leaving you for another woman, but something else to witness the humiliation firsthand in front of the entire town. Still, watching Trevor move among the guests, Lavonne could see why Eadie was still crazy about him. She could see why every woman in the place had perked up when he arrived.

"Here," she said to Nita, setting two glasses down on the table. "I brought you a margarita."

Nita, who had been looking up at the moon and wondering if Jimmy Lee was sitting somewhere looking up at it, too, colored slightly and said, "Thanks."

"As soon as this party's over we're going to have a talk, Nita, you and me, about what's going on in your life." Lavonne sat down. "I'm worried about you. You haven't seemed yourself lately."

Nita didn't want to get into this conversation so she changed the subject. "I'm glad Eadie's not here," she said, looking at Trevor and Tonya as they moved slowly among the buffet tables. It didn't seem right to her that a man who had stood up in front of an altar and made a promise to God to be faithful, could so easily break his marriage vows. She thought how wrong it was that a cheating husband could show up at a party with his girlfriend on his arm and no one thought much about it, but if a wife did the same thing she risked public condemnation and social exile.

"Oh shit," Lavonne said, staring across the crowd and holding her margarita glass to her lips the way a priest holds the communion chalice. "Here comes your damn mother-in-law. "

Virginia walked across the yard like a tiny ballerina on point. She stopped and chatted with those few she knew who were still sober enough to carry on a conversation, and waved when she saw Trevor Boone. She couldn't believe he had brought his slutty secretary, Sonya or Anya or whatever she was called. It was disgraceful behavior not befitting one of the founding families of Ithaca. Maureen Boone must be spinning in her grave. Actually, imagining Maureen spinning gave Virginia a little shudder of pleasure. Maureen had snubbed her on more than one occasion and it was pleasant to imagine her discomfort at seeing her only son with that bleach-haired trollop. Besides, it would give Virginia something else to gossip about tomorrow over lunch at the club, something besides the music and the margarita machine and the ridiculous caterers.

"Trevor!" she called gaily, standing on her toes to kiss his cheek. Trevor was blond and blue-eyed and stood about six foot one. He was just about the best-looking man Virginia had ever seen and she always got a little thrill of excitement just being in his presence. "Hello, Virginia," he said. The minute his back was turned Virginia gave the girl a withering glance. She at least had the decency to blush and look at her feet. Virginia turned and strolled across the lawn toward Nita and Lavonne.

"Shouldn't you two be seeing to your guests?" Virginia said briskly, sitting down at the table.

"We're taking a break," Lavonne said, scowling into her drink.

It hadn't taken Virginia long to get the word out that she'd had nothing to do with this tragic party. A well-placed word here, a raised eyebrow there, a shrug here and her disclaimer was complete; she had no doubt it would be all over town tomorrow. She could relax now and enjoy the spectacle going on around her. She leaned across the table and put her hand on Lavonne's arm for effect. "*Where* did you find those caterers?" she said.

"Help yourself to the brisket," Lavonne said, moving her arm. "It's good."

Virginia said, "*Brisket?*" and laughed, showing her sharp little teeth. Her steely eyes rolled in her head like ball bearings.

Lavonne sipped her drink and tried to pretend she was somewhere else. Stars littered the sky like shards of broken glass. Billy Idol belted out "Rebel Yell." Leonard's secretary, Christy, stumbled past the table, listing to one side like a sailboat on stormy seas.

"Good Lord, is that one of the office staff?" Virginia said, frowning at the woman who, inebriated past the point of decency, sported a short skirt and stiletto heels.

"That's Leonard's secretary," Lavonne said grimly.

"Well no wonder everyone is sleeping with the secretaries," Virginia said. "Whoever is doing the hiring over at the firm needs to be fired."

Lavonne was suddenly, undeniably, sober. She realized she needed to get this party closed down, get rid of Virginia, and drink another pitcher of margaritas, and not necessarily in that order.

Sunny Hawkins lurched over and putting both hands on the table, she leaned over and said loudly to Nita, "Oh my God, this food is fucking wonderful." Her eyes were bloodshot. Mascara ran down one cheek. She was having trouble getting the words out but she was determined. "I *love* the music, not like that boring shit you usually play, and I absolutely *love* the margaritas. This is the best party you ever had, Nita. I've been coming to these parties for fifteen years and I can honestly tell you this is the best one ever. Ever, ever, ever—" She noticed Virginia then, noticed her expression and her gray eyes glittering like bayonet points. She thrust herself off the table, giggled, and, giving Nita a little wave, stumbled off into the darkness.

No one said anything. Nita went back to staring at the moon and wondering what Jimmy Lee was doing right now. Lavonne, feeling optimistic for the first time all evening, thought that with any luck this party would be over in an hour with no more lasting repercussions than a few scattered hangovers. Virginia decided there was nothing worse than ingratitude and thought gloomily that if something terrible didn't happen soon, this party might actually wind up a success.

Over by the pool house, Dillon Foster kicked over one of the concrete garden urns and began to roll it across the lawn like a happy lumberjack.

Charles hurried past the table where his mother and the Zibolsky woman sat enjoying themselves while Nita picked obliviously at a plate of brisket. As if he didn't have enough to worry about trying to contain this damn party, it was obvious there was something wrong with his wife. Nita hadn't been herself lately. He had to give her instructions over and over again to get her to do them. Simple but important instructions, like picking up his shirts at the cleaners or rolling a tube of toothpaste the right way or making chicken for dinner when he had specifically told her he wanted beef.

Ed Trotter, one of his prep school comrades, passed him and shouted, "Great party, Broadwell." Charles thought, *Fuck you, buddy.* Charles said, "Thanks, Ed," and clapped him on the shoulder. So far, six people had told him what a great party it was, but Charles knew sarcasm when he heard it. Charles was an expert on sarcasm.

Sure everyone was having a good time now, laughing and whooping it up like a bunch of rowdy teenagers while a blood-red moon rose over the yard like a brushfire. But he knew that tomorrow, when they sobered up, they would remember the kugel and the matzo balls and the dreadlocked freaks and they would call one another on the phone and giggle and whisper and roll their eyes while they recounted the entire night. Charles's ears burned and his palms sweated, just thinking about it.

Not that he blamed Nita for the Rastafarian caterers. She would never have done anything so blatantly disloyal to him, something so sure to make him the laughingstock of Ithaca. No, the blame for the dreadful party did not rest on Nita's docile head—it rested clearly on the oversized shoulders of Lavonne Zibolsky. In the future, Nita would have to learn not to let people like the Zibolsky woman walk all over her. She would have to learn to be more assertive.

Charles stopped in the shadows behind the buffet tent, trying to catch his breath and watching his guests with a mixture of horror and repugnance on his face. Trevor Boone strolled across the lawn with his bimbo secretary. One of the hairy waiters, shirtless now, passed him carrying a tray of God knows what. Leonard's secretary, Christy, leaned over the pool and was sick. *Shit, it could be worse,* Charles thought, trying to cheer himself up.

Considering the music and the margarita machine and the excessive drinking his guests had been doing, it was an absolute miracle a fight hadn't broken out yet, and Charles supposed he should at least be thankful for that.

FIFTEEN MINUTES LATER, EADIE BOONE SHOWED UP.

"Oh dear God, no," Charles said, dropping his drink.

"Oh shit," Lavonne said.

"Oh my," Virginia said, rolling her eyes with delight. Her terrible miracle had arrived. Lavonne popped up out of her chair like a marionette and walked toward the deck where Eadie and Denton stood surveying the guests. Charles, who had personally witnessed numerous Boone altercations but never actually hosted one in his own home, swung around on his heel and hurried toward the buffet tent where he could see Trevor and Tonya talking to Adams Webb.

The minute Eadie and Denton arrived, the tone of the party changed. The air crackled with anticipation. Small groups stood around chattering behind their hands, watching Trevor and Tonya move among the buffet tables, watching excitedly as Eadie strolled down the steps and through the crowd like a movie star, wearing a dress that was cut low in front and high around the thigh, and trailing Denton Swafford behind her like a lapdog on a leash. Those few who hadn't heard were told about the country club dance two years ago where Trevor broke Chip Boatner's jaw for touching Eadie on the ass. Someone remembered the incident at the Tivoli Theatre during the early days of the Boone marriage, when, upon being asked to remove her feet from the seat in front of her, Eadie declined, and the usher, touching her briefly on the calf to make his point, was knocked over two rows of seats by Trevor.

Watching Eadie and Denton move toward her through the restless crowd, it occurred to Lavonne that this party was about to get interesting. This party was about to become legend.

"Where'd you stash the margarita machine?" Eadie called to her in greeting.

"Why didn't you tell me you were going to crash my goddamn party?"

"I knew you'd try and talk me out of it." Eadie grinned. "Where's the tequila?"

Realizing the machine was set up close to the tent where Trevor and Tonya were still circulating, apparently unaware of Eadie's presence, Lavonne said quickly, "Go rescue Nita. I'll bring you a margarita."

Eadie followed Lavonne's pointing finger and saw Nita sitting alone and helpless with her cold-blooded mother-in-law. "Oh Lord," Eadie said. "She looks like she needs rescuing." Over her shoulder she told Denton to fix her a plate and meet her at the table.

Lavonne stood where she was, watching Eadie stroll through the crowd and trying to figure out what she was going to do. Across the crowded yard, her eyes met Charles Broadwell's, held for a moment and then disengaged. Trevor and Tonya still hadn't realized that Eadie was here. Charles swung around and went over to the clueless couple, slipping an arm around both of their shoulders and propelling them toward the back gate, away from the buffet tent and the waiting guests, and Eadie.

FOR TEN MINUTES, THROUGH A MIRACULOUS COMBINATION OF FATE and timing, Lavonne managed to keep Eadie corralled at the table. If Eadie was aware of Lavonne and Charles's unspoken pact to keep her and Trevor apart, she gave no sign of it. She kept looking around the crowd but Trevor and Tonya hadn't been seen since they disappeared with Charles. Lavonne was hoping he'd somehow convinced them to leave.

A small candle in a glass globe flickered in the middle of the table. The women sat around nursing their drinks and trying not to listen as Virginia droned on about the weather and the difficulty of finding decent yard boys. Worland Pendergrass stopped by to chat with Virginia about the Ithaca Cotillion. Worland was small and blond with a long face and teeth that were large and slightly equine. She was a born social climber. She'd spent her whole life in Ithaca, sucking up to those she considered her social superiors and ignoring those she considered her inferiors. You could pretty much judge your social standing in Ithaca by how Worland Pendergrass treated you. Now that Trevor Boone was rumored to be finally divorcing Eadie, her social standing had slipped back to the gutter where it belonged. Worland no longer had to be nice to Eadie.

"Hey, who'd they name as king of the ball?" Eadie asked Worland. They always picked some old white guy, preferably of Anglo-Saxon heritage, to be the king.

Worland ignored Eadie. She had had her face done recently, and her lips, too. Her face, which had always had a slightly bowed appearance, now, with the recent lift, seemed even more pronounced. One eye sat up slightly higher than the other. The collagen in the top lip had plumped up slightly larger on the left side. The overall effect was terrifying. She looked like a flounder with a harelip. She looked like a Picasso painting gone bad.

"We took Mary Alice up to Atlanta to have her dress made," Worland said to Virginia. Worland's oldest daughter, Mary Alice, had been named Queen of the Cotillion Ball two weeks ago. Mary Alice was a freshman at Sanford who had managed to pledge Chi O. So far her life was on track to being everything her mother wanted her to be. To be named Queen of the Ithaca Cotillion Ball ranked right up there with discovering a cure for cancer or mapping the human genome.

Eadie sipped her margarita and said to Lavonne, "That whole debutante ritual is really just a throwback to virgin sacrifice."

"You mean, kind of like Persephone being kidnapped by Hades, God of the Underworld. That whole birth/death/sacrifice/rebirth cycle thing?"

"Kind of like that."

"Does the virgin have to kiss the old guy?" Lavonne said.

"Maybe in the old days," Eadie said, "but not now."

"She's not a virgin!" Worland said defensively, and then realizing what she had said, she flushed an ugly red color. Her face shone like fiberglass. "I mean, she's the queen," she said patting her hair in place. "That's what she's called." No one said anything. Eadie sipped her drink loudly. Worland seemed suddenly flat, deflated. She promised to call Virginia for a lunch date. "Oh, yes, do call me," Virginia said. They kissed each other on the cheek and after a few minutes Worland wandered off. "Good Lord, what did she do to her face," Virginia said, watching her go.

Eadie poked her head up and took a good look around. Lavonne knew she wasn't looking for Denton. She tried to think of something she could say to keep Eadie from leaving the table to hunt for Trevor.

"Speaking of debutantes, I might get to be one after all." It was all she could think of. Nita, who had barely said two words since they sat down, picked at her farfel cup. Eadie drummed her fingers on the table and looked around for Trevor. Virginia stared at Lavonne like she had spinach in her teeth. "I've been asked to the Kudzu Ball," Lavonne explained, grinning at her. "I've been nominated as the Kudzu Queen."

Eadie stopped scanning the crowd and looked at Lavonne. "You sly dog," she said.

The Kudzu Ball had been started five years ago as a parody of the Ithaca Cotillion Ball. The Kudzu Ball was open to everyone, and was a big favorite of the young professionals and corporate transferees who were slowly infecting Ithaca like a virus. The debs presented themselves and ranged in age from twenty-one to seventy. They wore thrift-store dresses wrapped in kudzu vines, and kudzu garlands in their hair. The queen, who was chosen by random lottery, chose her own king, the only requirement being that he must be at least ten years her junior. The women from her book club, all of whom had graduate degrees and could discuss literary symbolism and figurative language without batting an eye, had nominated Lavonne. When she told Leonard he had looked at her like she was crazy. "Don't even think about attending the Kudzu Ball," he'd said. "Don't even think about being Kudzu Queen. We'll be social outcasts if you do." And seeing the look on her face he wagged his finger and said, "If you won't think about us, at least think about your daughters. They'll be blackballed from the Cotillion Ball. They'll never make the Junior League. You'll ruin their lives forever." Lavonne wondered if her daughters would even care if they never made the Junior League. Even if she was asked to be a Cotillion Deb, Louise, who wrote articles for the school newspaper on the evils of the American Dairy Association, would probably turn up her nose at being a debutante, while Ashley, who had been on the Homecoming Court every year since seventh grade, would most likely jump at the chance.

Virginia took her little hands out of her lap and laid them on the table. She took a deep breath to steady herself. "You can't seriously be thinking about going to the Kudzu Ball," she said, frowning at Lavonne. "Surely this is just another one of your little jokes." Virginia had been trying to get the Kudzu Ball closed down for years. It irritated her that people would make a mockery of everything she held dear, that they would ridicule what took her years of scheming and hard work to achieve. And what was even worse, younger members of her own social class appeared to be going over to the enemy. If this alarming trend continued, the old traditions would eventually die out and social equality and anarchy would not be far behind. Virginia had done everything she could short of bribery and extortion to close the Kudzu Ball down, but when you're dealing with middle managers and college professors, what could you expect?

"When is the ball?" Eadie asked. She and Nita were not Cotillion debs. They had never been presented, Eadie because of her trailer-trash upbringing, and Nita because she was the last girl in the world Virginia had wanted Charles to end up with; she'd done everything possible to sabotage the romance between them, even going so far as to have Nita blackballed. Charles had gone as Lee Anne Bales's escort.

"It's the weekend our husbands get back from their little hunting trip."

"I'll go with you," Eadie said, the flickering light of the candle illuminating her face. "I've always wanted to go."

"Yes, well, what do *you* have to lose?" Virginia said, motioning for Little Moses to bring her another glass of wine.

"I don't like your tone," Eadie said.

"How about you, Nita?" Lavonne snapped her fingers but Nita wasn't listening. She was staring into the candle flame and imagining Jimmy Lee Motes standing by her pool with the moonlight shining in his eyes.

"Nita has more sense than that," Virginia said, squaring her little shoulders. "Besides, Charles would never let her go."

Eadie yawned. She put her hands over her head and stretched. She was tired of making small talk. She had a husband to find, and a marriage to save. "So, where's Trevor?" she said, finally asking the question they'd all been waiting for.

"I'm pretty sure he left," Lavonne said quickly.

"He's gone," Nita said.

"He's down at the garage behind the back fence," Virginia said, sweetly pointing toward the gate. Lavonne looked at her like *Die, bitch, die*. Virginia smiled and patted her smooth hair. "With his date," she added.

Nita couldn't believe Virginia had mentioned the garage, disguised as a storage shed, where Charles kept his father's old car—the Deuce. She and Virginia weren't ever supposed to talk about the car. Charles had given strict orders, and to her recollection, Nita had never disobeyed one of Charles's strict orders. For sixteen years she had followed all of Charles's orders. She had been loyal and faithful as an old dog. She had cooked his meals, washed his clothes, bore his children, and loved him as best she could. She had been a good girl. Now she could not trust him. She could not bear to have him touch her. She hated the sound of his voice. She hated the way his ears stood out on either side of his head, hated the whistling sound he made when he slept. Good girls did not do things like that. Good girls did not hate their husbands.

Eadie said, "What garage? What back fence?"

Trevor and Tonya sailed suddenly into the yard, dragging the hapless Charles behind them like an anchor. He was speaking and gesturing wildly, and looking around for Eadie, and when Lavonne saw him, she shook her head in disgust. Here she was hoping he had convinced Trevor to leave and he hadn't even managed to warn him that Eadie was here. It was up to her to keep Eadie and Trevor apart, to avert the inevitable tragedy that this party had been moving toward all evening.

Lavonne tried to think of something clever to say but her tongue went numb.

"Oh look," Virginia said, smiling sweetly and pointing. "There's Trevor and his date now."

Lavonne imagined herself wrapping her hands around Virginia's trim little neck and squeezing until her eyes popped. Her head felt swollen. She could feel her pulse in her temple. With her luck, it was an aneurysm and she'd be dead in ten minutes, facedown in a plate of kosher barbecue.

Eadie swung around to look, following Virginia's pointing finger. Her eyes locked onto Trevor and she smiled and rearranged the front of her dress. Denton came up carrying a plate of food but she shook her head impatiently and stood up. "You know what to do," she told him.

She started across the yard, but Denton just stood there holding the plate and watching her go. Eadie had warned him what to expect and he had agreed upon the price, but now that the moment was here he was having doubts. The truth of the matter was, he needed his face to make a decent living. Even one punch might break his nose, and then what was he supposed to do? Make ends meet as a personal trainer? Teach tennis for a living?

Trevor and Tonya stood with their backs to Eadie in front of a long buffet table. Charles watched Eadie's approach with the dull, dazed look of a cow caught in the headlight of an oncoming train. The crowd around the pool stopped shagging and began to cluster around the tent. Queen sang about that "Crazy Little Thing Called Love." Guests began to spill through the kitchen door onto the screened porch. Some watched from the family room windows.

Eadie moved up behind Trevor and Tonya, who had stopped in front of the buffet table. "There you are," she said.

Hearing her voice, Trevor swung around. Something flickered in his eyes and was quickly buried. Seeing this, Eadie smiled.

"Hey, Trevor," Charles said, moving up behind the buffet table and trying to draw his attention. "How about them Braves?" His voice trailed off feebly. This party had been a disaster from the first, and it was fixing to get worse. He looked around wildly for his mother.

Tonya tried to take his arm but Trevor shook her off. "Why are you here, Eadie?" he said and his voice had a cold metallic ring.

"Why shouldn't I be here?" Eadie said. "I've been here for the last fifteen years, except one. Why should this year be any different?"

Charles could smell tragedy the way a tethered goat smells a grizzly bear. It was coming and there was nothing he could do to stop it. "Can you believe what they're paying that Chipper Jones?" His voice rose, hung for a moment, and then plummeted. He tried again. "Can you believe how much money those guys make?"

Trevor and Eadie stood facing each other like gladiators. The air was heavy with the scent of pine tar and citronella. Charles looked around desperately for his mother. He could see her now, standing at the edge of the crowd, her small pale face looking almost . . . pleased? Nita stood beside her, watching Charles with sorrowful, accusing eyes.

"Come on, Trevor, let's go," Tonya said, trying again to take his arm.

"Not now, Tonya," he said.

"Do you mind?" Eadie said to her. "This is a private conversation."

Tonya looked at Eadie the way she would something blind and slimy found under a rock.

"You've chosen a very public place for a private conversation," Trevor said, tipping his head at the restless audience.

"Here's as good a place as any."

"Don't blame me," he said. "I wouldn't have wanted it this way."

Eadie didn't give a shit about the crowd and the look she gave them told them so. "You left me no choice," she said to Trevor.

"Now you're starting to scare me."

"Come home, Trevor."

"I don't want to do this here."

"What are you afraid of?"

"Jesus!" Trevor shouted and banged his fist on the buffet table. Dishes bounced and clattered. In the middle of the table, the ice sculpture of Tara had begun to melt. Scarlett O'Hara had shrunk noticeably. Beneath her wide crystal hat she looked like a humpbacked dwarf. After a minute Trevor sighed and shoved his hands deep in his pockets. "Goddamn it, Eadie," he began, and then stopped. Tonya looked nervously from one to the other. He pulled his hands out of his pockets and rubbed the bridge of his nose with two fingers. Dark half-moons swelled the skin beneath his eyes. Eadie put her hand up to touch his face, but he moved his head. "I'm trying to tell you some-thing," he said evenly. He studied her face a moment, and then sighed again. "I know I've been a shitty husband."

She grinned. It wasn't much, but it was a start. If he could admit he'd been a shitty husband, they could work from there. It was like one of those twelve-step programs. I am an alcoholic. I am a shitty husband. It was the same concept.

"Everybody makes mistakes," she said, feeling generous.

Trevor put his hand up to stop her. "Let me finish," he said. "Let me get this out. For once in your life, stop talking and just listen." She smiled indulgently and he took a deep breath, and continued, trying to keep his voice low. "I've been a lousy husband, but I'm going to be bet-ter," he said.

Eadie felt a sudden surge of hope and confidence. She could see Nita's pale, sad face in the crowd and Lavonne's sturdy one. Hadn't she known in her heart that he still loved her?

"I've learned a lot about commitment in the past few months. I know I can do better. I know I can be faithful."

She nodded and gave him a little smile, encouraging him to go on. She would forgive him. She knew already in her heart that she would. But he would have to fire Tonya. There was no other way she'd agree to take him back.

"I intend to start fresh. To be a good husband."

He'd have to fire Tonya and he'd have to agree to stop practicing law and write.

"Tonya and I are getting married," he said.

For a moment she didn't understand him. She stood smiling fool-ishly into his tired face. Overhead the insect light buzzed and flick-ered. The truth of what he was saying settled over her gradually. The glittering lights, the throng of guests, the entire lawn had the sudden shimmering quality of an underwater scene. Eadie felt as if she were sitting at the bottom of a deep lagoon, looking up toward some brightly lit world on the other side. Lavonne moved just within the watery perimeter of her vision, followed by Nita, moving toward her like slow somber swimmers.

"You cannot possibly mean that after twenty-one years of marriage you intend to divorce me to marry that child," she said in a distant voice.

"I'm sorry," he said.

We'll see about that, Eadie thought grimly. She swung her head over her shoulder and looked around for Denton. There was no mistaking her expression. Denton put the plate down on the table and trudged across the yard like a condemned man on his way to the chair. Eadie swung around to face him. Following her cue, he stopped and began running his hands up and down her bare back, which her daring dress left fully exposed. He was facing her but he was looking anxiously at Trevor over her shoulder.

"Come on, Trevor, let's go," Tonya pleaded.

"Is that the personal trainer you've been wasting my money on?" Trevor said. He smiled but didn't show his teeth.

"Oh, I wouldn't call it a complete waste of money," Eadie said, picking up a tray of stuffed mushrooms. She stood with her back to Trevor, feeding mushrooms to Denton, who stroked her mechanically, his cheeks plumped, his arm pumping like a compressor. Trevor watched him, his eyes the color of bone. Tonya held tightly to Trevor's waist.

Behind them, Charles said desperately, "If I had known there was so much money in baseball, I wouldn't have gone to law school—ha ha."

Denton's hand dipped and swirled and took refuge finally in the lower back of Eadie's dress. Trevor stared at him like a man in the midst of a psychotic episode. Charles rambled on like a lunatic.

"Who'd have thought there'd be so much money in baseball?" he asked anyone who would listen.

Trevor gave his drink to Tonya to hold. Her face crumpled suddenly like she might cry. Trevor stood motionless with his hands down against his sides, but there was something in his expression, some warning in the set of his shoulders that caused Denton to step back. Eadie spun around, her eyes wide, as though surprised to see her husband crossing the lawn with long, violent strides. With his hand still plunged into the back of her dress, Denton looked like a boy caught with his hand in the cookie jar.

"Don't do anything foolish, Trevor," Eadie said, smiling sweetly.

Denton finally managed to free his hand. He stepped back again, grazing the edge of the buffet table. Weasel picked up the punch bowl and moved it to safety just as Denton leaned into the table and went down, the table collapsing beneath him, leaving him spread-eagled on the ground while the remnants of Tara glistened around his head like a thorny crown. He lay there like a dead man, staring up at the big yellow moon.

Trevor pushed past Eadie and stopped, looking down at Denton. No one moved. The yard was quiet. Trevor snorted, a sudden, short, violent burst of laughter that shot up over the quiet yard like steam through a pressure valve. Hearing this, Charles began to giggle and slap himself, his frenzied laughter rising above the noise of the party as his guests joined in. He would later brag to his mother that this party could have been worse, that at least Denton and Eadie had been there to provide comic relief, that at least the whole affair hadn't ended in a drunken brawl.

Wave after wave of laughter washed over the yard. Denton rose slowly and, brushing his pants off, made a bow and held his arms above his head in a victory salute. The crowd applauded. Lavonne swam her way through the throng, moving slow and dreamlike toward Eadie. Nita floated behind her, her face pale and delicate as a sea urchin.

Beneath the neon glow of the bug lights, Eadie Boone looked dazed. She watched Trevor like a long-distance swimmer watches the horizon. She was no quitter. Eadie reminded herself of this, the words sloshing through the waterlogged corridors of her brain. *I am no quitter.* She could hear the voice in her head like a drowning woman.

"You'll never find a girl like me," she said to Trevor; and the moment she said it, she knew it was true. In that same moment she became aware of the moon shimmering over the trees like a mirage, and she thought with a sudden yearning for something better, *I should paint that.* A change came over her, her face softened gradually, and it was then that Eadie realized that loving someone, and being loved by them in return, isn't always enough.

Trevor saw her transformation and he stopped laughing. Eadie's eyes looked past him, fixed on some future that didn't include him, and it was so quiet and unexpected, this withdrawal from him, that it left him stunned. He had not expected her to give up so easily.

All around them the crowd, loosed from their enchantment, began to chatter and move around. Lavonne put her arm around Eadie and began to propel her gently but firmly toward the scuppernong arbor. Nita joined them on the other side putting her arm around Eadie. Little Moses passed carrying two water pitchers on a tray and Lavonne took the pitchers and dashed the water on the ground. "Do me a favor," she said, handing the empty containers back to him. "Fill these up with frozen margaritas and bring them to us in the arbor. Then unplug the machine and put an 'out of order' sign on it. This party's over."

Trevor and Tonya left, the gate banging shut behind them.

LAVONNE AND NITA SAT OUT ON THE PATIO DRINKING COFFEE AND watching Eadie and Little Moses dance slowly around the pool to the mournful crooning of Tony Bennett. The guests had left hours ago. Charles had long ago stumbled upstairs to bed. Leonard had gone to drive his unconscious secretary home. The Burning Bush boys had finished most of the cleanup and Little Moses had driven them and Mona home, and had come back to give Eadie a ride. Eadie had been drinking tequila shooters and he figured she might need a designated driver.

Nita watched Eadie and Little Moses dance slowly around the pool. He reminded her so much of Jimmy Lee Motes, with his dark hair and tall slender body. *That's what Jimmy Lee's arms would feel like,* she thought, seeing how tightly he embraced Eadie. *That's how gracefully Jimmy Lee would dance.*

Beside her Lavonne flipped absentmindedly through a photo album that Charles and Leonard and Trevor had compiled over the years of their trips to Montana. "See, here's Leonard when he had hair," she said, jabbing the page with her finger. "Look how young they were in this picture." She shoved the book at Nita, but Nita was watching

Eadie and Little Moses with a strange expression on her face. Lavonne looked again at the photo. They did look young. And hopeful, with their unlined faces and bright smiles. But Lavonne could see a change in each succeeding photograph. With the passing of the years their faces became less hopeful and more secretive, hardened into lines of resignation and distrust. Lavonne flipped to a photo taken on last year's trip. It was a close-up shot of all of them standing with their arms around one another's shoulders out in a field somewhere. Something about the picture was wrong, something flickered for a moment in her brain, an uneasiness, a warning, but she was tired and she could not focus on what it was that bothered her. She turned the page.

"Where's that tequila bottle?" Eadie said, letting go of Little Moses to look for it.

Lavonne watched her warily. "You might want to drink some coffee instead. I believe you've had enough tequila for one evening."

Eadie, looking more and more like the old Eadie and less like the dazed wounded woman at the party, grinned and lifted her glass. "One more shot," she said. "And it's all over."

Lavonne went back to the photo album. "This one is a little out of focus," she said.

"Let me see," Little Moses said. He sat down beside her and leaned in close. The candlelight flickered over his face. He squinted his eyes and pointed. "What's this?" he asked.

"What?" Lavonne leaned in closer.

"This." He tapped the photo with his finger.

Lavonne stared at the photograph. "Oh my God," she said. She flipped back to the picture that had bothered her. She pushed the album closer to the lantern, and leaned in close and looked down into the sly smiling faces of her husband and his partners.

"What's the matter?" Nita said.

Lavonne sat back in her chair. "Look at this picture," she said in an odd voice. Nita sighed. She leaned over the album. "What do you see?" Lavonne asked.

"I see . . . I don't know," Nita said. "It looks like a hand." It was a bit blurry, resting there on Leonard's shoulder like a furry animal.

"What kind of hand?"

"A hand with red fingernails," Nita said, still not comprehending.

"And here." Lavonne flipped through to the last photo and jabbed it with her finger. "What does this look like?"

Nita peered intently at something lying on the ground beside Leonard's hunting locker. "A shoe," she said.

"What kind of shoe?"

"A high-heeled shoe. A leopard-print high-heeled shoe."

Lavonne flipped back to a photograph taken fifteen years ago. There at the edge of a field sat a folding camp chair and draped across that chair, unmistakably, was a pair of lace panties.

"Leonard's hunting locker smells like cheap perfume," Lavonne said, remembering the day she came home to find him cleaning it out.

Nita stared at her, hard, for ten seconds. She blinked. "Charles has condoms in the pocket of his hunting jacket," she said.

Little Moses ducked his head and checked his fingernails for dirt.

"Either our husbands are transvestites, or they've been bringing women with them," Lavonne said.

Eadie quit looking for the tequila and lurched over to the table. "Let me see that book," she said. "Let me see that damn book."

"Maybe they found the shoe," Little Moses suggested. Being the only male present, he felt a certain obligation to play devil's advocate. "Maybe they picked it up in the woods."

"They picked up something in the woods," Eadie said darkly, looking at the photos.

"What about the panties?" Lavonne asked Little Moses. "What about the cheap perfume and the condoms?"

Little Moses was a musician in a Jewish reggae band. He had long ago learned to recognize futility. He shrugged and put his head back, and looked at the stars.

"I can't believe it," Lavonne said, trying desperately to believe it wasn't true even though, somewhere deep in the pit of her stomach, she knew it was. "Maybe there's some explanation." But she knew there wasn't. Not one she'd be willing to settle for, anyway.

Eadie set her shot glass down on the table and flipped slowly through the book. Coming so soon after the realization that her husband had walked out of her life forever, this revelation settled over

Eadie like a blow to the head. "How could we be so stupid," she wheezed. "How could we be so blind?"

Tony Bennett sang of love and heartbreak. Japanese lanterns flickered in the treetops like fallen stars. Lavonne had a sudden memory of her mother lying in an opened coffin, her face oddly pleasant, the sickly sweet odor of flowers and embalming fluid filling the room.

"All these years we've been sitting home worrying they'd catch pneumonia or accidentally shoot each other or die in a plane crash," Lavonne said. "And they've been bringing women along."

Eadie struggled to draw breath. "Well, this has been an evening we'll never forget," she said flatly.

"I wish I'd had more to drink," Lavonne said. "I wish I wasn't stone cold sober."

"It's not too late to fix that."

"I need to keep my wits about me while I figure out what in the hell I'm going to do."

Nita stirred and shook herself like a woman waking from a deep and implacable slumber. "Those bastards," she said. "Those lousy, cheating bastards."

CHAPTER

SIX

*T*HE NEXT MORNING THEY MET AT EADIE BOONE'S HOUSE TO plan revenge.

"The thing that gets me," Eadie said, setting a bottle of tequila and three glasses down on the table between them, "is that they got away with it for so long." She cut up some limes and poured salt on a plate in the middle of the table. "How stupid can we be?" she said. Eadie's eyes had a feverish quality. Her hair was unwashed and uncombed. She looked like a woman on the edge of something dangerous. Some women had a knack for decorating and some had a knack for picking wardrobes and some were real good with arts and crafts or gourmet cooking. Eadie Boone had a knack for revenge. She'd been practicing it, in one form or another, all her life.

"Why are we drinking tequila at nine-thirty in the morning?" Lavonne said. She still felt hung over from the night before. A plate of brownies rested on the table in front of her and, looking at it, Lavonne realized she didn't want one. She knew she would never again gorge herself on brownies or Rocky Road ice cream or Peach Paradise; that part of her life was over forever.

"We're drinking tequila because it feels like the right thing to do," Eadie said. If Eadie was hung over, she hid it well. "Tequila gets me in my revenge-planning mood."

Nita sat there with her hands clasped on the table. There was a stillness about her, a composure that seemed artificial and slightly sinister.

"I've got a few ideas for the revenge part, but before we talk about that, there's something else we need to talk about first," Lavonne said.

Eadie dipped the glasses in salt, poured out three shots of tequila, and pushed them around the table. Lavonne stared at hers. Nita picked hers up but didn't put it to her lips. Eadie swallowed her shot, and set the empty glass down on the table. She picked up a lime slice and sucked it, hard.

"I've got my own idea for the revenge part," Eadie said, grimacing. "I say we have them killed. I say we take out a contract on them or, hell, even do it ourselves."

"Let's be serious," Lavonne said.

Eadie stared at her steadily and Lavonne could see she was serious. "Forensic technology makes it real hard to get away with murder these days," she reminded Eadie.

"So you have thought about it," Eadie said.

"I've thought about murdering my own husband, but I've never considered murdering yours."

Eadie nodded as if she understood perfectly the logic of this statement. Nita said in a quiet voice, "You have to make it look like an accident."

No one said anything. After a moment, Lavonne patted Nita's hand nervously and said, "Yes, Nita, of course you're right. We could make it look like an accident if we murdered *one* of them, but not all *three*." Lavonne lifted the glass to her lips and sipped her drink. It tasted worse than anything she'd ever drunk. It was one thing to drink frozen margaritas; it was something else entirely to toss back straight shots of tequila.

Eadie, the tequila connoisseur, said, "Lavonne, you don't sip it. You down it in one gulp."

"You drink it your way, I'll drink it mine," Lavonne said stubbornly. She didn't want to drink it at all, but she felt it signified something meaningful, some important ritual blood sisters might do on a moonlit night in front of an open fire. Only instead of cutting themselves and sharing their blood, they were sharing tequila. It was the same concept. Beside her, Nita lifted the glass to her lips and put her head back. She slowly set the empty glass on the table. Her face was expressionless. Eadie offered her a lime slice but she shook her head, no.

"Nita, what do you think?" Lavonne said, noticing Nita's blank look. She hoped Nita wasn't getting ready to go postal on them. Wasn't it always the quiet ones who were the most dangerous?

"I think they should be punished," Nita said quietly.

"Well, all right then." Eadie poured herself and Nita another glass. "Maybe we could hire the Burning Bush boys to kill them. Hell, if we'd known last night we could have paid the boys to poison them."

"The Burning Bush boys are a Jewish reggae band," Lavonne reminded her. "They're not contract killers."

"That Johnny would do it," Eadie said, lifting her glass. "Or Little Moses. I could talk him into it. I could talk Little Moses into just about anything."

Lavonne lifted the shot glass to her lips and swallowed. The tequila ran down the back of her throat like battery acid. She could feel it burning a hole in the bottom of her stomach. "Good God," she choked. "That's nasty."

Eadie grinned and poured her another shot. "After awhile you get used to it," she promised. "After awhile, you don't feel a thing."

"Look," Lavonne said, suddenly all business. "We have to plan this revenge right. We have to plan this so those sons of bitches don't know what hit them. Murder is easy. Anyone can do it. We're intelligent women and we can plan something better than murder. Something creative and truly humiliating."

Far away, in the deepest recesses of the big house, a radio played. Eadie listened to the faint music. She stared despondently at her shot glass. She was a woman, now, without any illusions. It had felt courageous and noble to accept the fact her marriage was over in front of Trevor and the assembled elite of Ithaca. It had felt a little like the Christians facing the lions in the Coliseum. But realizing Trevor had been secretly cheating on her for years felt less like martyrdom and more like defeat. It felt . . . pathetic. "What do you have in mind?" she said to Lavonne, after a few minutes. She tapped her glass along the edge of the table. Nita stared out the bay window, watching a squirrel raid the bird feeder.

"We need to be organized about this," Lavonne said. "But before we talk about the revenge plan, we need to be clear on something else."

Eadie poured three more drinks. She raised her glass and Lavonne and Nita raised their glasses automatically. "Here's to revenge," Eadie said. They all clinked their glasses, downed their drinks, and set the empty glasses back down on the table. The tequila roared through Lavonne's brain like a monsoon. It was true what Eadie had said. After awhile she couldn't feel a thing. She couldn't even feel her feet.

Lavonne shook herself. "Okay, then," she said. Finding out her husband was a lying cheating bastard took a lot of the pressure off. It absolved her of any of the guilt she had felt over not being able to save her marriage. *My sins have been washed clean,* she thought. Only instead of sacrificial wine, it was tequila doing the washing. "The thing that occurred to me last night, was that our husbands have been cheating on us for fifteen years but no one's filed for divorce yet." She colored slightly and glanced at Eadie, but she seemed fine with this, so Lavonne went on. "I think they probably see their party in the woods as an annual transgression. They get to be bad boys once a year and the rest of the time they're good, hard-working lawyers. At least, I think that's how they see the whole hunting trip."

Eadie looked at her. "What in the hell are you talking about?"

"I'm talking about divorce. I'm talking about the fact that this cheating has been going on for fifteen years and not one of our husbands has seen fit to divorce us over it."

"What do *we* have to do with it?" Eadie was getting irritated trying to follow her convoluted logic.

"What I'm saying is, our revenge doesn't have to end in divorce. Whatever we decide to do to punish them doesn't have to include divorce, unless we feel our marriages are over, of course. Each one of us has to decide that for herself."

Eadie swirled her shot glass, spilling tequila on the table. It was bad enough Trevor had cheated on her openly twice, but to have cheated behind her back for fifteen years was more than Eadie could ever understand or forgive. "I think it was real apparent to ya'll last night that my marriage is over," Eadie said. "My marriage is so over I'm fantasizing how to have the cheating bastard killed."

"I thought about it all last night," Lavonne said. "And I've come to the conclusion my marriage was over years ago." She had slept like a baby and awakened refreshed, transformed by dreamless sleep and the knowledge she had stayed in her marriage because of boredom and fear, and for the sake of the children. She had, in effect, become her mother. "The only thing that's kept Leonard and me together is the girls, and they're nearly grown. I realize that now, and I'm guessing Leonard realizes it, too, or he wouldn't spend so much time away from home. He wouldn't be looking forward to this damn hunting trip so much when he hasn't been on a family vacation in five years."

They both looked at Nita. She sat staring out the window, watching the squirrel splash at the birdbath. Nita thought about the years she had spent trying to make Charles Broadwell happy. She thought about her children who headed for their rooms the minute they heard their father's footsteps in the hall, and she thought about the big house and the private school and the beach house and all the things her children were accustomed to having. She thought of those sad single women she had watched on afternoon TV talk shows, the ones who struggled to raise children on a secretary's salary or worked two jobs to pay the bills. She tried to remember if anyone in her family had been through a divorce and the only one she could think of was her Aunt Effie, the black sheep of the family who had run off to Daytona Beach with a dog track gambler. Nita shook her head and looked down at her little glass, watching the way the light caught in the clear-colored liquor. "I don't know about divorce," she said. "I just want him punished is all."

"We understand, Nita," Lavonne said, drawing little Mandela symbols in her Daytimer. "You've got more vested in your marriage than either of us, and your children are young." She beat the table with her pencil, flipping it between her fingers like a drumstick. "Okay, so it's decided. Eadie and I leave our marriages—Nita, you stay." She tapped out a sharp staccato beat on the table. "First thing is, we all have to agree to complete secrecy. We can't let the husbands know we found out about the women. I know Little Moses won't say anything if I ask him not to, and none of us can say a word to anyone either. We have to keep our plans for divorce and revenge secret until they leave for their hunting trip, because it won't work if they get wind of what's coming. I know it's hard, but we have to go on with our lives and act like nothing's happened. Act like we don't know a thing. We've only got four weeks until they leave for Montana; whatever we decide to do, has to be done within that time frame."

"You're rambling," Eadie said, pouring another round of drinks. "What has to be kept secret: the fact that we're leaving them, or the revenge?"

"Both," Lavonne said. "The first thing you and I have to do, Eadie, is figure out what assets we can get our hands on. Anything that doesn't have our husbands' name on it, bank accounts, stock certificates, you get the picture."

"Well, there won't be much of that," Eadie said. "Besides, Trevor's always been fair with me from a monetary standpoint."

"Look, Eadie, just because Trevor's been fair with you in the past, doesn't mean he'll continue to be fair. Remember, they're good lawyers and they'll fight us tooth and nail over any divorce settlement. I mean, eventually we'll prevail, but they'll tie the cases up in court so long we won't see a penny for years. And that's only *if* we can find an attorney in this town who'll agree to represent us."

"Rosebud Smoot will represent us," Eadie said.

"Well, she's the only one I know who will. You know how lawyers all stick together in times of trouble and divorce."

"Trust me, Rosebud's the only lawyer we'll need."

Rosebud Smoot was the first female attorney to practice in Ithaca. She had graduated number one in her class at Georgia forty years ago, and when she returned to town, had been offered a job as a legal secretary. Now she made a good living representing the ex-wives of corporate executives and lawyers who had a hard time finding legal representation among the closed, good ole' boy network that was Ithaca, Georgia. If it weren't for Rosebud, these women would have had to go all the way to Atlanta to find a lawyer.

"That's all very well and good, Eadie, but remember, a court case could take years to settle. Meanwhile, I want to get on with my life. And I need money to do that."

"Okay, so what are you saying?"

"I'm saying, make a list of assets. Start thinking of ways to get your hands on some quick cash." She remembered the pretty young financial adviser she'd watched on *Oprah*. Lavonne wished now she'd paid more attention that day to what the woman was saying. She looked at Nita. "I know you're not planning on divorcing Charles, but it's probably a good idea for you to start figuring out where the marital assets are, Nita, and maybe try to move a few into your name. Just in case. Just to be on the safe side."

Nita looked at her hands. She knew she wouldn't find any assets with her name on them. She had to beg Charles for money if she went twenty dollars over on the weekly grocery bill. She had to grovel and then she had to sit and listen while he lectured her on the importance of sticking to a household budget.

"We've got less than four weeks until our husbands leave for Montana; all this has to come together by then. If we can't figure out how to come up with cash, if we can't figure out how to punish them by the time they leave for Montana, then we might as well forget it. We might as well plan on staying married until we can get it all figured out, and that could take months."

"Obviously you aren't including me," Eadie said. "Trevor made it pretty clear he was going to marry that idiot Tonya, which means he needs to divorce me quick."

"Let him file the papers, Eadie. Don't you do it. Not yet, anyway. Maybe he'll be so busy trying to get ready for his hunting trip, he won't have time to file. Time is on our side—up to a point."

"I don't like all this secretive shit," Eadie said. "I like doing things out in the open. I like letting other people know where I stand."

"I know," Lavonne said. "I can barely stomach the idea of staying in the same house with Leonard for one day, much less weeks." The difficulty of this plan was beginning to dawn on her; she'd never been one to keep her mouth shut. She'd never been one to keep her feelings hidden. How in the world was she going to live with Leonard for four weeks trying to pretend nothing was wrong? "But we have to do this if we want everything to work out." She looked at Eadie to see if she understood. Eadie frowned and shrugged and Lavonne went on. "Okay, now that that's settled, let's move on to the next order of business, which is the revenge planning session." Lavonne raised her little glass in a toast and Nita and Eadie did, too.

"Here's to freedom," Lavonne said.

"Here's to revenge," Eadie said.

"Here's to love," Nita said in a voice that made the hair on the back of Lavonne's neck rise.

They tossed back their drinks and set the glasses on the table. No one bothered to pick up a lime slice anymore. "Let's think about this a moment," Lavonne said. "What is it these husbands all have in common?"

"They're all assholes," Eadie said.

"Besides that," Lavonne said. She paused dramatically, waiting for them to catch up and when they didn't, she said, "Pride. Male ego. They all have it in spades. That's where we strike."

"Look," Eadie said. "I've tried sleeping around. It doesn't work."

"Shit, Eadie, I'm not talking about sleeping around," Lavonne said. "We have to hit them where it hurts. We have to wound their pride."

"I'd like to wound something else," Eadie said.

"It's a control issue," Lavonne said.

"I still say we have them killed. Or at least maimed."

Sunlight slanted through the long windows. The old floor register hummed and belched a steady stream of warm humid air.

Nita tapped her glass with one finger. She chewed her lower lip. "What's the name of that place where they go each year?" she asked quietly.

"The Ah! Wilderness Game Ranch," Lavonne said. "A place where men go to feed their male desire to kill something."

The room was quiet. A tourist bus rumbled down the street. Clouds shaped like grazing sheep wandered across the blue sky.

"You're starting to sound like a feminist," Eadie said.

Lavonne put her pencil down. "What's your definition of a feminist?" she asked.

"A woman who won't take shit from anybody."

"Okay," Lavonne said. "I'm a feminist."

Eadie grinned at Lavonne and poured her another drink.

"I've been a feminist all my life," Lavonne said.

"Good old Ramsbottom," Eadie said. Lamar Ramsbottom was the owner of the Ah! Wilderness Game Ranch. "I'll bet he gets the girls. I'll bet that's part of the price."

Sunlight shone through the prism of Eadie's stained-glass window. A hummingbird hovered over the birdbath.

"You don't think they have girlfriends, do you?" Nita asked suddently. Eadie and Lavonne looked at each other and shook their heads.

"Naw," Lavonne said. "Leonard and Charles don't have time for girlfriends. Those women are once-a-year prostitutes. I'm sure of it."

"They must fill out a request form," Eadie said, stirring her drink with her finger. She stuck the finger in her mouth, and pulled it out again. "Kind of like filling out a sushi request form. You know, a check mark next to the California Roll, or the Crab Roll or the Tofu Sushi, only this time they're ordering women—blond, redhead, brunette." She was getting mad just thinking about it.

Lavonne sat up suddenly and slapped the table. "That's it!" she said. "That's the revenge part of our plan." It had come to her in a flash. She knew what they had to do. They would use the skills they had acquired through eighteen years of planning birthday parties, luncheons, and PTA meetings. "We'll plan their hunting trip for them. We'll set it all up before they even get there!"

Nita and Eadie looked at her. A muscle moved in Eadie's cheek. Nita sucked her lower lip. "I mean, hell," Lavonne said. "We planned the damn firm party. Why can't we plan the hunting trip?"

"You mean," Eadie said, beginning to catch on. "*We'll* be the ones placing the sushi order?"

"Right!" Lavonne said. "We'll put in the request for the girls." She frowned and drummed the table with her fingers. "But how can we get Ramsbottom to go along with it?"

"Simple," Eadie said, raising her glass. "We'll pay him twice what they do."

"We'll get the prostitutes ourselves?" Nita said.

"The ugliest we can find," Eadie said. "We'll tell him to get ugly women."

"Yeah. Very ugly women."

"Women who make us look good," Eadie said.

"Scary women," Lavonne said, getting the hang of this.

"Biker chicks."

"Feminists."

"Lorena Bobbit wannabes."

Nita lifted her drink, drained it, and then set it down. "Who says they have to be women?" she said.

LAVONNE DROVE HOME, HUMMING SOFTLY TO HERSELF. SHE FELT better just knowing they had a plan. She and Nita and Eadie had agreed to think about it and to meet again in a couple of days to discuss ways they could get their hands on some quick cash. Eadie had agreed to call Ramsbottom and Rosebud Smoot. Lavonne felt light on her feet, curiously elated, which was odd, she realized, for a woman who had just found out her husband had been cheating on her for years. She felt free for the first time since she quit her job and moved to Ithaca and started having children. Now she had only herself to rely on. Now she could be whomever she wanted to be. She could be an accountant or a waitress or a college student. She could be queen of the damn Kudzu Ball if she wanted to be, and no one could tell her what to do.

She drove past the Shapiro Bakery, lifting one hand to wave at Little Moses, who was hand-lettering a sign across the plate-glass window. *Bodacious Brownies,* the sign read. The thought of brownies made her slightly nauseous. She clenched the steering wheel and slowed for a group of tourists who ambled slowly across the street clutching brochures and bright blue bags that read *I Survived Shopping in Ithaca.* The bakery was closed on Saturdays and Sundays, which didn't seem like such a good idea to Lavonne, what with the tourist business and all, but it was Mona's store, not hers.

The girls were just getting out of bed when Lavonne arrived home. Leonard was in the family room reading the Sunday paper. He called to her as she came in. She had expected to find him sullen and angry over the catering fiasco, but he was obviously determined to keep up his cheerful front. He wasn't letting anything spoil his upcoming hunting trip. She was sure it was hard to be angry when you were looking forward to a week of good sex and animal slaughter.

"Where've you been so early this morning?" he called, rattling the newspaper.

None of your goddamned business, Lavonne thought. She sat down at the breakfast bar and poured herself a cup of coffee. A box of sweet rolls rested on the counter. Lavonne played idly with a corner of the tissue wrapping, pushing the box toward a bleary-eyed Louise as she came into the kitchen.

"Have a sweet roll," Lavonne said.

Louise yawned, stretching her arms above her head. She was wearing an old bathrobe and a flannel nightgown with a brown stain across the bodice. "Aren't you eating?" Louise said to her mother.

"Nope," Lavonne said.

Louise stopped yawning. She dropped her arms. "Are you sick?"

"No," Lavonne said, blowing on her coffee. "I feel great. I feel better than I've felt in a long time."

Louise shrugged and went to the cabinet to take down a mug. Her long ponytail hung down her back, almost to her waist. She had pretty hair like Leonard's, auburn colored with blond streaks, but she never wore it down. With her thick glasses and severe hairstyle, she looked like a middle-aged librarian. Ashley was cute and popular at school, but Louise wanted to be a writer. She had no social life to speak of.

Leonard came into the kitchen, whistling. He smiled at Lavonne but she stiffened and lifted her coffee cup to her lips. *Just don't look at him,* she told herself. *Just pretend he isn't even here.*

Ashley followed her father into the kitchen, her hair standing in stiff spikes around her sullen face like whipped egg whites. "Is there any coffee?" she said, plopping herself down at the breakfast bar.

"Good morning, Sunshine," Lavonne said to Ashley.

"Good morning, Puddin'," Leonard said.

"Don't call me Puddin'," Ashley said to her father.

"Don't drink coffee," Leonard said. "You're only sixteen years old," he reminded her. He was dressed in his Ralph Lauren bathrobe and slippers. He looked like the father in one of those 1950s TV shows where everyone in the family speaks politely and calls each other by pet names. "You're too young to drink coffee."

"Everyone I know drinks coffee," she said wearily, leaning to pour herself a cup.

"It will stunt your growth," Leonard said.

"I started drinking coffee at twelve," Lavonne said, holding her cup up with both hands, her elbows resting on the breakfast bar.

"I rest my case," Leonard said. Ashley and Louise thought this was funny. Leonard wasn't usually funny. He grinned at the girls, enjoying himself.

"I'm five feet six inches tall," Lavonne said stiffly. "That isn't short."

"Don't be mean to Mommy," Louise said pouring cream and sugar into her coffee. "She isn't feeling well."

Ashley picked at a sweet roll, bored. Lavonne tried to concentrate on a spot on the wall directly opposite her. It was difficult to look at Leonard in his Ralph Lauren robe and slippers. It was hard to be calm when all she wanted was to smash her fist into his cheerful face and knock every one of his shiny teeth down his throat. Lavonne fought a sudden urge to throw plates, cups, saucers, frying pans, and furniture. This secrecy thing was going to be harder than she had thought.

"Dolores Swafford called me yesterday," she said, casting about for something to say to take her mind off smashing Leonard's face. Dolores Swafford was a local realtor who had managed to build one of the biggest real estate brokerage firms in south Georgia. She billed herself as a Christian Real Estate Agent, and had biblical verses printed all over her business cards.

"What did that old dragon want?" Leonard said, reaching for a sweet roll.

"She says the Winklers have upped their offering price $20,000." The Winklers were Dolores's clients. They were moving here from New York and they desperately wanted Leonard's house. It seemed he wasn't the only Yankee with dreams of Tara.

"Damn those people," Leonard said. "When are they going to get it through their heads we're not selling this house." Leonard was getting mad just thinking about it. Some people just can't take no for an answer. Some people think money can buy anything. "I'll retire in this house," Leonard said. "I'll die in this house. They'll have to take me out of this house in a body bag."

"Materialism is the last refuge of scoundrels," Louise said to her father, quoting Nietzsche.

"I love this house," Leonard said, ignoring Louise.

Lavonne couldn't remember the last time Leonard had told her he loved her. Admitting his emotions had always been painful for Leonard. He had told her he loved her the first time they had sex, shuddering and whimpering against her shoulder, but Lavonne had known there was more gratitude than love involved. She hadn't really expected it. She had never heard her father tell her mother he loved her. She couldn't remember her parents ever saying, "I love you." The Schwagels had been too practical for all that crazy stuff. Too stoic and emotionally contained.

"Louise, I love you," Lavonne said suddenly. "And Ashley, I love you, too."

No one said anything. Louise set her cup down, leaned her elbows on the bar, and looked at her mother, blinking behind her thick glasses. Ashley looked suspiciously from one parent to the other. After a minute she said, "What are ya'll trying to tell me? I hope ya'll aren't trying to tell me something bad." Her voice rose. "I hope ya'll aren't trying to tell me you're getting a divorce or anything, because I have it on very good authority that I'm going to be named May Queen and there's never been a Barron Hall May Queen with divorced parents."

Leonard, who had been lost in some private reverie, woke up. "Of course we're not getting a divorce, Puddin'," he said quickly.

"Don't call me that," Ashley screamed.

"May Queen?" Louise said. "Don't you know that's just an old pagan fertility ritual?" She poured herself another cup of coffee.

"You're just jealous," Ashley said, "because you never got named May Queen."

"I never wanted to *be* May Queen," Louise said. "I never wanted to dance around the Maypole and worship that old phallic symbol."

"Louise!" Leonard wondered suddenly what it would be like to live in a house with no women.

"See how she talks!" Ashley shouted, flinging her arms wide like a stage actress. "She says words like that at school! She talks trashy at school!"

"What's trashy about *phallic*?" Louise said, stirring three table-spoons of sugar into her coffee. She looked at her father and shrugged. "It's Latin."

"Well I'm glad to see that prep school education has been put to good use," Leonard said. His ears were pink. His Adam's apple bounced up and down the thick stem of his throat like a buoy on stormy seas. "I'm glad to see I haven't completely wasted my money educating you."

"Everyone at school thinks she's weird," Ashley cried. "Of all the sisters in the world, oh why did I have to have her?"

"You and your moronic little friends," Louise said, sipping her coffee. "You're all just a bunch of snobs."

"Well I'd rather be a snob than an intellectual freak," Ashley said.

"You're just jealous because I'm smart and you're not."

"Oh, right. Like I'd rather be smart than popular."

"Are you listening to this?" Leonard said to Lavonne. He could feel his resolve to be calm and cheerful oozing through his pores like gravy through a sieve. His stomach felt lumpy. His heart felt thick and gluti-nous. "Isn't there anything you'd like to say to your daughter?"

"You're right," Lavonne said to Louise. "The Maypole is a phallic symbol."

"Go ahead and make fun of me in front of the children! Go ahead and treat this like a big joke!" Leonard's heart flopped around his chest like a wounded beast. He could feel it hammering against the tender bars of his rib cage. If he stayed married to Lavonne, he'd be dead of a heart attack before he was fifty. "I have to live in this town," he re-minded her. "I have to work in this goddamn town."

"Look, Leonard," she said. "You can't spend your whole life wor-ried about what other people think."

"Well, that's easy for you to say, Lavonne. When was the last time you brought home a paycheck?" He smiled at her in a manner she found particularly insulting.

Lavonne could feel something swelling beneath her breastbone, something monstrous and persistent. "It's kind of hard to bring home a paycheck, Leonard, when you're taking care of two babies and an enormous house."

"Oh, so now I'm to be blamed for buying you a big house?" He looked at the girls, protesting this injustice.

"You didn't buy me this house, Leonard. You bought *you* this house."

"Well, you sure didn't object when we moved in. You sure didn't ask for something smaller. I didn't hear you complaining that the house was too goddamned big."

"Actually, Leonard, I did complain. Numerous times. You just didn't listen. You didn't listen because you wanted this house, because this house means more to you than anything else in the whole world."

Lavonne and Leonard faced each other across the breakfast bar. Leonard's eyes were wild. His pulse raced. One side of his face twitched. The fullness in Lavonne's chest was beginning to move up the column of her throat. She could feel it when she swallowed, swelling like a tumor. A man who betrayed his wife with prostitutes was capable of anything. She wondered what other secrets Leonard had locked up in his dark cramped little heart.

Leonard shook his finger at Lavonne. "If you think it's so easy to make a living and support a family, why don't you try it for a while?"

"Get your finger out of my face," Lavonne said.

Louise took a napkin and began to write things down. You couldn't make up dialogue like this. Louise figured the greatest gift parents could give an aspiring writer was a dysfunctional childhood. She was beginning to believe being born a Zibolsky was a true blessing from God.

"You go to work and I'll stay home and play tennis and go to the beach and spend money," Leonard shouted.

"You wanted me to stay home with the girls, you asshole! You wanted me to quit my job and move down here to this godforsaken banana republic."

Louise was writing furiously on her napkin. "Is *'Godforsaken'* with a hyphen?" she asked.

"Goddamn it, you better not be writing any of this down!" Leonard shouted at Louise. "This is our business! This is our family business! You go to your rooms!" He waved his arms wildly at his daughters. Both girls sat where they were. Ashley munched a sweet roll. Louise reached for another napkin. Lavonne stared at Leonard like she would a lunatic stranger. All those years of thinking him an ally, a partner, thinking she knew him inside and out, when, really, she didn't know him at all. He could be capable of anything. All he cared about was himself. All he cared about was this house. Hell, for all she knew, her name wasn't even on the title. This thought pushed itself up suddenly into her consciousness. Her breathing slowed. There was a metallic taste in her mouth. She couldn't remember attending when they closed on the house. She had been saddled with a baby who needed nap time. She couldn't remember closing on the beach house, either. A warning went off in her head. A sense of foreboding settled ominously in her belly.

Leonard could see a change come over Lavonne's face, but he was too angry to stop. Any other woman would appreciate what he had given her. Any other woman would be grateful. "You can go back to work anytime you want, Lavonne," Leonard said, leaning across the breakfast bar and shoving his angry face close to hers. Foam flecked the corners of his mouth. His eyes were wild and dilated, black-rimmed around the pupil. She could see herself reflected there, small and still.

Leonard, sensing suddenly that the mood in the room had changed, forced himself to calm down. He forced himself to breathe slowly and deeply. The kitchen wall clock ticked like a time bomb. Something about Lavonne's determined expression made Leonard uneasy. He remembered Dillon Foster's advice: "You have to be like a commando behind enemy lines. She can't know a thing is wrong until you serve her with the papers." After awhile, Leonard forced himself to smile. "Sorry," he said, pushing himself off the breakfast bar. He smiled wider, showing his teeth. "Of course I wanted you home with the girls." He opened his hands, palms facing her. *See,* he seemed to say, *I'm carrying no weapons. I'm unarmed.* He looked at the girls. "Sometimes mommies and daddies argue," he said. "That's normal. That's what happens in every family."

"Gee, Dad, you don't have to talk to us like we're three years old."

"Just be quiet, Louise!" His voice was harsh but he managed to keep grinning, like a clown with a painted smile. The effect was terrifying. "We're not angry anymore, are we, Mommy?" he said soothingly. Lavonne looked at her fingers. Her mouth moved like she was adding sums in her head.

"I tell you what!" Leonard said brightly, trying to draw her attention. "Why don't we all go out to brunch?"

Ashley sniffed. "You mean like one big, *happy* family."

"We are a happy family," Leonard said. He put his arm around Ashley's shoulders. "We're just like every other happy American family."

"Happy families are all alike; every unhappy family is unhappy in its own way," Louise said. Her father and sister stared at her like she was retarded. She pushed her glasses up on her nose. "Tolstoy," she explained. "That's the opening line from *Anna Karenina.*"

Ashley made a move toward her sister, but Leonard tightened his arm around her, restraining her. It was taking every effort at self-control for Leonard to handle this situation. It was taking every bit of sly conceit and artifice that he had learned through twenty years of practicing law, to manage his family. "You girls go on upstairs and get ready and we'll go over to the Pink House for brunch," he said cheerfully.

"I'm not going if she goes," Ashley said, pointing at Louise.

"I'm not eating at that Temple to Middle-Class Status," Louise said.

"It'll be just like old times," Leonard said. He gave Ashley a little push toward the door. "Won't it, Mommy?" he asked, grinning at Lavonne and motioning for Louise to go and get dressed.

They all looked at Lavonne. She stopped adding numbers in her head. "Oh yes, Daddy," she said, forcing herself to look at him. "It'll be just like old times."

IN THE END, SHE CONVINCED THEM TO GO WITHOUT HER, PLEADING a headache. Leonard seemed happy enough to comply, but Louise wouldn't go until Lavonne promised to meet them later. Lavonne waited until they had driven away, and then she took the spare office key Leonard kept in his dresser, and went down to the office. One or two young associates were working; she could hear the low murmur of their voices as they bent over their tape recorders. She went down the hallway without saying hello to anyone.

Leonard's office door was closed but unlocked. It took her just a minute to locate the filing drawer marked *Personal*. The drawer was unlocked. Anyone could have gone through their tax returns, receipts, stock portfolio, and real estate files. He had the whole story of their lives together out there in the open for anyone to see. *Anyone but me*, she reminded herself as she began to go through the drawer.

It took her an hour. She didn't find a single document with her name on it, except for the joint checking account, which didn't have near the balance Leonard's accounts did. She made copies of what she needed, closed the drawer, and pulling his office door quietly shut behind her, she left.

CHARLES AWOKE THE MORNING FOLLOWING THE PARTY TO FIND Nita gone. The children had spent the night sleeping at their friends' houses. The house was quiet. He went downstairs and found the kitchen empty, no coffee brewing, no breakfast cooked, no table set, no note from Nita telling him where she was. These were all ominous signs, confirmation that his wife was not in her right mind. They left Charles with an unsettled feeling, a premonition that his life was fixing to change, and not necessarily for the better.

The feeling persisted, intensified, as he hurried into his study, took the key to the shed from his desk drawer, and went through the backyard to check on the Deuce. While he walked down the garden walk he paid careful attention to the soil, trying to spot footsteps in the damp earth, trying to see if anyone from the party had stumbled accidentally onto his treasure. There were footsteps in the soft soil near the fence, left, he supposed, by him and Trevor and Tonya. The men from the tent and awning rental place were taking down the white canopy and long buffet tables. The sky was blue. There was no threat of rain. Charles walked down the path past the pool, past the army of workers, and through the back gate. The garage stood wreathed in kudzu vines and Virginia creeper, hidden in a tall stand of Johnson grass. A stranger passing down the back alley would not even notice it. He looked over his shoulder as he turned the key in the lock and swung the door open, stepping into the darkened garage and allowing his eyes to adjust to the dim light.

The car was covered by a canvas tarp. He could see its long clean lines clearly under the cloth. He walked over to the grille, pulled the canvas back, and ran his hand along the sleek fender like he was running his hand along a woman's thigh. The Deuce had belonged to his father. It was the only thing the old Judge had ever genuinely valued, the only thing in his life that truly seemed to give him pleasure. As he lay dying, he called Charles in and told him he had arranged to sell the car to his college roommate. He gave final instructions for the sale and asked Charles to handle it. Charles promised he would.

Two weeks after his father's death, Charles called the roommate, a wealthy doctor in Atlanta, and informed him he would be keeping the car. There was a period of unpleasantness during which the jilted roommate threatened a lawsuit. Charles took the threat seriously. He guarded the Deuce, his possession now, zealously. Even eighteen years after his father's death, there were few in town who knew of its existence. He never drove it. He kept it hidden in this little garage disguised as a garden shed, hoarding it like a miser hoards his gold. He lived in fear it would be taken from him, stolen in the night by a shadowy figure that haunted his dreams like an angry ghost.

Charles replaced the canvas cover carefully and stepped outside, turning the key in the lock. He made a mental note to hang a sign on the back gate, *Wet Paint,* or *Beware of Dog,* anything that might discourage people from wandering through the back gate and stumbling on his treasure.

COMING UP THE PATH HE SAW NITA'S CAR IN THE DRIVEWAY AND suddenly Charles's world was normal again. All was as it should be. The sun was shining, the Deuce was safe, and his wife was home to make him breakfast. He hurried up the path, whistling.

But Nita was not in the kitchen making breakfast. Nor was she in the family room. Distantly, he could hear the sound of running water. He called her name, but there was no answer. He climbed the stairs, the sound of running water growing louder, and stepped into the bathroom.

Nita was taking a bath. He stood in the doorway and said, "What are you doing?"

She looked at him. One eyebrow rose slightly. "I'm taking a bath."

"Yes, Nita, I'm not stupid, I can see that. But *why* are you taking a bath?"

She was soaking in bubbles up to her chin. She blew gently on the surface of the water. "Because I want to," she said.

Charles rubbed his fingers over his forehead like he was massaging a migraine. He sighed. "Okay, let's try this again," he said. "Where have you been?"

"I've been at Eadie's."

"At this hour? On Sunday morning?"

She made little splashing movements on the surface of the water. "Yes," she said.

He had heard of postpartum depression. He knew it made women strange and unpredictable. But surely, eleven years after the birth of her last child, Nita was too far along to be suffering from that condition. Was there such a thing as middle-age schizophrenia? Charles made a mental note to check on that. "You didn't leave a note. You didn't tell me where you were going. I woke up and you were gone."

She pulled the bubbles toward her like she was gathering roses in her arms.

"I woke up and I was hungry for a big breakfast. Bacon and eggs and grits. Where are the children?"

"At the Mitchells's. She's taking them to Sunday school and then bringing them home."

"Thank God for Anne Mitchell." He had meant it as a cutting remark, but Nita did not seem offended. She did not seem concerned in the least. She built a pyramid of soap suds, a floating pyramid she sculpted with her hands. "What about you?" he said. "Aren't you going to Sunday school?"

Nita looked at him steadily. "When was the last time you went to Sunday school?" she said.

He felt like a stranger in a strange land. He felt as if he had stepped into some bizarre life not his own. "I've decided I don't want you spending so much time with Eadie Boone or Lavonne Zibolsky," he said. "I think they may be bad influences. I think they may be leading you down the wrong road. Goddamn it, Nita, are you listening to me?"

She wondered how hard it would be to build a real pyramid. She had read somewhere that pyramids were known to cure all sorts of human ills, from brain tumors to multiple sclerosis to asthma. She wondered if a pyramid could cure a broken heart.

"Nita! Are you listening to me?"

What was he blithering on about now? She forced herself to concentrate. "I'll make you some breakfast in a minute," she said. She wondered if Jimmy Lee could build her a pyramid. Maybe she should call him and ask him.

Charles stood there staring at the strange woman in his bathtub. "I'm hungry," he said finally.

"I'll be down in a minute," she repeated, shaving one side of her own pyramid to make it even.

He swung around and plodded downstairs to wait. He picked up the channel changer and scrolled through political commentaries, evangelical ministers preaching the end of the world, and a documentary on the Australian wombat. Ten minutes later he went to the foot of the stairs and shouted, "Nita!" He heard the sound of movement overhead. A minute later she appeared, wrapping a towel around her head, wearing her bathrobe and slippers and taking her time coming down the steps. "Did you hear what I said about Eadie Boone?" he said.

"Eggs, bacon, and grits?" she said.

"And coffee," he said. "And toast."

He sat on the sofa watching the wombat documentary while behind him Nita set the table for one and made the coffee and put the bacon in the skillet. Whatever was wrong with Nita would take professional intervention; that much was clear to him. With the annual hunting trip coming up he only had four weeks to clear his calendar and get the summary judgment filed on the Wray case; there would be no time to fix his wife, too. He would have to do that after he returned. There was no way he would give up his hunting trip, the one thing he looked forward to all year, to stay home with an emotionally unstable wife. Guilt flared briefly in his heart, and was quickly extinguished. Maybe there was something his mother could do. Maybe she would be willing to take Nita in hand, so to speak, since he would obviously not have the time.

The aroma of frying bacon and fresh-brewed coffee put him in a better mood. What was that old saying? The way to a man's heart is through his stomach. Never were truer words spoken. No matter what her faults, her little quirks and eccentricities, the one thing you could always count on with Nita was that she was a great cook.

"Breakfast is served," she said in an odd little voice.

He turned the TV off and sat down at the table and she put his plate in front of him. His eggs, which he liked sunny side up, were scrambled. His bacon strips, which he liked brown and crispy, were rubbery. His grits were gray and lumpy as old socks. Coffee bubbled out of the automatic coffeemaker and ran over the counter and down the sides of the cabinets like a lava flow. Toast burned in the toaster.

"Why don't you play golf this afternoon?" she said, standing beside the table with a blank expression on her face. She was still holding the spatula. There was something slightly menacing in her posture, something subtle but obvious. "Why don't you play golf and have dinner at the club? I'll take the children to the park and then to my folks' house for supper." He opened his mouth to complain about the scrambled eggs and lumpy grits and rubbery bacon, but thought better of it. How do you complain to a woman who's holding a spatula the way an Iroquois warrior holds a war club? A woman who might not be quite right in the head, as it is, who might suddenly snap and see nothing wrong with bashing her husband in the back of the head with a spatula or a pair of barbecue tongs or some other sharp kitchen utensil. He wondered if dementia ran in Nita's family. He wondered if there was a great-aunt or great-uncle or fourth cousin locked up somewhere in some out-of-the-way asylum. He wondered if he should really be leaving his fragile wife to go off to Montana and cavort with whores. Guilt blazed again but was quickly extinguished by his willingness to absolve himself of all blame.

Charles had learned long ago that guilt was a useless emotion.

CHAPTER

SEVEN

*L*AMAR RAMSBOTTOM SAT IN HIS OFFICE LOOKING OUT OVER a field of buffalo grass. In the distance, a herd of horses grazed, tiny specks against the wide brown fields and gentle rises of the Montana landscape. The sky was blue and streaked with thin wisps of trailing clouds. Ramsbottom pushed himself back in his chair and slowly stretched his booted feet up on top of the desk. Papers littered the dusty surface of the desk. A half-finished cup of cold coffee collected mold. A loud metallic hum told him Bentley Nash, his Sioux ranch hand, was using the Gravely to move trash down to the landfill.

Ramsbottom pulled his collar up around his neck and settled himself down in his chair. The morning was cold and clear. Steam rose around his face with his breathing. A calf bawled in the stockade. From down in the creekside pen, old Humphrey, the moth-eaten circus lion, coughed at the moon. Ramsbottom knew he should be up, readying himself for the next onslaught of guests, but on cold mornings his arthritic limbs refused to move and he found himself thinking about the fire crackling in the grate up at the ranch house. He was getting old. Too old to be dragging his ass around the Montana countryside with a pack of churnhead guests who couldn't hit the side of a barn with a cannon. It made him sick just thinking about it.

What had made him think a hunting ranch for wealthy Easterners would be the life for him? Desperation, probably. He squinted his eyes, trying to remember himself as a youth, full of optimism and ideals and determined to hang on to the land that had been in his family since 1878. The land that his father had mortgaged and then killed himself over during the Great Depression. The land Ramsbottom almost lost to foreclosure. Yes, of course that was it. Desperation had driven him to open the game ranch.

And now here he was fifty years later, old and arthritic and dreading the next group of Nancy-boys that was at that very moment circling the skies above Push Hard, drunk, no doubt, and ready to descend upon the Ah! Wilderness Game Ranch and prove themselves—ready to prove their manhood by slaughtering droves of tame mule deer and antelope and quail so docile they lay on the ground like trussed hens waiting to be killed. It made him sick just thinking about it. How could a man take pride in something like that? He remembered the old days, before jet service came to Bozeman, when the town was small and sleepy and filled with hardened characters. A little backcountry, washed-out refuge for criminals and prostitutes—that's what Push Hard, Montana, had been before the Hollywood People discovered it, and ruined it. Now all the shops and restaurants had striped awnings and names like La Petite Couchon, and a man had to drive all the way to Big Ridge to get a pan-fried steak. Where once the dusty boardwalks had swarmed with hardened men and brazen women, now the concrete sidewalks were thronged with businessmen wearing Orvis field gear, and skinny stuck-up women pushed baby strollers and haggled with merchants over silver jewelry.

It made his blood pressure rise just thinking about it. Only last year another Hollywood Star had bought the ranch adjoining the Ah! Wilderness Ranch and brought in a herd of buffalo to trample the grazing lands, and now there was talk of him reintroducing the timber wolf on his property. He'd been in Push Hard only one year and already he and a bunch of his rich Hollywood friends had staged a downtown demonstration against the Ah! Wilderness Game Ranch, which they had decided was inhumane and immoral. Paparazzi from all over the world had come and clicked pictures of the beautiful people and a few of Ramsbottom himself, looking dazed and sluggish, like a white tail caught in the headlights of a semi-truck. These sons of bitches made more money than God, and here they were protesting an honest man making an honest living the best way he knew how.

"Hey, Boss, you want me to take the truck over to the airport to pick up those Nancy-boys?" Bentley Nash stood just inside the door, his hat in his hands. Bentley was what you call movie-star handsome. He had long black hair that he wore in a ponytail, and chiseled features, and he was tall, for a Sioux. He was dumb as a stump, but he was good-looking. "You want me to go into town and pick up those skim-milk cowboys?" Bentley asked, dusting his jeans with the brim of his hat.

Ramsbottom took careful aim and spat into the cup of cold coffee. "Yeah," he said, in disgust, "they'll be landing right about now. Look for them in the bar."

Bentley grinned and nodded his head. He knew the routine.

"And don't let them drive this time," Ramsbottom shouted after him, as he closed the door.

Shit. He stretched his legs gingerly. There was plenty to do before they got here. This bunch was coming in from Dallas, Texas. Texans were the worst, always bragging about how manly they were, always bragging about being from Texas. The only good thing about putting up with Texans for four days was that they were usually pretty good tippers. He'd have to call Pinky to get those girls up here before the Texans arrived. They liked a good fuck to start the weekend off right. "Good whiskey, good huntin', good food, good fuckin'" was their motto.

The only really good thing about this weekend was that he was going to get to tell the Texans he was retiring. This was their last trip to the Ah! Wilderness Game Ranch, their last chance to wreak havoc on a bunch of tame wildlife. From now on, they'd have to find someplace else to do their pitiful hunting. It made Ramsbottom grin, just thinking about it. The rich Movie Star had offered to buy two thousand acres and pay him four times what the land was worth, if he agreed to give up the game ranch. That's the way these people were. They had no concept of what money was really worth. They had so much they could just throw it away to suit their ideals. That was fine with him. He would keep the ranch house and the other five hundred acres and he would retire. Bentley, too, if he wanted. He'd have only one other goddamn hunting party after the Texans—those rich-lawyer Georgians, who were coming out in four weeks.

He didn't much like to think about them. On second thought, the Texans weren't so bad. If he hadn't already spent the lawyers' deposit money, he would have canceled. Thinking back to all the years of pain-in-the-ass guests, he figured this bunch was the worst. Charles Broadwell. Biggest asshole he'd ever known. The old Judge must be spinning in his grave to see how his son had turned out. Ramsbottom would not be sorry to tell Broadwell he was retiring after this trip. One more month of business, one more week of putting up with Charles Broadwell, and then he would be free forever from the Charles Broadwells of the world.

He put his feet down squarely on the floor. He leaned forward slightly, testing his knees, letting his weight settle gradually and pushing himself up with one hand leaning on the desk. His bones creaked. He groaned and stretched himself gingerly, like an old dog. He took one step, and then another, gradually adjusting to the pain that always came after long periods of inactivity. He fixed his eyes on the door and forced his legs to move.

He was almost to the door when the phone rang.

EADIE DIDN'T WASTE ANY TIME. ONCE SHE FOUND RAMSBOTTOM'S name and phone number among the receipts, she called him. He was hesitant, at first, as if he suspected a joke was being played on him. But after awhile, under Eadie's persistent questioning and after it became clear to him that she was, indeed, legitimate in her desire for revenge against the lawyers, he began to give her the information she wanted. Under Eadie's skillful prodding, Ramsbottom unburdened himself of the frustration of working fifty years for a bunch of rich pallet heads who were slick as owl snot when it came to making money, but who didn't have the sense God gave a saddle horn when it came to hunting game.

Eadie let him talk. After awhile she began to throw out a few ideas she had for this year's hunting trip. Ramsbottom thought the idea she had for the "girls" was hilarious. Female impersonators were something he didn't get many requests for, but he was pretty sure he could rustle up a few through his contacts in Vegas. And he was pretty sure he could work it so the hunting trip was a little rougher this year than it had been in the past, filled with a little more danger and hardship than the lawyers were usually accustomed to.

"Do you want me to take pictures?" he said.

"What?"

"Pictures of the greenhorns with the male prostitutes. You know. For insurance purposes."

She couldn't believe this hadn't occurred to her. Obviously, parts of her brain were still frozen and not working properly after the shock of finding out her husband was a lying, cheating bastard, or she would have thought of the compromising photographs herself. With photographs, Leonard and Charles would do whatever Lavonne and Nita asked. They would do anything to keep those photographs from becoming public and ruining their reputations. Trevor probably wouldn't care what the public thought, but he might care what Tonya thought. "Can you take videos, too?" she said, feeling a little throb of excitement in the pit of her stomach. This was turning from a bitch-fest into a definite plan for revenge. She couldn't wait to tell Nita and Lavonne.

"Sure," Ramsbottom said. "It'll cost you extra, but I can do it." Hell, he'd have done it for free just to see the look on those slack-jawed pissants' faces, but if she was willing to pay, why not? "Now, you don't mean for these old boys to be maimed or permanently injured during the trip, do you?" he asked Eadie, trying to determine how far she was willing to go.

Eadie thought about it for a moment. "No," she said. "We don't want them maimed or permanently injured. We just want them whittled down some."

"You're a girl after my own heart," he said in admiration of Eadie's resolve. She was the first female he'd ever met who even came close to having his penchant for getting even. He didn't have to see her to know she was a fine-looking woman. He knew just from talking to her she was the kind of woman could make a man plow through a stump. "Ole' Boone must be crazy for letting you go," he said.

"Oh, he's crazy all right," Eadie said. She wished she could be there to see the whole thing go down. She wished she could be there when Trevor found out the hookers were really boys. "I'll call you next week to firm up our plans. Just make sure you take lots of pictures," she said to Ramsbottom. "Make sure they know the female impersonators were our idea," she said, and hung up.

TWO DAYS LATER, EADIE WENT TO SEE ROSEBUD SMOOT. ROSEBUD had worked with Eadie for years, doing pro bono work for women in domestic violence situations. On the way to Rosebud's office, Eadie stopped first at the bookstore and bought a book on Frida Kahlo. She figured Frida would be good reading considering her current marital situation.

"What you got, Eadie?" Rosebud asked after her new secretary, Stephen, showed Eadie into her office.

"You have a *male* secretary?"

"Yes. He couldn't get into graduate school so he took the job with me."

"Score one for gender equality," Eadie said.

"Yep. What can I do for you?"

"It's a divorce matter."

"One of the women at the shelter?" Rosebud asked, reaching for her legal pad.

"No, me."

Rosebud smiled. She put the top back on her pen and leaned back in her chair. "Are you telling me, after all these years, you're contemplating divorce from the great Trevor Boone?"

"I'm doing more than contemplating it," Eadie said.

"What happened?"

Eadie told her. Everything except for the hunting trip revenge part. She didn't want to give Rosebud a chance to talk her out of something she'd already put her heart and soul into. "Can you believe it?" Eadie said, when she had finished. "Prostitutes. For fifteen years. Have you ever heard anything so pathetic?"

After forty years of practicing law, Rosebud had heard it all. After forty years of representing women in domestic violence and divorce cases, she'd heard every disastrous tale of love gone wrong you could imagine. She'd been accosted twice on the courthouse steps by irate husbands or their family members. She walked with a limp from a bullet she still carried in her hip, the result of a shooting from a wife beater distraught over his wife's removal from their happy home. Still, the image of Trevor Boone, Leonard Zibolsky, and Charles Broadwell betraying their wives with prostitutes was disturbing. They were, after all, colleagues. They were, with the exception of Trevor, by all outward appearances, happily married men; pillars of the community. It made Rosebud wonder at the treachery and capacity for self-deception of the male sex. It made her glad she had never married.

"Are you serious about this?" Rosebud said.

"Serious as a heart transplant," Eadie said.

"Okay. I've known you long enough to know that once you've made up your mind, there's no changing it. I guess you've thought about your options. I know you and Trevor have patched up your differences in the past, but I do understand the concept of the straw that broke the camel's back." She raised her eyebrows and gave Eadie a chance to jump in here, but Eadie wasn't changing her mind. She stared resolutely at Rosebud. Rosebud sighed. "Okay," she said briskly. "I need you to sit down and list all the assets you can think of. Everything, from the furniture to the house, beach house, boat, cars, stocks and bonds— you get the picture. Put it all down on a piece of paper. And then I need you to come in and meet with me again as early as possible so we can get the ball rolling."

"What about Lavonne?"

"What about her?"

"Can you represent her, too?"

"Of course. But she needs to call me."

"Can we get a group discount?"

Rosebud grinned. "Don't worry about that. Your husbands will foot the bill, eventually anyway."

"I like your optimism."

"Now, Eadie, I don't want you to think this is going to be easy. Trevor Boone is a damn fine attorney. This could drag on awhile. It could get real messy. You may need to work out some other source of income for awhile."

Eadie thought about this. "Can I sell the house?" she said.

"Not if it's in his name. Not if it's in both your names."

"Shit," Eadie said.

"I may be able to get you temporary alimony, but without children it's getting harder and harder to do that these days."

"Okay," Eadie said. She wasn't really worried, but she couldn't tell Rosebud why. She was pretty sure that once Trevor and Leonard got a look at the photographs she and Lavonne and Nita were going to wind up with, they'd jump through hoops to get the divorces over with. She was pretty sure they wouldn't put up much of a fight. "I don't think we need to worry about Trevor dragging this thing out," Eadie said. "I'm pretty sure he'll be happy to get this little episode of his life over with."

"I like your optimism," Rosebud said, motioning for Stephen to bring them another cup of coffee. "But what makes you think he'll settle?"

"It's a gut feeling," Eadie said.

"I'm curious," Rosebud said, swinging around in her chair with her elbows resting on the armrest and her hands tented in front of her. "What did Trevor say when you confronted him about the prostitutes?"

"He didn't say anything." Eadie picked a piece of lint off her jacket. "He didn't say anything because I didn't confront him." She looked at Rosebud and grinned. "Hard to believe, isn't it?"

"Yes, it is." Rosebud frowned and bumped her index finger against her bottom lip. Stephen brought their coffee and closed the door quietly behind him. "But how do you know he was involved? I'm playing devil's advocate here, but shouldn't you give him a chance to explain what happened before you hit him with divorce papers?"

"I'm through with explanations."

"Things aren't always what they seem."

"Do you want to represent me, or not?"

Rosebud smiled and lifted her cup. "It'll give me great pleasure to represent you," she said. She sipped the steaming coffee and set it back down on her desk. "Just promise me you'll call me if you change your mind."

"I won't change my mind," Eadie said.

*   *   *

LEAVING ROSEBUD'S OFFICE, EADIE FELT LIKE A SPRING THAT HAD come unsprung. Caught up in the adrenaline high of phone calls and revenge planning, she hadn't had much time to think about Trevor. She hadn't had time to dwell on his treachery and what it might mean to her and her future. Until now. She walked through the parking lot aimlessly looking for her car. Her feet were not reliable. She felt like she was walking on marbles. She felt like she was pushing something heavy up a steep hill. If she stopped to breathe, the momentum would be lost. If she stopped to rest, the monstrous weight would roll back down and crush her.

As she drove home through the slow-moving traffic, the frenzy she had felt since she discovered her husband's betrayal continued to subside. The zeal she had carried faltered and ebbed to a vacuous emptiness that thickened and spread like formaldehyde through the hollow cavity of her abdomen. Her heart was numb. Her spirit was dead. Everything she had ever thought true was false.

She had thought Trevor an equal, a worthy adversary, someone she could build her life around, and he had proved himself no better than Charles Broadwell and Leonard Zibolsky. No better than Luther Birdsong and Frank Plumlee, the men her sad mother had loved and lost. She could understand the open cheating, could even, on some unexplainable irrational level, respect the courageousness of it, and could understand why Trevor felt compelled to do it. She understood that it opened him up to the pain of her reciprocal betrayal. It was complicated, and she knew, to many people, it appeared sick and psychologically unsound. But as long as the betrayal had been open, as long as it had been reciprocal, a balance had been maintained between them that allowed their marriage, with its periods of estrangement and reunion, to continue. She couldn't explain it in any terms other than some weird yin/yang thing. It would not work for most people, but it had worked for them.

And now Trevor had fucked it all up by keeping his dirty little secret all these years. He had upset the delicate balance that was necessary for their marriage to continue. He had lessened himself as a man and made her ashamed to love him. Even if the thing with Tonya didn't work out, Eadie would never take him back now.

She stopped at a red light. She picked up the book on Frida Kahlo and began to thumb through the glossy pages, stopping on pictures of Frida with a monkey, Frida with her heart clipped and bleeding, Frida dissected on a hospital bed. There was in Frida's solemn mustachioed face, her anguished eyes, an expression of patient and deliberate suffering that reminded Eadie of her mother. Her mother had worn the same expression all those years ago when she watched Luther Birdsong's big feet go stomping past, when she waited for Frank Plumlee to come in for dinner.

It startled Eadie, remembering this, and it disturbed her, too, because it occurred to her suddenly that in her relationship with Trevor Boone, she was more like her mother than she cared to admit.

EADIE HAD NO CLEAR RECOLLECTION OF HER FATHER. HE HAD left when she was still a baby, leaving her and her mother to the enduring poverty of the Shangri-La Trailer Park. Her mother, Reba, worked a number of jobs to put food on the table. From time to time she worked as a beautician, a waitress, a maid out at the Holiday Inn, a cashier at the Piggly Wiggly, and a laborer on a construction road crew. It was on this road crew that she met her second husband, Luther Birdsong.

Luther was a quiet steady man given to fits of violent rage when he drank, which turned out to be every Friday evening. Eadie would lie beneath the bed with her mother watching Luther's big feet pass back and forth, the floor trembling and the walls rattling with his bellowed rage. After Luther left, Friday nights at the Shangri-La Trailer Park got quiet again for a while, but Eadie's mother got sad and nothing Eadie could do would cheer up her. Eadie guessed Reba missed the Friday nights huddled beneath the bed while the tiny trailer rattled like a metal box in a gale. After awhile Reba began to dress herself up and go out on Friday nights, leaving Eadie propped in front of the television with a Coca-cola and a bag of chips, and orders not to stay up too late. Eadie didn't mind too much. It was still better than hiding beneath the bed watching Luther Birdsong's big feet go stomping past.

Eadie didn't much care for the steady procession of men her

mother brought home. It seemed to Eadie that men were nothing but trouble. It also seemed to Eadie that Reba could not live without them. She resigned herself to this, and when Reba came home one morning, eyes shining, dragging behind her a small thin man in a plaid suit whom she introduced as "your new daddy," Eadie extended her arm with as much grace as possible, and shook hands. She was eleven years old and too cynical to believe that this one would last much longer than the others had.

His name was Frank Plumlee. He was a manic-depressive Broderbund Encyclopedia salesman who sold books door to door. In those first few weeks he came to live with them he was a good influence on Reba, who learned to iron his shirts and cook meals that didn't come out of a box or a plastic tray. Those first few weeks were smooth sailing, but after Frank ran out of his medication, he quit going to work and began sitting around the trailer all day in his underwear. Reba had to go back to work at Miss Eula's House of Hair to pay the bills, and Eadie would return home from school in the afternoons to find Frank sitting in the darkened trailer watching TV soap operas that showed people too good-looking to be real rolling around together in bed. Her mother didn't seem to mind that Frank didn't work. Eadie didn't know what was worse, listening to the racket Luther Birdsong made on Friday nights or listening to the racket her mother and Frank made every night from the dark fetid recesses of the cramped bedroom. After ten weeks with Frank Plumlee, Luther Birdsong was starting to look pretty good.

To make matters worse, Frank had begun to bother Eadie. She would wake some nights to find him standing over her, his sour smell wafting through the trailer like some sinister disembodied shape. He had begun to follow her with his eyes, leaving her with the feeling that he had run his dirty hands over her and left smudges in places she didn't like to think about. She tried to tell her mother, but all Reba did was look around wildly and say in a panicked voice, "What are you saying, Eadie? What are you saying?"

Eadie thought it was pretty clear what she was saying. Still, she had learned by now that women could be divided into two groups; those who were miserable and couldn't do anything about it, and those who were miserable and could. Her mother definitely fell into the former category, but Eadie didn't blame her for this. She set about planning how to get rid of Frank Plumlee on her own.

She bought a pearl-handled pocketknife and practiced stabbing things with it: upholstered furniture, cereal boxes, her pillow, the sandy creek bank. One Friday afternoon she returned home from school to find her mother's Pinto parked in the yard. Frank's El Dorado was gone. The weight that sat constantly on Eadie's chest like a cement block lifted, and she was whistling when she opened the trailer door and stepped inside.

"Mama!" she called, throwing her book bag on the floor.

"She ain't here," Frank said.

Her heart slammed against her ribs. She could see him now, her eyes slowly adjusting to the darkness of the room. He was sitting over by the kitchen in a metal chair wearing nothing but his underwear. His slit was opened in front and his thing was plopped out on the side of his thigh like a dead fish.

"Her car wouldn't start. She took mine to work." While he talked the fish began to move slightly. "It's just you and me," he said. Frank's eyes glowed in the dim room as if lit by something deep and powerful.

Eadie reached in her pocket and took out the little pearl-handled knife. Across the room Frank began to chuckle softly. His thing had left his thigh, rising up out of his shorts and quivering like a harpoon embedded in flesh. Eadie tried not to look. Bile rose in her throat. Her bladder swelled like a balloon. She opened the blade of the little knife and began to wipe it on her sleeve.

Frank stood up. "You gonna poke me with that little bitty knife?" he said in a thick voice.

"Frank," she said in a loud calm voice. "I've got a proposition for you."

He chuckled slightly and took a step toward her. She looked up to meet his gaze, hefting the knife in her hand and closing her fingers over the handle, remembering how she had plunged the tip into her pillow at night, imagining the point embedded deep in Frank's soft white belly. "The way I look at it," she said. "You've got two options. You can take the money I've saved and pack your bags and leave to start a new life in Alabama or Mississippi, or you can come over here and let me poke you with my little knife and then wait while I put on my Girl Scout uniform and go down to the station and tell Sheriff Cox and those two big deputies of his how you stood there and dropped your thing out of your pants for a little girl to see." She held her two clenched fists up like a scale swaying to balance. "Think about it," she said. "Jail or Mississippi. Jail or Alabama. What do you choose?"

It turned out Frank Plumlee was an easy man to fool. Eadie didn't even have a Girl Scout uniform. He stood there with his face setting up around his eyes like cement around two rotten stumps. Suddenly he twitched. His shoulders slumped. After a moment the sinister light in his eyes flickered, and went out.

When Reba came home an hour later to find Frank gone, she went into the bedroom to cry.

TWO MONTHS LATER EADIE ENTERED HER FIRST BEAUTY CONTEST. She did it to please her mother, who had grown increasingly despondent after Frank Plumlee's hurried departure. It seemed Reba could not be happy without a man around to make her miserable. She threw the ironing board out in the woods behind the trailer, she quit cooking, and she cut back on her hours at Eula's House of Hair. Nothing Eadie did cheered her up. Finally, on a hot humid day in June, Eadie came into Eula's to find her mother and the other beauticians bent over a printed flyer that read in giant letters across the top *Little Miss Mag Wheels Beauty Pageant! Sponsored by Clyde Purvis Auto! $50 in Cash to the Winner! Free Tires! Free Lube and Oil Change! Free MoonPie with Every Fill-up! Come on down to Clyde Purvis Auto for Details!*

"Who-ee," Martha Agnes said. "I sure could use them tires."

"You're a little old for a beauty pageant, ain't you?" Thelma said.

"Shut up," Martha Agnes said.

"You know who's pretty enough to win one of them pageants is your little girl," Betty Lee said to Reba, who was picking despondently at a hairbrush.

"You think so?" Reba said doubtfully.

"Shit yeah," Betty Lee said. "She don't never come in here when one of my customers don't say 'My goodness Betty Lee, who is that beautiful child?' "

"Miz Eva Bedwell noticed her yestiddy," Martha Agnes said.

"Miz Hampton said she was pretty enough to be out in Hollywood in one of them Hollywood pictures," Thelma said.

"You think so?" Reba said, frowning.

"Let's go ahead and enter her in old Clyde Purvis's contest," Thelma said.

"I don't know," Reba said. Eadie stood quietly just inside the door watching them. The ceiling fans hummed and clanked, stirring tiny clumps of hair that littered the floor. Over in the corner the icebox whirred.

"I can do her hair," Martha Agnes said.

"I can do her face," Thelma said.

"She'll need one of them pageant dresses," Betty Lee said.

"I don't have no money for a pageant dress," Reba said.

"Hell, maybe we can sponsor her," Miss Eula said, leaning against Thelma's chair and idly scratching at her monstrous hip. "She'd be good advertising for the shop. A girl that pretty's bound to attract attention even if she don't win the damn contest."

But Eadie did win the Little Miss Mag Wheels Beauty Pageant. And she won or at least placed in the top three spots for most of the pageants her mother entered her in thereafter. For the next six years she and Reba toured the South, pulling Eadie out of school when necessary and driving everywhere in a beat-up old Ford Mustang. In between beauty contests, she made TV commercials. By the time she was sixteen, Eadie had made enough money to buy her mother a little house over on the south side of town, and by the time she was eighteen, Eadie had won a scholarship and set aside enough money to get through the University of Georgia without ever having to enter another damn beauty contest. It was while she was at U. of Georgia that she fulfilled her childhood dreams of glory and destiny by becoming an artist just like she had dreamed of all those years before. It was also here that she met and married the rich and handsome Trevor Boone, which had never figured into her childhood dreams and, seen now, with the bright clear vision of hindsight, might not have been such a good idea after all.

❀   ❀   ❀

EADIE DROVE THROUGH THE TRAFFIC LIKE A ZOMBIE, REMEMBER-ing her sad childhood and how she had vowed to make a better life for herself. Was this the better life she had envisioned as a girl sitting on the bank of the creek that meandered behind the Shangri-La Trailer Park? If she had it to do all over again, would she look down favorably on Trevor Boone from her perch on the Georgia Homecoming float, or would she turn her face and ride away without a second glance? It was futile to think this way, Eadie knew, but she couldn't help herself.

Behind her a car beeped and she punched the accelerator and followed the stream of traffic through the intersection. The car in front of her, an old Volvo sedan, sped up and veered erratically from lane to lane. The driver watched her from the rearview mirror. The passenger turned around to look at her and for a moment Eadie thought, *I know that woman*. The Volvo's brake lights flared and Eadie slowed and said, "What the hell?"

She realized suddenly that the driver of the car was Trevor and the passenger was Tonya.

Eadie put her foot on the brake and let her car drift to the shoulder of the road while the sedan sped up. Tonya turned again to look at her just before they slipped behind a poultry truck and Eadie imagined the two of them, terrified that she was following them, Trevor, tight-lipped and hunched over the steering wheel as he drove; Tonya, white-faced and nervous, urging him to hurry.

Eadie sat on the shoulder of the road while the traffic roared past. Construction workers leaned against the concrete abutment and smoked cigarettes. One of them raised his hand and waved at her. She wanted to weep with humiliation. She wanted to call Trevor on the phone and tell him she wasn't following him. She could hear his voice, thick with pity, warning Tonya to stay down, warning Tonya that she was dangerous, that she was crazy and capable of anything. She could hear Tonya's voice, small and frightened but with a hint of triumph, too, as she urged him to drive faster.

Fuck them. She sat for a long time watching the traffic pass. Steppenwolf played on the oldies station. Eadie felt the cold lump of sorrow that was frozen around her heart beginning to thaw. Courage and out-rage, her old companions, swept through her like a brushfire. Some-time during the mortifying realization that her husband still thought she was stalking him, Eadie had made a final decision. She had decided that everything that happened to her from now on, every aspect of her life, her hopes, her art, her future, depended solely and entirely on her.

She would go through with the hunting trip revenge, she would commit herself to divorce, she would find a way, somehow, to work again, and when it was all over she didn't care if she ever saw Trevor Boone again.

*L*AVONNE ROSE EARLY, ATE A BRAN MUFFIN AND SOME YO-gurt, and went for a walk. She walked briskly. The morning air was cool and damp against her face and fragrant with the sharp scent of pine. The sky brightened gradually as she walked, washing the yards and houses with a faint golden tinge. Cars zoomed past her; husbands on their way to work clutched steaming cups of coffee, their eyes fixed wearily on the road.

She had dreamed last night she was flying. High above the roofs and treetops of Ithaca, she soared like a great black bird, gliding peace-fully over the sleeping town. It was like swimming, really. Flying. Like moving through water, her body grown suddenly light and supple, mak-ing movement effortless. She had awakened to an incredible feeling of lightness and hope. She had awakened to a feeling that everything was going to be all right.

When she got home the girls had already left for school. She stood in the kitchen and stretched for a while, giving her worn muscles a chance to relax. She poured herself a cup of coffee and sat down at the breakfast bar to read an article on women business owners she had found in one of Leonard's magazine. *By the year 2010, one out of every two small businesses will be owned by women.* It made her feel good to read that. She finished the article and sat for a long time, drinking her coffee and contemplating her future.

It occurred to her suddenly that she no longer had to live in Ithaca. Louise was in her last year of high school. Ashley had another year to go. They would both be leaving in the next two years to go off to college. There would be nothing to keep her in Ithaca except her friendship with Eadie and Nita. Nothing, she reminded herself, except a potential business opportunity.

She went to the phone and called Mona Shapiro to set up an appointment to see her at two o'clock. Then she called Dolores Swafford, the town's leading Christian Real Estate Agent, and made an appointment to see her the following day.

UNTIL SHE MET EADIE AND NITA, LAVONNE HAD NEVER HAD CLOSE girlfriends. She had never been one of those giggly feminine girls who surrounds herself in high school and college with other giggly feminine girls. Except for the odd loner she met during debating events or at school clubs, Lavonne's only true childhood girlfriend had been Teresa Cuplink, her next-door neighbor. The Cuplinks were Catholic and there were nine children ranging in age from two to eighteen, including Teresa, who was a year older than Lavonne but similar to her in temperament and social status. They were both smart and athletic, and at a time when girls were not allowed to wear pants to school or play organized sports, they considered themselves "tomboys." They would spy on the Cuplink boys, or build forts in the woods, or play Bad Barbie, a role-playing game where they dressed Barbie in revealing outfits and had her perpetrate acts of cruelty on a willing and submissive Ken. It wasn't much of a childhood, but it wasn't as bad as some, and when the Cuplink grandmother died and Ralph and Enid moved their swarm to her big crumbling house across town, Lavonne lost her best childhood friend, put on twenty pounds, and went back to reading comic books alone in her attic.

High school was a blur of homework, honors classes, debating events, and the occasional club meeting. Lavonne had little time for socializing. College, which she attended on an academic scholarship, was little different, except that she managed to lose forty pounds her senior year and met and began dating Leonard Zibolsky. They were both studious and ambitious and socially awkward; it seemed a match made in heaven. Lavonne's mother died of a heart attack three years after she graduated from college and her father, who had never in his entire married life made himself a sandwich or washed his laundry or made a bed, died six months later. Lavonne and Leonard married that same year, the year Leonard graduated from law school and took a job with a small Cleveland law firm. Three years later, they moved to Ithaca.

Until they moved south, Lavonne and Leonard had lived quiet, conservative lives. They had not done a lot of socializing. But within their first week in Ithaca they went to three dinner parties, a luncheon, and a brunch. Lavonne had never known people who partied as much as these Southerners did. They'd take any opportunity to have a "throw down." She couldn't imagine how anyone ever got any work done.

The people Lavonne met were kind and polite; they were so friendly and sweet it made her teeth hurt just talking to them. She had never met people who seemed so outgoing and neighborly. The women especially had a way of making you feel like you'd been good, good friends all your lives. They were always saying about one another, "Oh, she's a *good, good* friend of mine," right before they spilled some juicy bit of gossip about the good, good friend involved.

At every party, Lavonne saw the same people. At every dinner party, every supper club, every barbecue, the same small group of people congregated. They were an island in the great rushing river of social equality. They were an evolutionary disaster waiting to happen.

To make matters worse, Leonard had gone completely native. She hardly knew the man anymore. He had managed to pick up a really bad Southern accent, the kind that TV actors use. She caught him practicing one morning, standing in front of the bathroom mirror, drawing out his vowels and talking like he had cotton batting stuffed in his mouth. It was embarrassing. It made Lavonne feel as if she had been dropped suddenly into the middle of a Tennessee Williams play and everyone but her had been given scripts. It made her feel as if she had been transported to a Southern version of *The Stepford Wives*.

But then Lavonne met Eadie Boone, and her opinion that Southerners were all alike and unoriginal changed forever. It was early June,

their second week in town, and she and Leonard were at the "get acquainted" party the Boones had thrown to welcome the Zibolskys to
town. They had arrived at the Boone mansion to find Eadie standing on
a table singing the "Georgia Fight Song." Trevor was trying to convince
her to climb down but he was looking around, too, and grinning like a
man who knows he's the luckiest son of a bitch in the world. It was obvious he was crazy about his wife. Lavonne thought Eadie was the most
beautiful woman she had ever seen.

Lavonne stood awkwardly beside the bar that had been set up on
the patio and watched Leonard move among the guests like he had
lived here all his life. He was wearing khaki pants and a pink polo shirt
and loafers with no socks. He'd only been here a little over one week
and he was already saying "ya'll."

Lavonne sipped her wine and watched the party and tried not to
say too much. Leonard had warned her to just listen for a while, to
smile and be polite, and for God's sake, to keep her voice down.

Eadie Boone did a high kick and one of her shoes, a stacked sandal
with a stiletto heel, shot off and smacked Dolph Meriwether in the
back of the head. He swung around violently, one hand, the one not
holding his drink, clenched in a fist. Eadie put her hand over her
mouth. The party got real quiet except for Trevor's loud chuckling.

"Death by stiletto," he shouted, and Dolph, seeing it was Eadie
who had smacked him in the head, relaxed and unclenched his fist and
drawled, "I don't mind you singing the 'Georgia Fight Song,' Eadie, but
try not to kill me while you're doing it."

For some reason, maybe it was nerves, maybe it was boredom,
maybe it was three glasses of wine, Lavonne found all this very funny.
She snorted loudly, and the whole party turned to look at her. Leonard's
face fell. From across the patio, Eadie grinned at Lavonne and lifted
her glass in a silent toast.

Nita James, the shy sweet girl who was dating Charles Broadwell,
moved up beside Lavonne and touched her lightly on the arm. "Mrs.
Zibolsky, how're you settling in?" she asked. Lavonne was glad for her
support. Nita seemed genuinely sweet and she was very pretty and, like
Lavonne, seemed nervous around these people, as if she knew she
didn't really fit in.

"Call me Lavonne," she said. "When I hear Mrs. Zibolsky, I immediately think of my mother-in-law." She rolled her eyes comically and Nita laughed. Nita was engaged to the Tyrant Charles, which is how Lavonne, who had only known him briefly, had already begun to think of Charles Broadwell. Having grown up with an autocratic father, Lavonne could always spot a tyrant, and avoided them if at all possible, a lesson she wished the unfortunate Nita had also learned.

Worland Pendergrass and another woman stopped by to say hello. "Hi Laverne, I'm Lee Anne Bales," the woman said, smiling brightly. She had the whitest teeth Lavonne had ever seen. She was wearing a diamond tennis bracelet that she kept twisting around her wrist and holding up to the light so everyone could get a good look at it.

Lavonne wished she had chosen something a little stronger than white wine to drink. She wished she was drinking whatever Eadie Boone was drinking. "It's Lavonne," she said to the woman with the blinding teeth.

Lee Anne frowned and leaned in close like she suspected Lavonne might have a speech impediment. "Excuse me?" she said.

"My name. It's Lavonne, not Laverne."

"I just love your outfit," Worland cooed, her eyes traveling from Lavonne's shoes to her hairstyle with one darting glance. It was like the flickering of a serpent's tongue, that glance, and it deduced everything there was to know about Lavonne, from her weight (165), to the kind of schools she attended (public), to the kind of people she came from (blue collar).

"Thanks," Lavonne said, trying not to be put off by the woman's probing eyes, trying not to appear too vain or pompous. She had recently lost fifteen pounds and she was feeling pretty good about herself. She wasn't fashionably thin, but she wasn't fat either, and the woman at the department store had promised her navy blue was slimming.

Later, Lavonne overheard them talking about her in the bathroom. She was waiting outside the locked door, standing in the wide hall that ran from the front to the back of the Boone house. Tall doors opened onto the formal rooms on either side of the hall, which were filled with huge sculptures, slightly menacing female shapes that glimmered in the lamplight like an army of Chinese tomb figures. Lavonne remembered that someone had told her Eadie Boone was an artist.

She could hear Worland Pendergrass and Lee Anne Bales from behind the heavy door.

"My God, the Yankees are coming."

"Can you believe that suit?"

"Can you believe she's wearing *white shoes with a blue suit*?"

"Can you believe she snorts when she laughs?"

"Yes, I can believe it. Look at how she *looks*."

"And the husband's even worse."

"If that's possible."

Lavonne went upstairs to find another bathroom. When she came back out onto the patio, Eadie Boone was standing beside Nita James with her arm draped around Nita's shoulders. Lavonne made her way through the crowd toward them. She could hear Leonard's loud laughter from somewhere across the pool, and she could tell from the sound that he was already drunk.

Eadie saw her coming and grinned. "Hey, I'm Eadie." She stuck her hand out and Lavonne shook it. "Sorry about all this," she said, lifting her hands to indicate her guests. "These whores, cheats, and backstabbers are the best Ithaca has to offer in the way of social entertainment, and if you're like me you'll learn to get through it by drinking as much as you can stomach and ignoring as many people as you can. Later on I'll introduce you to the few, besides my husband and Nita here, who are worth knowing."

A waiter passed and stopped to take Lavonne's drink order. "I'll have whatever she's having," she said, pointing to Eadie's glass.

AFTER THAT, EADIE AND LAVONNE BECAME BEST FRIENDS. THEY went everywhere together, and under Eadie's influence Lavonne became the wild and crazy girl she had never dared be in high school and college.

Once they got drunk at a bar in Atlanta and Eadie took a piece of blank paper and scrawled *For a Blow Job You'll Never Forget—Call Worland*. She put Worland's home phone number on the paper and then they called a cab and drove to the nearest Kinko's and made five hundred copies of the paper. They had the driver stop at a parking lot in downtown Atlanta and they took turns throwing reams of paper into the air. Two weeks later Worland tearfully told them she had been receiving obscene phone calls from as far away as Tokyo and she'd had to change her phone number. She confessed that her husband, Connelly, had been looking at her real funny lately. She was pretty sure she must have somehow gotten listed on some Internet porn site. Eadie raised her eyebrow when Worland said this, but Lavonne frowned and shook her head, no. She figured they'd done enough damage.

Sometimes they'd go out to Bad Bob's to drink Coors long-necks and swing dance with the cowboys and carpenters and peanut farmers who congregated there. Bad Bob's was out on the river close to the concrete plant. It was the kind of place that showed up in every bad movie about the South ever made. It had concrete block walls painted shit brown and a big yellow door and no windows. Someone had tried to brighten the place up a bit by painting a cowboy scene on the front wall, complete with grazing cattle and cowboys on horseback and dancing señoritas. A sign above the door read *Beer, Food, Dancin.* The parking lot was always filled with the usual assortment of pickup trucks and Pintos and Camaros. It was the kind of place where Lavonne would never have set foot if she weren't with Eadie Boone.

Usually, if they drank too much, they'd call Trevor to come get them, but once they called Leonard. He pretended to be good-natured about the whole thing in front of Eadie, but once they got home, he shouted at Lavonne about responsibility and social standing and the importance of keeping a good reputation and in general acted the way she suspected her father might have acted if she'd been a bad girl in high school.

Lavonne lay down on the spinning sofa with a pillow over her head so she wouldn't have to hear Leonard while she pondered the mysteries of friendship and centrifugal force. Right before she passed out, she realized that being Eadie Boone's friend had opened her up to a whole world of opportunities and experiences she might never have had if she hadn't pulled up her Cleveland roots and set them down again, tenu-

ously, in Ithaca, Georgia, and for one brief moment between consciousness and oblivion, she was deeply and earnestly grateful.

EADIE AND LAVONNE WERE INSEPARABLE THE FIRST SIX MONTHS
after Lavonne moved to the banana republic of Ithaca, and then everything changed. Lavonne got pregnant.

She wasn't even supposed to be able to get pregnant. She'd been
afraid to tell Leonard after her last medical exam that the doctor had
told her she would never conceive. She was stunned. "Never?" Never.
The young doctor seemed bored. She protested, "Are you sure?" Very
sure. "But I'm still young." Perhaps you should consider adoption.
"You're not God—you don't know whether I'll get pregnant." I'd stake
my career on the fact you will not.

Two months later she was pregnant. She thought of the pregnancy
as a miracle, not only because of the young doctor's dire pronounce-
ments, but also because of the infrequency of her and Leonard's sex
life. The fact that a pregnancy would occur, that life would renew itself
against such obstacles, had a profound effect upon Lavonne. She
stopped drinking alcohol and caffeine. She began to plan and cook only
healthy meals. She began an exercise routine.

Eadie was supportive, up to a point. She had made it clear that she
and Trevor would never have children, that her life would always re-
volve around Trevor and her art. Those were her priorities. Eadie knew
what it was like to grow up in a house where children are not valued,
where they come a dismal last in the long line of parental priorities.

Gradually, Lavonne saw less and less of Eadie Boone. By the time
her second child was born, they saw each other at dinner parties or the
occasional luncheon or the annual beach vacation. Lavonne's whole life
revolved around her two daughters. They were like twin suns and she a
doddering old planet that circled, endlessly entranced, within their ra-
diant orbits. Somewhere off in the farthest reaches of cold deep space,
Leonard circled them all like a rogue satellite. He was often gone, but
Lavonne didn't care. She got used to it being just the three of them.
She liked the sameness, the carefully measured routine of their days together. They were the friends she no longer needed. The sisters she

never had. The career she would never return to. She thought it would always be like this.

Time passed like the flashing of a comet. The girls, her playmates and confidantes, the center of her life, were suddenly grown. They locked their bedroom doors against her. They grew sullen and private. They did not want her sticking her nose in their business. They wanted her to "get a life" of her own. The illusion of a purposeful life that she had built so carefully around herself crumbled.

Now, she was forty-six years old, teetering on the edge of divorce, and driving to an appointment with Mona Shapiro to see if she could figure out what she was going to do with the rest of her life.

LITTLE MOSES WAS CLEANING THE PLATE-GLASS WINDOW WHEN she arrived.

"Hey, Lavonne," he said. He was wearing a T-shirt that read *Shofar, So Good.* "My mom's in the kitchen. Go on back."

The kitchen was cozy and warm with the fragrance of rising bread. Lavonne stood just inside the swinging door, breathing deeply and watching Mona Shapiro scamper around the small room. Her sleeves were rolled to her elbows, and her face was pink with the heat and the exertion of lifting bread pans into the ovens. She was singing to herself as she worked, a tune Lavonne did not recognize.

"Well, hey, Miz Zibolsky," she said, her bad eye bouncing over Lavonne and rolling, slowly, to one side.

"Hello, Mona."

"Excuse my appearance," she said, patting her hair back up into her hairnet and wiping her floured fingers on her apron.

"It sure smells good in here."

"Does it? I guess I'm so used to the smell, I never notice it."

"It makes me hungry just standing here."

"Here, try some of this." She lifted a plate holding small squares of cut bread and offered it to Lavonne. Lavonne took one of the squares and popped it into her mouth. It was delicious.

"Pumpkin bread," Mona said.

"I love the cream cheese icing," Lavonne said. She stood there holding her briefcase. "Should we meet in here or out front?"

Mona indicated a little table in front of the window. "Let's sit here," she said. "That way I can keep my eye on the ovens."

Lavonne sat at the table and opened up her briefcase. She shook her head when Mona asked if she wanted a whole piece of pumpkin bread. "I'm dieting," she explained.

"Good for you," Mona said. She sat down and began to pick pieces of dough off her apron.

"Did you say you owned the space next door, too?" Lavonne asked, taking out a file and a legal pad and setting them on the table.

"Honey, I own the whole building."

"Why don't you rent it out?" Lavonne took out a pencil and set it down beside the legal pad.

"It needs to be fixed up before I rent it out. And I need money to fix it up, which I don't have. Your husband says it'll take more to fix it up than it's worth."

"Is that what he told you?" Lavonne said.

"He told me he'd give me a good price."

"Can I ask what he offered you?"

Mona told her. Lavonne chewed the eraser end of the pencil. She could see Little Moses through the opened doorway, still cleaning the glass.

"Did you get an appraisal?"

"A *what*?" Mona rolled the pieces of dough into little balls. She stacked them neatly like she was building a wall out of miniature stones.

"Never mind," Lavonne said, putting her pencil down and leaning forward with her arms resting on the table. "Mona, have you ever thought about taking a partner?"

Mona frowned. "A partner?"

"Yes. Someone who could bring you some operating capital. Someone who could run the business while you do what you enjoy doing, which is running the kitchen."

"Well, I don't know about that." Mona laughed, her weak eye rolling toward the ovens. "Who would I get? Who would want to buy into this dusty old place?"

"Me," Lavonne said. Dust whorls hung in the sunlight slanting through the window. A refrigerator hummed in the back.

Mona looked at Lavonne like she was listening to a joke and waiting for the punchline. After a minute, she said, "You, Miz Zibolsky? You don't need to work."

"I do need to work," Lavonne said. "You don't know how badly I need to work." She let Mona have a few minutes to think about it. "Look, you mentioned the other day that you're still using a ledger book. Mona, that's crazy. A computer with the right software would save you hours in accounting time, not to mention it can track your sales, keep track of your inventory, list your depreciation—I'm sure you're depreciating all this equipment." She looked around the kitchen. Some of the equipment looked new.

Mona looked doubtful. "Depreciation?" she said.

"Who does your taxes?"

"Cousin Solomon over in Valdosta."

"Well, I'm sure he knows about depreciating your equipment, but with a computer it would be so much easier to track. I'm an accountant, Mona, that's what I do. I find loopholes, I find tax incentives, I pore over your numbers to find ways to be more cost-efficient. Marketing is new to me, too, but I've been reading a lot about it and I'm certain we can come up with a marketing plan that will double your sales immediately."

"Double my sales?" Mona said, astounded. "Why would I want to do that?"

Lavonne smiled and looked down at her arms. She opened up the file and took out a sheet of paper. "Do you know what this is?" she asked.

Mona shook her head, no.

"It's a list of people who've called me about you catering one of their parties. There are twelve names on the list, Mona, and that's just the beginning."

"Well I'll be," Mona said, reaching for the paper.

Lavonne took out another piece of paper and pushed it toward Mona. "You know what this is."

"Uh-huh," Mona said. "It's my bill for your party." She'd handwritten it on a piece of stationery that looked like it was printed in 1948. *Shapiro's,* it read across the top. *Good Food, Good Times.*

"And this?" Lavonne pointed with her finger.

"The total you owe me," Mona said, getting the hang of this.

"It's not enough, Mona," Lavonne said gently. "You're not charging enough."

Mona patted her hair. "It's what I always charge," she said. "It's what Big Marvin always charged."

"How long's Big Marvin been dead now?"

Mona understood what she was trying to say. She patted her hair with a trembling hand. "Catering's hard work," she said defensively.

"Which is exactly why you should charge more for it," Lavonne said. "Your food is excellent. It's worth double this amount." Lavonne pointed again at the total. "That's the amount I'm going to submit to Leonard's law firm. Double what you wrote down right here."

"Double?" Mona said, her good eye fluttering over Lavonne's face. "Double?"

"It's hard to find caterers in this town, Mona. Believe me, I've tried. There's that woman that works out of her home, but you can never get her, and there's the Pink House Restaurant, but their food is terrible and overpriced. Most people hire someone out of Atlanta. Until now. Now everyone in town knows there's a top-notch caterer right here in Ithaca and your phone will be ringing off the hook."

"It already is," Mona said. "I took five new appointments but I had to tell the others no."

"See what I mean?" Lavonne sat back in her chair, smiling. "I know it's a lot to think about, Mona, and I want you to take your time and talk it over with Little Moses. I'm going to leave you a copy of my business proposal." She took it out and laid it on the table.

"That's a real pretty color," Mona said, pointing to the cover.

"The way I see it, we could start out slow, just adding a few catering events until we get ourselves fully staffed and I get the systems up and running. But eventually, we'll move out of the bakery business and more into the deli business. You know, sandwiches, lunch items, maybe even breakfast items."

"It used to be a sandwich shop, back when Big Marvin first started up," Mona said.

"You've got a ready market, not only with the locals but also with all these tourists coming down from Atlanta," Lavonne said, pointing through the opened doorway toward the street. "They need a good place to eat lunch. They're used to delicatessens in the big city. We wouldn't even have to open for the evening meal. Just lunch and maybe, eventually, breakfast."

Mona went to check the oven and then came back and sat down. She had the tender attentive look of a woman listening to distant music.

"But do you know what excites me the most, Mona?" Lavonne tapped her fingers on the table like she was running numbers on an adding machine. "The Internet. The Internet could make us rich."

"What are we going to do?" Mona said, grinning sheepishly. "Sell sandwiches on the Internet?" She giggled and shook her head.

Lavonne opened up her file and took out a computer-generated logo she had made last night. She'd scanned a photo of her grandmother into the computer and circled the photo with the label: *Grandma Ada's Kosher Barbecue Sauce.*

Mona's jaw dropped. She frowned. "That doesn't even look like Grandma Ada," she said.

"I know. It's just an example. We can make up any label you want. But think about this, Mona: How many places can you get authentic kosher barbecue sauce?" She didn't wait for Mona to finish. "I'll tell you: *none.* I couldn't find a single Web site on the Internet that sells kosher barbecue sauce. We can set up a Web site and make a fortune!"

"You know," Mona said, shaking her head, "there aren't a whole lot of Dixie Jews."

"That's not our only market, Mona. Here, look, here's some data showing the number of Jewish people in the United States broken down by geographical area."

Mona put on her reading glasses and took the printout from Lavonne. "Well, I'll be," she said after a few minutes, hiding her mouth with her fingers.

"But it's not just Jewish people that we'll market to, Mona. With all the concern these days over the chemicals and preservatives being pumped into our food supply, kosher products made with all natural ingredients are being bought by a growing percentage of American consumers. Here, look at these figures."

Mona shook her head and looked at Lavonne, her eyes magnified behind the black-rimmed glasses. "I had no idea there were so many Hebrew folks in this country," she said.

"We can make up bottles and sell them here in the store. The sauce is delicious, and with the right marketing—maybe smaller bottles packed in some kind of an unusual gift box—we could sell to the tourists all day long." Lavonne put the documents back in the file and closed it up, pushing it toward Mona. She smiled at Mona and leaned over and patted her arm. "I know it's a lot to think about," she said. "But you and Little Moses read the business plan and think about it. I'd love to be your partner, and the amount of operating capital I could bring to the deal is set out in my proposal. I made some guesses about your sales figures and we'll have to make some adjustments there, but this is a good starting point." She thumped the folder with her fingers. "You know me, Mona, you know what working with me would be like, but if you decide not to go through with this, I'll understand. If you do decide to sell to my husband, I'd appreciate you letting me know beforehand, because it'll change my plans, too. Whatever you do, though, don't sell to my husband or Redmon until you get a fair market appraisal of this property. I can tell you right now, my husband's not offering you enough. I mean, hell, Mona, if you wanted to, you could sell this property and retire tomorrow."

"Oh no," she said, taking off her hairnet so her curls tumbled about her face. "What would I do if I didn't work? I've worked all my life." She wiped her hands on her floured apron. "Well" was all she could think to say. "Well."

"Don't make a decision yet," Lavonne said, rising. "Just think about it. I'm willing if you are. I think we can make a go of this, but you have to be certain, too." She held out her hand to Mrs. Shapiro. "In the year 2010 one out of every two businesses will be owned by women," she said.

Mrs. Shapiro looked at Lavonne, a look of dubious admiration on her face. "Lord," she said, shaking her head. "Is that right, Miz Zibolsky?"

"Lavonne."

"What?"

"It's past time we got on a first-name basis." Lavonne slid her purse strap up her shoulder. "Call me Lavonne."

"Well, all right then," Mrs. Shapiro said shyly.

"Think about it, Mona. And don't sign anything with my husband until then." Lavonne stopped in the open doorway. "And Mona," she said, turning.

"Yes, Lavonne?"

"This is our little secret, okay? The partnership. Discuss it with Little Moses, but no one else. We have to be careful until the plan's all set."

Mrs. Shapiro grinned and made an "X" over her heart. "Cross my heart. I won't tell a soul but Little Moses," she said.

"I'll call you in a few days." Lavonne waved at Little Moses as she went out, glancing again at his T-shirt. *The Shofar So Good Deli,* she thought, closing the door behind her. *I like the sound of that.*

*C*HARLES WAS SERIOUS ABOUT USING HIS MOTHER TO TRY AND talk Nita back to her senses. In the weeks leading up to his ill-fated hunting trip, he spent less and less time at home. He was becoming more and more uncomfortable in Nita's presence, more and more aware that mental breakdowns sometimes involve violence and running amok with sharp instruments. And there was *something* about Nita that hadn't been there before the firm party; he was sure of it—a stillness, a sense of contained fury, which made him nervous in her presence. Just yesterday, at breakfast, he had told her he wanted pork tenderloin for dinner and she had looked at him over the edge of her book and in a strong steady voice that brooked no argument, she had said, "We're having chicken."

It left him stunned and shaken.

The Saturday after Lavonne met with Mona Shapiro, Virginia Broadwell pulled into Nita's driveway. It was ten o'clock and Virginia had a luncheon appointment at twelve. She really didn't have time to run around trying to straighten out Charles's messy domestic affairs—she had warned him years ago not to marry Nita James—but, being a dutiful mother, here she was. She went in through the garage door, which Charles had left unlocked for her. The children were in the den watching Saturday morning cartoons. Nita was on the screened porch reading *Wuthering Heights*.

"Don't get up," Virginia said, noting that Nita made no effort to get up.

She was wearing blue jeans and a blue V-necked sweater. Her hair was pulled back into a ponytail and she was wearing very little makeup. "Charles isn't here," Nita said, not bothering to look up from her book.

Virginia stared at her steadily, her mouth puckered in a perfect little *o*. "Do you have any coffee?" she asked pleasantly.

Nita kept her eyes on the book. "In the kitchen," she said.

Really, this was too much. Nita might as well have been a complete stranger dropped suddenly onto the bosom of the Broadwell family. Virginia tugged on the hem of her jacket and went into the kitchen to pour herself a cup of coffee. This was going to take more work than Virginia had imagined, and might, after all, require the professional services of Dr. Guffey and his arsenal of antidepressants.

She came back out on the porch and sat down. "Nita," she began tentatively, settling her cup of coffee on her lap and searching for just the right words. "Charles is worried."

"He should be," Nita said.

Something in the way she said it startled Virginia. It made her feel that she should warn Charles of something, but she wasn't sure what. Virginia's little chin trembled. She stared at her daughter-in-law like she was trying to read tea leaves in the bottom of a cup.

A few minutes later, Lavonne and Eadie showed up to take Nita to Logan's soccer game. Virginia wasn't happy to see them, and this time she made no attempt to hide it. "I really need to speak with Nita in private," Virginia said, as they came noisily onto the porch.

Nita looked at Virginia over the edge of her book. "If you wanted to speak to me privately, you should have called me and not just shown up. I have plans today. I don't have time to talk to you."

Lavonne and Eadie looked at each other and sat down on the willow sofa.

Virginia, dazed and uneasy, stared at the sunlight that slanted through the porch screens. She had become accustomed, over the years, to bullying and riding roughshod over Nita, but the woman sitting across from her did not seem the type who could be easily intimidated. Virginia felt suddenly and curiously timid.

Lavonne looked at her watch. "I'd go with you guys to the soccer game, but I've got a twelve-thirty appointment. Are we still on for to-morrow?"

"Yes." Nita stretched her legs out along the lounger, ignoring her mother-in-law's dazed look. "Mama baked a pecan pie and she was wondering if we'd like to meet over at her house around two-thirty. She says she hasn't seen you and Eadie since Moby Dick was just a min-now."

Lavonne grinned. "That sounds like something she'd say."

"Meeting?" Virginia said.

Nita looked at her coolly. "School meeting," she said.

Eadie poked Lavonne with her elbow. "Hey, I talked to Kari over at the bookstore about the Kudzu Ball and she said it was an absolute blast. She says it's the best throw down this town has to offer."

Lavonne hadn't thought much about the Kudzu Ball lately. She'd been too busy planning divorce and revenge to think about much else.

"I think you should go," Eadie said without waiting for her to reply. "I'll go with you."

Now that Lavonne was no longer trying to be the dutiful wife, there was no reason why she couldn't go to the Kudzu Ball. It was the same night the husbands returned from Montana, and either everything would have worked out by then or everything would have turned disastrous. Either way, Lavonne figured she'd probably be needing a tequila binge.

"Okay," she said. "It might be my only chance to be a debutante. It might be my only chance to be a queen."

Virginia wasn't about to let herself get drawn into this argument again. She didn't really care if they went to the Kudzu Ball or not. If Lavonne wanted to ruin what little social standing she had, so be it. And as for Eadie Boone, once Trevor divorced her she'd be out of the social loop anyway. She might as well go ahead and meet some new friends, because none of her old ones would be calling. Virginia glanced through the French door to the kitchen wall clock. She didn't have much time left. If she was going to get on with this intervention, she'd have to work fast. "You look a little pale," Virginia began, leaning toward Nita and touching her on the knee. Nita moved her leg out of the way. "Maybe it's time you saw Dr. Guffey."

"We've already had this conversation," Lavonne said.

"Lavonne, I'm not talking to you, I'm talking to Nita!"

"There's nothing wrong with me that Dr. Guffey can fix," Nita said, and Lavonne tapped the edge of Nita's lounger with her foot and Eadie gave her a little smile.

Virginia continued as if she hadn't heard her. "It's amazing what a little Zoloft can do to lift the spirits. It's amazing what a low-dose prescription of Prozac can do."

"Tequila is my drug of choice," Eadie said.

"Yes, we're all aware of that."

"Bite me, Virginia."

Virginia, stunned, stopped talking. Her little mouth opened and closed. She looked like a carp hauled up on a riverbank. She wasn't sure what "bite me" meant, but she was pretty sure it must be crude and disrespectful. Here she was trying to fix her son's defective wife and all she got for it was criticism and hostility. Well, she was through trying. She forced herself to calm down. She forced her tremulous heart to be still. Let Charles fix his own problems. Virginia turned her head and looked through the French door at the kitchen clock. "I've got a twelve o'clock luncheon," she said.

"Don't let us hold you up," Lavonne said.

Virginia stood up and smoothed her skirt. "I'll just run to the little girls' room before I go," she said to no one in particular. She put her sharp little nose in the air and stalked off.

Eadie waited until Virginia had closed the door and headed down the hall and then she leaned forward and said excitedly, "Okay, listen. I talked to Ramsbottom. And he said we needed to take pictures. You know, of the husbands with the male prostitutes or female impersonators or whatever the hell you call them. It was his idea but he said he'd do it for the agreed upon price. Videos, too."

"That's illegal," Lavonne said.

"I know," Eadie said. "Isn't it great?"

"I have to think about this," Lavonne said. "Extortion isn't something I planned on."

"It's not extortion," Eadie said. "It's blackmail. I mean, if you want to get technical about it. Besides, what do you think the husbands are going to do when they find out we've cheated them out of money behind their backs? Trust me, we're going to need those pictures as insurance."

"Let's not talk about this right now," Nita said, looking down the hallway where her mother-in-law had disappeared.

"All I'm saying is we better have a good backup plan," Eadie said, taking her keys out of her purse. "And those pictures would be added insurance."

No one said anything. A few minutes later they heard the sharp clacking of Virginia's heels on the hardwood floor.

"I'll think about it," Lavonne said quietly to Eadie. "But remember, we mustn't talk about this, even among ourselves, unless we're all together. The more we talk, the more likely it is to get around town. We'll discuss it again tomorrow at Nita's mother's house, but not a word to anyone until then."

THE SOCCER FIELDS WERE CROWDED. THEY HAD TO PARK IN THE back lot and walk up from the lower fields, past the creek that flowed parallel to the road through a grove of beech, sycamore, and red oak. The water was slow and brackish. Logan skipped rocks across its dark green surface, his soccer bag banging against his knees as he walked. Through the chain-link fence ahead, Nita could see his team warming up on the practice field. "Honey, you better hurry," she said.

"Have a good game," Eadie said, ruffling his hair affectionately.

He smiled at her but didn't move, standing in the middle of the road and kicking his toe in the sand. "Do I have to play?" he asked his mother. He hated soccer, but his father had pulled every string imaginable to get him on this select team. Quitting was not an option, and he knew it.

Nita stopped in the road and looked at him. "Of course you don't have to play," she said. "If you don't want to."

He squinted at his mother, holding his arm up against the sun. "Are you saying I can quit?" -

"Anytime you want."

He dropped his arm. The expression of relief that flooded his face made Nita think about all the ways she could have been a better mother. Why had she let Charles bully Logan into doing something he didn't want to do? Why had she let Charles bully all of them over the past sixteen years? "We can go home now if you want to," she said, pointing toward the parking lot. "I mean it."

He frowned and looked at his feet. He dug the toe of his shoe in the sand. "Naw," he said. "I'm already here. I better play. Besides, you never know, dad might show up." He gave his mother and Eadie a little wave and headed off toward the field. At the edge of the green he turned around and shouted, "But this is the last time. I'm quitting after this game."

They stopped at the concession booth and bought some popcorn and Cokes, and then they climbed up into the stands to wait for the game to begin. The day was cool and breezy and the warm sun felt good on Nita's face.

"I'm working again," Eadie said, tugging her straw in and out of the plastic lid of her Coke. It made a sound like wind whistling through a stovepipe.

"I'm glad," Nita said. "You look good. Really rested. I think work agrees with you."

"I'm trying a mixed medium," Eadie said. "Oil and doilies." She laughed and Nita thought how pretty she was with the sun shining on her face and the breeze in her hair. "I guess that's what you'd call it. It's kind of a cross between painting and collage. I haven't painted in years, but it feels right to me now."

Neither one mentioned Trevor or Charles or the fact that their worlds had, in a little over a week, gone completely topsy-turvy. Nita thought again how rested Eadie looked, not at all like a woman who had faced public humiliation and was soon to be embroiled in a contentious divorce. She wished she had an artistic outlet like Eadie had, or a hobby, something she could throw herself into to take her mind off her appalling marriage. She thought, briefly, of Jimmy Lee's offer to teach her woodworking, and she smiled, remembering the silly hopeful woman she had been that day in the garden. She thought of Jimmy Lee less and less now, and she knew there would come a time when she would not think of him at all. Nita was too cynical now for romance.

Eadie stood up and poked her fingers in her jeans pocket. "Hey, do you want to split a bag of boiled peanuts?"

"Sure," Nita said. She sat in the stands while Eadie went back down to the concession booth. Bright sunlight washed over the fields and the distant fringe of trees, glittering on the metallic roofs of parked cars and trucks. A thin cloud of dust rose over the parking lot as people continued to arrive. The Ithaca Raptors, in neon blue and white, were just finishing their game with the YMCA Dominators, in red and yellow. The Raptors were ahead 1–0. Players flowed and receded across the field like a red-blue tide. Mothers sat in the stands and gossiped and pleaded with small children who hung from the metal bleachers like monkeys. Fathers paced the sidelines, shouting instructions and pumping their fists in the air. Across the field, Nita could see Logan's team warming up.

Eadie sat down beside her, holding a small sack of wet, steaming peanuts. "Who are they playing?" Eadie asked, nodding toward Logan's brightly colored teammates.

"Reverend Bob's team," Nita said, in a low voice. She could see Reverend Bob sitting one bleacher row down and to their left. He was hard to miss.

"Oh God," Eadie said.

The Reverend Bob Hog was six feet five inches tall. He had played basketball at Duke and engaged in drink and other assorted sins of the flesh until one night in a drunken orgy at Myrtle Beach with a group of Kappa Delt girls, he heard the call of the Lord.

"*Bob Hog,*" the Lord said. "*Why do you ignore my Word? Why do you wallow in the trough of sin and despair?*"

"Is that you, Lord?" Bob said. He sat, stunned and bloated with sin, pinned to the sofa like an arrow-riddled Saint Sebastian.

"*Why do you conspire with harlots?*"

"They're not harlots, Lord. They're Kappa Delts."

"*Go and sin no more, Bob. Preach my Word to the wicked.*"

Bob Hog stood up and shook off the Kappa Delts like a dog shaking off fleas. After that he attended seminary at Bob Jones University, and now he was youth minister down at Ithaca First Baptist Church. The Reverend Bob liked to coach Little League and soccer and town basketball and city league football. He liked to teach boys about sports on one hand and fill them with the fear of the Lord on the other.

On this breezy Saturday afternoon in October while they waited for the soccer match to begin, the Reverend Bob sat in the bleachers with Tammy Purvis and talked about the Lord. Tammy had been a cheerleader up at UVA and had smoked pot and slept with a boy named Mule before she got the call from the Lord. Now she was married to Chester Purvis, had three children, attended Bible study four times a week, and spent her spare time purging the school library of books she found inappropriate, and passing out leaflets to schoolchildren on the evils of Halloween. Tammy Purvis believed donning a Halloween costume was the closest thing possible to opening up your heart and inviting Satan to enter. She had been denying her own children the sinful joys of trick or treating for years, and now she felt compelled to deny other people's children. Tammy figured it was her Christian duty.

Nita tried not to listen to their conversation, which was hard because Reverend Bob always talked as if he was standing in a pulpit. His voice carried up the stands and across the field and probably across two counties as well. He and Tammy were talking now about Chester's new car.

Chester Purvis was a steady, God-fearing man. He sold insurance out of his basement and attended huge prayer meetings in Atlanta where Christian men go to learn how to take back control of their families. "It's an eighty-four Mercedes," Tammy said, flipping her bleached blond hair over one shoulder. "I prayed about it and prayed about it and the Lord told me we should buy it."

"Praise the Lord," Reverend Bob said.

Over in the parking lot, Reverend Bob's team stood methodically kicking a soccer ball into the side of his truck. Reverend Bob had a Ford truck with a bumper sticker that read *I am a Christian and I have a Gun.* Seeing the boys, Reverend Bob stood up and shouted in a thundering voice, "Nathan, get those boys out on the practice field and ya'll start warming up."

Nathan Hog stood apart from the other boys, watching in dignified silence. He was a tall thin boy who looked out at the world with an abiding sense of one who is preordained to failure. He was a minister's boy and his last name was Hog. It didn't get much worse than that.

Reverend Bob sighed and sat down heavily. Across the field, Nita saw Logan take a shot on goal and miss. He put his head down and loped back to the sidelines. She wanted to go out and put her arms around him and tell him everything was going to be all right. She wanted to tell him that life could be better than succeeding at soccer and trying to live up to impossible standards, and that he mustn't give up hope. But then, who was she to talk?

Reverend Bob wiped his sweating face with a handkerchief and nodded his head while Tammy droned on about the Mercedes. She had told Chester no, he couldn't have it, it was too expensive, and then they prayed about it and the Lord sent an answer in the form of a 1978 Honda Civic driven by a crowd of unruly teenagers. The teenagers plowed into the passenger's side of the Mercedes and the lady who owned it, shaken and unharmed but realizing she was ninety-four years old and too old to drive, had called Chester and told him the car was his.

"I just know the Lord meant for Chester to have that Mercedes," Tammy said, bobbing her head like one of those little dashboard dolls. "He gave me a sign, plain as day."

Eadie, who had somehow managed to keep quiet throughout this entire conversation, leaned over and said loudly, "I hope you don't seriously think the Lord would cause an accident between a little old lady and a carload of children just so Chester could get himself a fucking Mercedes." Several people looked over their shoulders. Nita kicked Eadie with her foot, but Eadie ignored her.

Tammy swung around, her eyes narrowing when she saw Eadie. Reverend Bob glanced at Eadie and then away, ducking his head between his shoulders. Eadie Boone was one of the biggest contributors to the Baptist Boy's home. She served Christmas dinner to the homeless down at the Interfaith Outreach Program and helped pay for the new ten-bed building addition. Reverend Bob didn't want any trouble with Eadie Boone.

"This is a private conversation!" Tammy said, her little beaked nose turning bright red. She had a shrill voice when she was calm, but when she got excited it sounded like seagulls fighting over a dead fish. "We weren't talking to you, were we, Reverend?" she shrieked.

"Excuse me, ladies," Reverend Bob said, rising. "I see our game is about to begin." He nodded without looking at any of them and hurried out of the stands.

Tammy stood up, quickly gathering her belongings. She made little short jerking movements and her hair stood up around her face like ruffled feathers. "You're just jealous," she hissed at Eadie over her shoulder. "You've been jealous of me since the day I made pom-pom squad, and you didn't."

Eadie smiled sweetly. "Of course, you're right, Tammy, I never stood a chance competing with you."

Tammy tossed her hair over one shoulder, her little dark eyes glittering with pride and vindication.

"After all, you were sleeping with the whole football squad." Eadie smiled, showing her teeth. "What chance did I have?"

Tammy made a squawking sound deep in her throat, and turning, she sailed down the long row of bleachers, stepping over people who got in her way, and dragging her purse behind her like a broken tether.

"Bye, Tammy," Eadie called.

"Well, that was pleasant," Nita said.

"Yes, wasn't it?"

Nita watched Tammy stomp down the bleacher steps. "And I guess this doesn't have anything to do with the pom-pom squad?" she said to Eadie.

Eadie took a small mirror out of her purse and carefully applied her lipstick. "She *was* sleeping with the football team." She closed the mirror, slid the lipstick into its sheath, and put both into her purse. "I always got blamed for things like that. Sleeping with the football team, I mean. No one ever believed I was a virgin the day I graduated, and it was girls like Tammy spreading the rumors." She smiled at Nita and smoothed her hair. "I'm just setting the record straight, is all."

Logan's team was lining up on the field opposite Reverend Bob's team. Logan sat on the bench, waiting. He usually got sent in for a few minutes at the end of the second half, but only if they were ahead by three goals, or losing so badly it didn't matter.

The referee came out onto the field to start the game. There was something familiar about him, something familiar about the way he moved. He raised his arm and blew the whistle and in that instant, Nita recognized him. Blood flooded her face, pulsing delicately beneath her skin. Watching his lanky figure run up and down the sidelines it seemed foolish that she had ever thought she could forget him.

"Hey." Eadie nudged her with her shoulder. "Isn't that your good-looking carpenter? Billy Ray? Johnny Bob?"

"Jimmy Lee," Nita said quietly.

AT HALF TIME EADIE WENT TO THE CONCESSION BOOTH TO BUY AN-other Coke. Nita sat in the stands, trying not to feel self-conscious. If Jimmy Lee had seen her, he gave no sign of it. He stood over on the sideline drinking water from a bottle. She tried to send him a telepathic message, willing him to look at her. A cool breeze fluttered his hair. Nita wondered if he had forgotten her in the two weeks since she saw him last. She wondered if she had imagined their little flirtation that day in the garden. The insistent voice in her head reminded her she was often naive and easily duped. She had, after all, been faithful to a man who cheated on her for fifteen years, and she never had a clue. Maybe Jimmy Lee was just another way she had of fooling herself.

A tall blond girl wearing faded blue jeans strolled across the field. He saw her coming and grinned, wiping his face on a towel. The girl put her hand on his shoulder and they stood talking for a few minutes while the players from both teams slowly resumed their positions on the field.

"What's the matter with you?" Eadie said. She sat down beside Nita, holding out another sack of boiled peanuts. Steam rose from the sack and curled, thick and wet, around Nita's face.

"Nothing," Nita said.

"Do you want some peanuts?"

"No thanks."

High-flying clouds scuttled across the sun. The day, which had seemed so bright and promising just a short time before, grew gray and dismal. Nita tried not to let it all weigh her down. She tried not to think about all the things she had to worry about, but they fell into place anyway, lining up in her mind like missiles in a silo. She was married to a man she could no longer love or respect. Her children would need therapy. She had no skills or training that would enable her to find a job that could support both her and the children. She had fallen for a boy who probably couldn't even remember her name.

Nita longed suddenly for the escape of her porno romance novels. She longed for the days when she had been able to immerse herself in thrilling tales of love and adventure on the high seas, in castle boudoirs, in lonely teepees, when all around her the world had seemed safe and knowable and miraculously uncomplicated, and the only problem she had had to worry about was whether to make chicken or fish for dinner.

AN HOUR AND FIFTEEN MINUTES LATER, THE GAME WAS OVER, A perfect rout by Reverend Bob's Raiders. The two teams lined up on the field to shake hands. Logan's team filed by the stands like prisoners on their way to execution. One of the boys was crying. Logan came up the rear, whistling. He saw his mother and waved. In a strange twist of reasoning known only to bored housewives, death-row felons, and lonely adolescents, other people's misery made Logan happy. He passed the crying boy.

"Good game, Randy," Logan said.

"Shut up asshole," Randy sobbed.

Nita could see Jimmy Lee across the field, packing his bag. The blond girl went across the field to meet him. Nita moved slightly behind Eadie, shielding herself from Jimmy Lee and his girlfriend. A stream of slow-moving people clogged the stands. Nita motioned for Logan to go on. "We'll meet you at the concession stand," she shouted. She wanted to get out of there before Jimmy Lee saw her.

They followed the crowd out of the stands, nodding at people they knew. Logan was waiting for them at the concession stand looking relaxed and happier than Nita had seen him in a long time. "You meant what you said, right?" he said to Nita. "About me dropping out of soccer?"

She put her arm around him. "Of course I meant it."

Eadie put her arm around him, too, and the three of them strolled through the crowd. Nita wanted to run, wanted to push them to hurry, but she couldn't drag them along without having to answer a lot of questions she didn't want to answer. "Hey, Mom," Logan said. "Did you see who the referee was?"

"Look," Nita said, pointing. "There's Jake Hendricks."

Eadie grinned at her over Logan's head but Nita ignored her. Nita thought, *Maybe I can brush up on my secretarial skills and get a job out at the college. Maybe I can get a job clerking at one of the department stores out at the mall.*

"Nita!" His voice boomed out over the throng of people. For a moment she pretended she hadn't heard him, but Eadie and Logan stopped immediately and swung around. They let go of each other, standing in the road while curious people streamed by on both sides. Eadie touched her on the shoulder. "We'll wait for you at the car," she said.

"No, don't go," Nita said.

Jimmy Lee trotted through the crowd with a slow easy gait, dodging people like a running back. About ten feet from them he slowed to a walk. He put his hand up. "Hey," he said, looking at Nita.

Logan put his hand out and Jimmy Lee took it. "Good game," he said.

"Thanks for not calling that handball," Logan said.

"What handball?" Jimmy Lee said.

Eadie wasn't used to being ignored, especially by good-looking young men. "Hi, I'm Eadie," she said, giving him her hand. "I may have some work I need you to do around my house. It's an old house and there's a lot of repair work that hasn't been done in a long, long time." She gave him the full impact of her eyes and smile, shooting out pheromones in all directions.

"Great. I'll give you my card," he said, taking out his wallet.

"It's a lot of work," she said. "It's probably at least three or four weeks worth of work." She stood there in the middle of the road, smiling, while all around her people got caught up in that wash of pheromones and slowed to gawk.

"That's okay." He grinned, handing her his card. "My schedule should clear up in the next couple of weeks."

"Why don't you wait for me at the car?" Nita said to Eadie.

Eadie grinned and stuck his business card in her purse. "Good idea," she said. She put her arm around Logan's shoulders and turned, pulling him along with her. "Come on, kiddo. It's just you and me."

Nita stood in the middle of the road, smiling and nodding at people she knew, feeling like the whole town had caught her in some flagrant act of misconduct, feeling like they were all watching and whispering behind their hands. Her face burned. Her knees trembled. Goose bumps rose on her arms.

"How have you been?" Jimmy Lee said. His hair was loose about his shoulders. He had grown a mustache and one of those little goatees the young wear nowadays, the kind that closely covers the chin. Nita didn't know what it was called, but it looked good on him.

"I've been okay," she said. She could see Eadie and Logan up ahead, their heads bobbing in the crowd. Jimmy Lee stood with his sports bag resting against one hip, the strap wrapping his chest like a bandolier.

"Really? Just okay?" They stood in the middle of the road looking at each other. She turned and began to walk slowly along the road and he followed, slowing his steps to match hers. "How's the pool house holding up?"

"It collapsed at the party and killed two people," she said.

"You're funny," he said. He grinned and slung his sports bag to the opposite hip.

Sunlight fell through the arching branches of the trees. Fish jumped in the creek. Nita was happy again.

"Hey, I was going to ask you, is there anything else you need done around the house—a bathroom remodeled, a kitchen updated, a basement finished?" He pushed his hair behind his ears, smiling at her. "My workload is slowing down over the next few weeks and I can probably fit you in."

"What about Eadie?"

"Oh, I'd fit you in ahead of Eadie. I'd fit you in ahead of anybody."

Most of the crowd had reached the parking lot and began to disperse in a cloud of dust and moving automobiles and pickup trucks.

Only a few people passed them on the road now. "I don't think I'll be doing much else to that house," Nita said absently.

"Have you thought about the woodworking?" They walked from beneath the trees into a clearing. The sky behind him filled with light. Great frothy clouds sailed across the horizon. She had not felt this way in years. She had never felt this way. "Woodworking?" she said.

"Oh, don't tell me you forgot." He put his hand on his chest like she had wounded him. They were walking so close together she could see the small jagged scar running beneath his lip. "You said you wanted a hobby and I told you I could teach you to make wooden trivets, and cigar boxes, and maybe even furniture. Remember?"

They reached the parking lot. His cleats made sharp little metallic sounds in the loose gravel. Across the lot she could see Eadie and Logan sitting in her car. Logan was sitting in the driver's seat, pretending to drive. Eadie had her head back against the headrest like she was sleeping. The lot was deserted except for her car and four or five others. "What about your girlfriend?" she said, stopping.

He frowned. "My girlfriend?" He put his thumbs under the strap of his bag and looked at her. "What girlfriend?"

Nita shrugged and waved one careless hand toward the fields. "The tall blonde. The pretty one."

He grinned and shook his head. Nita thought, *This is crazy*. She thought, *What am I doing?* "She's not my girlfriend," he said. "She's my cousin. I'm teaching her to be a soccer referee."

It was hard to think straight with him standing so close. It was hard to see the big picture with his mouth so close to hers. A sudden breeze blew her hair across her face.

"I'm still married," she said.

He said, "I know that."

"I'm a wife and a mother in a town where everybody knows everybody else's secrets."

"Hell, Nita, it's an offer to learn woodworking, not a proposition."

She flushed, but felt compelled to finish. "I'm the wife of a bitter and vindictive man."

"I'll keep my hands to myself," he said, grinning and holding them up so she could see them. "I promise."

She thought of Eadie and her joy in her art, and Nita thought, *Oh, what's the harm in a little woodworking?* "Okay," she said, pushing past him. "I'll call you."

"I've heard that before."

She turned around, walking backward for a few steps so she could see his face. "This time I mean it," she said, and smiling, she turned around and headed for the car.

*T*HE NEXT MORNING NITA WENT OUT TO HER PARENTS' HOUSE early so she could explain to them how she had caught her husband of sixteen years cheating on her. It wouldn't have done any good to try and keep it all secret; Nita never was any good at keeping secrets from people she loved, it just wasn't in her nature—besides, her mother would have taken one look at her and known something was wrong. Nita would have preferred not to tell her daddy; Eustis James was an old-school Southerner who believed in shotgun weddings and shotgun funerals, but Nita knew her mother would tell him anyway. It seemed best he hear it from her. Maybe she could keep him calm by reminding him Charles was her husband in the sight of God, and father to her children. Maybe her daddy would go easy on Charles if she reminded him she had no intention of breaking up her family by divorcing her husband or becoming a thirty-nine-year-old widow.

She told them everything except the part about Jimmy Lee and the fact that she had a date with Jimmy Lee to learn woodworking the following week. There were some things Nita wasn't willing to share with her mother, at least not yet.

Loretta's round chin trembled with rage and her face got pink and her hair stood up around her head like a nuclear explosion. "Those low-life bar dogs," she said, meaning the husbands of course. "So, are you going to quit him?" she asked fiercely.

"Mama!" Nita was surprised her mother had even mentioned it, given her Baptist upbringing and the fact there hadn't been a divorce in their family for years. "I'm not planning on leaving my husband. I've got two children to think about."

They sat at the kitchen table drinking coffee and watching Logan and Whitney stuff a scarecrow out of straw and leaves in the backyard.

Eustis James rose, kissed her gently on the forehead, told her he loved her, and went out into the backyard to help his grandchildren with the scarecrow. He came back a minute later and stuck his head through the door. "I admire your courage and determination to stay, honey, but you know I'd be happy to shoot him if you want me to. It wouldn't bother me one little bit. I'd do it and serve my time and not think a thing of it."

"I appreciate that, Daddy."

He nodded and went out. Loretta patted Nita's hand and said, "Don't you worry about a thing, honey. It'll all come out in the wash, you'll see. I've watched you for years living in misery up to your armpits married to that low-life stump sucker, and I can't say I'd be sorry to have you wash your hands of him." She thumped her fingers for a moment on the table, thinking. "Your daddy's right, though. A funeral's cheaper, and a hell of a lot less messy than a divorce. At least, that's always been true in our family."

Nita wasn't quite sure what her mother was trying to say. Her grandmother had been widowed at an early age, as had her great-grandmother and two great aunts on her mother's side. "Mama, there's only been one divorce in our family I can think of, and that was Aunt Effie. I don't want to become only the second woman in generations to divorce her husband! What about all those proud Sweeneys and Gordons that came before us? What would they say?"

"Lord, child, what are you rambling on about?" Loretta wore her hair pulled back from her face and twisted into a small bun at the nape of her neck. She'd never been a slave to fashion. She'd worn her hair exactly the same way for forty years. "Of course there haven't been many divorces in our family. What do you think happened to a woman who divorced her husband, for any reason, forty or fifty years ago? She lost her home, her children, and her good name. My great-grandfather beat my great-grandmother every night of their married lives, and what did she do about it? Did she divorce him? No, she did what every other unhappily married wife of her generation did, or at least the ones with spunk. She fed him poke root or rat poison or dried bleeding heart in his soup."

"Mama, what are you saying?" Nita was horrified to imagine the white-haired, saintly looking great-grandmother she'd seen in family photographs as a murderess.

"I'm saying funerals are a hell of a lot easier than divorces." Loretta got up and went to turn on the oven. She always made a big dinner on Sundays, with lots of fresh vegetables and corn bread and fried chicken or pork chops. If Charles was out of town, or busy playing golf, she and the children would sneak out and join Loretta and Eustis at the midday meal.

Nita sat there, stunned, and watched her happy children drive the golf cart around the yard. She didn't like to think of her family tree peopled with poisoners and murderesses. If these were the kind of women she came from, it made her wonder what she herself might be capable of.

After awhile, Loretta came back and sat down. "Of course, honey, I'm not recommending that you murder your husband." She laughed reassuringly and patted Nita's hands. "You girls nowadays are lucky, because you don't have to stay in a bad marriage, you can leave with your children and your good name and, if you're lucky, a little money, too, and start all over again. I'm not trying to tell you to leave your husband, you'll have to make that decision yourself. But I am telling you I don't want you staying with him because of some mistaken idea that you'll be letting your family down if you do leave. You worry about yourself, and your children, and nothing else."

"Okay, Mama," Nita said, worried that Loretta still seemed so worked up. "Me and Eadie and Lavonne are going to punish the husbands our own way, and you've got to keep quiet or you'll ruin everything. Eadie and Lavonne are coming out after dinner and we're going to talk about what we have to do. It's okay, Mama. We have a plan."

Loretta shook her head and leaned her elbows on the table as if she hadn't heard her. "Those slack-jawed hyenas," she said. "Those dirty low-down clinkers." She hunched her shoulders and took a deep breath. "I hope your plan's a good one," she said.

LORETTA WAS STILL ANGRY WHEN EADIE AND LAVONNE SHOWED up two hours later. She stalked around the kitchen like a miniature pit bull, growling to herself and slamming pots and pans and throwing silverware in the drawers. Eustis had quickly excused himself after dinner, and he and Logan and Whitney had jumped on the golf cart and headed down to the pond to do some fishing. Nita helped her mother clean up. Later, she explained to Eadie and Lavonne that she'd told her mother everything.

"You can keep a secret, right, Loretta?" Lavonne said. "Because if any of this gets out before our husbands leave for the hunting trip, we're sunk. The only chance we have for revenge and an equitable settlement is to take the sons of bitches by surprise."

Loretta poured them all a cup of coffee and sat down at the table. Her apron was a bright red color and read *Roosters Crow, Hens Deliver* in big black letters across the front. "You girls can count on me. I'll keep it secret as an old maid's dreams," she said, hunkering down over her coffee. "Okay, what's the plan?"

Lavonne told her, explaining how they were going to hire the prostitutes for this year's trip themselves, mentioning Ramsbottom's plan to take photographs, and confirming that she and Eadie were divorcing their husbands as soon as they returned and therefore had to get their hands on as much cash as they could in the meantime.

Loretta especially liked the taking-pictures-to-use-as-blackmail part of the plan. That was a scheme right up her alley. "You gotta grab them by the short hairs, girls," she crowed, slapping the table. "And yank."

"I don't know," Lavonne said, shaking her head. "I'm not sure about the photographs."

"I don't think we should take pictures," Nita said. "That'll make Charles so mad he's likely to do anything." It wasn't hard to imagine Charles divorcing her and taking the children so she was only able to see them on the occasional holiday or weekend. Nita was beginning to rethink this whole revenge plan.

"Taking pictures kind of takes it to a whole new level of dirty-dealing," Lavonne said, shaking her head. "Hell, we might as well be terrorists. We might as well be Republicans."

"I am a Republican," Nita said.

"Then act like one," Loretta said. "Those pictures will knock the boys off their high horses. Those pictures will make sure they play fair when it comes to monetary responsibility."

Nita looked at her mother with love and admiration. "Mama, I want to be just like you when I grow up," she said.

"Honey, you are just like me," Loretta said, patting her arm. "You just don't know it yet."

Lavonne showed them the financial data she'd pulled from Leonard's personal files. "Good Lord," Loretta said, pointing with her finger. "Is that really what the old boy's worth?"

"Trevor was worth more than that," Eadie said, grinning. "Until I started spending it all."

"Let's only use the pictures as a backup," Nita said, imagining how angry Charles would be if they went through with this. "Let's only use the pictures if Trevor and Leonard won't agree to settle."

"Fair enough," Lavonne said. "You guys have to remember there's a lot of money at stake here. Even so, I'm not trying to take Leonard for everything, which is what he's trying to do to me by putting it all in his name. I'm just trying to make sure he plays fair, financially speaking, which is something you need to be concerned about, too, Nita. I know you're not planning on leaving Charles, but you still need to find out where the money's hidden, you still need to come up with some way of having your own bank account."

They all looked at her. Everyone knew Charles was a tightwad miser. Loretta patted Nita again. "She's right, honey. Charles Broadwell wouldn't loan a beggar a nickel unless the Lord and all his disciples cosigned the note."

"Mama, you're talking about the children's daddy," Nita reminded her.

"I'm just telling you, you need to look out for yourself. A woman without her own money will always be dependent on her husband."

"Okay," Eadie said, trying to get them back on track. "So it's agreed. We'll tell Ramsbottom to take the pictures and videos, too."

"What's to keep Ramsbottom from blackmailing them?"

"Ramsbottom is retiring. He's selling his ranch to a movie star for more money than he can spend in three lifetimes. The pictures are just his little parting shot. It turns out we're not the only ones wanting revenge on our darling husbands."

"Even if he agrees to take the photos," Lavonne reminded them, "there's no guarantee they'll come out. There's no guarantee the camera won't jam, or the film get overexposed or lost in the mail."

"There's no guarantee any of this will work," Eadie said cheerfully. "But we have to have faith it will."

"Okay, the pictures are a definite yes," Lavonne said. "Now how about the money—Eadie, have you figured out some way to get your hands on a large chunk of cash?"

"I'm not worried. Trevor's never cut me off before."

"Yes, well, Eadie, Trevor's never planned on getting married again before. His fiancée might have something to say about you spending all his money. She might just convince him to put the brakes on your lifestyle."

This was something Eadie hadn't considered. "He wouldn't dare," she said, getting mad just thinking about it. "He wouldn't dare cut me off. I've put up with him for twenty-one years and that ought to count for something."

Lavonne told them her plan to sell the house out from under Leonard.

"My God, you're a genius," Eadie said.

"Do you really think it'll work?" Nita said.

"That plan's got more holes than a banker's heart," Loretta said.

"It's a long shot," Lavonne agreed, "but it's the only chance I've got. Everything else will take years and I can't wait years. I've got a business I'm hoping to invest in."

"I've made arrangements with a gallery in Atlanta to take some of my best pieces," Eadie said. "I've kept the girls around long enough; it's time for them to go out into the world. The gallery will sell them on commission, so eventually I'll make some money, but probably not right away. I've been kicking around the idea of renting out some warehouse space downtown and maybe opening up a gallery myself. You know, to sell to the tourist trade."

"That's not a bad idea," Lavonne said. "I may be able to help you out there. I know of some space that should be opening up pretty soon that would make a great art gallery." Lavonne went to the counter and poured herself another cup of coffee. She sat back down. "But how are you going to come up with the money to finance the gallery?"

"Simple," Eadie said, having just thought of it. "I'll sell off the antiques."

"Oh Eadie, you can't sell off his family pieces," Nita said. "Some of that stuff has been in his family for generations."

"He doesn't give a shit about those old things. He's always talking about how he wants to sell everything and make a clean start."

No one said anything. Loretta got up and went to check on a load of laundry. Eadie scowled and looked at her hands. "Oh all right, I won't sell everything. I'll just sell some of it."

"You could have an estate sale," Loretta said, coming back into the kitchen. "You could have an estate sale the weekend they're gone."

Nita pursed her lips and nodded. "Virginia and Myra Redmon will be out of town that weekend, too. That just might work."

"The problem with an estate sale is you have to advertise," Eadie said. "Someone will read the advertisement and figure out who's having the sale, and then it'll be all over town, and before you know it, we're screwed. I've got the name of a woman who comes in and buys everything in a house, the whole kit and caboodle, for one price, and then hauls it all away. I think she's our best bet."

"Will she give us a fair price?" Lavonne asked, making notes.

"Shit, no. But we may clear a few thousand each, and I mean, hell, it's a start. I'll probably sell the family silver to the history museum because they've been after us for years to sell, and since Trevor and I won't ever have kids, and there's no one to inherit it anyway, I might as well go on and sell the whole collection intact." No one mentioned the obvious, which was that Trevor and his new wife might have kids. After a minute Eadie looked at Lavonne and said, "I could probably make enough selling the silver and the Jefferson letter and the Nathan Bedford Forrest medical kit to live on for a while." The Boone family had a letter written by Thomas Jefferson to Trevor's great-great-great-great-grandfather framed and hanging in Eadie's dining room. She had a traveling medical kit used by Dr. Cincinnatus Boone, Nathan Bedford

Forrest's personal physician during the Mississippi Campaign, displayed in her living room. "I think you've got the best plan, Lavonne. You're the one who stands to make the most."

"I'm also the one who's risking the most. It'll be a miracle if Leonard doesn't suspect something and refuse to go through with it."

"What are you going to do with the money?"

Lavonne hesitated a minute and then said, "I'm going into business with Mona Shapiro. We're changing her bakery to a deli that serves breakfast and lunch, and opening up a catering service."

Eadie looked surprised and excited at the same time. "That's brilliant," she said. "In that location, you'll make a fortune."

"I wish I could figure out something to do to make some money," Nita said wistfully. "I wish I could figure out something to sell."

"Do you have anything that might be valuable?" Eadie said. "Something like the Jefferson letter or the Nathan Bedford Forrest medical kit?"

Nita shook her head. "My mother-in-law has most of the family antiques. All I've got is a bunch of furniture and a big-screen TV and stuff like that."

"There has to be something else," Lavonne said, making scribbles on her notepad. "Something that maybe has your name on it. I don't suppose the house is in your name?"

"Oh I don't think so," Nita said.

"The cars?"

Nita shook her head. "Charles always buys the cars," she said. "He just brings a new car home whenever he feels like it. I never know what he'll buy." She played idly with her hair. Outside in the yard, her father's old Jack Russell terrier, Winston, chased a squirrel up a pecan tree. He got halfway up the tree trunk before age and gravity forced his descent. "I think my name's still on the title for that old car, though," Nita said absently.

"What old car?"

"The old car that belonged to Charles's daddy that Charles keeps in the storage shed out at the back of our lot."

"There's a car in that building?" Lavonne said. "I thought it was a garden shed."

"Yeah, everybody thinks that. I'm not supposed to talk about it."

Lavonne looked at Eadie. "What kind of car?"

"Just some old car," Nita said. She knew the name but in the excitement of the moment she had forgotten. "Charles calls it the Deuce."

"How do you know your name's on the title?"

"Because I found it the other day in a stack of files on Charles's desk. He had written, 'Nita—Change Title Over,' on the outside of the file and when I looked inside there was this piece of paper that had my name on it. I *think* it was a car title, I don't know, maybe it wasn't. I don't even know what a car title looks like, I guess."

Lavonne looked at Eadie and shrugged. "It bears further investigation, don't you think?"

"Hell, yes. Even if it's only worth a thousand bucks, every little bit helps."

Loretta got up and went to the sink to stir a pot of soup she had left simmering. She had calmed down considerably once she heard the women's plan for revenge. She looked less like a pit bull now, and more like a kindly grandmother. She grinned and stirred the pot. "You girls are nutty as a Claxton fruitcake," she said. "Remind me never to get on your bad side."

"Where's Charles right now?" Lavonne said to Nita.

"He's playing golf with Dolph Meriweather and Ed Trotter and then they're having supper at the club."

"Can you get into the shed where he keeps the car?"

"He keeps the key in his desk." All this made Nita nervous. She was beginning to worry this revenge might not work out after all. She was beginning to realize what she had at stake. Charles was a bad man to underestimate. He had enough of his mother in him to be dangerous when crossed. "Ya'll don't think we're making a mistake, do you?" she said, fingering the hem of her shirt nervously. "You don't think we're going to make them so mad they come after us with everything they've got."

"Don't worry," Eadie said, putting her arm around Nita. "Everything will turn out all right. You'll see."

Lavonne closed her notebook and reached for her purse.

"Are we going somewhere?" Eadie said.

"Let's take a little ride over to Nita's house," Lavonne said, gathering her purse and notebook in her arms. "Let's go over and see what kind of car Charles has been keeping locked up in his little faux garden shed."

IN THE END, THEY HAD TO TALK LORETTA OUT OF COMING WITH them. She was determined to be part of their revenge planning, and it was only by reminding her that Eustis would ask a lot of questions if she wasn't around, when he and the kids got back from fishing, that they managed to convince her to stay home.

Nita retrieved the key and they went down the garden path to the back fence. A sign reading *Wet Paint* hung on the gate, but Nita pulled the latch and they went through. Lavonne had never been back here. She could see the faint tracks of a sandy road running across the heavily wooded lot toward the county road that stretched some miles behind the subdivision. "How many acres do you have, Nita?"

Nita shrugged, trying to fit the key in the lock. "Two or three, I think. It's a double lot."

They went in through the small side door, and Nita switched on the light. She opened the window blinds so they could see better. Eadie grabbed one side of the tarp, and Lavonne grabbed the other, and they pulled it back over the roof of the car like they were pulling a blanket over a sleeping child.

"Oh, my God," Lavonne said. The Deuce, all chrome bumpers and flaring fenders, gleamed like a scepter in the dim interior of the garage. Dust motes swirled on the beams of sunlight slanting through the windows. The air was thick with the scent of paste wax and leather.

Eadie whistled. "That's some old car," she said.

"It's not just a car," Lavonne said, walking around to the front grille. "It's a Duesenberg." She was so excited her voice cracked. The hand lightly stroking the front grille trembled. "And it's worth a hell of a lot more than one thousand dollars."

"How much more?" Eadie said.

"I'm not sure." Lavonne walked slowly around the car. "Leonard was watching an antique car auction on TV the other day, and they had a car like this one featured. I wish I had paid more attention now to what it sold for, but I'm pretty sure it was close to seventy-five thousand dollars."

Nita looked from one to the other. Eadie grinned and put her arm around Nita's shoulders. "Do you know what this means? If your name is on the title and it's worth seventy-five thousand dollars and we're able to sell it—well, all right then. There's your little nest egg."

"I can't sell this car," Nita said. "Charles loves this car more than anything in the world."

"When was the last time he drove it?" Eadie asked, arching one eyebrow. "When was the last time he took it out for a spin?"

"Never," Nita said. Whether or not he enjoyed owning the car was not the issue. The issue was that Charles would be furious that Nita had sold something that belonged to him without asking his permission. *Still*, Nita thought, selling the Deuce was a symbolic gesture that needed to be made. It put Charles on notice that their marriage, although continuing, was changing to something he might not like. In renegotiating the terms of her marriage, Nita felt she should speak softly and carry a big stick. And a seventy-five-thousand-dollar bank account in her name might be just the stick she needed.

Eadie let go of Nita and turned to Lavonne. "The question is who do we sell it to? And how quickly can we do it?"

"First we've got to find the title and make sure it's in Nita's name. Then we have to figure out how to have it appraised without Charles knowing about it, and *then* we have to figure out how to sell it quickly." She stepped back and knocked over an oilcan.

"Is this an example of goddamn synchronicity or what?" Eadie said, grinning. "I mean can you believe how this is all coming together?"

"Don't get too cocky," Lavonne said. "We haven't pulled it off yet."

Nita put her hand over her mouth and giggled like a schoolgirl. "Charles will be so mad if I sell this car," she said. "Ya'll, he might leave *me*."

Eadie and Lavonne looked at each other. "Look, Nita, we don't have to do this if you don't want to," Lavonne said. "We don't have to sell the car."

Nita thought about it for a moment. She couldn't imagine Charles leaving her no matter what she did to him. Who else could he find to dominate and bully, who else would cater to his every whim like a docile slave girl?

She looked at Lavonne and grinned. "Let's do it," she said.

THE FILE WAS WHERE NITA REMEMBERED SEEING IT LAST, SITTING in a stack on the corner of the library desk. Lavonne sat down in Charles's chair and opened the file and Nita said nervously, "Just make sure you put everything back the way he had it or he'll know we've been in here." Eadie went down the hall to use the bathroom, and Nita went into the kitchen to check messages on the answering machine. A few minutes later she heard a metallic coughing sound, followed immediately by a high-pitched yodeling scream, the closest Lavonne Zibolsky would ever come to a rebel yell. Eadie and Nita sprinted down the hallway to the library.

The file was opened on her lap. Lavonne held a piece of paper between two fingers like she was holding a winning lottery ticket. "Do you know what this is?" she said, her hard metallic voice vibrating. They both shook their heads. "It's an appraisal Charles had done six months ago. That car's a 1931 Duesenberg Model J Sedan, and it's worth—are you ready for this, are you fucking ready for this—it's worth *seven hundred and fifty thousand dollars.*" She set the file on the desk and looked at them in wonder and amazement. Eadie took Nita in her arms and began to dance her around the room. "And what's more," Lavonne said, putting her reading glasses back on and shuffling through the file, "not only is Nita's name, solely, on the title, but there's correspondence in the file to indicate that Charles was supposed to sell the car when his father died to a doctor in Atlanta, a doctor by the name of"—Lavonne checked the file—"Marshall Osborne, and when he didn't, the doctor threatened to sue, which explains why Charles transferred title over to Nita. There's also correspondence in the file, dated three years ago, indicating the doctor is still interested in purchasing the car, should Charles ever decide to sell it. He must have realized he'd never get it by suing, so he decided to try the honey approach."

Eadie stopped twirling Nita around the room. "So, all we have to do is contact the doctor and make arrangements to sell the car to him, and Nita is pretty much set for life."

"By the year 2010, one out of every two businesses will be owned by women!" Lavonne shouted.

Nita's eyes were bright as a little bird's. "But I couldn't keep all of the money," Nita said hesitantly to Eadie. "Could I?"

Lavonne and Eadie looked at each other and then back at Nita. "Honey, with seven hundred fifty thousand dollars, you could do whatever you damn well please," Eadie said.

*J*IMMY LEE'S HOUSE WAS JUST THE WAY NITA HAD PICTURED it. He lived in the older section of town, not too far from the antebellum mansions of the rich, in an area of small, shotgun-style raised cottages. The house had a wide porch that extended across the front and around one side, overlooking a small, well-kept yard. Azalea bushes rimmed the lawn. An old live oak stood in the middle of the side yard, spreading its huge branches protectively over the house. A peeling concrete bench rested against its trunk.

Nita parked at the end of the drive closest to the garage, hoping no one she knew would drive by and see her car. If anyone saw her and asked questions, she would tell the truth. She was there to learn woodworking. She was there to learn a hobby.

An old yellow lab ambled across the yard to greet her, his tail swinging back and forth with each step. Nita's heart fluttered in her chest like a wren throwing itself against a plate-glass window. She combed her hair with her fingers, took a deep breath, and climbed the steps to the front porch. The front door was open. She stood at the screen door and called timidly, "Hello?"

There was a smell of bacon in the air, and fresh-brewed coffee. She could hear noises from deep inside the house, the clatter of silverware, the clanging of pots, the distant whine of a radio. A wide hallway ran the length of the house. On one side, through an opened doorway, she glimpsed a bedroom, and on the other side, a formal room filled with tall bookshelves and a leather armchair and floor lamp. She opened the screened door and stepped inside. "Hello," she said loudly.

"Hey, come on in," he shouted. He stuck his head around a corner at the end of the hall, wiping his hands on a towel. "Are you hungry? Do you want some breakfast?" He came out to greet her.

"Just coffee," she said, following him down the long hallway. He wore jeans and a T-shirt and his feet were bare.

There was another bedroom on the left and to the right a room filled with two sofas and a TV in a tall armoire. The back of the house was an enclosed porch with a bathroom on one end, and the kitchen on the other. She followed him up a step into the kitchen. Tall windows overlooked the yard. A small table and four chairs nestled in a corner between two windows. The ceilings in the house were high, at least fourteen feet, and covered in beadboard. She sat down at the table and he poured her a cup of coffee, then sat down across from her.

"I like your house," she said, reaching for the creamer.

"Thanks." He put one foot up on his chair and rested his arm across his knee. His hair was still wet from his shower and curled slightly at the ends. "Did you park out front?"

"No." She shook her head and sipped her coffee. "At the end of the drive."

"That's probably best," he said. He cleared his throat and she realized he was as nervous as she was. "Did you tell your husband you were coming over here?"

"No. I didn't think it mattered," she said, looking at him and trying not to feel guilty.

He tapped his spoon against the creamer, a blue ceramic dish in the shape of a cow. "It might have mattered to him."

Nita watched the yellow dog amble across the backyard. "He's got a lot on his mind right now. He's going hunting in two weeks."

"Really?" Jimmy Lee tapped his knee with the spoon. There was a frayed hole in the fabric just above his shin. "Where does he go?"

"Montana. For six days."

Jimmy Lee put his foot down and dropped his hand to the table. It rested inches from her own. She picked up the spoon and stirred her coffee.

"Men are fools sometimes."

She put the spoon down and looked at him over the rim of her cup. "Not all men," she said.

LAVONNE AGREED TO NEGOTIATE THE SALE OF THE DUESENBERG with the wealthy doctor from Atlanta. She figured she'd be better at lying than Nita. She took the file home with her with instructions that should Charles ask for it, Nita was to say that perhaps the housekeeper had misplaced it. Lavonne figured, correctly, that Charles had more pressing things on his mind to worry about than the Duesenburg file, which he assumed to be safely in his possession.

The doctor from Atlanta was quick to figure out what was going on. "Broadwell doesn't know a thing about you selling this car to me, does he?"

"He doesn't need to know. The title's in his wife's name. And he signed the transfer himself."

"Selling behind his back, while perhaps not illegal, is certainly immoral and unethical."

"Yes," Lavonne said. "It's similar to what Broadwell did to you eighteen years ago when he reneged on the promise made to his father. I guess it would fall under the category of 'what goes around, comes around.' "

The doctor laughed. They dickered for a while over price. Lavonne was a shrewd negotiator. She convinced herself that it didn't matter whether Nita sold the car to him or not, and by doing so, bargained from a position of power. He politely declined her price, and hung up. Forty minutes later he called back.

The final price, a compromise, was less than the appraised value but more than enough to give Nita a powerful bargaining chip when it came to renegotiating the terms of her marriage. A renegotiation was probably the best Nita could hope for since Lavonne was sure she would never seriously contemplate leaving Charles. Nita was one of those women who wrap themselves up in one man and then stay until the bitter end, or at least until the children are grown. Kind of like her mother had been. Kind of like Lavonne herself had been until she found out about the prostitutes and her husband's hidden bank accounts.

"I can have my attorney draw up the bill of sale or whatever other legal documents we need," he said.

"I think the title transfer alone will suffice. As you can understand, the fewer legal documents she signs, the better. I'll schedule the closing here at the bank. You can choose the time convenient to you since you'll have to drive down. We'll need to close either Tuesday or Wednesday the week of the twelfth. And, of course, we'll need a certified check made payable to Juanita James Broadwell."

"I'll call you tomorrow and we can discuss the final details."

"Fine. Needless to say, I trust you'll be discreet."

"You can trust me," he said, laughing. "I would never cross you. Women like you scare me."

"I must admit," Lavonne said, closing the file. "Sometimes I scare myself."

THE FOLLOWING MORNING, EADIE CALLED THE ITHACA AWNING Company and ordered a tent to be set up on the front lawn. Then she called Denton Swafford. She hadn't talked to him since the night of the firm party.

"Yeah?" he said, sounding like he was still in bed even though it was almost one o'clock in the afternoon.

"I need you to get over here," Eadie said. "Now."

"Look, Eadie, I'm real tired. I can't be expected to perform at just the drop of a hat."

"I don't want to sleep with you, peckerhead. That's over. Period. I need you to help me move some furniture is all."

"What furniture?" he said, his voice thick with sleep and resentment. The last thing he needed was to throw his back out moving furniture. Then how would he make a living?

"The furniture I've got stored in my attic and cellar. The furniture that belonged to my sorry-ass husband and his sorry-ass family for the last two hundred years."

"I can't afford to throw my back out," he began.

"I'll give you five hundred dollars," she said.

"I'll be over in fifteen minutes," he said.

⬦   ⬦   ⬦

IT TOOK ABOUT THREE HOURS TO GET THE CHINA, VINTAGE CLOTH-ing, trunks, mahogany and rosewood furniture, and oriental carpets out onto the front lawn. Eadie had put aside those pieces she thought Trevor might want to keep; no matter how hard she tried, she couldn't be heartless enough to throw away heirlooms that might have senti-mental value for him. Still, many of the heirlooms had spent the last fif-teen years locked away in the cellar and the attic without so much as a visit from Trevor, so she was pretty sure if she hadn't insisted they store them, he would have sold them long ago. Trevor never was one to dwell in the past. He wasn't sentimental that way.

Eadie made a large hand-lettered sign advertising antiques and heirloom collectibles. It didn't take long for the tourists to congregate like pigs around a trough, and by the end of the afternoon she'd made enough money to last her three months, if she economized, and that didn't include the family silver and the Jefferson letter and the Nathan Bedford Forrest medical kit she had arranged to sell to the history mu-seum, or the jewelry she had yet to pawn. The assets on her asset list had dwindled considerably but she figured it was better she get the money now before Trevor and Tonya got wind of what was up and tried to cut in for their share.

She remembered and went upstairs to the spare bedroom where Trevor kept his clothes. It was an old trick of his, leaving clothes in the bedroom closet that he would return for later. He had been doing this for years. It was one of the ways she always knew he planned on com-ing back, because he never came for the clothes, he just eventually moved back in.

There were several Brooks Brother suits and a stack of sweaters, some nice leather shoes, two big boxes of books, a golf bag, and a tele-scope that had belonged to Trevor as a child. Eadie stood just inside the closet door, smelling the faint scent of his cologne, and trying not to think about love and loss and the absurdity of fate.

She heard the shelter truck pull up to the curb, its brakes squealing loudly, and she went to the window and looked down at the lawn still dotted with tourists. Whatever she didn't sell today she was donating to the women's shelter. Denton saw her and waved. She opened the window.

"Do you want us to start loading this stuff in the truck?" he asked her.

"Yes." Eadie stood on her tiptoes and shouted, "Folks, everything left is half price. You've got five minutes to make up your mind before it all gets hauled away."

"How much for the portrait?" one woman asked, pointing to a full-length painting of Trevor's mother done the year she graduated from high school.

Eadie thought, *I'll give you ten thousand dollars to take it off my hands.* Eadie said, "Sorry, that one's not for sale." She motioned for Denton to bring the portrait up to her. "Come up here and get the rest of this shit out of the closet," she said.

"What shit?"

"Some Brooks Brothers suits. Sweaters. Shoes."

"Brooks Brothers suits?" Denton was interested. It was hard to afford decent suits on his income. It was hard to afford anything on his income. He was beginning to realize he was going to have to find a better way to make a living. "Can I have them?" he said, coming across the lawn to stand under the window. "The suits, I mean."

Eadie didn't hesitate. "I won't need them," she said, and closed the window.

NITA HADN'T TOLD HER MOTHER ABOUT JIMMY LEE, BUT SOMEHOW Loretta just knew. "Bring him around," she said to Nita, the Friday before Charles left for Montana.

"Bring who around?"

"Whoever it is that's putting the roses in your cheeks and the smile on your lips," Loretta said.

Nita told her. When she had finished, she said, "Do you think daddy will get mad?"

"Honey, daddy just wants you to be happy. Daddy knows that love may not make the world go round but it sure makes the trip a lot more pleasant."

"I can't help the way I feel."

"I just hope you're being careful is all. I hope you haven't done anything to give Charles Broadwell the right to take those children away from you."

"I'm being real careful, Mama. Nothing's happened between us. We're just good friends, is all."

"Uh-huh," Loretta said. "Do the children know?"

"That me and Jimmy Lee are friends? Of course. I can't tell them everything until after the hunting trip and this mess is all cleared up. At least I hope it'll all be cleared up after the hunting trip, if everything works out the way we planned. Pray for us, Mama. Pray it all works out the way we have it planned."

"Bring him around so I can meet him."

"We're supposed to take the children fishing tomorrow. I told them we were going fishing with a friend."

"That seems kind of risky. If Charles asks them, and they tell him, won't it look suspicious?"

"Charles won't ask. He's hardly ever home anymore. He spends all his time at the office getting ready for his trip. He doesn't even get home until the children are in bed and he leaves before they get up."

"Bring him around. Your carpenter, I mean."

"We'll come tomorrow for dinner, after the fishing. Tell daddy to be nice."

THE NEXT MORNING JIMMY LEE MET NITA AND THE CHILDREN at the public boat ramp. It was still early; fog rolled in over the surface of the Black Warrior River, and the air was cool and thick with the scent of pine. They took Jimmy Lee's boat into the coves where the catfish liked to sleep, where the bank was slick and overgrown with tall trees and the water was dark with tannin. The catfish were big as puppies, and almost as friendly, and after awhile Jimmy Lee and Logan quit catching them and throwing them back, and instead sat watching as Whitney fed them small pieces of the sandwiches they had brought along for lunch. Jimmy Lee taught Whitney the magical "Catfish Song," which had been used by generations of fishermen to lure the big fish, and soon, whether from the "Catfish Song" or the feast of sandwiches, the water around the boat was teeming with fish that wagged their tails and raised their whiskered snouts out of the water.

"I didn't know you believed in magic," Nita said, laughing at him from the stern of the boat while her happy children hung over the bow and patted and stroked the glistening fish.

"Magic happens every day," Jimmy Lee said, looking at her like she was proof of this very statement.

"You shaved off your goatee," she said.

He shrugged. "I thought you'd like it better," he said.

They went back to her parents' house for dinner. Loretta James had cooked a big meal, and they sat down to collard greens and squash casserole and field peas with stewed tomatoes and fried chicken and biscuits, washed down with gallons of sweet tea. For dessert there was peach cobbler. The children ate like field hands and entertained them with tales of the catfish. Eustis James and Jimmy Lee had worked together on several projects over the years, and pretty soon Eustis began to thaw toward the young man, and include him in the conversation. After awhile Eustis and Jimmy Lee began to exchange fishing stories, each more wild and fantastic than the last as they tried to outdo each other. The children laughed and slapped the table and rolled their eyes at their mother with each new whopper. Jimmy Lee had second helpings of everything and praised Loretta's cooking skills until she turned beet-red and gushed like a schoolgirl.

When it was time for him to go, Nita walked him to his truck. They stood together, side by side, looking at the stars. Nita had never seen such a pretty night sky.

"Look how clear it is," she said. "You can see every star like it was painted on."

His breathing was slow and rhythmic. She could feel his breath on her cheek. "Do you know in the city you can't even see the night sky?" he said. "All the reflected light keeps it hidden. It's one of the reasons I never could stay in Atlanta. I had to get back to a place where I could see the stars."

"I didn't know you lived in Atlanta," she said, glancing at him. His face, so close to hers, gleamed in the moonlight. "I probably should be getting home," she said.

"Will Old Chuck be waiting up?"

"Who?" she said.

He took her in his arms and kissed her so long and so slow that she lost track of time and space and the whole world seemed to collapse around her like a black hole. She had never, in her whole life, been kissed like that. When he finished with her mouth, he kissed her neck and then he dropped his head on her shoulder and lifted her up in his arms, holding her there just a few inches above the ground.

"Damn," he said, nuzzling her neck.

"Put me down before you hurt yourself," she said softly.

"I've already hurt myself." He kissed her again and set her down. "I'll call you tomorrow."

"Okay," she said.

When she came into the house later, her body light and freed from the weight of gravity, her mother was waiting for her.

"Now that one," Loretta said, wagging her finger in the direction of Jimmy Lee's disappearing truck, "is a keeper."

CHAPTER

TWELVE

*T*HE SUNDAY NIGHT BEFORE LEONARD LEFT FOR HIS HUNTING trip, Lavonne walked around the house and waited, restlessly, for Mona Shapiro's phone call. They had worked it out that Mona would call late, too late for Leonard to have time to think about what he would do, but Lavonne realized now she hadn't specified what "late" meant. Late to Mona might mean eight o'clock. She could hear Leonard downstairs in the family room. She prayed their plan would work, but the voice in her head relentlessly calculated the odds for failure. She did a load of laundry, checked the clock at seven-thirty, folded a load of laundry, cleaned the bathroom, and checked the clock again at eight-fifteen. Her stomach throbbed. A rash broke out along her neck and her right arm. At eight-thirty the phone rang and Lavonne jumped like someone had touched a hot poker to her back. She let Leonard answer it, and then went to the top of the stairs to listen.

She could hear him a few minutes later, stomping down the hallway in his bare feet.

"Lavonne!"

"Yes. I'm up here." She leaned over the banister so he could see her.

His face was red and slightly puffy. "That woman from the Kudzu Ball called again. She says she needs to talk to you about your duties as queen." He wrapped his hands around the banister post like he was wrapping his hands around Lavonne's neck. "I told her there was a mistake, that you wouldn't be able to attend the ball but she said you have to call her." His nose quivered. His bald spot shone like wet linoleum. "I thought we decided this was something you wouldn't do. I thought I made it clear this was something I didn't want you to do."

Lavonne thought, *I'll be the goddamned Kudzu Queen if it's the last thing I ever do.* Lavonne said, "Sure, I'll call her."

Mona Shapiro called at ten-thirty. Leonard answered the phone in the kitchen and Lavonne could hear him arguing with her. After awhile he slammed the phone down and came into the family room.

"Goddamn it," he said, throwing himself into a chair. He stared despondently at the blank TV screen. From time to time his lips moved as if he were arguing with some phantom adversary. Lavonne pretended to flip through a magazine. She yawned. "Is there a problem?" she said finally, trying to sound casual.

Leonard groaned and leaned forward, his elbows resting on his knees, his face hidden in his hands. He looked the very picture of rage and dejection.

Lavonne waited a minute and then asked again, "What's wrong?" She forced herself to sound uninterested, her eyes fixed on the glossy pages of the magazine in her lap.

"You spend your whole year working your ass off, just so you can have this one week of relaxation," Leonard said. "Fifty-one weeks of drudgery for one week of pure bliss." He was working himself into a frenzy. He sounded like he might cry. Lavonne had never heard Leonard refer to a family vacation as "pure bliss." She supposed family vacations would fall under the category of "drudgery." "My one week of relaxation and now I'm going to have to miss it because of one crazy old woman who can't make up her mind what in the hell she wants to do. It's not fair. It's just not fair."

Lavonne clamped her lips together and flipped through the magazine. If she sounded too interested, he'd know something was wrong. Normally, she didn't give a shit about problems he brought home from the office.

Leonard leaned back in his chair, his hands dropped in his lap like slabs of raw meat. The vein in his forehead pulsed. After awhile he said, "I've been after her for three months to close. I've had the documents

ready and just sitting in a file, waiting for her to make up her goddamned mind. We were supposed to close last week and then she
called at the last minute and postponed."

"Who?" Lavonne said.

"The Shapiro woman who owns the bakery on Broad Street. The
one you hired to cater the party."

"What do you want with a bakery?"

"I don't want a goddamn bakery!" He waved his hand at her like
she was purposefully missing the whole point. "I want the real estate."

Lavonne didn't say anything. She fanned the corners of the magazine, letting them slap against the palm of her hand.

"I've been waiting for three months for her to make up her mind
and close, and now, the night before I'm supposed to leave town, she
decides she has to close tomorrow, and it has to be at one o'clock, or she
walks." Leonard shook his head. He wiped his face with one hand,
dropped it again in his lap. "I mean, who is she to dictate terms to me?"
he asked an imaginary audience.

"Maybe she's had a better offer."

Leonard looked at her like this hadn't occurred to him. The dishwasher hummed in the kitchen. A shrub in the shape of a rabbit
pressed against the window. "Whose side are you on, Lavonne?" he
asked evenly.

"I'm not on anyone's side, Leonard," she said. "I really don't give a
shit who buys the bakery. I'm just trying to figure out why you're getting so worked up over something so stupid."

He stared at her, forcing himself to count to ten, forcing his turbu-
lent heart to slow. "I'm getting worked up, Lavonne, because I have to
be at a closing tomorrow at one, which means I'll miss my flight to
Bozeman."

"So take a later flight."

"There is no later flight. Do you know how hard it is to make
arrangements to fly into Push Hard, Montana?"

"So go a day late."

"A day late!" He jumped up and began to pace the room. "If I go a
day late, I'll miss a day of hunting. They won't wait for me. They'll ride
up to base camp without me and I'll miss all the action. I don't want to

go a day late!" She wouldn't be a bit surprised if he suddenly threw himself on the floor and began to kick his feet and howl like a two-year-old.

"Okay." Lavonne put the magazine down. She leaned forward, trying to look as sincere as possible. "Okay," she said. "How about this?"

He stopped pacing and looked at her. She glanced down at the floor, pretending she was winging it as she went along. *I should win an Academy Award for this performance*, she thought. *I should win a goddamn Oscar.* "You said you had all the closing documents prepared, right?"

Leonard nodded miserably. "Yes," he said.

"So sign a power of attorney and let one of the young associates in the firm close for you."

"No," he said, so quickly that she knew what she had suspected all along was true. Leonard didn't want the firm to know the details of his close dealings with Redmon.

"Okay," she said, feeling like this was too easy, like it was all falling into place like clockwork. "Make the power of attorney out to me and I'll close it for you. I'll sign the documents, give the check to Mrs. Shapiro, leave the documents in the file, and you can clean everything up when you get home." She reached for another magazine on the coffee table. She didn't look at Leonard. She could hear him breathing in the quiet room.

"The power of attorney has to be notarized," he said, shaking his head.

She couldn't believe he had fallen for it. He had to be desperate. She took a long slow breath and said, "So go in early, call your secretary to meet you there and have her type the power of attorney and notarize it."

"She's not going to get up at six-thirty to type a power of attorney!" He had a sudden mental picture of Christy's angry face. Since the firm party, it was getting harder and harder to get any work out of her. With any luck at all, he could have her transferred to another attorney when he got back from Montana.

"Okay, I'll type it," Lavonne said. "I'll go with you and type it up and you can get her to notarize it as we're leaving. Surely she'll come in early to notarize your signature?"

"I can get someone else to notarize it," he said, as if the plan was beginning to make perfect sense to him.

"Okay," Lavonne said, sitting back with the magazine in her lap. "There you go. Problem solved."

Leonard sat down. He wasn't accustomed to Lavonne offering to help him. It was shocking and left him speechless. He thought about his plans to leave her for a younger woman. "Are you sure you don't mind?" he said. What would she do without him? He was certain no one else would marry her. She would become one of those sad, lonely, middle-aged women who sit alone in a darkened house drinking scotch and talking to the cats. *No, no, this wouldn't do.* He was too far along his course to turn back now. It was every man for himself in this marriage. He forced himself to smile at his wife.

"I don't mind at all," she said. "Don't miss your trip because of something so stupid."

He relaxed. The color crept slowly back into his pink baby cheeks. His tiny lips stopped twitching. "Okay," he said, beginning to feel cheerful again. "Okay."

"That's settled, then," she said. She forced herself to smile. Her top lip felt glued to her teeth.

Across the street, the Redmons' old dog coughed like a cat throwing up a hairball. Moths as big as hummingbirds flung themselves at the porch light. After awhile Leonard got up and went to the window to turn off the light. He touched her shoulder awkwardly as he passed. "Thanks," he said. "I really appreciate this."

Lavonne held the false smile as long as she could. She thought, *So this is what it feels like to be a lying, cheating, low-life dirty dealer.* She thought, *I could get used to this.*

"Don't mention it," she said, going back to her magazine. "It's the least I could do."

CHAPTER
THIRTEEN

*T*REVOR WATCHED ATLANTA GRADUALLY DISAPPEAR BELOW
him. The city reminded him of the Emerald City in the *Wizard
of Oz,* with its gleaming skyscrapers rising up out of the treetops. A
pretty city, but big, spread out in all directions with rows and rows of
little houses and looping expressways and tall, glass office buildings,
and here and there, patches of trees sprouting up like fungi among the
asphalt. He could not live in a place as big and spread out and imper-
sonal as Atlanta. In Ithaca, he was Trevor Boone, grandson of wealthy
planters and pine barren speculators, great-great-great-nephew of that
other famous Boone who had forged trails into the Appalachian wilderness. In Ithaca, he was a Boone, he was somebody, but in the vast
gleaming city of Atlanta he would be a nobody, another of the millions
of nameless faces that hurried about their business below him, a legion
of small scurrying ants. No, he decided, staring through the small
cramped window at the landscape below, it was not a change of location
he craved.

So what was it? It depressed him at his age to find himself floating
aimlessly, one of those pitiful, self-indulgent, middle-aged men he used
to make fun of. His life, which had started out so promising, had begun
to flounder, had seized up and ground down upon itself like some monstrous, overloaded machine. What had happened to the young man so
sure of himself, so certain of his dreams of the writer's life, the old

house on Lee Street overflowing with writers and artist friends? Where had that boy gone? And who had taken his place? The law had been a substitute, a concession to his mother, a safe place to channel his energies until his first novel sold, but it had also been a diversion, an anchor he had dragged through life until it wore him down, made him doubt himself and his dreams. Made him tired.

Three rows behind him he could hear Leonard and Charles and Redmon whooping it up like college boys. "Hey, honey!" Redmon shouted to the stewardess, "bring us another drink." It had been Leonard's idea to invite Redmon. They usually brought along the client with the most billable hours, and this year Redmon was the winner. Trevor couldn't stand him and had made some excuse so he wouldn't have to sit with them. Sunlight glinted off the wing of the plane. Fragments of cloud drifted past the window. The landscape below was flat and gray.

It seemed to Trevor his whole life had been a diversion, a futile attempt to elude truth. He had hidden behind the law the same way he had hidden behind his box of unfinished manuscripts, protecting himself from his own sense of inadequacy, his fear of failure, his fear of the ordinary life. He saw that clearly now. His writing was like being a Boone; it was a way of being extraordinary, a way of making himself feel like he was more than one of those faceless scurrying ants always looking for something else, for something better.

Three rows back, Charles and Leonard and Redmon were beginning to annoy the stewardess. "Put that down, sir," she said in a tired voice.

"Okay," Leonard said.

"Hey, baby, why don't you sit down and have a drink with us?" Redmon said.

"Sorry, sir, I'm on duty."

"Come on! One little drink."

"It's a federal offense to touch me there, sir."

"A federal offense," Redmon said. "Good thing I've got my lawyers with me!"

The woman in the seat next to him glanced at Trevor over the top of her book. She was pushing fifty, he guessed, with thinning brown hair and a face that had once been pretty. She smiled at him. "Friends of yours?" she asked.

"Not really," he said. He turned again to the window. His women, too, had been a diversion; even Tonya. Sweet, gentle-hearted Tonya, who couldn't argue and drove him crazy with her suffocating love. Like drowning in molasses, that love, like sinking in a thick syrup that clung to you and held you down no matter how hard you tried to swim. He had left her for good. She deserved someone better. Someone who would appreciate her love. Someone who could love her back.

Beneath him the plane rolled and shuddered and dipped. The woman next to him had begun to doze. Her book slid into her lap. Trevor held himself close to the window trying not to touch the sleeping woman, who was beginning to spread out in her seat and ooze over the armrest. He listened to the woman's snoring and watched the clouds drift over the plane's wing, and thought about Eadie.

He had seen her yesterday, crossing the street in front of the little bakery along Broad Street, and she had looked so young and pretty and happy, that for a moment his heart had stopped. It hung in his chest like a great weighted pendulum, suddenly still, and then she had seen him, too, and his heart had begun to move again, swinging in a wide gradual arc. He honked the horn and waved, and she looked right at him, and then away. She went into the bakery and left him sitting in the traffic, his hands clenched around the steering wheel. He wanted to follow her into the bakery and take her by the shoulders and shake her. He wanted to tell her she had been right all along. He wanted to make her love him again.

Now it was too late. He had called her twice, and both times she hung up on him. She had loved him for as long as she could, and then, with that steady courage he had always admired in her, she had let him go. Her love for him, he saw now with the painful clarity of hindsight, had always been good and true. She had always pushed him toward his better self. Rising as she had from that dismal trailer on the south side of town, she had not understood his own fear of failure, his inability to act. She had a defiant spirit and the gift of losing herself completely in her art and he had been jealous of this. He had tried to punish her. It was all hopeless and humiliating and he had no one to blame but himself. He closed his eyes and leaned his head back wearily against the headrest. Remorse settled over him like a wave of nausea. He felt feverish.

Behind him, Charles and Redmon had begun to sing the "Georgia Fight Song." The other passengers looked embarrassed and tried to ignore them. A stewardess poked her head from the front cabin and began her slow procession toward the back of the plane. She passed Trevor, her face set in lines of weary resignation, eyes hollow, mouth drawn up tight.

"Hey, baby, where you been?" Redmon said. "We missed you."

"Sirs, I'm going to have to ask you to quiet down," she said. "You're disturbing the other passengers."

"Okay," Leonard said.

"We're not disturbing them," Redmon said. "We're entertaining them."

Trevor concentrated on the patch of blue sky outside the window. He wondered what Eadie was doing right now. He wondered if she was working. He wondered if she was still sleeping with that goddamned personal trainer. *God*, he thought. *I've been a fool.*

THEY LANDED IN BOZEMAN AROUND FOUR O'CLOCK, AND FROM there picked up a commuter flight to Push Hard. The plane, an Embraer Turbo Prop, was crowded with a backpacking group from the University of Texas, and they seemed a little less aggravated by Redmon and Charles than the last group of passengers had been. They applauded politely after the "Georgia Fight Song," and when Redmon broke into his rendition of "Up Against the Wall, Redneck Mothers," several joined in, and one ordered another round of drinks. "You know," Redmon said, leaning across the aisle and draping one arm around the neck of a tall, curly-haired boy. "You Texas boys is family. And I don't say that about just anybody." Leonard sat next to him, smiling like an indulgent father with an unruly child. He'd been drinking steadily since they left Atlanta, but he was still sober, trying to pace himself, trying to keep Redmon and Charles from getting them kicked off the plane, or worse. He was on duty until they arrived at the Ah! Wilderness Ranch. He felt certain that once they arrived, the good times would begin. He'd be able to relax then. All his life he'd been the responsible one who did what was expected of him, but he felt sure this trip was fixing to get better. His whole life was getting ready to change in a very big way. He just knew it.

Charles slumped in his seat, nursing a bourbon and Coke and watching a girl with long brown hair who perched along the armrest of one of the seats facing the idiot Redmon. She was clapping and singing along to "Rollin' in My Sweet Baby's Arms." She was not really pretty, but her face was pleasant and clean of makeup, and she had an attitude about her that Charles found compelling and mildly irritating. He had seen it in other young women her age, this attitude of knowing they were not pretty and not really caring, as if whatever motivated them went beyond caring whether or not they could catch a husband. These younger generation females were frightening to Charles. Knowing that they could choose any career, knowing that the traditional male worlds of law, medicine, and engineering lay open before them, that high incomes and sperm banks had made the necessity of a husband a thing of the past, they were an anomaly to Charles. They were an unsettling vision of a future where men like himself would have no power over women. Charles scowled and sipped his drink.

Trevor watched the girl with the long brown hair. She smiled at him, and he raised his glass in a salute. She reminded him of Eadie. Not pretty in the same way that Eadie was pretty, but confident. Sure of herself. The quality Trevor had always admired in his wife. The quality he had always found irresistible.

The captain came on to announce their arrival in Push Hard and the students scrambled to take their seats. Below them the runway lights twinkled merrily, surrounded by the tall dark ridges of the Gallatins. The lights of Push Hard glowed in the distance and the headlights of cars traveling down the mountain highway fell like shooting stars into the valley. The Embraer shuddered once and began its descent, bucking and lurching in the updrafts like a paper plane on a string. They felt it slip to the right, and hang for a moment, before plummeting the final distance, the cabin loud with the roar of engines and subdued laughter and tinkling glass. Five hundred feet from the ground the runway lights suddenly went dark.

The pilot's loud expletive, followed by the roar of the engines as the pilot attempted to slow the descent, was the only sound in the cabin. The small plane clattered and shook like a roller coaster on a wooden track. It dropped suddenly and the passengers came up off their seats, luggage banging in the overhead racks, engines screaming. Redmon began to cry and blubber like a baby. "Oh Jesus!" he wailed. "Oh Lord, I've been a sinner but I have a good heart!"

Trevor had a sudden clear picture of the way his life could have been if only he'd had the courage to live.

Leonard had an immediate sense of the irony of dying before he ever got a chance to be a winner.

Charles had an instant vision of his wife and children inheriting millions and living a life of peace and happiness without him.

"Save us, Jesus!" Redmon wailed. "Save us!"

The runway lights flickered and came on suddenly, sparkling below them like a Christmas tree. The plane steadied and began its slow climb.

"Jesus!" Redmon said. "Sweet Jesus."

"Let's try that again," the pilot said cheerfully.

Charles leaned over, put his head between his knees, and was sick. Leonard thumped himself on the chest with his fist, trying to get his lungs to draw. Trevor stared out the window at the blinking lights of Push Hard like Moses at the Burning Bush.

In the back of the plane, Redmon began to giggle.

*T*REVOR TRIED TO CALL EADIE FROM THE PUSH HARD airport. Her phone rang and rang, but she didn't pick up. He hung up and stood in front of the long plate-glass windows overlooking the airfield. Gray mountains rose against the dark sky. A plane taxied slowly down the runway, the lights inside the cabin illuminating the passengers who went about their business, unaware that life could change in the blink of an eye, in the time it took an Embraer Turbo Prop to drop five hundred feet. Trevor shook himself like a man coming out of a heavy sleep. "Boys," he said, turning around to Redmon, Charles, and Leonard, who stood watching him suspiciously. "I have a plane to catch. I'm going home to my wife."

They stood looking at him, not really comprehending what he was saying. Redmon grinned and leered at a group of college girls who eyed him with disgust.

"But we just got here," Leonard said, beginning to feel like this was all falling apart. He'd spent years bragging to Redmon about how great these trips were, and now here Trevor was ruining it for everyone.

"She'll never take you back," Charles wheezed, trying to get his asthmatic lungs to draw.

"We'll see about that," Trevor said.

It was four o'clock in the morning when Trevor landed at Hartsfield in Atlanta. He picked up his car and headed south. Traffic was light. He sped along the highway trying to figure out how he was going to talk to her, how he was going to convince Eadie to take him back if she wouldn't take his calls. The thought that she might not forgive him made him reckless. He drove like a madman. He had to see her tonight. He had to make her love him again.

Darkness rolled away from his headlights. A harvest moon hung over the trees like a rocket flare. Trevor sped down the lonely highway thinking of Eadie and wondering at the terrible and relentless power of unrequited love.

EADIE SLEPT FITFULLY. SHE DREAMED SHE WAS CROSSING A GREAT river in a small rowboat. She rowed and she rowed but she never got any closer to the far shore. Finally she stopped rowing. She let go and felt herself drift with the current, past throngs of people and grazing sheep and strange trees that grew like mushrooms along the banks of the river. She heard someone calling her name and leaning over the edge of the boat, she looked down into the dark water and saw a city of light filled with tiny fish-people who swam and sang her name. There was a sudden loud noise, an abrupt sound of wood striking metal as the boat scraped against a rock. Eadie woke up.

Trevor was standing in the doorway. He had turned on the hall light so she could see it was him. "Eadie," he said, stepping into the room with his hands raised in front of him. "Eadie, don't shoot me. I had to see you. You won't take my calls and I'm desperate. I can't go on like this, baby."

Eadie, still foggy with sleep but feeling a gradual, swelling fury come over her, was, for the first time in her life, speechless. She sat up and picked up a picture frame and flung it at him. It crashed on the wall beside his head, shattering into pieces.

"That's okay, baby," he said, advancing slowly. "Get it all out. Say whatever you want to say, do whatever you have to do. I deserve it. Throw whatever you have to throw. Hell," he said, grinning. "I won't even duck."

She picked up a heavy volume of Sylvia Plath's *Johnny Panic and the Bible of Dreams* and threw it. It caught him over the left temple. Trevor sagged to his knees like a sack of wet sand, and went down.

THE SYLVIA PLATH VOLUME DID MORE DAMAGE THAN TREVOR HAD anticipated when he made the courageous decision not to duck. It took seven stitches, administered at the Ithaca County Hospital Emergency Room, to close the gash in his forehead. Eadie drove him over, cursing him the whole time. You had to admire someone who could curse for ten minutes straight without stopping to breathe. It took a steady concentration and a great deal of intelligence to string together long looping sentences using four-letter words without stuttering or stammering or ever missing a beat. Trevor found himself holding his bleeding head and watching Eadie with love and admiration. *That's my girl,* he thought, wiping away the blood that dripped steadily into his left eye. *That's my beautiful girl.*

They pulled up in front of the emergency room just as the sun was coming up and Eadie went around to the passenger door and opened it. Trevor just sat there looking foolish, a bloody Kleenex stuck to his forehead.

"You're incredible," he said.

"Get out of the car, you idiot," Eadie said. "You're lucky I don't keep a gun in the house or you'd have a lot bigger hole in your damn head."

He followed her in through the sliding doors. She was wearing a short nightgown that barely covered her ass, and no shoes. The effect on the orderlies was immediate. They hurried over to help.

"What are you looking at?" Trevor said, trying to step between his wife and the two young men.

"See if you can stitch up his mouth when you stitch up his forehead," Eadie said to the orderlies, and without another word, she swung around and headed home.

MONDAY EVENING JIMMY LEE TOOK NITA AND THE CHILDREN OUT to the Rebel Yell Go-Cart Track. The children were leaving Tuesday morning to go to the beach with Loretta and Eustis for fall break, and Nita had promised them a special treat before they left. Logan had lived his whole life in the South, and had never been to a go-cart track. When Jimmy Lee heard this, he put his arm around Logan's shoulders and said, "Son, there are three things a Southern boy should know how to do, and one of them is drive a go-cart."

"What are the other two?" Logan asked.

"I'll tell you when you're older," Jimmy Lee said, and Logan grinned, and Nita blushed and looked at her feet.

The track was owned by twin brothers, Floyd and Lloyd Pickett. The Picketts were friends of Jimmy Lee's and they let Logan and Whitney have extra-long runs around the track, it being a slow night and all. Two hours later, Logan was hooked. Right then and there, Dale Earnhardt became his own personal hero. Looking out at the glistening track as the overhead lights came on and "Free Bird" blared from the loudspeaker, Logan made up his mind that one day, come hell or high water, he'd win the Winston Cup or die trying.

After they took the kids to Nita's parents' house, Jimmy Lee and Nita drove out to the river and sat in the back of Jimmy Lee's truck under a red-gold moon drinking Coors long-necks and talking about God and quantum physics and life on other planets. It seemed to Nita that she was another person when she was with him, that the world was opened up to possibility, and she could say anything, however personal or absurd, and he would understand what she was trying to say, and not judge her for it.

He had his arm thrown around her shoulders and she was nestled up close to him to keep warm, and pretty soon one thing led to another, and before long they were stretched out in the bed of the truck. Nita caught her shoulder on something sharp and the stabbing pain brought her abruptly back to her senses. She jumped up and buttoned her shirt and went to sit at the opposite end of the truck, with her back up against the tailgate. Jimmy Lee sat across from her, breathing heavy. He had his shirt off but he didn't seem cold.

"I can't," Nita said, pulling her collar up around her neck. She pushed her hair out of her face and looked at him. He had his head back against the cab but he was watching her. His chest moved up and down with his breathing. "If I do, I'll be no better than him. I'll be breaking my marriage vows as easy as he broke his, and that isn't my way. You know that, Jimmy Lee. If I do this with you now, you'll remember it later, and you'll never trust me. You'll always be wondering, you'll always be saying to yourself: She cheated on Charles Broadwell, why can't she cheat on me?"

He shook his head. "I wouldn't think that, Nita."

She put her hand up to stop him. "I have to think about my children," she said. "If he catches me sneaking around with you, if he finds out, I'm scared of what he might do." This was true. She had been thinking a lot about what Charles would do when he returned home from Montana; she had been imagining his anger over her setting him up with transvestites and selling the Deuce behind his back. Charles Broadwell was not a man to cross, and like all the Broadwells, he was sure to carry a grudge. It sounded so easy when she and Nita and Lavonne had planned all this, but the truth was, even if everything worked out, even if every little piece fell into place the way they hoped and prayed it would, Charles was still likely to find a way to punish her. Even if he didn't divorce her, he would still find a way to make her miserable. She was sure of that. God help her if Ramsbottom wasn't able to come up with those photographs. God help her if Charles found out about Jimmy Lee.

He sat up and reached for his shirt. "I can't stand all this sneaking around. I want to be able to take you places. I want to take you dancing, and out to dinner, and to the movies. I don't want to always have to hide what I feel."

She shook her head. "You knew I was married."

He pulled his shirt over his head. "Why can't you just tell him you're leaving him?"

"I don't know that I am leaving him. I don't know what I'm going to do." She put her head in her hands. "When he gets back from Montana, I'll decide what I have to do. I have to think about my children."

He pulled his knees up and rested his arms across the top. "This is getting complicated," he said.

"I never promised it'd be easy," she said.

He stood up and folded the blanket they had been lying on. "We better go." He put out his hand to help her rise.

She rose unsteadily to her feet and leaned against him for a moment. "Do you still want me to come over tomorrow morning to help you get ready for the Kudzu Festival?"

He climbed over the side of the truck and put his arms up to help her down. "Aren't you afraid one of my neighbors will see you?" He put his arms around her and pushed her up against the side of the truck. His breath was warm against her neck.

"It won't always be like this," she said, sliding her hands into his back pockets.

"Bring some breakfast when you come," he said, and kissed her.

*I*F CHARLES, LEONARD, AND REDMON HAD BEEN MORE INTU-
itive, if they had been more attentive to the signs and warnings
of fate, they might have taken the near-death experience on the Em-
brauer Turbo Prop and Trevor's desertion as a warning. They might
have noted the fact that their luggage and rifles didn't arrive, that their
gear seemed to have disappeared inexplicably somewhere over the
Rockies, and taken this as a bad omen. Instead, they searched for Bentley in the airport bar.

Bentley, who by now had been let in on Ramsbottom's plan for revenge against the lawyers, was, for once, glad to see them. He sat at the
bar nursing a boilermaker and nodded as they came in. He had spent
the last several years carting these sorry-ass yahoos through the Montana wilderness and he was not sorry they were finally going to get what
was coming to them. He was especially glad that Trevor Boone seemed
to have skipped the trip; Bentley had always liked Trevor, and he would
not have wanted to see Trevor undergo the dismantling Ramsbottom
had planned for the rest.

"They can't find our luggage," Charles said by way of greeting to
Bentley. "Or our guns." He had spent the last thirty minutes bullying a
reservation clerk, but so far it didn't seem to have done much good
other than to alert security to a possible terrorist threat.

Bentley downed his drink. "That's too bad," he said.

They sat at the bar drinking kamikazes. Redmon tried to pick up two girls sitting at a table behind them but one of the girls said, "We don't party with old guys."

"What the fuck?" Redmon said, rising unsteadily to his feet. "Who you calling an old guy?"

Bentley set his empty glass down on the bar and stood up. "Let's go," he said.

It was cold walking to the Range Rover, and Charles wished he had thought to wear his hunting jacket on the plane instead of packing it away in his suitcase. His sinuses shriveled and throbbed in the cold dry air. Leonard had his arm around Redmon's shoulders still trying to calm him down after his exchange with the snotty college girls. "Trust me, there'll be plenty of girls at the Ah! Wilderness Ranch," Leonard said. "Girls a lot prettier than those two."

"Goddamn," Redmon said, rubbing his hands together. "It's cold enough to freeze the stink off a monkey. How much longer till we get there?"

When they reached the Rover, Charles walked around to the driver's side but Bentley shook his head and said, "I'll drive." He took the keys out of his pocket and pushed past Charles who stood there with his hand out.

"No, I'll drive," Charles wheezed.

Bentley swung around to face him. He was smaller than Charles by a couple of inches but he was broader through the shoulders and used to backing down cowboys and pickpockets and other assorted petty criminals. Backing down a lawyer was no big deal. "Boss said I was to do the driving this trip."

Charles took a deep breath, feeling his throat constrict. If he hadn't been dealing with asthma he might have noticed the menace in Bentley's tone, he might have realized the Indian boy was treating him the same way Nita had been treating him ever since the firm party.

"Let's you and me go back into that bar for one more little bitty drink," Redmon said, leaning heavily on Leonard's shoulder.

"Get in the car," Bentley said.

"Let's go back in there and given them snotty college girls hell."

"Get in the car *now*," Bentley said, and Leonard jumped and opened the door and shoved Redmon inside and climbed in beside him. Charles went around and got into the passenger's side. They were so stunned at the way Bentley had spoken to them it was miles before anyone thought to say anything. Bentley drove slowly, following the taillights of the car in front of them that glowed and arced through the darkness like twin comets heralding the beginning of some dire and long-awaited prophecy.

Charles, who wasn't sure now what he had heard Bentley say, shook himself and said, "If you drive this slow we won't get to the ranch until morning."

Bentley looked at him. In the backseat, Redmon sang "Lonely Women Make Good Lovers." "You saying you want me to drive fast?" Bentley asked the hapless Charles.

"I'm saying I'm cold and I'm hungry and I want to get into a warm bed sometime tonight."

Bentley buckled his seat belt. He checked his rearview mirror. "Whatever you say, Kemosabe," he said, and clamped his foot down on the accelerator.

THEY ROARED UP TO THE RANCH IN A CLOUD OF DUST. RAMS-bottom had heard them coming and was standing on the porch to greet them. Two small lamps cast their spindly light across the planked porch, patched here and there with new pine boards. Ramsbottom stood at the top of a small flight of steps. Sheba, the old Ridgeback, was with him. She looked up at him and whined deep in her throat as the Rover spun around the drive and came to a sudden stop, its momentum arrested, dust-covered flanks swaying in the lamplight.

A rear door opened and Redmon fell out onto the drive on his hands and knees. He vomited steadily for several minutes. On the other side Charles Broadwell climbed out and stumbled around the back of the Rover, his face pinched and bloodless in the lamplight. Behind him Leonard emerged, clutching his chest.

"Evening," Ramsbottom said cheerfully, putting on his game face, his "welcome to my home, you skim-milk cowboys," face.

"He tried to kill us," Charles wheezed, pointing at Bentley, who had climbed out and was calmly unloading groceries and supplies onto a pushcart. "He left the road." Charles sounded like he was sucking bbs through a straw. "We went airborne. Twice."

"You said you wanted to go fast," Bentley said. "I took a shortcut."

Charles looked as if someone had punched him in the stomach. He tried, desperately, to draw a breath. "Fire him," he said to Ramsbottom. "Fire him right now."

"Now, now, Mr. Broadwell," Ramsbottom said, coming down the steps with his arms wide. Sheba climbed stiffly down the steps beside him. "There's no need for all that." He clapped Charles on the shoulder and pulled him up close. "Bentley was just trying to do what you asked him to do," he said in a low, soothing voice. "You know old Bentley. You've known old Bentley for years. Surely you don't think old Bentley would do anything to make you mad."

"Old Bentley tried to kill me."

"Naw," Ramsbottom said, like he was trying to coax a smile from a colicky baby. "You know that ain't true! Bentley would never try to kill one of the guests. That'd be bad for business!" Charles could understand the logic of this. Beneath the old man's steady voice he was beginning to thaw, was beginning to breathe easier. After all, he *had* asked Bentley to drive faster.

"Well," he said, smoothing his sweater with his hands. "Well."

"Right," Ramsbottom said, and clapping him once again on the shoulder, he let Charles go. "Now, let's get on up to the house and have a nightcap and then we need to turn in. We've got a busy day ahead of us." He walked over to Redmon who was climbing up the side of the Rover, trying to stand up straight. Ramsbottom stuck out his hand, stepping discreetly over the vomit stain, and said, "You must be Mr. Redmon."

"Where's the girls?" Redmon croaked.

"The girls missed their flight in Vegas. They had a late show."

"These are *Vegas showgirls*?" Redmon said, already feeling better. Leonard grinned and gave him a look that said "See, I told you so."

Bentley looked at Ramsbottom. Down in the creek pens Sambo, the old toothless circus lion, coughed at the moon. "I guess you could say they were showgirls," Ramsbottom said, and Bentley made a sound like he had swallowed a golf ball, and pushed past them with the luggage cart.

RAMSBOTTOM'S PLAN FOR REVENGE WAS SIMPLE. INSTEAD OF doing anything overtly brutal, they just weren't going to intervene to make sure things went smoothly for the lawyers. There would be no gourmet food, no penned animals waiting patiently to be loosed and slaughtered, no carefully planned expedition into the mountains. Ramsbottom had lived in Push Hard, Montana, all his life and he knew from experience that nature could be cruel and devious. Mother Nature didn't like puffed-up hombres who went around thinking they were better than everyone else. The Greeks had a word for it—hubris. Mother Nature had a tendency to curb-stomp anyone foolish enough to enter her wilderness carrying more than their fair share of hubris. All Ramsbottom had to do to get revenge on the clabber-heads was to sit back and let Nature do her work.

The morning after they arrived at the game ranch, Ramsbottom got the hunters up early. Leonard, Charles, and Redmon had sat up late the evening before drinking bourbon, and they were all slightly hungover. They ate buffalo sausage and fried eggs and Texas toast washed down by pots of black coffee. Carlos, the chef Ramsbottom had used for years, had left to open his own restaurant, and Ramsbottom had recently hired William to do the cooking. He came out on the porch wearing a dirty apron and carrying a pot of coffee. He was big and bald and he looked like what he was: an ex-felon from Oklahoma who had done time in McAllester for grand theft auto and assault. So far William's cooking skills had been somewhat limited, but Ramsbottom believed in giving a man a second chance. William poured coffee and sucked a toothpick but he kept quiet.

Bentley had been up since sunrise getting the pack animals loaded. He came up on the veranda to join the others around eight o'clock.

"When do the girls get here?" Redmon whined, reaching for another piece of toast.

Ramsbottom had promised the wives he wouldn't let the husbands catch sight of the girls until Thursday evening at the earliest.

They needed the week to plan whatever it was they were doing to punish the husbands, and he needed the week to watch Nature whittle the husbands down to his satisfaction. He'd make excuses and string them along until then. "The girls have been delayed," he said, tapping the edge of his coffee cup with his spoon. "They had another show to do, so they're probably not even going to get in until Thursday night. But that's okay, because that'll give you boys time to get some hunting in before the female entertainment gets here." He winked at Charles who scowled and looked out at the distant Gallatins. Their luggage had still not arrived and the men were wearing a mishmash of hunting gear, whatever Ramsbottom had been able to dig up for them from the lost and found he had collected over the years. Charles was wearing a khaki army jacket and a furred hat with earflaps. Redmon had on a camouflage jumpsuit and matching stocking cap. Leonard wore a field coat that hung nearly to his knees, a pair of ear warmers, and a baseball cap that read *Gun Control Is Hitting Your Target*.

"We'll get an early start," Bentley said, brushing the dust off his knees, "and be at Big Nose Pass by noon. We should reach the Boot by five o'clock, with any luck."

"Good," Ramsbottom said, rubbing his palms together. "The weather should hold until the middle of the week. You'll be back before then."

"We'll be back long before then," Charles said, looking from one to the other. "I don't plan on being caught up above tree line in a snowstorm."

Ramsbottom laughed as if Charles had said something funny. Bentley grinned and poured himself a cup of coffee. He passed the pot to William, who stood sucking his toothpick and gazing at the blue cloudless sky, his black face inscrutable. Ramsbottom and Bentley looked at each other and giggled like a couple of teenagers. Charles wasn't sure what they were laughing at, but he found their behavior extremely unprofessional. He looked from one to the other, scowling his displeasure. If the foreboding William hadn't been standing right behind Ramsbottom's shoulder he would have berated Ramsbottom for his behavior and the fact that the girls hadn't shown up as scheduled, but something about the big black man made him nervous. Charles sat there and didn't say anything at all.

BY MIDAFTERNOON THEY WERE UP IN THE HIGH COUNTRY. THE SUN was warm against their backs, but from time to time a damp wind blew from the north, bringing with it the scent of snow. They followed a trail beside a splashing stream lined with cedar and willow, the sound of their horses' hooves deadened in the thick carpet of moss and pine needles. The sun could not penetrate the trees in some places and the air here was as cold and prickly as the inside of a freezer chest. Bentley led the way, followed by Leonard, who rode Big Mama and, as the most inexperienced rider, was having trouble keeping the horse on the trail. Redmon followed him, then Charles, and William came up the rear dragging the pack mules, their packsaddles clanging and rattling like ball bearings in a washtub.

About half a mile up the trail, Bentley's horse picked up a stone and went lame. From that point on, things began to go steadily wrong. The sky, which up to now had been blue and clear, began to darken and fill with gray clouds. A cold wet wind blew in from the northwest. Big Mama tried to dislodge Leonard by running him into a tall pine, trying to scrape him off in the branches and managing to pin his knee while Leonard screamed in pain. Bentley shouted and jumped into the thicket to grab her bridle, and Big Mama rolled her eyes and stamped her feet and shook her skin like an elephant trying to shake a tethered monkey.

Redmon, who seemed oblivious to what was going on around him, said, "Time to drain the snake," and fell off the side of his horse. He was having trouble breathing in the high altitude and his face was the color of oatmeal. He stumbled off into a stand of wild raspberry and was sick. The mules put their ears back and showed their teeth. Charles scowled at the overcast sky. Redmon came out a few minutes later, wiping his face on the sleeve of his jumpsuit.

"I hope you remembered to pack that tequila, Uncle," he said to William.

William took a toothpick out of his pocket. "Who you calling 'uncle,' motherfucker," he said.

❀   ❀   ❀

THEY STOPPED FOR LUNCH AROUND THREE O'CLOCK AND ATE PI-
mento cheese sandwiches washed down by cold beer. The sky had
darkened and the wind had picked up, moving through the tall grass
and the tops of the trees, and bringing with it the scent of snow. No one
said much. Huddled in their odd clothes, their fingers stiff with cold,
Charles, Leonard, and Redmon clustered along a fallen log like fungi,
watching William as he cleaned up and repacked the basket with the
leftover beer.

"You boys get off your asses and go out and get them horses,"
William said.

"Yes, sir," Redmon said.

Sensing the change in the weather, the horses grew restless. They
threw their heads up and stamped their feet, blowing out their bellies
so it took the men several tries to get the cinch straps tight.

It was dark by the time they reached the Boot and took the left trail
toward camp. Bentley led the way, with Charles bringing up the rear. A
slanting, sleeting rain fell, stinging the men's hands and faces and stiff-
ening the horses' manes and tails. They followed the trail through thick
stands of alder and willow where it diverged in a stand of wild raspberry
into two trails, and then back into one, and up into a wide flat meadow.
The creek skirted the meadow, a pale ribbon in the moonlight. Beyond
the meadow they could see the camp set up in a stand of cedars. Two
canvas tents had been set up on wooden platforms raised several inches
above the ground.

"Jesus Christ," Redmon said, as they reined up in front of the tents.
"Is that where we're sleeping?"

"This is a wilderness trip," Charles reminded him. He'd had just
about enough of this whole experience. He was cold and he was hungry
and he was tired of trying to keep his mouth shut around the big black
man who was obviously a serial killer in waiting. He made a mental
note to add this to the lawsuit he planned to file against Ramsbottom.
"This is a hunting trip, not a country club jaunt," he said harshly to
Redmon. "What did you expect?"

"For what we paid, I expected a goddamned heated cabin with
clean sheets and a warm bath," Redmon said.

Leonard laughed nervously.

"This is the kind of trip that separates the men from the boys," Charles said.

Bentley looked at William. William sucked his toothpick. Far off across the meadow beyond the trees, it began to snow.

RAMSBOTTOM LIT HIS CIGAR AND LEANED BACK IN HIS LEATHER chair with his feet stretched to the fire. "How long do you think the snow will fall in the high passes?" he asked Bentley on the mobile phone.

"Hard to say." Bentley's voice was scratchy with static.

Ramsbottom took a drink, swished it around in his mouth, and swallowed. "I expect you'll have sun by morning," he shouted, grimacing as he eased his legs over. "The storm's supposed to move on sometime tonight."

In the bunkhouse across the way he could hear the "girls" dancing to the soundtrack of *Saturday Night Fever.* He had lied when he told the tenderfoots the girls weren't coming in until Thursday. He yawned, looking at the fire. "You think you can keep those churnheads from killing themselves before Thursday?" he shouted into the mobile.

"It's not the churnheads I'm worried about. It's William. He's got an awfully big bowie knife strapped to his waist. The dude's scary, man."

Ramsbottom hoped William wasn't close enough to hear what Bentley was shouting. "Remind him those boys are to be whittled down some but not killed or permanently maimed."

"I best take the bowie knife away from him then."

Outside the window the snow fell steadily. The cheerful fire hissed in the grate. The room was warm and fragrant with the remains of supper. "You doing any hunting tomorrow?" Ramsbottom said, drawing on his cigar.

"I guess. They want to go up to the aspen meadow in the morning, but I told them we'd have better luck up higher."

Ramsbottom chuckled. "Did you tell them why?" Normally, they fed the elk at the aspen meadow for several weeks before a big hunt to get them used to coming there to feed, but this time, of course, they hadn't bothered. It made Ramsbottom sick, thinking about all the times he'd had to practically truss an animal and leave it staked in a field just so these banty-rooster lawyers could take home a trophy.

Outside he heard the clatter of high-heeled shoes on the wooden porch and the door burst open with a gust of snow. Stella, wearing a faux leopard fur coat, stepped inside, and closed the door behind her. She stood for a moment, brushing the snow out of her long red wig. "Hi," she said, smiling.

Ramsbottom swished his brandy. "Hi, Stella," he said.

She had her coat opened in the front, revealing a black miniskirt and the longest legs Ramsbottom had ever seen. He got a boner just looking at her legs. It was amazing that a girl that looked that fine could not be a girl. It was amazing, and it was scary.

"Do you have any fingernail polish remover?" Stella said.

"Nope," Ramsbottom said. "I'm fresh out."

"Damn it," she said, waving her big hand in front of her face.

"I've got some paint thinner in the shed," Ramsbottom said, grinning.

"Shit," Stella said, splaying her fingers so he could see the chipped nail. "I need a touch-up."

"How about a drink instead?" Ramsbottom said.

"What you got?" She walked over and picked up the bottle. "Ooh, Courvoisier. Very chic."

"So how about it?"

"Let me get the other girls. I'll be right back."

"It's a party, then," Ramsbottom said.

Stella grinned and raised her eyebrows. "Honey, it's always a party," she said. She wrapped her coat around herself and hurried out.

"You still there?" Bentley shouted.

"Just tell me this," Ramsbottom said, clearing his throat. "Are those bastards sitting up there talking about how they're going to sue my ass?"

"They did mention it a couple of times," Bentley said.

"Motherfuckers."

"Yep," Bentley said.

Ramsbottom raised his glass and drained it, looking at the video camera resting on the bookcase. The fire crackled merrily. He grinned and set his glass down. "When I get through making my little movies, they won't be suing anybody," he shouted, and clicked off.

Sleet scoured the window and distantly, faintly, he could hear Sambo howling at the storm. Ramsbottom poured himself another drink, stretched his feet to the fire, and settled down to wait for the girls.

CHAPTER

SIXTEEN

*T*UESDAY MORNING NITA ROSE EARLY, SAW HER CHILDREN AND her parents off to the beach, and went over to Jimmy Lee's. The sun shone brightly on the tree-lined streets; the day seemed fair and full of promise. She had lain awake most of the night, worrying, but today everything seemed better. By two o'clock tomorrow afternoon she would have closed on the Deuce and would have enough money in her bank account to raise her children without ever having to take another penny from Charles. The power and confidence she derived from this thought amazed her. She had never had money of her own, she had never really cared about it, but she could see now why people went to such lengths to have it. Money gave you the power to make your own decisions without having to be dependent on anyone else. On Saturday evening Charles would be home from Montana and she would tell him she knew about the women. She would tell him she had sold the Deuce, and they would have to agree to forgive each other and move on from there for the children's sake. If he bullied and threatened her she would, God willing, have photographs sure to silence him. And once she and Charles had decided what to do about their faltering marriage, she could decide what to do about Jimmy Lee. The plan, which in the dark closed bedroom last night seemed doomed to failure, seemed now, in the bright clear sunshine of a new day, fail-proof.

Jimmy Lee was back in his garage working on his entry for the

Kudzu Festival recliner chair race. The Kudzu Ball was held every year in a vacant lot beside the Wal-Mart. Over the years it had evolved from a dance celebrating single, married, widowed, divorced, or soon-to-be divorced women, to a daylong Kudzu Festival celebrating Southern culture, in general, and white-trash culture, specifically. It had been started originally by a group of college professors out at the university, people who in their professional lives wrote articles like "An Empirical Analysis of Price Dispersion in the Automotive Industry," or "Environmental Assessment Using Bayesian Inference," but whom, in spite of all that, still knew how to plan a pretty good throw down. The Kudzu Festival was held on Saturday and included games such as the Hubcap Throw, Bobbing for Pigs' Feet, Possum Toss, Hillbilly Jeopardy, and Name That Hick; a Beer Can Art Exhibit; the ever-popular recliner chair race, dubbed NASCHAIR by the festival organizers; and several cooking contests including the Betty Cracker Cook-Off and the White Trash Iron Chef event. The Kudzu Festival culminated Saturday night in the Kudzu Ball, complete with live music and a deadly alcoholic concoction known as Kudzu Koolaid that was guaranteed "to take the chrome off your bumper."

Jimmy Lee was putting the final touches on his recliner, a blue velour Barcalounger he had mounted on a pallet with wheels and decorated with NASCAR decals and a giant number 3 painted across the back in honor of Dale Earnhardt. He was calling the chair *The Intimidator.*

"Hello," Nita said, stepping into the garage.

"Hey." He leaned and kissed her. He tasted of Cinnamon Toast Crunch and Nita took her time kissing him. "You better stop that," he said. "Or things might get out of hand."

She walked around *The Intimidator* admiring his work. "That's a real work of art," she said. He tried to grab her but she moved out of his way.

"Come on, baby, be my copilot," he said, grinning.

"I can't. I've got things to do on Saturday." She looked at the Barcalounger and said, "How do you make this thing go?"

"Someone pushes me. If you won't be my Pusher, I'll have to get someone else."

"You think you have a chance of winning?"

I'm gunning for the Pickett boys," he said, wiping his fingers on a rag. Floyd and Lloyd Pickett had won NASCHAIR three years in a row. "They win every damn year, but this year I'll give them a run for their money, so to speak."

The recliner race was a big favorite with everyone, and consisted of teams of two, the Pusher and the Pushee, who maneuvered wheeled recliners through an obstacle course for the prized Kudzu Kup. Teams were judged not only on speed, but on the creative concept of their recliners. The Pickett brothers' creation last year was a faded plaid La-Z-Boy that had been outfitted with a beer cooler, a remote control carry case, a crude steering wheel, and a drop down table tray onto which had been glued a plate, a NASCAR beer coozie, and a fork on a chain.

He leaned back against the tool bench with his arms crossed over his chest. "You should come with me to the festival," he said. "It's a lot of fun. Last year I won second place in the Betty Cracker Cook-Off with my entry—Elvis's Fried Nanner Samich."

She laughed. "That sounds awful," she said.

"Hey, I beat out the Ho-Ho Log and the Twinkie Torte in the Best Sweets category." He took a recipe card out of his pocket and handed it to her. "Here's my entry this year."

The card read, *Heart Thumper Breakfast Shake*. It called for a handful of ground coffee (not brewed); 2 cigarettes (remove the casings and drop the tobacco in the blender); 1 can of Mountain Dew. Across the bottom it read, *This one'll put the hair on your chest, by God. Any yuppie Hilfiger can drink a Starbucks Latte but it takes a real man to keep this one down.*

"Very nice," she said, giving him back the card.

He slipped it into his pocket. "You'll have fun. I promise."

"I can't." This time she let him grab her and pull her into his arms.

"At least go with me to the Kudzu Ball."

She shook her head slowly. "You know I'm meeting with Charles Saturday night," she said, not really wanting to talk about it. She had thought about it last night until she felt sick to her stomach.

"I feel like a condemned man waiting for a call from the governor." He frowned and ran his finger along her cheek.

"I'm sorry," she said. "It's the best I can do for right now. I won't know until Saturday night if the Deuce sells, if Charles still wants to stay married to me, if I still want to stay married to him. It's all complicated and it makes me sick to have to think about it, but there's nothing else I can promise right now. Either things will work out or they won't. I just can't do better than that."

Seeing her distress and not wanting to get pulled into this argument again, he kissed her lightly on the forehead, and let her go.

TREVOR HAD MOVED OUT OF THE APARTMENT HE SHARED WITH Tonya, and he was staying out at the Holiday Inn. The day he got home from the hospital after having his head stitched up, he spent all afternoon planning how to make Eadie take him back. It would take longer, probably a lifetime, to make her trust him again, but Trevor was willing to do whatever it took. He had never been so committed to anything in his whole life as he was to making his wife love him again.

He called every florist within a hundred miles. He ordered calla lilies and bird of paradise and orchids and tropical helitonia from Hawaii, and scheduled a dozen of each for delivery over a twelve-hour period. Then he went to the Hallmark store and bought three dozen cards. He spent the rest of the day writing notes on the cards, things like *Forgive me. I'm an ass. There's only one girl like you in the whole world. Give me another chance. You won't be sorry,* and other such things, one line to a card. Then he went to the post office and mailed all the cards at once.

He ordered one of those flashing portable billboards and had it delivered to the driveway of the vacant house across the street from Eadie, so that every morning when she woke up, and every evening when she went to bed, she could see his public affirmation—*I love you Eadie*—spelled out in bright, flashing neon bulbs.

He called the house and left long messages on her answering machine, filling it up with quotations from *Sonnets from the Portuguese* and Keats. In the middle of "La Belle Dame Sans Merci" she picked up the phone and said, "Stop calling, Trevor. This isn't going to work."

But something in the way she said it made him think it just might.

❀   ❀   ❀

THE MORNING AFTER THEIR FIRST NIGHT AT CAMP, THE MEN GOT up early and trudged up to the aspen meadow on foot to hunt for elk. They followed the stream up through tall rocky cliffs, through a spruce grove and into a meadow of tall grass and aspen. They found elk scat here and Charles and Leonard got excited, but Bentley could see it was weeks old. They milled around in their excitement and trampled over the most promising trail, but Bentley said nothing. He wasn't there to help them find game or lead them to the best hunting spots; he was there to make sure they didn't accidentally shoot themselves or fall into a ravine.

By mid-morning Redmon had had enough. "I'm hungry as a goat on a concrete pasture," he said. "Let's get back to camp and eat."

"We're not here to eat, we're here to hunt," Charles said, brandishing the Remington Wingmaster he had borrowed from Ramsbottom.

"I could eat," Leonard said.

"Goddamn it," Charles said.

"Hey, buddy, you best simmer down," Redmon said. "You've had a bee in your bonnet since we started this trip."

They could smell food as they came down into the pine grove that ringed the camp, and Redmond clapped his hands together and shouted cheerfully to William, "Goddamn, I'm hungry as a woodpecker with a sore pecker! Is that steak you're cooking there, 'cause I'm definitely in the mood for a big old juicy steak!"

"We having chili," William said, slamming the lid on the pot. He was wearing the same dirty apron he'd worn yesterday over his camouflage jacket. A cigarette dangled from the edge of his mouth.

"How much longer till it's ready?" Redmon said, holding his big hairy nose over the pot.

William took the lid off and stirred the chili, his face set with the determined expression of a man contemplating murder and mayhem. "Hey, man, it's ready when it's ready. Why don't you sit your sorry ass down over there by that fire and peel me some potatoes, you looking for something to do."

Redmon had never in his entire life had a negro talk to him in such a way. It was the way his own daddy used to talk to him. It made Redmon feel like he was a little boy back home in the Alabama pine lands. It made him feel like he and the black man were developing some kind of special bond out here in the wilderness, some kind of macho fellowship that transcended race and creed and economic status.

"I think I'll have me a beer," Redmon said.

"Don't look at me, motherfucker," William said.

"Well, all right then," Redmon said, and grinning at William, he went to get himself a beer.

THAT AFTERNOON, THEY DECIDED TO TRY THEIR LUCK FARTHER UP. They took Bentley's advice and followed a trail that led north from the aspen meadow they had unsuccessfully hunted that morning. The trail skirted the creek, which narrowed to a trickle through thick stands of wild brush, and then widened again as the trail and creek bottom converged. Tall stands of pine and alder crowded the creek as they walked single file, Bentley in front, followed by Charles and then Leonard, with Redmon bringing up the rear. Bentley had been quiet, with the exception of reminding the gentlemen to keep their safeties on.

Pine needles deadened their footsteps as they climbed. It had stopped sleeting but the sky was overcast again, and beneath the tall trees the air was cold and damp and thick with the scent of rotting humus. They had walked for the better part of two hours and had seen nothing, not even a bird. Redmon had complained steadily of the cold and the weight of his rifle and the lack of game. Leonard limped ahead of him, coughing politely from time to time, and trying to be supportive.

The trail opened up on a wide meadow strewn with boulders. The creek here was wide and slow-moving, and they followed its banks as it rose through the tall grass into a stand of pine, where it narrowed and tumbled over smooth boulders.

A half-mile up they came upon a bear cub crouched low in the water, and before anyone could stop him, Redmon swung the Rigby to his shoulder and fired in the air over the cub's head. The recoil of the elephant gun knocked him flat. The shot echoed through the mountains and across the quiet meadow. The cub rose up on its hind legs, sniffed the air, and ran bawling up a small ridge.

"You idiot," Charles cried.

"Who you calling an idiot, you Pencil Pusher?" Redmon said, climbing with Leonard's help, to his feet.

"The mama can't be far away," Bentley said, his eyes anxiously scanning the ridge. "You better hope that cub wasn't a grizzly."

It was. The sow appeared minutes later, a huge monstrous shape standing upright on the ridge.

"Dear Jesus, what we gonna do now?" Redmon cried.

"Run," Charles said.

They took off at a sprint across the meadow before Bentley could stop them, Charles moving like a world-class athlete, followed by Leonard who limped along at a good pace, and Redmon who made little grunting squeals as he ran. Bentley watched them in disgust. He leaned over and picked up the Rigby, cradling it in his arms as he walked across the field slowly, his eyes fixed on the sow.

Charles was already in the top of the tree. Leonard, afraid of heights, was climbing slowly. Redmon stood at the base of the tree, holding the stock of Leonard's rifle up to him.

"Goddamn it, boy, move it," Redmon shouted at Leonard. Seeing Bentley move up beside him Redmon cried, "Help me, Sport. I can't get my leg up over that first branch."

"Shut up," Bentley hissed, still watching the bear. "You got us into this mess. Get your own ass up that damn tree."

Redmon looked like he was having a stroke. His face turned purple. His eyes bulged and rolled in his head like marbles. He grasped the lower limb with his free hand.

"I think that bear's fixing to charge," Charles said from the top of the tree, trying to be helpful.

"Give me my rifle," Leonard squealed, and the sow swung her head around toward the tree.

"Shit," Bentley said.

Redmon raised the stock of Leonard's rifle like a blind man raising a torch and Leonard clutched the stock with a trembling hand. There was a sudden loud *boom* as the rifle discharged. The bullet sliced through Redmon's hunting boot and creased the side of his left heel before piercing the sole of the boot and burrowing several inches into the frozen ground. For a moment, no one moved. Then Redmon dropped to the ground and began to roll around clutching his heel and bleating like a slaughtered sheep. Leonard, realizing he had just shot his biggest client, leaned over and was sick.

Bentley lifted the Rigby, and sighting carefully, aimed at the sow. She stood watching them from the ridge, the rifle shot still echoing through the canyons. The sow dropped to her feet, and turning, disappeared over the ridge with the cub following closely behind.

Bentley lowered the Rigby and turned around slowly. "Didn't I tell you to put the safety on?" he said to Leonard. "Didn't I tell you over and over to put the damn safety on?" He set the Rigby down and knelt beside Redmon. Blood had begun to seep through the hole in Redmon's boot. Seeing this, Redmon began to scream.

"Shut up, man!" Bentley said. "You want that grizzly coming back?" Redmon clamped his hand over his mouth and watched Bentley, wild-eyed, as Bentley carefully untied the boot and slid it off Redmon's foot. The sock was soaked in blood, but when he took it off Bentley could see Redmon's wound was superficial. "It's just a scratch, man," he said, shaking his head.

"I'll bleed to death," Redmon said, "way up here in the wilderness."

"No, man, you ain't gonna bleed to death over this little scratch." Bentley took a handkerchief out of his pocket, wrapped it tightly around Redmon's heel, and then put the sock back on. He lifted the boot but Redmon shook his head. "You don't wear the boot, you can't walk," Bentley said to him.

"I can't walk anyway," Redmon wailed. "I'm shot!"

Leonard climbed down slowly out of the tree. His face was white. His lips moved soundlessly. Charles climbed down behind him.

"You boys will have to carry him," Bentley said to them, rising.

Charles looked at Leonard. "You carry him," he said. "He's your client."

"GODDAMN," RAMSBOTTOM SAID, WHEN BENTLEY CALLED THAT night to tell him. "Are you telling me one of them actually shot the other?"

"Yeah, but it's only a flesh wound. I bandaged him up, gave him a bottle of whiskey, and the yahoo is sitting in front of the fire singing some song about rednecks and mothers and goat ropers. We'll leave in the morning and be back at the house by mid-afternoon or thereabouts."

"Hell, we don't even need to worry about Nature whittling them down," Ramsbottom said, chuckling. "They seem to be doing a pretty good job of that themselves."

CHAPTER
SEVENTEEN

*B*ACK IN ITHACA, THE WIVES WERE DEALING WITH THEIR own disasters.

Nita spent Wednesday morning housecleaning and at eleven o'clock she stopped and went to shower before the two o'clock closing at the bank. But at one o'clock her cell phone rang and it was Dr. Osborne telling her he had been unable to transfer the funds and they would have to push the closing off until tomorrow.

An ominous feeling settled over Nita. She wasted no time calling Lavonne.

"Goddamn it," Lavonne said, scratching relentlessly at the rash on her arm. "What's his number?" She forced herself to calm down before she called him. If he heard panic in her voice, the whole deal would collapse. She forced herself to believe she had another buyer waiting in the wings, and when she had somehow managed to convince herself of this falsehood, she called Osborne.

"We're not playing around here," she said. "Either you want the car or you don't."

"I don't think you understand how hard it is to move such a large sum of money. I can wire transfer the funds, although they won't guarantee fund availability until Monday, but if you want a certified check, it's going to take a day or two."

"A day or two? You've known about this for over a week."

"Look, it's a short time frame. I'm doing the best I can do."

"How many 1931 Duesenburgs do you know that have gone on the market recently? Call Nita in the morning to confirm you're ready to close. If you don't show up tomorrow at two o'clock with a certified check, we'll sell to the other buyer."

"What other buyer?"

"The other buyer who's ready to close tomorrow at two o'clock," Lavonne lied.

DALLAS PADGETT, THE ASSOCIATE LAVONNE HAD ARRANGED TO handle the closing with Delores Swafford and the Winklers, called Thursday morning to say he needed to postpone the closing until Monday. Lavonne scratched furiously at the hives that now covered her chest and stomach. She tried to keep her voice calm.

"I told you, Dallas, we have to close tomorrow. Friday morning at eleven o'clock. That's the deal. That's what the contract says."

"I'm just not comfortable with it, Lavonne. I've never done an all-cash deal, especially one that involves such a large amount of cash. I mean, Leonard didn't leave me any instructions, which isn't like him. He didn't leave me a memo or an e-mail or a phone message, nothing."

"So what are you saying, Dallas, that I made the whole thing up?"

"No, no of course not, Lavonne."

"You saw the power of attorney. You've got a contract, right? The title is clear, right?"

"Well, yes." She heard the hesitation in his voice. "But normally, there's a bank involved and a closing like this takes weeks to put together. I don't know, it just seems so *hurried*."

Lavonne thought, *There's a reason for that, you pinhead.* She curled her fingers into a fist to keep from scratching and tried to convince herself she had the power to pull this off. She made herself believe she didn't care if the closing went off or not. She told herself she didn't need the money; that her business partnership with Mona Shapiro, that her own financial security, wasn't dependent on this closing. She pretended she had just won the lottery.

"Look, Dallas, you do whatever you have to do." Her voice sounded surprisingly confident and unconcerned. "I'm just telling you the Winklers have been after us for months to sell the house to them, and Sunday night they called with a cash offer we couldn't refuse. It was late or Leonard probably would have called you then. He was in a hurry to get out of town Monday morning or he probably would have sent you a memo. All he could do was sign the power of attorney and then ask me to handle it while he's away."

"I just wish I could talk to Leonard."

"Well you can't, Dallas. He's where he can't be reached by cell phone. That's part of the appeal of the place." She thought, *I don't need this closing.* She thought, *Please, God, let this closing come off as planned.* "You saw the contract. The contract is clear. We have to close by Friday or the deal's off."

"That's another odd thing," Dallas said. "I've never seen a contract with a five-day closing stipulation."

"Look, Dallas, you've obviously made up your mind not to do the closing, which makes it kind of difficult for me because who else am I going to get to close it at such a late date, but if that's your decision, fine. I'll just try to explain to Leonard when he gets back that the Winklers have walked and the huge amount of cash he expected to see in his checking account isn't there because you got cold feet about doing the closing. I'm sure he'll understand."

"Goddamn it. Let me think about it."

"Call me in an hour." She hung up. She drove to the bakery feeling like she was standing in the shadow of Mount St. Helens minutes before it detonated. The day was cloudy and rainy, which matched her emotional state perfectly. Wet leaves littered the pavement. Woodsmoke curled from chimneys and hung like a dense fog over the tree-lined streets and rows of neat houses. She was supposed to be meeting Nita and Eadie to go over last-minute details, but all Lavonne could think about was how terrible it was going to be trying to pay rent on a bookkeeper's salary, assuming, of course, she could even find a job. Assuming it didn't take Rosebud Smoot ten years of litigation to squeeze out of Leonard whatever money she had coming to her.

NITA HAD ASKED JIMMY LEE TO DROP HER OFF BEHIND THE BUILD-ing and let her walk, but he insisted on dropping her off at the front door so she wouldn't get wet. When he insisted on anything, she was powerless against him. It was only because he was an honorable man that their lovemaking hadn't progressed beyond the kissing and cuddling stage, because the truth of the matter was, if he had insisted on moving things to the bed, she would have been powerless against that, too. There were times when she regretted her decision not to sleep with him until after she had confronted Charles. Until after she had decided what to do about her marriage. There were times when she thought about the way his hair curled against the nape of his neck, or the way his arms felt around her, or how sweet his breath was upon her face, times when she thought: *Charles hasn't been faithful to his wedding vows, why should I be faithful—technically at least—to mine?* But she was a good girl. She had been a good girl all her life. She couldn't go and change who she was now, even though her husband was a faithless bastard, even though she was in love with someone else.

Nita looked over her shoulder as she climbed out of the truck. She and Jimmy Lee tried to be careful, but it was dangerous being seen with him. Charles wasn't the kind of man to forgive her for anything, especially Jimmy Lee. He was the kind who would take her children away from her for spite and pure meanness. If the sale of the Deuce didn't go through and she was forced to stay with Charles until she could figure out a way to leave and take the children, her relationship with Jimmy Lee would have to end. She couldn't risk Charles finding out and punishing her through the children.

And it was beginning to look increasingly as if the sale of the Deuce was not going to take place. The closing was supposed to happen this afternoon at two o'clock, but Dr. Osborne hadn't called to confirm this. She had called him twice and left messages and he hadn't returned her call either time. The thought of failure depressed her. The idea that she might have to give up Jimmy Lee thundered through her head, slow and somber as rain on a tin roof.

Eadie and Lavonne were already waiting for her. Nita shook her umbrella out and left it sitting just inside the door.

"Don't tell me," Lavonne said when she saw her face. "Dr. Osborne hasn't called you to confirm the closing."

Nita shook her head and sat down. "He hasn't," she said.

"Damn." Lavonne scratched dejectedly at her stomach.

"You really need to get someone to look at that rash," Eadie said.

"It's just nerves. I always break out in hives when I'm nervous. I always break out in hives when my life is falling apart around me and I'm powerless to stop it."

"You just need a drink." Eadie waved at Mona. "Hey, Mona, do you have any alcohol in here?"

"Alcohol?" Mona was busy rearranging the glass case.

"Scotch, whiskey, tequila?"

"I've got some Mogen David in the back."

"That'll do. Bring it up front."

"No," Lavonne said. "I'll just have a cup of coffee." She rose but Mona shooed her away and said, "I'll bring ya'll a cup. You just go on with your revenge planning."

Lavonne scowled and looked at her hands. Eadie laughed and said, "Isn't this supposed to be a secret? The revenge planning, I mean. I wonder how many people in town know about it now."

"What difference does it make?" Lavonne said. "I'm pretty sure the closing with the Winklers is off. I'm pretty sure the sale of the Duesenburg is off." All Lavonne wanted was what was fair. She was pretty sure she could make her daughters understand the necessity for the divorce without having to tell them about Leonard's cheating ways. She had let them go to Costa Rica with friends for the fall break and she planned on telling them when they got back. She hated having to move so quickly and so furtively but she had no choice. Leonard had left her no choice. The money she would receive from the sale of their house almost equaled the money Leonard had hidden away in his secret bank accounts. She could go after that money, and after Leonard's partnership interest in Boone & Broadwell as well, but Lavonne didn't want to be vindictive. All she wanted was enough to make a fresh start. All she wanted was what was fair. She wanted the proceeds from the sale of their home and she wanted the beach house sold and the proceeds put into a college fund for the girls. Other than that, Lavonne wanted nothing else from Leonard Zibolsky.

"I hate to be the bearer of more bad news," Eadie said cheerfully.

"But Billie Stubbs, the woman who's buying our household goods, can't get a truck until Saturday."

"Good God!" Lavonne said. "There's no way she'll be able to load up two households of furniture and do it before the husbands get back. Their flight gets into Atlanta at four o'clock. That means they'll be home around seven-thirty."

"Yeah, I know it'll be a tight fit, time wise and all," Eadie said.

"Mona," Lavonne shouted, "bring me that Mogen David." She tapped the table with her fingers to keep from scratching. "You seem pretty chipper considering all the bad news," she said to Eadie.

"I'm just more used to dealing with heartache and disappointment than you are."

"This doesn't have anything to do with Trevor being back in town, does it?"

Eadie checked her nails for flaws. "What makes you think that?"

"Lee Ann Bales saw him out at the flower store buying truckloads of calla lillies for Tonya."

"He wasn't buying flowers for Tonya, he was buying them for me," Eadie said quickly.

"Okay," Lavonne said. "I get it."

Mona set a nearly empty bottle of wine and three glasses down on the table and Eadie poured them all a jigger-full. "I'm not taking him back, if that's what you're implying," she said. "I'm just saying I'm not as worried about money as I once was because I know I can get him to be fair. As long as Tonya's out of the picture, I'm not worried. Which is a good thing because it turns out the history museum isn't interested in buying the Thomas Jefferson letter or the Nathan Bedford Forrest medical kit without Trevor's signature on the bill of sale." Eadie looked at Lavonne. "I'll stoop to anything but forgery," she added apologetically.

Lavonne shook her head. "You know, theoretically you're no longer a part of this little scheme. You don't need to cheat your husband to get him to be fair to you, and you won't have photos of him with female impersonators to bargain with anyway."

"Don't be bitter, Lavonne," Nita said.

Lavonne sighed. She pulled her sleeve up and scratched despondently at a red patch near her elbow.

Eadie swirled her wine in her glass. "I talked to Ramsbottom this morning."

"Oh God, don't tell me the husbands are already on a plane headed home."

"Relax." Eadie patted Lavonne's arm. "No wonder you've got hives. Ramsbottom promised me he wouldn't let them leave before Saturday."

Lavonne took a deep breath and sighed. At this time, any good news was welcome.

"Ramsbottom said Leonard had actually managed to shoot Redmon."

"What?" Lavonne set her glass down.

Nita put her hand over her mouth. "Is he dead?"

"No, he said he just winged him, whatever that means. He says they're still up at the camp and won't be headed down until tomorrow morning, so it can't be that bad. The female impersonators are already at the ranch, but Ramsbottom swears he'll keep them all apart until Thursday evening."

"Pray they don't decide to head back early," Lavonne said dejectedly. "Pray the closing with the Winklers goes off and the closing with Dr. Osborne goes off, and Ms. Stubbs shows up with the truck and the money she owes us."

Eadie put her glass down and, leaning forward, gave Lavonne a little shake. "Now listen, we have to be honest here. The plan's pretty complicated, we knew that from the beginning, and we didn't have a lot of time to pull it off, so we all knew the chances of success were slim. You can't beat yourself up over this, Lavonne."

Lavonne pulled her sleeve down. "If this is your idea of a pep talk, it isn't working."

"Maybe Ramsbottom will wind up getting us pictures we can negotiate with, and maybe he won't. Maybe all of our little plans for coming up with ready cash will pan out, and maybe they won't. Whatever happens, I still say—good for us! I'm glad we didn't just sit back and act like victims. I'm glad we did *something*, even if it fails, even if it all goes to hell in a handbasket—"

"Even if we all go to prison?" Lavonne said.

"Even if we all go to prison. It was still worth the risk. Even if we wind up broke and lonely and it takes Rosebud ten years to get the money that's coming to us, I still say we did the right thing by trying to embezzle money and humiliate our cheating husbands."

"This is beginning to sound a lot like the 'As God Is My Witness, I'll Never Be Hungry Again' speech from *Gone with the Wind*."

"I tell you what," Eadie said. "If more women acted like Scarlett O'Hara there wouldn't be near the divorce, poverty, and spousal abuse there is in the world today."

The door opened and a woman dressed in black slacks and a black turtleneck with a green sweater tied around her neck came into the store. "Do you serve anything besides baked goods?" the woman said to Mona, who was standing at the counter. "Do you have a lunch menu?"

"No, ma'am, not yet. But we're opening up a deli real soon that will sell sandwiches and stuff like that."

"Can you tell me what that green vine is growing all over everything?" The woman had the hard clipped accent of a New Englander. Lavonne was guessing Boston or New York.

"Green vine?" Mrs. Shapiro asked, her little nose wrinkling as she tried to understand the woman's accent.

"It looks a little bit like English ivy but it has broader leaves."

"Does it have purple flowers in the spring and summer?" Mrs. Shapiro said, shaking her head. " 'Cause if it does, it's wisteria."

"No," the woman said. "I know wisteria. It doesn't have flowers. It's just green. It seems to cover everything."

"It's called kudzu," Lavonne said.

The woman turned around and said to Lavonne, "Where can I get some?"

Behind the counter Mrs. Shapiro stared at the back of the woman's head, a blank expression on her face. "What do you want it for?" she said.

"I want to take a clipping home." The woman turned her shoulders so she could look at Lavonne and Mona at the same time. "I want to hang a pot of it in my sunroom."

Mona Shapiro blinked. She arched her brows and looked at the woman like she might look at an escaped lunatic from the mental hospital.

"You don't want a clipping of that," Eadie said. "You'd go to bed and wake up the next morning and your whole room would be covered in vines."

"Oh?" the woman said.

"It grows up to a foot a day," Lavonne said.

"It won't grow up north," Eadie said. "And even if it did, you wouldn't want it. It's hard to kill."

Lavonne looked at Eadie and grinned. "It takes over everything that gets in its way," she said.

"It's tenacious as hell," Eadie said.

"Oh really," the woman said, obviously feeling they were making fun of her. "A foot a day," she said flatly, looking at Mona, who slowly nodded her head in agreement, her bad eye rolling toward the wall. "Okay, thanks," the woman said, turning abruptly to leave. The door banged shut behind her. They watched her walk hurriedly down the street, her little green sweater flapping against her back like wings.

"You know she'll take a clipping home with her," Lavonne said, watching her disappear in a crowd of tourists.

"Serves her right if it takes over her whole damn house," Eadie said. "I don't think she believed a word we said."

"Speaking of kudzu," Lavonne said, trying not to think about the fact that Dallas hadn't called her back and it had already been more than an hour since she talked to him. "The Kudzu Ball is Saturday and I'm assuming you're going with me, Eadie, because I sure as hell don't want to go by myself. It starts at seven-thirty, but the queen doesn't arrive until later. If we're lucky, and everything goes according to plans, we'll be able to meet with the husbands and still get to the ball on time."

"I like the way that sounds," Eadie said. "Of course I'm going. I got my dress yesterday down at the Goodwill Thrift Store and I can't wait to wear it. Aren't you supposed to pick somebody to be the Kudzu King?" she said to Lavonne. "Aren't you supposed to have an escort?"

Lavonne jabbed her thumb at Little Moses, who had come out of the back carrying a tray of Texas sheet cake. "I've always wanted to be a king," he said, grinning.

"You're not the king," Lavonne reminded him. "You're just the queen's consort."

Little Moses slid the tray into the display case. "What exactly is a Kudzu Debutante?" He stood up, wiping his fingers on his apron.

"It's a cross between a feminist and a homecoming queen," Eadie said.

"It's a woman who thinks for herself and won't do as she's told," Lavonne said. "Are you going, Nita?"

Nita shook her head. "I don't think so." She'd be lucky if Charles ever let her out of the house again. If she wasn't able to sell the Deuce and come up with some money of her own, she'd be a virtual prisoner in her own house, dependent upon the generosity of a husband who would probably never forgive her for setting him up with female impersonators. It was a dismal thought.

Lavonne reached out and patted her hand. "Don't worry, Nita, everything will work out. No one's blaming you for anything you do. It's your decision, not ours. You'll always be our friend and we'll support you no matter what you decide to do."

"Even if you decide to stay married to that asshole Charles Broadwell, we'll still love and support you," Eadie said. "Even if it all falls apart and we wind up broke and incarcerated, you'll still be our special friend."

"Whether you want to be or not," Lavonne said.

They raised their glasses in a toast.

"Here's to friendship," Nita said, trying to imagine life without Jimmy Lee.

"Here's hoping our husbands get what's coming to them," Eadie said.

"And here's hoping we get what's coming to us," Lavonne said, tapping her glass against the other two.

*B*ENTLEY AND WILLIAM AROSE EARLY THURSDAY MORNING. The snow had melted, showing the scattered remains of camp utensils and packs that littered the ground like a sacked and abandoned city. The charred tower of the fire pit rose from the center of the clearing. From the dim interior of one of the tents, the Nancy-boys watched them with the fish-eyed, hunger-crazed look of plane-crash survivors who've lived three weeks on roots, berries, and beetles. They hadn't slept in two nights. Redmon had moaned all night in his sleep and William snored like a buzz saw, but Bentley was a heavy sleeper and he had awakened feeling cheerful and refreshed.

"Morning, boys," Bentley said.

William got the fire started and fried up some bacon and some moldy biscuits he had brought in his pack, while Bentley cleaned up the camp. He whistled while he worked and spoke cheerfully to William, ignoring the strained silence of the lawyers who had refused to give up their sleeping bags, and settled their raggedy asses around the fire like a gang of lumpy scarecrows. They had been here two days and hadn't shot anything other than Redmon. Bentley assumed their silence was from shame, but in actuality, Charles had admonished both Redmon and Leonard to keep their mouths shut so as not to damage their chances of retribution in a court of law.

They started down the trail around two. The storm had cleared; the sun shone from a blue and cloudless sky. Redmon, anesthetized by whiskey, rolled in his saddle and chattered like a magpie. Leonard, perched atop the perverse Big Mama, found that although she had been loathe to climb the trail, she seemed now, as they headed home, inclined to break into a trot at the slightest pressure of his heels against her flanks. He rode behind the stiff-backed, morose Charles Broadwell, and daydreamed about the new life he would have when the girls were grown and he was no longer saddled with Lavonne.

Bentley rode in front of Charles, feeling the greenhorn's hatred like a cold wind on his back. He kept throwing out little comments meant to wound Charles, tales of other greenhorns who, unable to hunt for food, had perished in the wilderness. Charles didn't say anything but Bentley could imagine each tale piercing the chucklehead like an arrow point. He could feel his words embed themselves deeply in the lawyer's tender flesh. He imagined Broadwell riddled with arrows, like a member of the Seventh Cavalry at the Little Big Horn, flayed and tortured and pierced like a pincushion. This mental picture made him so happy that Bentley put his head back and began to sing "Oh Lord, Won't You Buy Me a Mercedes-Benz." They were almost to the bottom of the trail, where the trees thinned before breaking into a wide meadow in front of the ranch, when Charles, unable to stand it any longer, burst out, "Are you going to sing, or are we going to ride?"

Bentley reined his horse and turned around in the saddle. Redmon, remembering the trip in the Range Rover, fell suddenly quiet. Leonard fought a rising sense of panic while Big Mama pawed the earth with her hoof, throwing her head up wildly.

"Hey man, I'm draggin' these sorry-ass mules," William said, trying to diffuse the situation.

Bentley pushed his hat back on his head. He squinted at Charles, chewing on the inside of his cheek. "You saying you want to run back to the ranch, Kemosabe?"

"Sure," Charles said, gathering his reins. He'd taken dressage in college and he figured he could handle a sway-backed trail pony. "The sooner I get back to the ranch so I can have you fired, the better."

"Sweet Jesus," Redmon said.

"Oh dear God, no," Leonard said.

"Giddyap," Bentley said, touching his heels to his horse's belly.

RAMSBOTTOM AND THE GIRLS WERE SITTING OUT ON THE FRONT porch drinking beer and watching the sun set behind the distant mountains.

"Just look at that sunset," Stella said.

"It's totally awesome," Tawny said.

"I'm bored," Cherry Blyss said.

"When do we get to meet the movie stars?" Morganna said.

Ramsbottom had promised them if they cooperated he would take them next door to meet the Enviro Nazi Movie Director and some of his Hollywood friends. "Don't get your panties in a wad," he said, running his hand up Morganna's stockinged leg. "You do something for me, I'll do something for you."

"I've heard that before," Morganna said, pouting.

"I'll bet you have," Ramsbottom said, turning his head toward the distant fringe of trees. He had heard something.

Stella had heard it, too. "What the hell's that?" she said.

Ramsbottom grabbed the railing and hauled himself rigidly to his feet. "Stampede," he said.

They burst through the trees, coming across the field at a dead run like a cavalry charge in a B western, only this time the charge was being led by a crazy Indian. Bentley stood in his stirrups swinging his hat from side to side and yelling like a madman. To his right William rode standing in his stirrups, the mules loosed from their tethers and coming up on either side of him with their packs flopping like corpses. Directly behind him rode Charles Broadwell, his hat gone, the reins loosed, both hands clutching the saddle horn, his face pale and contorted with fear. The fat one rode to his left; his saddle had slipped to the side and he rode perpendicular to the ground like a trick rider, his head inches from Big Mama's thundering hooves. Redmon brought up the rear. His feet had slipped from the stirrups and he clung to the saddle horn and flopped around like a rag doll, screaming the whole time, his voice echoing down the darkened canyon and spurring his horse to new feats of speed and daring.

They came across the field and veered to the right of the ranch house, Bentley standing in his stirrups and doffing his hat to the girls like Buffalo Bill, William racing up beside him, his hat flattened, his face stretched in a wide grin, enjoying himself. Behind them followed the mules and the other three, still in the saddle by some miracle of God; their horses' hooves pounding the ground and throwing up great clods of earth. It was a thrilling spectacle worthy of any Wild West Show. The girls jumped to their feet and began to cheer and clap their hands.

Ramsbottom limped to the steps and shouted, "Goddamn it, Bentley, you're fired!" He hurried down the steps and around the side of the house, expecting to see the ground littered with the bodies of dead or injured lawyers. He had spent weeks planning his little revenge and now Bentley was going to fuck everything up by killing them before he had had a chance to videotape them with the female impersonators.

Ramsbottom limped around the side of the house, his legs stiff, joints wrenched in pain, and headed toward the stable just in time to see Big Mama clear the stable fence, Leonard's head missing the top rail by maybe three inches. Charles Broadwell's horse pulled up short and Broadwell swung around in front of him, his arms still clutching the horse's neck. He stood there for a moment, slumped against the sweating animal in an awkward sort of embrace, and then he collapsed like he'd been hit between the eyes with the butt end of a pistol. Redmon's horse dropped to a trot and followed Bentley and William into the corral. The horse stopped and waited patiently for Redmon to dismount, but the man refused, clenching the saddle horn and blubbering until William and Bentley came over and lifted him forcibly out of the saddle.

IN THE END, IT WAS THE GIRLS WHO MANAGED TO GET THE GREEN-horns calmed down. Charles Broadwell had walked around in a stupor for nearly an hour after the stampede incident and the fat one had sat on a stool in the stable yard and cried like a baby. After they dragged Redmon from his horse, they plopped him down on a bale of hay and he grinned and chattered like a monkey, asking for tequila and cigarettes.

The girls went into the bunkhouse to freshen up, and came out forty minutes later in full regalia. Ramsbottom had to admit, watching them troop into the stable yard in their high heels, they did look good. Pretty as a speckled pup. Pretty as a scorpion with her tail up, and just as dangerous.

AFTER A HOT BATH AND A HOT MEAL, THE TENDERFOOTS BEGAN TO look better. The fat one's left eye was swollen to a slit and one of his hands had frozen into a clutched position, the result of having hung upside down beneath his horse on that wild ride across the field, but other than that, he looked okay. Charles Broadwell had developed a tic in the side of his face and a slight stutter, but seemed fairly normal otherwise. Redmon seemed to have aged about twenty years and one shoulder set up higher than the other one, which, for a man his age, considering what he had been through, probably wasn't too bad. Overall, they were whittled down some, but still standing.

After dinner they all went out on the front porch to party. The tequila had been flowing freely for two hours and the girls were still looking pretty good, especially under the dim porch lights. Redmon sat between Tawny and Morganna, who had perched precariously on the arms of his chair, and kept leaning forward to press their bosoms to his face. He looked happy as a pig in slop. His eyes rolled from side to side of his big bald head. Drool spilled down the front of his shirt.

Cherry Blyss sat on the porch swing squeezed up beside Charles Broadwell, but it was obvious to everyone that Charles had his sights set on Stella, who was sitting on Leonard's lap and feeding him olives by hand.

Stella was the prettiest girl to ever sit on Leonard's lap. He had lost the contact in his swollen eye, which made it kind of hard to see her clearly up close, but he was enthralled by the length of her legs and her voice, which had a deep, throaty quality, and the playfulness of her teasing. She flattered him every way possible, told him how smart he was, how sexy, how funny, and by the time she finished buttering him up, Leonard was feeling pretty good about himself. The demoralizing memories of the past few days were beginning to fade under Stella's careful guidance. *She's just the kind of girl I will marry once I get rid of Lavonne,* Leonard thought, happily nibbling olives from her rather large hairy fingers. *Someone who appreciates the things I will give her. Someone who appreciates me for who I am.*

Charles stared at Stella like a man in a trance. She was the most desirable girl he had ever seen. But why was she flattering that fat buffoon, Zibolsky, when she could be sitting on *his* lap? Charles knew he was still a damn fine, good-looking man. Someone had told him once he looked a little like Robert Redford.

Cherry Blyss was not accustomed to being ignored. She pouted and poked Charles in the ribs with a sharp finger, and when he did nothing but continue to stare at Stella, she yawned and said, "I'm bored." She stretched her legs out in front of her but Charles didn't look. "I think I'll go sit with him," she said, rising and walking over to plop herself down on Redmon's lap.

"Wa-wa-whatever," Charles said, embarrassed by his stutter. He hadn't stuttered since kindergarten, since his mother sent him away to a school in Boca Raton that specialized in stutterers, sufferers of Tourettes syndrome, and idiot savants.

"Hey," he said to Stella, patting his lap with both hands. "Why don't you c-c-come over here and sit?"

"What's the matter, honey?" Stella said. "Cherry Blyss not good enough for you?"

"I'm picky," Charles said. "I like the c-c-cream of the c-c-crop."

Stella couldn't help but be flattered by this. She stroked her hair and crossed her long legs dramatically.

Charles stood up. "C-c-come on," he said to her. "Let's take a walk."

She stood up and went down the steps with Charles, arm in arm, before Leonard could think to say anything. "Hey," he said, lifting his frozen hand like a lobster lifts his claw. "What about me?"

"You take Ch-Ch-Cherry Blyss," Charles said over his shoulder.

Rage ricocheted through Leonard like a bottle rocket. All his life he had been taking second best. All his life boys like Charles Broadwell had been taking the prize away from him. All his life he had sat back and let it happen. "No," he shouted, standing up suddenly.

Charles and Stella turned around in surprise. "What did you s-s-say?"

"I said no!" Leonard bellowed, coming down the steps like a madman. He grabbed Stella's arm with his good hand and pulled her behind him. Charles's face twitched and spasmed, and he reached out to take Stella back, but before he could touch her, Leonard had clubbed him in the head with his lobster claw hand. Charles stood for a moment, stunned, staring into his squinty-eyed partner's enraged face, and then he put both hands around Leonard's throat, and they went down in a pile of swinging fists and kicking feet.

Ramsbottom videotaped them rolling around in a big pile of steaming horse shit and pummeling each other, and then he motioned for Bentley and William to break it up. He convinced Stella to take both of them back to the ranch house for a friendly little game of strip poker, and it was after that that things got interesting and Ramsbottom managed to snap some photos and film some of his best footage. He was amazed at how long it took the lawyers to figure out that the girls weren't girls, and he really wasn't sure they ever did, because Leonard passed out sometime around eleven o'clock, and Redmon fell asleep soon after, facedown in a plate of chicken pie. Charles had more stamina; he lasted until nearly twelve-thirty.

Ramsbottom waited until he had stumbled off to bed and then he downloaded the photographs and e-mailed them to Eadie. He checked the video, sealed the mini DV in a package, and then handed it to Bentley who had volunteered to drive it into Push Hard to the overnight courier office.

*T*HE FLIGHT HOME TO ITHACA WAS CONSIDERABLY MORE SUB-
dued than the flight to Push Hard had been. Charles sat by himself near the front of the plane, and Leonard and Redmon sat near the
back. Redmon had his foot bandaged and stretched out in the aisle and
Leonard spent a good deal of time adjusting Redmon's blanket, prop-
ping his leg on a stack of pillows, making sure the stewardesses were
prompt and attentive, and in general, trying in every way possible to assure Redmon the shooting had been accidental and very regrettable,
and that he hoped their business relationship would continue as before.

"Prop it a little higher, Sport," Redmon said, as Leonard attempted
to adjust the injured limb, "and get me another one of those Percocets
out of my pocket."

Charles put his head back and gazed wearily at the fog rolling past
the window. He felt feverish, his stomach was still queasy, and he had
not been able to keep anything down in twenty-four hours. Not since
waking Friday afternoon to find Stella and the other girls gone. Not
since his brawl with Ramsbottom where he demanded a partial refund
for the dismal hunting trip and the man, perhaps too readily, complied,
seemed even to be trying to keep himself from chuckling as he wrote
out the check.

The party with the girls was a blurry memory. He could remember
the fistfight with Leonard over Stella, could remember snatches of the

strip poker game, could remember Leonard passing out, and Redmon, could remember Stella rising to take his hand. But after that it got smeared and indistinct like images seen through a foggy window, strange figures, flickering lights, snatches of memory—or was it a dream? A dream of something . . . unpleasant. Charles shuddered and shook his head.

He couldn't even remember if he had slept with Stella. Often they didn't sleep with the girls Ramsbottom provided, but sometimes they did. The point was, they had paid for the girls' company and they had not received what they paid for—even Ramsbottom realized that or he would not have been so eager to refund their money.

In any case, the tradition begun by his father was over; Charles had made up his mind this would be his last trip to the Ah! Wilderness Ranch. It had gone on far longer than it should have, and he was not even certain why. His trips in the future would be with his family, he decided. Maybe he would take them skiing at Christmas. Maybe he would take Nita to Europe. It had been a bad year for the firm financially, billable hours were down considerably and Leonard had managed to lose the Moretti case, which should have been a slam dunk, but Charles could come up with the money if he tried. He could take out a second mortage on the house, or hell, even sell the Duesenberg. He'd been shocked to find out how much the car was worth, and the truth of the matter was, it meant little to him outside of the obvious symbolic value it held; the fact he had defied his father in order to keep it, but really, who was around now to see his defiance? He never drove the car, he worried incessantly that someone would steal it or sue him for possession—why not sell it and be done forever with that part of his life?

He found the idea of unloading the Duesenberg oddly comforting. He found the idea of spending more time with his family strangely compelling. The children were old enough, now, not to be annoying in public and Nita, well she was lovely and supportive in an all-American-girl-next-door kind of way. If he could get her the counseling she needed to snap out of her recent surliness, if he could medicate the children so they were quiet and focused and better able to carry on conversations in a sedate and adult manner, this family renewal policy might work. Hell, Dick Melton had put his wife and children on Ritalin and claimed it had made all the difference in family harmony.

Charles put his head back and dozed. He awoke thirty minutes later with a start, his chest pounding and sweat breaking out on his brow and the palms of his hands. He had dreamed again that disturbing dream of long legs and garter belts and frilly underwear and hidden somewhere in that frilly feminine underwear something . . . wrong. Something that shouldn't be there.

No, no, it isn't a memory, he told himself, sitting forward and wiping his mouth on his handkerchief. *It's a dream, a nightmare, something Freudian and bizarre and to be expected from a man in the grips of a fever.*

In the back of the plane Redmon's leg rolled off the stack of pillows and landed with a loud *thump* on the floor of the plane. He cursed Leonard loudly and profusely and it took two stewardesses and a steward to get him calmed down.

THE SOMBER FEELING OF WAKING IN THE GRIPS OF A NIGHTMARE persisted as they landed in Atlanta and discovered there was no one there to meet them. They had driven up with Trevor earlier in the week and with him gone, Charles had had no choice but to call Nita to pick them up. He had called from the Push Hard airport and the Bozeman airport and had not been able to reach her either time, but he had left clear and concise messages when and where she was to pick them up at Hartsfield. He tried her on her cell phone thinking she might be caught in traffic, but there was no answer. Redmon had himself wheeled to the curb in a wheelchair, and without a word to either Charles or Leonard, he took a cab. They waited thirty minutes and then went to the desk to rent a car.

They were quiet on the trip to Ithaca, Charles worrying about his wife's erratic behavior and Leonard wondering how he was going to be able to keep his income up now that he had lost Redmon as a client.

Traffic was light and they made good time, speeding along the expressway past scattered herds of grazing cattle, and cornfields, and soybean fields, and a barn that read *See Rock City* in big black letters across its roof. Darkness descended gradually, rolling in like ominous clouds of billowing smoke.

IT WAS DARK BY THE TIME THEY REACHED ITHACA. THEY HAD DEcided not to stop for dinner and they were both hungry and tired and eager for a hot shower. Charles swung into the subdivision and slowed as he reached their block.

Something was wrong. Charles knew it instantly as he pulled into their street. Both houses were dark and there was a sign in Leonard's front yard that read *Another Sale by Delores Swafford—Your Friendly Christian Real Estate Broker.*

"What the hell?" Leonard said, as they drove slowly past his house and pulled into Charles's driveway. Leonard didn't even wait for the car to stop before he opened the door, rolled out, and limped at a fast clip across the lawn toward his front door.

Charles stood in his driveway feeling like he was caught in some bizarre parallel universe; this *looked* like his house, but it was not his house, something was wrong, something was terribly wrong. Nita's car was not in the garage. Where was his wife? Where were his children? He wondered suddenly if there had been some kind of an emergency and he picked up his cell phone to call his mother before remembering that she was in the Bahamas with Myra Redmon.

Leonard stood at his front door trying unsuccessfully to open it with his key. He gave up finally and went around to the garage but that door wouldn't open either, nor would the French doors in the back. He peered through the glass but the house was dark and seemed suddenly cavernous. He called Lavonne on her cell phone. She picked up after the third ring.

"I can't get in the house," Leonard shouted. "There's something wrong with my key."

"Meet me at the Pink House Restaurant at eight. Bring Charles," she said.

"I think we've been robbed!" he screamed into the phone, but she had already hung up. He tried to call her again but the line went instantly to voice mail.

✤   ✤   ✤

CHARLES OPENED THE KITCHEN DOOR AND STEPPED INSIDE, NOTing that his footsteps sounded odd, that they had a strange ringing quality in the darkened house. He switched on the light. Everything was as it should be. Dishes gleamed in the glass cabinets, the appliances sparkled, the floor shone. But there was an oppressive quality to the stillness of the house, a lingering sense that something was wrong. Behind him he could hear Leonard stumbling through the garage.

Leonard stepped into the house and said, "Oh my God, I've been robbed." He was out of breath and his face was the color of bone. "Lavonne says I'm to meet her at the Pink House Restaurant and bring you. I need to call the police."

For some reason he didn't yet understand, Charles said, "No, wait." They went through the house, room after room, and everything was as it should be, neat and orderly. But coming back into the kitchen, he saw a note lying on the breakfast bar addressed to him. It was in Nita's handwriting. *The children are with my parents at the beach. Meet me at the Pink House Restaurant at 8:00. Bring Leonard.*

"What does this mean?" Leonard shouted, looking wildly at his partner. "What the hell does this all mean?"

Standing in the kitchen door, Charles suddenly realized what it meant.

He ran through the back door and the screened porch, and down the deck steps with Leonard limping behind him like an old stiff-legged dog. "I can't get into my house," Leonard kept shouting. "What in the hell's going on?"

Leonard followed him through the yard to the back gate, down a garden path to a small garage at the rear of the property. His knee ached with each step and his lungs felt like he had swallowed a dagger that pierced and sliced his chest with every breath. He stumbled into the garage just as Charles flipped on the light.

Charles stood there looking at the empty garage. There was a sound in his head like angry bees. Cobwebs hung in the corners of the room like tattered lace. Looking at them, Charles felt suddenly bereft, lonely.

"What does this mean?" Leonard cried, overwhelmed by the panic in his own voice and the thought that everything he had ever worked for, everything he had ever hoped for was on the verge of ruin and collapse. He had survived four days in the wilderness with a morose partner, an ungrateful client, a grizzly bear, a bad-tempered felon, and a wild Sioux Indian only to return and find that the real danger to his health and sanity lay here in the civilized world he called home.

Charles's face had hardened. He looked like a man on the edge of something dangerous and unpredictable. His eyes glittered. His arms hung down from his shoulders like sledgehammers.

"I can't get into my house." Leonard's swollen eye throbbed and pierced his skull like a hot poker. "I can't get into my house and my wife wants you and me to meet her at eight o'clock at the Pink House Restaurant. Tell me what's happening here, buddy. Tell me what I'm supposed to do." His teeth chattered. His heart pounded his chest wall like a battering ram. "Tell me I'm having a nightmare and all I have to do is wake up and everything will be back the way it was."

A muscle moved in the side of Charles's face. The fingers of one hand twitched uncontrollably. "I knew your wife was trouble," he said, and violently switched off the light. Leonard stood for a moment allowing his good eye to adjust to the darkness, and then, without a word, he followed his partner out into the chilly night.

WHEN CHARLES AND LEONARD ARRIVED AT THE PINK HOUSE THEY were ushered into a private room at the back of the restaurant. Lavonne, Nita, Eadie, and Trevor were already there, seated around a large table with the women on one side and Trevor on the other. There were two empty Corona bottles on the table in front of him. He looked up at the other men as they came through the door, and chuckled.

"What in the hell is going on?" Charles said.

"Sit down, Charles," Lavonne said. "And you, too, Leonard."

The women were drinking Tequila sunrises. The waitress came in to get their drink orders but Charles shook his head and Leonard said, "Do you have any Maalox?" The waitress was nineteen years old and she had never heard of Maalox. "Just bring me some water." He leaned across the table and said to Lavonne, "My key won't fit in the lock. There's a 'Sold' sign in front of my house. I want to know what's going on. I want to know right now."

Lavonne waited until the waitress had gone out and then she leaned across the table and said, "I think you should calm down, Leonard, and you, too, Charles. We're going to discuss this like civilized adults and if you two don't want it getting all over town, I'd suggest you keep your voices down."

"Goddamn it, Lavonne, don't you tell me to calm down!" Charles slammed his hand against the table. He pointed a long finger at her. "I know you're behind this. You and *her*." He jabbed his finger at Eadie and Trevor said, "Get your finger out of my wife's face."

Eadie stared at Trevor. "Mind your own damn business," she said. "I can handle this myself."

Charles took a deep breath. His mouth drooped at one corner. "Where's my c-car?" he said, looking at Lavonne. "I want my car. I want my Duesenberg."

Trevor raised one eyebrow. "Duesenberg?" he said.

"That's *my* car." Charles thumped his chest. "That's my car and I want it back. I know you two are behind this," he pointed again at Lavonne but not Eadie. They sat patiently waiting for him to finish venting. "I know you took advantage of Nita and talked her into doing something she didn't want to do."

"The only one who took advantage of Nita is you," Eadie said.

"You shut up!" Charles said. "That's none of your business!"

Trevor swiveled around in his chair and looked at him steadily and there was in his expression a warning that could not be ignored. Charles made up his mind to leave Eadie Boone out of it from this point forward.

"I want my car! That car belonged to my daddy and I want it back. It's worth a lot of money and if you think—"

"We sold the car, Charles," Lavonne said. "The car is gone. Deal with it."

The waitress came into the room carrying Leonard's glass of water. "Can I get ya'll anything right now?" she asked cheerfully and Lavonne said, "No. We'll order later. Check back in about fifteen minutes."

The girl seemed confused. "Okay?" she said and went out, closing the door softly behind her.

Charles stared at his wife, dumbfounded. "Nita, is this true?"

Nita looked at her hands.

He leaned across the table and shouted at Lavonne, "You took advantage of my wife while I was out of town and you talked her into doing something she wouldn't normally have done. My wife was a good simple girl until she started hanging out with the two of you, and don't think I don't know you put her up to this. Don't think I don't know she never would have come up with this on her own. I won't have it. I simply will not have it. I'll sue both of you. I'll sue you for everything you've—"

"Shut up, Charles," Nita said.

Charles stopped shouting. His looked at his wife. His jaw bunched and sagged around the column of his throat like an old sock. "Honey?" he said.

"The sooner you be quiet the sooner we can get through this mess and be on our way," Nita said.

"Why is there a 'Sold' sign in my front yard?" Leonard, who had been sitting stunned and bloated as a toad, stirred and pointed at Lavonne and Eadie. "Why are you dressed like that?" he croaked. Eadie was wearing a purple taffeta prom dress she had picked up down at the Goodwill Store. Lavonne was wearing a strapless, pastel pink, satin bridesmaid dress with a big bow that rode just above her ass. Mona Shapiro had lent her a fur stole that was supposed to be fox, but with its sharp nose and beady little black eyes, bore an uncanny resemblance to a giant wharf rat. Both debutantes were wearing tennis shoes and kudzu vines in their hair.

"We're dressed like this because we're going to the Kudzu Ball."

"No you're not! No you're not!" He glared at his wife with his good eye and said, "I made that clear two weeks ago. You are not going to the Kudzu Ball."

Lavonne leaned over and pulled a scrapbook out of her briefcase. She set it on the table and pushed it toward Leonard. "You're through giving me orders," she said.

Charles stared at Nita like he was trying to figure out who in the hell she was. "Look, honey," he said, stretching out his hand, but she shook her head and said, "Look at the scrapbook."

They sat there looking stupidly at the book and then Trevor pulled it toward him and opened it up. He flipped through the pages slowly and when he was finished he shoved it at Charles and Leonard. "Is this what we've come to?" he said to Eadie. He looked angry now, not at all amused. "Blackmail? Could you possibly have sunk this low, Eadie?"

"Don't you lecture me on morality," Eadie said. "It's only because you came back early that you're not in those pictures, but don't think I don't know what happened in years past. Don't think I don't know all about your little escapades at the Ah! Wilderness Game Ranch."

Trevor frowned. "What in the hell are you talking about?" he said.

"What's going on?" Leonard said, looking around wildly. "For the love of God, what's going on?"

Lavonne told him. She told him about the smell in his hunting locker, and the condoms in Charles's hunting jacket, and the conversations with Ramsbottom about the girls he had provided in past years. She told him how she had used the power of attorney to sell the house rather than close on Mona Shapiro's bakery, and how Nita had sold the Duesenberg and how she and Eadie had sold all the household goods they could get their hands on. She told him that Rosebud Smoot had a list of additional assets, including hidden assets (she looked at Leonard when she said this), with instructions to begin divorce proceedings immediately. She told them that she hoped they would agree not to prosecute over the items already disposed of, and to settle fairly with any other assets. She told them at this time she and Eadie had no intention of going after partnership assets, nor had they any intention of making the scrapbook photos public, but all that could change, of course, depending on how the husbands conducted themselves.

When she finished talking, no one said anything. Leonard huddled over the photos, slowly turning the pages. Charles looked like he had swallowed battery acid. Trevor put his head back and laughed.

Eadie finished her drink. "I'm glad you think this is funny."

Trevor slapped the table with one hand.

"You wouldn't think it was so funny if we had photos of you."

"You girls are something else," Trevor said finally, shaking his head and raising his Corona in a mock toast. "Hell, I should quit trying to write legal thrillers and write about you Kudzu Debutantes instead."

Charles grabbed the edge of the table with both hands and leaned toward Nita. "I'm confused," he said. "Are you telling me you're going to divorce me, or not? I hear Lavonne saying *we* but I don't know if she means *you*."

They all looked at Nita. This was the moment she had been dreading for weeks. The moment when she could no longer lie to herself about what it was she needed to make herself happy. The moment when she had to admit that being a good girl was not all it was cracked up to be, when she had to face the guilt of a failed marriage and the fear and uncertainty of an unknown future. It helped that she was in love with Jimmy Lee Motes. It helped that she had a bank account with six hundred fifty thousand dollars in it.

"I'm leaving you, Charles," she said finally.

Charles took the scrapbook from Leonard and slid it across the table. "Those pictures won't prove anything," he said to Lavonne. "Photos can be digitally altered these days and that's what we'll claim you did."

Lavonne opened her laptop and slid it to the middle of the table so they could all see the screen clearly. She took a DVD out of her purse and slid it into the computer. They watched Leonard and Charles rolling around in horseshit while they pummeled each other over Stella; watched some footage of the strip poker game; watched Leonard strap on a bra and a pair of high-heeled shoes and do his imitation of Cher singing "Do You Believe in Life After Love." They watched while Stella pulled an obviously intoxicated Charles to his feet so forcefully that Stella's wig slipped to one side and her face, pushed close to the camera in embarrassment, showed clear signs of razor burn and five o'clock shadow.

"Oh my God, is that a *man*?" Leonard said.

Charles slammed the laptop closed. It was all becoming clear to him now, the hazy images of him and Stella climbing the stairs, the disturbing dream of frilly underpants and something unpleasant hidden there. His stomach spasmed. Bile rose in his throat. He put his hand over his mouth.

Lavonne slid the laptop back in its case, and then leaned forward and folded her hands on the table. Leonard, who at the moment was having an out-of-body experience, who in the shock and horror of realizing he had French-kissed another man had popped out of the top of his head and was floating somewhere near the ceiling, noticed, looking down at his wife in a distant and detached way, that Lavonne had lost weight. She looked good.

"Here's the deal," Lavonne said patiently. "You can claim those photos have been digitally altered, you can even claim the videos were digitally altered, but what you have to ask yourself is this: Do you really want anyone in this small loose-lipped town to actually *see* those photos or that video?" Lavonne looked from one to the other. "No, I didn't think so," she said. "We're not trying to be unreasonable here. The proceeds I got from the sale of the house roughly equal what you've got stashed in your secret accounts, Leonard, and the proceeds from the sale of the Duesenberg mean that Nita doesn't want alimony from you, Charles, or her interest in your home, only child support and insurance and educational costs for the kids. We're trying to be fair here. We're trying to be reasonable." She looked at Trevor and said, "Of course, you've always been fair and reasonable and we expect you to continue to be so even though we don't have any blackmail photos of you."

"Naturally," Trevor said, lifting his Corona and looking steadily at Eadie.

"If you won't contest the divorce, if you won't try to come back against us legally for selling the house and the car, then those photos get locked up in a safe-deposit box where no one will see them. And in addition to legal amnesty for us, I also want legal amnesty for anyone who assisted us; Ramsbottom, Dallas Padgett, Mona Shapiro. You get the picture."

"Nita, you can't be serious about all this," Charles said, trying to take her hand, but she moved it away. "You can't tell me you're going to leave your husband and your children . . ."

"I'm not leaving my children," Nita said coldly. "That's part of the deal. I get sole custody, although I'm willing to grant you visitation rights as long as you behave yourself and don't try and punish me through the kids. As long as you're nice to the kids and pay their child support, you're welcome to see them as much as you like."

The pedestal he had built for Nita shattered and broke into a million pieces. The illusion of his wife as a good, simple girl, the dream he had carried with him all these years evaporated and crumbled like chalk. Compared to his treacherous wife, his mother was starting to look like Mother Teresa.

"And there's something else you need to know," Nita said, in a strong clear voice. "I'm in love with someone else. Someone who treats me nice and makes me happy. Someone who's nice to the kids and makes me feel like my life has meaning and purpose."

Lavonne and Eadie exchanged glances. Eadie grinned. "I know who it is," she said in a singsong voice.

"It's Jimmy Lee Motes," Nita said, looking Charles squarely in the eye. "He's the carpenter you hired to fix the pool house and I love him and he loves me and I haven't slept with him yet but I plan to. I thought you should know."

"*What?*" Charles shouted.

"We're going to need to extend that amnesty to cover Jimmy Lee, too," Lavonne said.

"You sly dog," Eadie said, grinning at Nita.

"I hope you're not getting ready to tell me you've fallen in love with that goddamned personal trainer," Trevor said to Eadie. "Because in case you haven't heard, I've given up Tonya."

"Well aren't you special," Eadie said. "Aren't you the most special dirty cheating swamp rat there is."

He grinned at her. "You keep sweet-talking me like that, I might think you still care," he said.

"Fuck you," Eadie said.

"Where am I supposed to live?" a bewildered Leonard asked Lavonne. "What am I supposed to do about furniture and stuff like that?"

"I kept some of your stuff and put it in storage. You're welcome to pick it up whenever you like. I've rented a house for me and the girls and once my business takes off, I'll probably buy something smaller."

"What business?" Leonard said.

"If you want to sell the Boone house that's fine with me, honey," Trevor said to Eadie. "I don't care where we live. I don't care where we live as long as we're together. You know," he reminded Eadie, "I've left Tonya for good."

"You already said that," Eadie said, and threw her empty glass at Trevor's head. He ducked and it shattered against the wall. "You think just because you're not sleeping with your secretary anymore I should take you back? What about all those other women?"

"What other women?" Trevor said.

Charles had had time to collect himself. "If you think I'm going to let you humiliate me in this town by running off with a pool house carpenter, you better think again," he said grimly.

"No, *you* better think again," Nita said, standing up so violently her chair banged the wall. "You better think about what's more humiliating: me running off with a carpenter, or you showing up in an X-rated movie with a man wearing a garter belt."

Charles had a sudden clear picture of the way his life was going to be from here on out.

The waitress came back into the room to take their order. She smiled and said, "The special tonight is roast duck with horseradish sauce."

"I might as well just go ahead and kill myself," Charles said.

"Oh it ain't that bad," the waitress said. "It's a little on the greasy side but you get used to it after awhile."

"I think we'll skip dinner tonight," Lavonne said, closing up the scrapbook and gathering her purse. "Go ahead and tally the bill and give it to that gentleman," she said, pointing at the bewildered Leonard. She stood up and Eadie rose with her. "Now gentlemen, if you'll excuse us, we have a ball to attend."

NITA DIDN'T WASTE ANY TIME. AFTER THE MEETING AT THE PINK House Restaurant she had Lavonne drop her off at her car and she drove as fast as she could to Jimmy Lee's house. He was sitting in his little den watching TV. The lights were on and the room looked cozy and neat. She stood at the door feeling her heart pound her chest like a jackhammer, and when he didn't get up from his chair, she knocked again. He heard her this time, and when he saw it was her, he jumped up and crossed the room with a few long strides.

He swung the door open and pulled her inside. "Hey, baby," he said, taking her in his arms. His touch was like an electrical current, and she understood suddenly and completely the concept of magnetic force and attraction. They stood for a while, wrapped in each other's arms, his chin resting on top of her head. "How'd it go?" he asked her, finally.

She told him, briefly, about the meeting at the Pink House. She had promised him that after the meeting, after she told Charles the truth, things would be different between them, that all the barricades that stood in the way of them taking their relationship to the next level, would be down. But here she was and they were suddenly shy with each other.

"I just got home from the Kudzu Festival and I haven't had a chance to shower yet," he said.

"How'd it go?"

"I took fourth place in the recliner race but came in third place in the Betty Cracker Cook-Off with my Heart Thumper Shake." His chest was hard and flat beneath his Austin City Limits T-shirt.

She laughed and he leaned over and kissed her, long and slow. "I thought for sure you'd win the breakfast category," she said, sliding her hands into his back pockets.

He grinned, looking down at her with his eyes half-closed and his head tilted slightly. "First prize went to White Trash Breakfast, a one-skillet meal of eggs, Spam, butter, and Velveeta."

"Oh my God," she said.

"Second prize went to Uncle Homer's Deep Fried Baloney Sandwich with Velveeta."

"People don't actually have to *eat* their recipes, do they?"

His arms tightened around her. "Well now, honey, of course they do. I'm sorry you missed it. Don't worry, though. I'm thinking of making White Trash Breakfast tomorrow morning. If you stay, that is."

"Well, I just might stay in spite of breakfast," she said and he kissed her again and this time she could feel the kiss all the way down into the soles of her feet. He kissed her neck and said, "I really need to take a shower." He picked her up in his arms and then set her down again. "I'll be right back," he said. "Don't go anywhere."

He switched the TV off and went over to a tall bookcase and pushed a button on the CD player. "Make yourself at home," he said, watching her from the doorway.

"Okay," she said. The feeling of having taken hold of a live wire persisted. Her body vibrated. Her pulse raced. *This is how I should have felt on my wedding night,* she thought.

She stood in the middle of his den listening to Jerry Jeff Walker sing about love and loneliness and sangria wine. She heard a door close, and the distant sound of water running. She walked across the wide hallway into his bedroom. His boots were on the floor. A *Commander Cody and His Lost Planet Airmen* poster hung on the wall above his bed. He had the long windows opened a crack and a cool breeze blew through the room, chilling her as she undressed. She could see the hooks in the ceiling where they used to hang the quilting frames. A thick carpet covered most of the pine-planked floor. His bed was unmade and she climbed in, making a nest of the blankets to warm herself. A small fireplace stood on the opposite wall, with signs of a recent fire. *I'd like a fire right now,* she thought. *A fire would be just about perfect.*

The bathroom door opened and she heard him padding down the hallway and into the den. The high ceilings of the house echoed his footsteps. "I don't want to rush you," she heard him say. Then, silence. "Nita!" he shouted, and she heard him go to the side door and open it.

"I'm in here," she called, snuggling down in her warm nest, and there he was, standing in the doorway in a pair of gray sweatpants and a T-shirt. His hair was loose and damp against his shoulders.

"Will you make me a fire?" she said.

He walked around the bed slowly, wrapping his arm around the tall bedpost and looking down at her like he couldn't believe she was really here. "Are you cold?" he said.

"Yes. But don't close the window. I like the smell of wet leaves. I like the smell of wet leaves and wood smoke."

He went out and came back in carrying a bucket of wood. She

watched him lay the fire, watched the kindling take light. He pulled his shirt over his head. In the living room, Jerry Jeff sang about London and English girls and homesickness. Jimmy Lee came back to the bed, untying the string of his sweatpants. The fire crackled merrily behind him.

"Why are you looking at me like that?" she teased, opening the blankets for him.

"I think I've died and gone to heaven," he said, reaching for her.

He got up later and went into the kitchen to get a beer and Nita rolled over on her side so she could watch him. She liked the way he could walk through the house naked, like it was the most natural thing in the world. He stood in the middle of the bedroom and said, "Whoee. Where'd you learn to do those things?"

"I read a lot," she said, pulling the sheet up to cover her mouth.

He grinned. She was every man's dream. The kind of girl who could do the things they had just done and still blush about it.

She sat up on her elbow and pushed her hair out of her face. "What time is it?"

"Nine-thirty. Why?"

"I promised Lavonne and Eadie I'd make it to the Kudzu Ball."

He offered her the beer and she took a swig, and passed it back.

Nita looked up into his handsome face and thought about how those romance novels and sex manuals had the female orgasm all wrong, how they didn't come close to describing it as it really was. It was birth and death and pleasure and pain all rolled into one big bang experience. It was the Creator's little joke on mankind. Nita figured there wasn't a whole lot she could be certain about these days; she wasn't certain how her children were going to take the news of the divorce, or where they were going to live, or whether Charles would agree to her terms, and let her live in peace. She wasn't even certain how her relationship with Jimmy Lee would work out, given the thirteen-year age difference and the fact she had responsibilities he didn't have, and the fact that love affairs have a tendency to get complicated over time.

The only thing Nita was sure about was that, for the first time in a long time, she had a chance at happiness, and she was going to take that chance. She had a chance at happiness and she would never again have to sit at a Passion Party and listen to all those little Jeza-bells going off around her while her little bell stayed still and silent.

In the future she'd be doing plenty of bell-ringing herself.

LAVONNE AND EADIE MET LITTLE MOSES AT THE WAFFLE HOUSE parking lot at eight forty-five. Tradition called for the Kudzu Queen to arrive at the Kudzu Ball in the back of the Kudzu Kruiser. The Kruiser was the brainchild of Clayton Suttles. At the beginning of every summer Clayton covered his Bonneville convertible with chicken wire and parked it in his field at the edge of a good stand of kudzu. The day of the ball, Clayton cut the car loose and drove it into town. With its thick covering of greenery, the car was a strange and wonderful sight. It looked like a moving shrubbery. It looked like a giant Chia pet on wheels. The only mishap had occurred last year when Clayton forgot to mark where he'd parked the Bonneville and they'd had to go in there with a metal detector to find it.

Lavonne and Eadie and Little Moses stood out in the parking lot waiting for Clayton to arrive in the Kudzu Kruiser. Little Moses was barefoot and wearing the same blue tux he had worn to cater the firm's party. Lavonne had insisted it would be perfect for the ball.

"Aren't your feet cold?" she asked Little Moses.

He was wearing a baseball cap that read *Why Ration Passion?* over his dreadlocks. "Naw," he said. "I'm okay."

Eadie adjusted Lavonne's wharf-rat stole around her shoulders. "Are you nervous?" she asked Lavonne.

"No," Lavonne said. "Should I be?"

Eadie shrugged and took a pair of elbow-length gloves out of her purse. "I heard at the last Kudzu Ball the queen got so drunk she fell off the stage and broke her leg in two places."

"Damn," Lavonne said.

"She just sat there laughing and feeling no pain. They figured she must have drunk nearly a gallon of Kudzu Koolaid."

"Well, that explains it," Lavonne said.

The recipe for Kudzu Koolaid was a closely guarded secret passed down from one master of ceremony to the next. It was rumored to be laced with all kinds of potent ingredients, from cough syrup to ground-up sleeping pills, but Eadie was pretty sure it contained a goodly amount of Curtis Peet's homebrewed corn whiskey. Curtis made it in the back of his greenhouse from an old family recipe passed down for generations. It went by the innocuous name of Old Bull and was said to kill head lice and take the stains out of concrete. "Just make sure you don't drink too much of the Koolaid," Eadie warned her, "and you'll be okay."

"Words to live by," Lavonne said. She smoothed the front of her pink satin dress. "Okay, tell me again what to expect during this throw down." It had been years since Lavonne did any public speaking and she was nervous she might have to make a speech after her crowning. Eadie had called a couple of the girls she'd worked with down at the women's shelter to get the scoop on what to expect.

"It's real simple," Eadie said. "Clayton will pick us up here and drive us over to the Wal-Mart, where he'll let us out in front of the tent. That's the signal for the band to start playing "Kudzu Limbo," which is the theme song, and the party's on, baby."

"So when does the crowning occur?"

"The crowning occurs toward the end of the evening after every-body's gotten liquored up enough to throw their inhibitions to the wind," Eadie said. "The debutantes go up on stage for the promenade toward the end of the evening, right before you're crowned. Wendell decides when he'll call everybody up." Wendell Stamps was this year's master of ceremony. Wendell's daddy was a dentist and he had sent Wendell to one of the finest boarding schools in Virginia. Despite Wendell's prestigious liberal arts education, he had come back to Ithaca to raise his family. This was his second tour as master of ceremony. "What name are you using?" Eadie asked her.

Somewhere along the line it had become tradition for the Kudzu Debutantes and their escorts to use false names. Over the years, these false names had become an art form in themselves.

"I'm going as Ima Badass," Lavonne said. "And Little Moses is Bushrod daToilet."

"I'm Aneeda Mann," Eadie said, sticking out her hand. "Glad to meet you, Ima."

"Likewise, I'm sure." Lavonne shook her hand. "How about Nita?"

"You don't really think those two are going to climb out of bed long enough to attend the Kudzu Ball, do you?" Eadie said, snorting through her nose.

"She better," Lavonne said. "She's part of my damn Kudzu Kourt."

"I wouldn't hold my breath," Eadie said.

"What names are she and Jimmy Lee using?"

"Blanche and Cooter Benclipped."

"That figures," Lavonne said.

THE BALL WAS SCHEDULED TO BEGIN AT EIGHT O'CLOCK, BUT WHEN Lavonne, Eadie, Little Moses, and Clayton pulled up in the Wal-Mart parking lot at nine-fifteen, people were still straggling in. A big striped circus tent had been set up with a stage at one end for the presentation promenade of the debutantes, many of whom crowded the entrance and the parking lot dressed in their cheap ball gown finery with their heads wreathed in kudzu garlands. Their escorts, dressed in an assortment of overhauls, bad-fitting leisure suits, and camouflage gear stood with them. Some sported Billy Bob teeth and NASCAR caps. Up on the stage, the Mississippi Swamp Dogs were warming up with their rendition of "Daddy Was a Preacher But Mama Was a Go-Go Girl."

The crowd had spilled out into the parking lot to await the arrival of the Kudzu Queen, and when the Kudzu Kruiser pulled slowly into the parking lot, they went wild. Wendell Stamps was waiting for them outside the tent. He was dressed like Colonel Sanders, all in white linen with a black string tie and a panama hat wreathed in kudzu vine. He held his hand out for Lavonne and she stood up, trying not to feel foolish at the applause and the attention, but feeling happy, too, and not just because she had a tidy sum of money waiting in her checking account and a good business plan and a feeling that her life was fixing to change in a very big way. She knew she looked good in her bridesmaid dress, size 14, and she felt good about that, too. Damn good.

"Good evening, your majesty," Wendell said. He was wearing a nametag that read, *Hey, my name is* Uwuz Worned Aboutme—*what's yours?*

Lavonne gave him her hand. The crowd settled down respectfully to hear what she had to say. Someone thrust a wax cup filled with Kudzu Koolaid into her hand. Wendell handed her a microphone. She raised the cup, looking around the crowd. She only knew one toast.

"Love is blind," she said, "but marriage is a real eye opener."

The crowd hooted their approval. Wendell grinned, a wide slow grin that split his handsome black face into perfect hemispheres. The Swamp Dogs launched into the "Kudzu Limbo," followed by "Drunk and Lonesome (Again)," as Wendell led Lavonne into the big tent, which had been strung with colored lights in the shape of shotgun shells and streamers and posters of Famous Rednecks from History. Wallace Spurlock, who owned the local Kinkos, had produced a number of computer-generated posters that showed the heads of famous people wearing camo caps superimposed on a pair of overhauls. There was George Washington and Queen Elizabeths I and II, Shakespeare and Amelia Earhart, and of course, Bill Clinton and George W. Bush, among others. Tables sporting camo tablecloths and centerpieces that looked like miniature double-wides were crowded along one side of the tent. On the other side was a long buffet table stacked with dishes of fried chicken, squash casserole, mashed potatoes, collard greens, corn fritters, and every other example of good Southern cooking imaginable. Corporate sponsors had paid for the food, which was being catered by various restaurants, and Lavonne made a mental note to add the Shofar So Good Deli to the approved list for next year.

EADIE WAS OUT ON THE DANCE FLOOR WITH LITTLE MOSES WHEN she saw Trevor sitting alone at a table over by the door. She hadn't seen him come in and she had no idea how long he had been sitting there. He gave her a little wave. He was wearing a bright orange jumpsuit, the kind the prison trustees wear when picking up trash beside the highway, and he had his hair combed back with enough grease to deep-fry a turkey. "I'll be right back," Eadie said to Little Moses and began to make her way slowly through the crowd. He saw her coming and stood up.

"What are you doing here?"

"I think you know what I'm doing here."

"Does the word 'stalker' mean anything to you?"

"Desperate times call for desperate measures," he said, pulling out a chair for her but she didn't sit down. "I need to tell you something," he said. "Something I realized back at the Pink House, and if you'll just sit down and listen, if you'll just give me a few minutes, I promise I'll never bother you again. I promise I'll agree to whatever divorce terms you set and I won't have you prosecuted for blackmail or extortion or whatever the hell it is you women call what you're doing."

"Insurance."

"Okay, insurance. I won't have you prosecuted for insurance and I'll agree to any divorce terms, if you'll just sit down and listen to me." He put his hand on the chair but she stood there looking at him. The back of his jumpsuit read *Ithaca Correctional Facility* in bold letters. "Please, Eadie," he said. She sat down.

Trevor hunched his shoulders and sat forward with his forearms resting on the table. He reached across the table and tried to take both her hands but she slid them into her lap. "Look at me, Eadie," he said. She looked at him. "I have never in my entire life slept with prostitutes. The old Judge started the tradition of bringing women along years ago and I just went along with it because it was tradition and it seemed to give Broadwell and Zibolsky so much fucking joy. But I never, ever slept with those women myself. And Ramsbottom and Bentley will back me up on that if you call them."

The minute he said it, she knew it was true. She had known all along, she supposed, but it had been easier to hate him for sleeping with prostitutes than it had been to admit she was loosing him to Tonya. It had been easier to write him off as a bastard than to admit her relationship with Trevor was like her mother's relationships with Luther Birdsong and Frank Plumlee.

"Tonya was a mistake. I don't even know why Tonya happened, really. She was a distraction, a way to make me feel better about myself." He shook his head and looked at the cup of Kudzu Koolaid that rested on the table between his hands. "I'm not making excuses. I'm just telling you everything's going to be different from now on. Even if you don't take me back, I'm still quitting my law practice. I'm going to write. I'm forty-five years old and if I don't try now, I'll never have the courage to try. I don't know how I'll live. I don't know how *we'll* live. There won't be any money. We'll have to sell the house."

"I didn't sell everything," Eadie said. "I want you to know that. I kept some of the antiques and the portrait of your mother."

"I don't care about any of that shit." He shrugged and lifted his paper cup. "Well, maybe the portrait of my mother." He grimaced and set his drink down. "I want you to know, the only women I've slept with outside of our marriage are Rosemary Crouch, that waitress out at the Thirsty Dog, and Tonya."

"That doesn't exactly make you a hero, you asshole."

He chuckled and sat back in his chair with his hands resting on his thighs. "No, it doesn't. But it makes me honest." He didn't want to get her angry. If she got angry she'd start throwing things, and then he'd never get her to take him back.

Eadie took her hands out of her lap. She played with the edge of the camo tablecloth. "Honesty isn't enough anymore," she said.

He frowned and looked at his hands. "And the only men you've ever slept with are Bobby Summerfield, that cowboy out at the Thirsty Dog, and that sonofabitch personal trainer?"

"Denton."

A muscle moved in his jaw. He took his hands out of his lap and laid them on the table. "Yeah, Denton," he said.

The Swamp Dogs were playing "Damaged Goods." "Listen," Eadie said. "They're playing our song."

"I don't expect you to take me back, I know it's probably too late for that, but I want you to know I love you. You're the only woman I've ever really loved and if you take me back I'll spend the rest of my life proving that."

"I've gotten used to the idea of not having you in my life, Trevor. I've gotten used to the idea of being alone. I found a gallery in Atlanta that's going to sell my goddesses. I've been working pretty steadily the last few weeks."

"Eadie, that's great. I mean it." He reached for her hand again and this time she let him take it.

"I don't want to go back to that old life," she said. "I don't want to go back to all the chaos and the distractions."

"Just give me another chance."

"I'm not putting up with infidelity anymore," Eadie said. "I'm tired of that shit."

"I'm through with all that," Trevor said. "I know what I need to make me happy, and it isn't another woman."

Wendell Stamps and his beautiful wife, Amalie, danced past the table wrapped in each other's arms. Eadie thought about love and forgiveness, and how, if you were lucky, you could live with someone most of your life and still get to find out something new about them every day. And she thought about herself and Trevor, and Nita and Jimmy Lee Motes, and Lavonne and Mona Shapiro and Little Moses, and how everyone's definition of happiness was different, and you had to work it out for yourself and not let other people tell you what was right. "I'll have to think about it for a while," she said, trying to prolong the feeling of independence, trying to buy herself time. "I'm not making any quick decisions."

"I don't expect you to." He leaned forward and tried to kiss her.

She turned her face away but let him keep her hand. "I can live without you if I have to," she said.

"It kills me to hear you say that."

"Just so you know," she said.

BY TEN O'CLOCK MOST OF THE DEBUTANTES AND THEIR ESCORTS were liquored up enough for the presentation ceremony to begin. Wendell Stamps strolled across the stage and took possession of the microphone. The Swamp Dogs took a beer break. The crowd hooted and screamed and Wendell put his hands up to settle them down. "Ladies and gentlemen," Wendell said. "Kudzu Debutantes and Redneck Escorts." This brought some shouts from the crowd. "What, you might ask, qualifies someone for membership in our fine debutante society? Well, to put it bluntly, there are a number of stringent qualifications. First, she must *look* like a female." This comment brought several whistles from the gay community, who over the years had begun to attend the debutante ball in ever-increasing numbers, driving in from Mobile and Birmingham and Atlanta.

"She can be married."

"Yeah boy," someone shouted.

Wendell raised his hands. "She can be single or single for the evening!"

"Hallelujah!"

Wendell lifted one finger and held it over his head like Moses parting the Red Sea. "Hell, she can even be widowed."

"You tell us, brother!"

Wendell was into it now, walking back and forth across the stage and doing his best impersonation of a televangelist. "She can be longtime divorced, newly divorced, or soon-to-be divorced." This brought the loudest applause and stamping of feet. "She can be a divorcee in any sense of the word, or, as we say in the South, she can be drinking double, but sleeping single."

The crowd went wild. Wendell mopped his face and waited for the noise to subside. "Ladies and gentlemen," he said, opening his arms wide, "I give you the fifth annual Kudzu Debutantes. Ladies, come up to the stage, give your names and the names of your escorts to the name caller, and line up for your promenade. If you think you might have trouble with the promenade, raise your hands for assistance." This brought a roar of laughter from the audience. Several people raised their hands.

The Swamp Dogs straggled back onto the stage while the debutante line formed. There were about twenty debs being presented this year. Lavonne stood at the end of the line with Little Moses behind Eadie and Trevor, and Nita and Jimmy Lee, who had shown up around ten o'clock. Nita was barefoot and she was blushing like a bride. Lavonne had never seen her look so pretty or so happy. Lavonne was halfway through her third Koolaid when she realized she couldn't feel her hands and there was a sound of jungle drums in her head and she was happy, happy, happy. She wasn't nervous at all. If she had to give a speech, she'd be fine. If she had to, she could give the Gettysburg Address. She could recite the damn preamble to the Constitution and never skip a beat.

Vernon Caslin, who in the real world was an auctioneer for the Mertis Slack Real Estate Company, went to the microphone with his list of debutantes and their escorts. The Swamp Dogs began playing "Pomp and Circumstance" with a slight backbeat. Vernon held up his hands.

"Simmer down, simmer down," he said. "Let's get this show on the road. Okay, first up we got Miss Flossy Bedweder and her date Mr. Dewayne deBoner." Wild applause followed. "Next, is Miss Ivana daMoan and her date Gnarly Davisson." More applause. "Miss Mozelle McCrotch and Homer Damnright. Miss Ophelia Sticks and Bocephus Abcess."

The list went on and on, with the applause and cheers remaining pretty constant up until the moment Wanda Mosby was presented. Wanda had been a cheerleader in high school. She hadn't cheered in thirty years but under the influence of Kudzu Koolaid and the heady encouragement of the crowd, Wanda bounced across the stage, did a cartwheel, and went into the splits right in front of the microphone. She got a standing ovation that lasted for several minutes and it wasn't until the cheering had begun to die down and Wanda still sat there with her legs apart and a funny look on her face that the crowd realized she was stuck. Her escort hurried over to help but it took him, Vernon, and one of the members of the Swamp Dogs to get Wanda on her feet. She grinned and gave the crowd a victory sign as she limped off the stage on the arm of her escort.

Lavonne watched it all like a dreamer watches a dream, kind of half in and half out of consciousness. The loss of feeling in her hands had spread through her limbs and was slowly moving into her head. The shotgun-shell minilights glittered like diamonds in the top of the circus tent. The voices of the crowd were dampened, like distant music. All around her was a sea of happy faces and Lavonne realized she was one of them, that whatever had come before was over with and whatever came from now on would be of her own making. She thought of her parents, of her mother's acquiescent suffering and her father's selfish-ness, and she forgave them both. She thought of her daughters and the guilt she would feel upon telling them she had left their father, and she let that go, too. She thought of the sacrifices she had made to bring her here, to this one moment in time, and she did not regret a single one and would make them all again if she had to. And she thought, briefly,

of Leonard, of the hopeful boy he had been before time and circumstance and character wreaked their gradual disintegration, and she forgave him, too. But mostly she thought of herself, of the girl she had
once been, of the woman she was now, and of the woman she would
one day become, and it seemed to Lavonne that everything had a purpose, every trauma and heartache and joy, and she was living proof of
all that.

"And now, the moment we've all been waiting for," Vernon said,
and Lavonne saw the faces of the crowd turn her way and this was the
moment she had been waiting for all her life. Nita stood at the side of
the stage and smiled and beckoned for her to come on. Eadie grinned
and gave her a thumbs-up. The Swamp Dogs launched into a rousing
rendition of "Liquored Up and Lacquered Down," and Lavonne Zibolsky, aka Miss Ima Badass, went forward to claim her crown.

Acknowledgments

I am indebted to Lee Boudreaux, whose guidance and belief in my work helped forge this novel, to Linda Marrow, Dan Mallory, Bert Yaeger, and all the other editors at Ballantine/Random House whose patience, advice, and good humor were unfailing.

I would like to thank Kristin Lindstrom and Joel Gotler, whose early appreciation of my story kept me writing, and whose hard work made this whole experience possible.

Thanks to all those fine teachers and professors who taught me how to read and appreciate good literature, who encouraged me, and saw something in me that probably made most people nervous.

To Sam, Lauren, and Jordan, who put up with burned biscuits, unmade beds, missed P.T.A. meetings, and all the other baggage that goes along with having a mother who is a writer, and to Mark, whose honesty, encouragement, and love have sustained me for nearly thirty years.

And finally, thanks to my parents, who taught me to appreciate the magic of the written word and to believe that being a little different is a good thing.

Eadie, Nita, and Lavonne return in
The Secret Lives of the Kudzu Debutantes.
Published by Ballantine Books in August 2007.

Read on for a preview.

$\mathcal{V}$IRGINIA BROADWELL WAS ANGRY. AND ANYONE WHO KNEW Virginia, knew she was a dangerous woman when riled. Her first husband, the Judge, had learned this lesson long before he died, and her only son, Charles, had experienced the sting of her self-contained fury enough times over his forty-five years to be gun-shy. And her new husband would learn it, too, although Virginia would wait until the last thank-you note had been written and the ring was securely settled on her finger before showing Redmon that side of her nature. She would give him a chance to settle into the traces and take the bit firmly between his teeth before applying the whip the first time.

Downstairs she could hear the wedding guests milling about. She looked around the flowered chintz bedroom she had shared with the Judge for nearly twenty-six years, and then spent the next twenty years enjoying in solitary bliss. It would be sad to leave this house, the one she had insisted the Judge build for her all those years ago, before she would agree to marry him. The scene of so many of her social triumphs, the place where she had plotted and schemed her way to the top of the wobbly Ithaca social ladder, and which now, sadly, must be sold to pay her debts. Redmon, like the wily redneck businessman he was, had insisted she enter the marriage debt-free. He had insisted she sign a prenuptial agreement. Despite herself, Virginia had felt a kind of grudging admiration for him then. She would have done the same thing had their circumstances been reversed.

She had survived an unfortunate childhood, widowhood, scandal, near financial ruin, and now Y2K, and it had seemed only fitting that she set her wedding date for January 20, 2000. Let others worry about computer crashes and social anarchy; Virginia had endured enough turmoil in her life to know that victory belonged to the bold and the cunning.

There was a knock on the door and her son, Charles, stuck his head in. "Mother, are you ready?" He wore the same, whipped-dog expression he had worn since his meek wife of sixteen years walked out of his life a little over a year ago, taking with her his children, his pride, and nearly six hundred thousand dollars of his assets. His defeatism irritated Virginia beyond words.

"Yes, I'm ready," she said. "I'm ready to do my duty, to do whatever is necessary to hold this family together—"

"Good." He knew where this was headed and he wanted no part of it. "I'll give the signal then." He tried to close the door but Virginia inserted her slim little foot. Charles sighed and swung the door open again. "Yes, Mother?" he said, rolling his eyes skyward like a martyr on his way to the stake.

"Come in and close the door behind you," she said fiercely. He did as he was told and followed her into the center of the room, where she stood looking at herself in a cheval glass. She lifted a well-manicured hand, indicating a wingback chair by the window.

"Do we really have to do this now?" he said, and when she said nothing, only stared at him steadily in the glass, he sighed and slumped down with his feet stretched in front of him.

"You brought this on yourself," she said. She sniffed, looking at herself critically in the mirror. There weren't many women her age who could still wear designer clothes and heels. Hadn't she caught the bag boy at the Piggly Wiggly staring at her legs yesterday as he loaded her groceries into the car? And hadn't some ruffians in a pickup truck whistled at her last week as she crossed the street in front of the Courthouse?

Charles slumped in his chair and stared despondently at a spot in the center of the oriental carpet. It was his newest technique, this passive-aggressive slumping, this lumpish inertia, like a sack of grain propped against a table leg. Virginia frowned at him in the glass. "You won't return my phone calls, you hide behind locked doors when I show up at your condo—don't think I haven't seen you peering from behind the blinds—you refuse to see me when I show up at that ratty little place you call an office."

Good. She had drawn blood. She noted the way his ears flushed, the way he lurched forward with his elbows pinned to the arms of the chair. "That ratty little office is all I can afford," he said tersely.

"Whose fault is that?"

"Surely, Mother, you're not blaming me for the breakup of Boone and Broadwell." He lifted his top lip, looking more like the old Charles, more like the surly, sarcastic boy she had raised and tutored, so much like his father, but so much more like her.

"Who should I blame?" she said, lifting one eyebrow. "Who should I blame for the breakup of your father's law firm, for the loss of my annual income and partnership assets."

He smirked in a way she found particularly offensive. He said, "Well, you're managing to survive pretty well, considering you're marrying one of the wealthiest men in Georgia."

"I'm doing what I have to do given the circumstances," she snapped. "And you'd be well advised to do the same."

His eyes clouded suddenly and he shrugged and went limp again, and in that moment of surrender Virginia knew the breakup of Boone & Broadwell had something to do with Nita. Something had happened between Charles and his soon-to-be-remarried ex-wife. Something secret but underhanded—and Virginia knew a thing or two about secrets, not to mention underhandedness.

"Speaking of marriage," she said, smoothing her hair with one hand. "I understand Nita is getting remarried next week."

Charles stared at his feet. A muscle moved along his jaw. "So I heard," he said evenly.

"You should have put a stop to all that when you had a chance."

"This isn't the dark ages, Mother. I couldn't have stopped her from divorcing me if she wanted to."

"Yes, but you could have made it more difficult for her. You could have tied the case up in court for years and bled her dry, financially and emotionally. You're a good attorney, or at least you used to be."

He laughed bitterly and put his hands on the arm of the chair as if to rise. "Are we about finished here?"

She looked at him suspiciously. Why hadn't he opposed the divorce? Why hadn't he stopped Nita from running off with that good-looking young carpenter she hired to fix her pool house, an action that made the Broadwells the laughingstock of Ithaca, Georgia?

Virginia smelled a rat.

And she knew it had something to do with Nita and her two devious friends—Eadie Boone and Lavonne Zibolsky. Some scheme they had cooked up a year ago when Nita and Lavonne left their husbands, and Eadie ran off to New Orleans with her husband, Trevor, to live the life of bohemian artists.

Virginia adjusted the sleeves of her jacket. "Tell them to give me five minutes and then start the wedding march. You can wait for me at the foot of the stairs. And for God's sake, stand up straight and stop slouching."

Charles went out without another word, pulling the door closed firmly behind him. No, it had been a bad year for everyone but Nita, Lavonne, and Eadie, who had somehow managed to turn everyone else's bad luck to their advantage. And Virginia was determined to get to the bottom of what had happened no matter what it took. But first she must put her own affairs in order. She tucked her bobbed hair behind one ear and looked at her smooth skin appreciatively. *Keep your face out of the sun.* It was the one bit of childhood advice her mother had given her that actually proved useful, besides her admonition to Virginia on her wedding night, to "close your eyes and think of something pleasant." Virginia had laughed bitterly then, and she laughed bitterly now, remembering.

She stared at herself in the mirror, somewhat disgusted at the predicament she found herself in now—a bride at sixty-five. Still, beggars can't be choosers, she reminded herself. Desperate times call for desperate measures. She had married beneath herself both times, first, to the Judge, the son of a sharecropper, and now to Redmon, the son of a pine barren hog farmer, but she had done what well-brought-up women of her generation were taught to do: she had married for money. She had her work cut out for her this time, though. Redmon didn't seem the type likely to submit to the crop and bridle of matrimony, although Virginia was certain she would prevail in the end.

She would prevail in bringing her new husband to heel and then she would turn her attention to Nita and her renegade girlfriends. Virginia had never, in her entire life, let anyone get the best of her, and she wasn't about to start now. She stared balefully at herself in the mirror, trying to remember that brides should appear virginal and not homicidal. Her tiny hands curled into fists. Her tiny teeth clenched. Twin spots of color appeared on her cheeks. Below her the wedding march began, low and plaintive as a cow stuck in a bog, slow and ponderous as a funeral dirge.

Virginia forced a bright, artificial grin. She checked her teeth for lipstick stains.

Vengeance is mine, saith the Lord, but Virginia had never been one to turn her responsibilities over to someone else.

PHOTO: SHANNON FONTAINE

CATHY HOLTON was born in Lakeland, Florida, and grew up in college towns in the South and the Midwest. She attended Oklahoma State University and Michigan State University and worked for a number of years in Atlanta before settling in the mountains of Tennessee with her husband and their three children.